ARCADE WORLD

DRAGON FLAMES

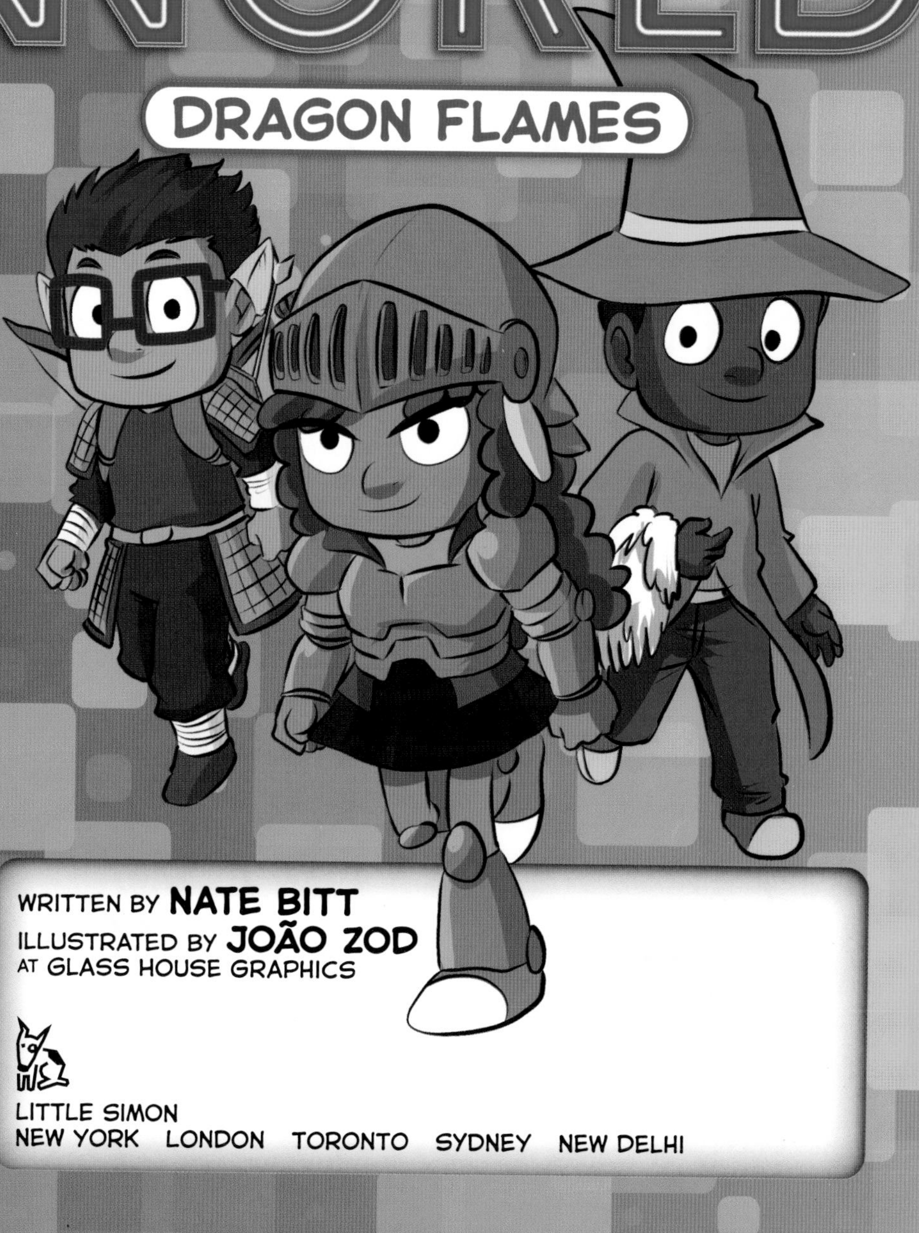

WRITTEN BY **NATE BITT**
ILLUSTRATED BY **JOÃO ZOD**
AT GLASS HOUSE GRAPHICS

LITTLE SIMON
NEW YORK LONDON TORONTO SYDNEY NEW DELHI

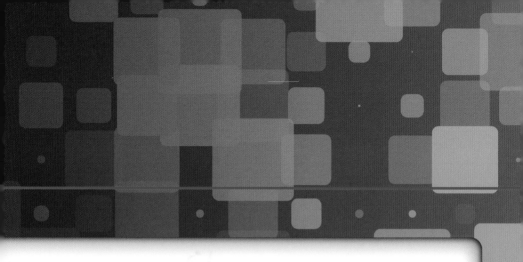

LITTLE SIMON
AN IMPRINT OF SIMON & SCHUSTER CHILDREN'S PUBLISHING DIVISION • 1230 AVENUE OF THE AMERICAS, NEW YORK, NEW YORK 10020 • FIRST LITTLE SIMON EDITION FEBRUARY 2023 • COPYRIGHT © 2023 BY SIMON & SCHUSTER, INC. • ALL RIGHTS RESERVED, INCLUDING THE RIGHT OF REPRODUCTION IN WHOLE OR IN PART IN ANY FORM. • LITTLE SIMON IS A REGISTERED TRADEMARK OF SIMON & SCHUSTER, INC., AND ASSOCIATED COLOPHON IS A TRADEMARK OF SIMON & SCHUSTER, INC. • FOR INFORMATION ABOUT SPECIAL DISCOUNTS FOR BULK PURCHASES, PLEASE CONTACT SIMON & SCHUSTER SPECIAL SALES AT 1-866-506-1949 OR BUSINESS@SIMONANDSCHUSTER.COM. • THE SIMON & SCHUSTER SPEAKERS BUREAU CAN BRING AUTHORS TO YOUR LIVE EVENT. FOR MORE INFORMATION OR TO BOOK AN EVENT CONTACT THE SIMON & SCHUSTER SPEAKERS BUREAU AT 1-866-248-3049 OR VISIT OUR WEBSITE AT WWW.SIMONSPEAKERS.COM. • TEXT BY MATTHEW J. GILBERT • DESIGNED BY NICK SCIACCA • ART SERVICES BY GLASS HOUSE GRAPHICS • ART BY JOÃO ZOD, MARCEL SALAZA & WATS • COLORS BY MARCOS PELANDRA & KAMUI • LETTERING BY MARCOS INOUE. THE ILLUSTRATIONS FOR THIS BOOK WERE RENDERED DIGITALLY. THE TEXT OF THIS BOOK WAS SET IN CC SAMARITAN. MANUFACTURED IN CHINA 1022 SCP
10 9 8 7 6 5 4 3 2 1
ISBN 9781665904773 (HC)
ISBN 9781665904766 (PBK)
ISBN 9781665904780 (EBOOK)
THIS BOOK HAS BEEN CATALOGED WITH THE LIBRARY OF CONGRESS.

INSERT COIN

CREDIT 999

CONTENTS

LITTLE SIMON 2023

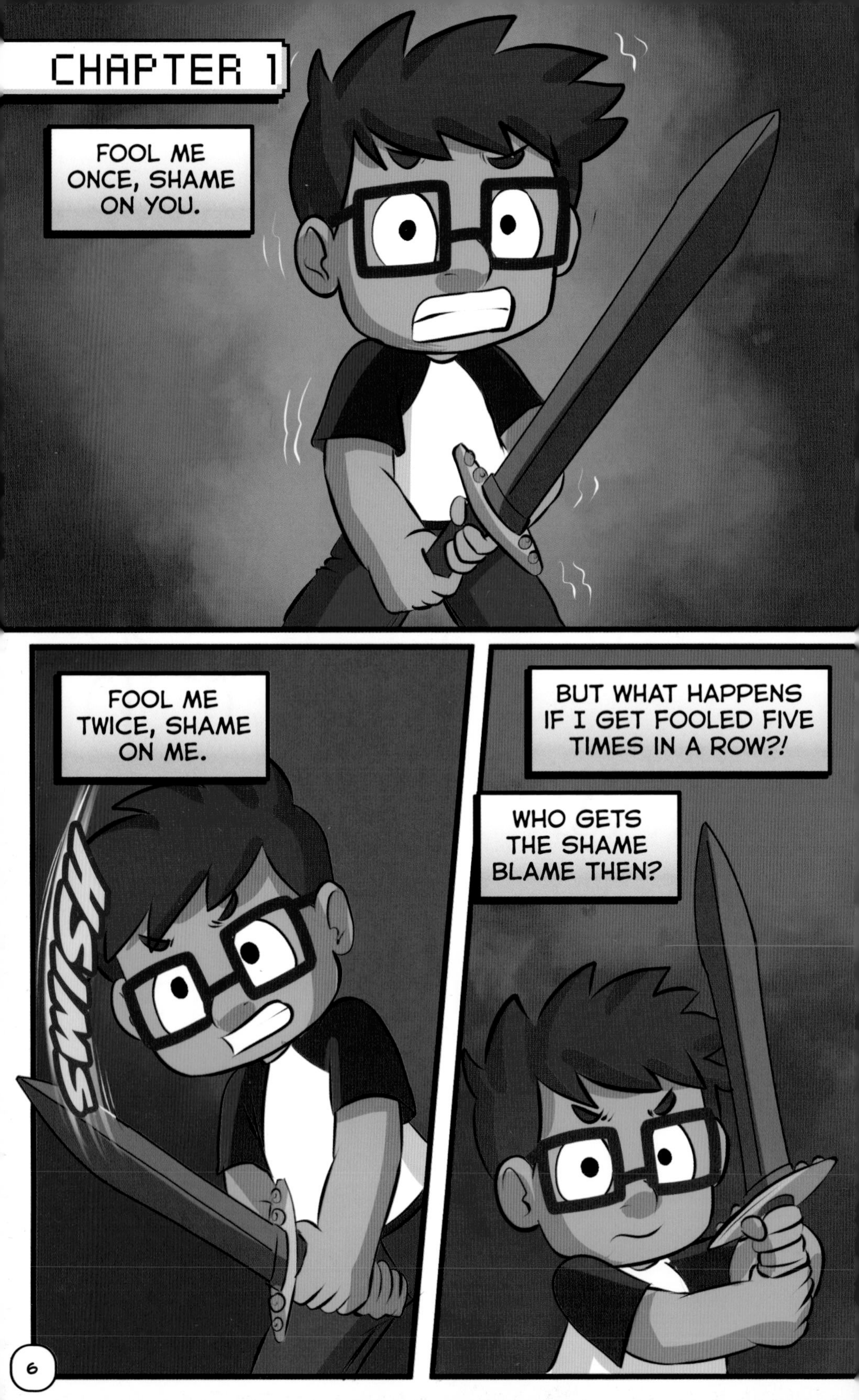
CHAPTER 1
FOOL ME ONCE, SHAME ON YOU.
FOOL ME TWICE, SHAME ON ME.
SWISH
BUT WHAT HAPPENS IF I GET FOOLED FIVE TIMES IN A ROW?!
WHO GETS THE SHAME BLAME THEN?

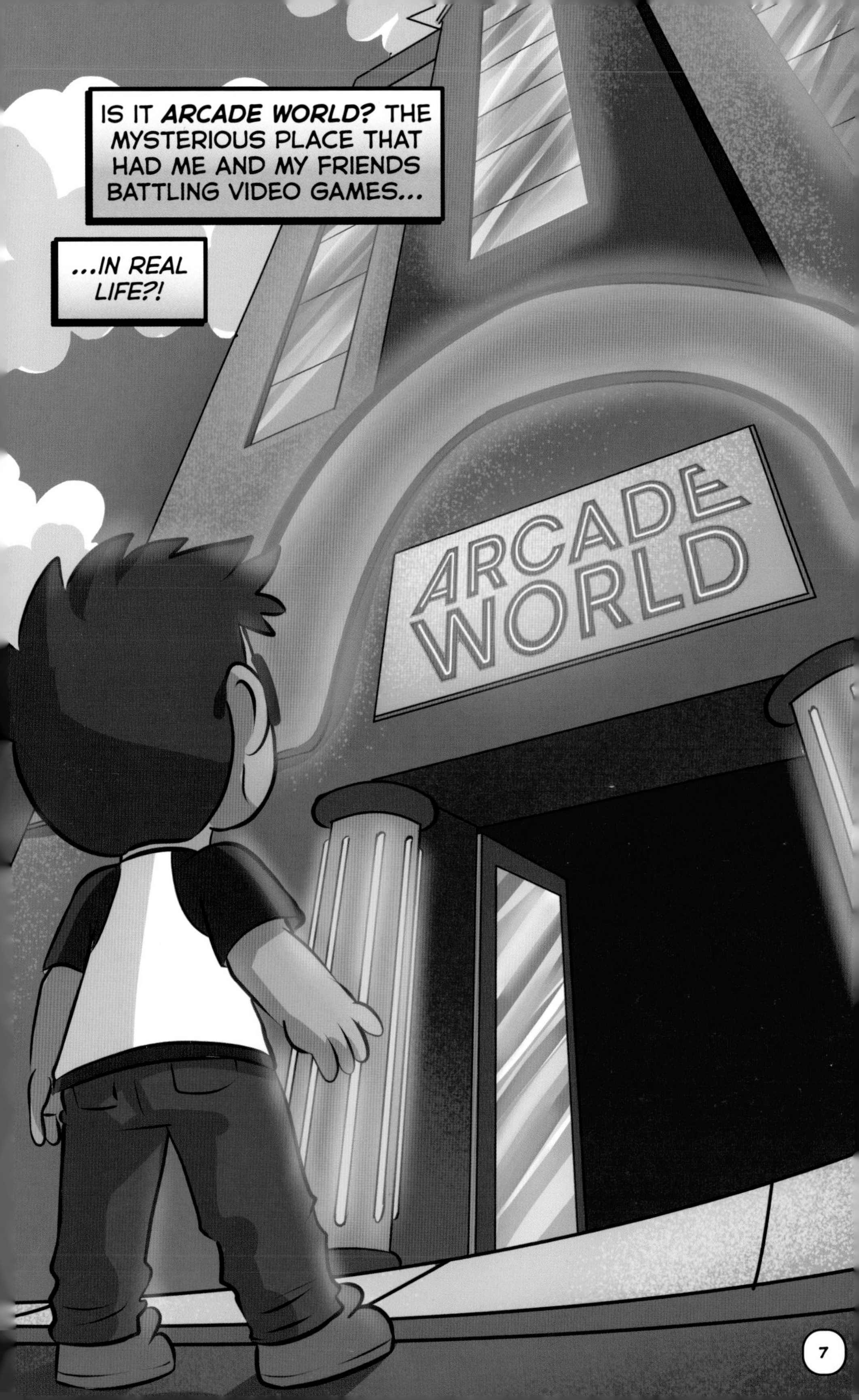
IS IT ARCADE WORLD? THE MYSTERIOUS PLACE THAT HAD ME AND MY FRIENDS BATTLING VIDEO GAMES...
...IN REAL LIFE?!
ARCADE WORLD

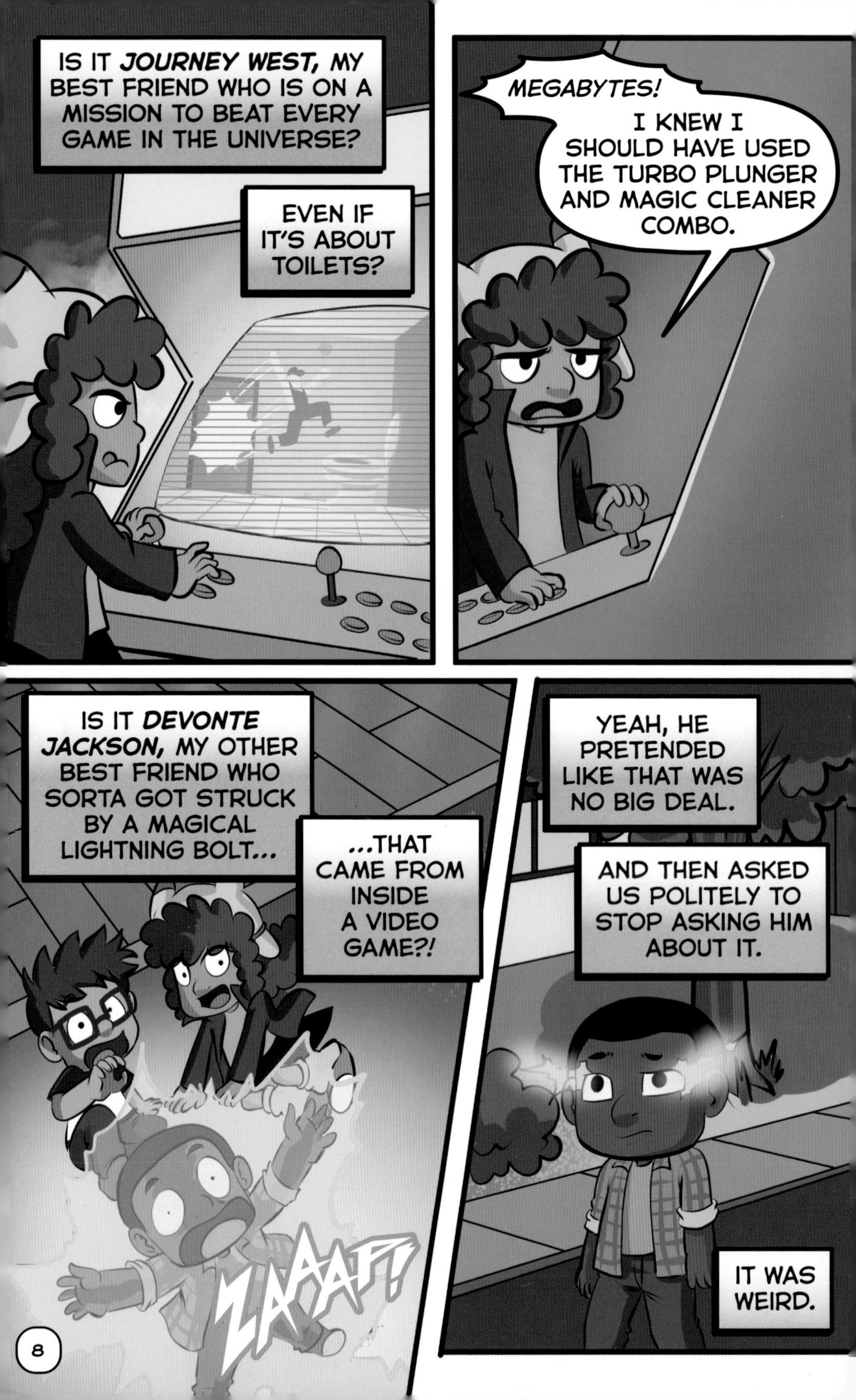
IS IT *JOURNEY WEST,* MY BEST FRIEND WHO IS ON A MISSION TO BEAT EVERY GAME IN THE UNIVERSE?
EVEN IF IT'S ABOUT TOILETS?
MEGABYTES!
I KNEW I SHOULD HAVE USED THE TURBO PLUNGER AND MAGIC CLEANER COMBO.
IS IT *DEVONTE JACKSON,* MY OTHER BEST FRIEND WHO SORTA GOT STRUCK BY A MAGICAL LIGHTNING BOLT...
...THAT CAME FROM INSIDE A VIDEO GAME?!
ZAAAP!
YEAH, HE PRETENDED LIKE THAT WAS NO BIG DEAL.
AND THEN ASKED US POLITELY TO STOP ASKING HIM ABOUT IT.
IT WAS WEIRD.

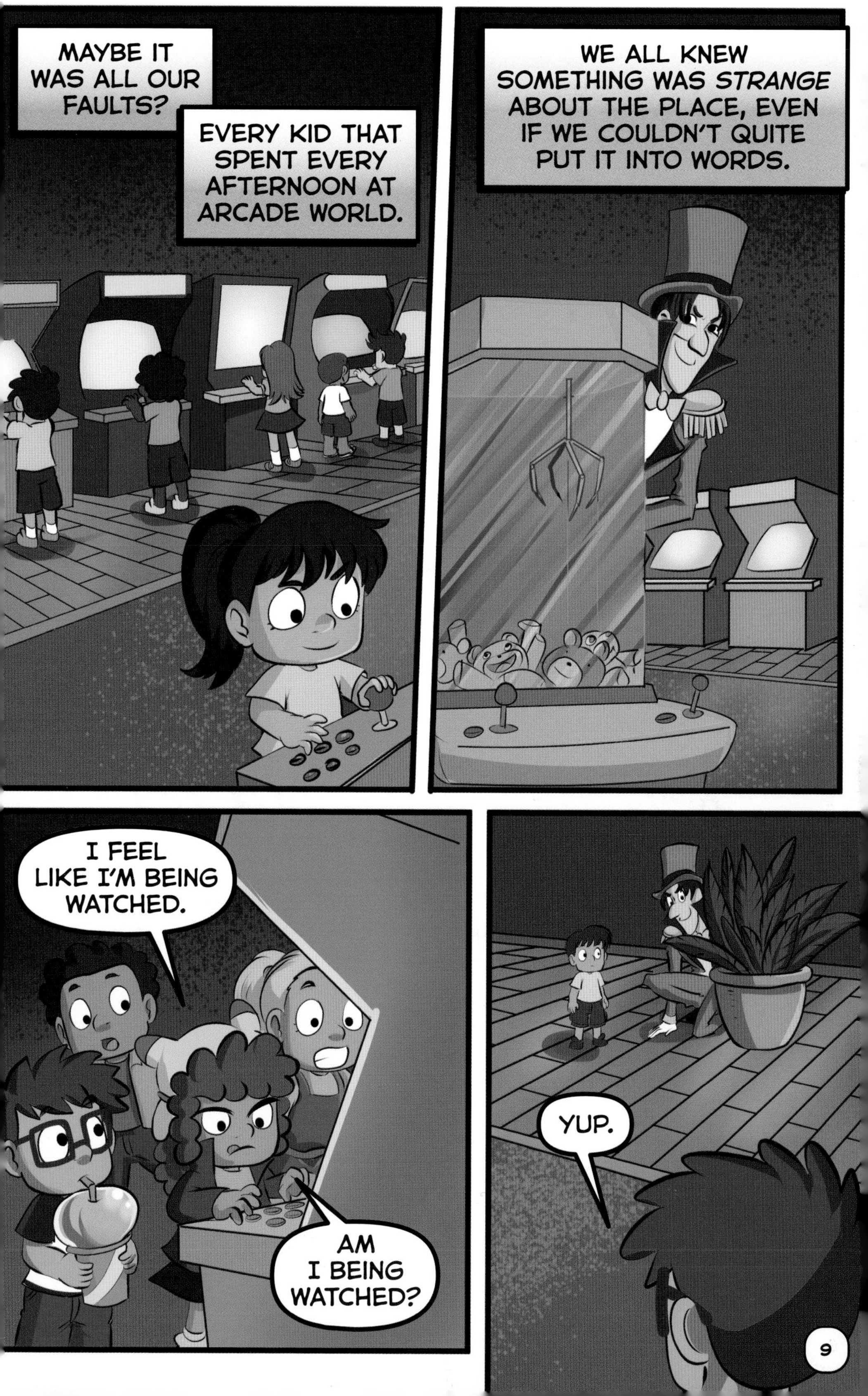
MAYBE IT WAS ALL OUR FAULTS?
EVERY KID THAT SPENT EVERY AFTERNOON AT ARCADE WORLD.
WE ALL KNEW SOMETHING WAS *STRANGE* ABOUT THE PLACE, EVEN IF WE COULDN'T QUITE PUT IT INTO WORDS.
I FEEL LIKE I'M BEING WATCHED.
AM I BEING WATCHED?
YUP.

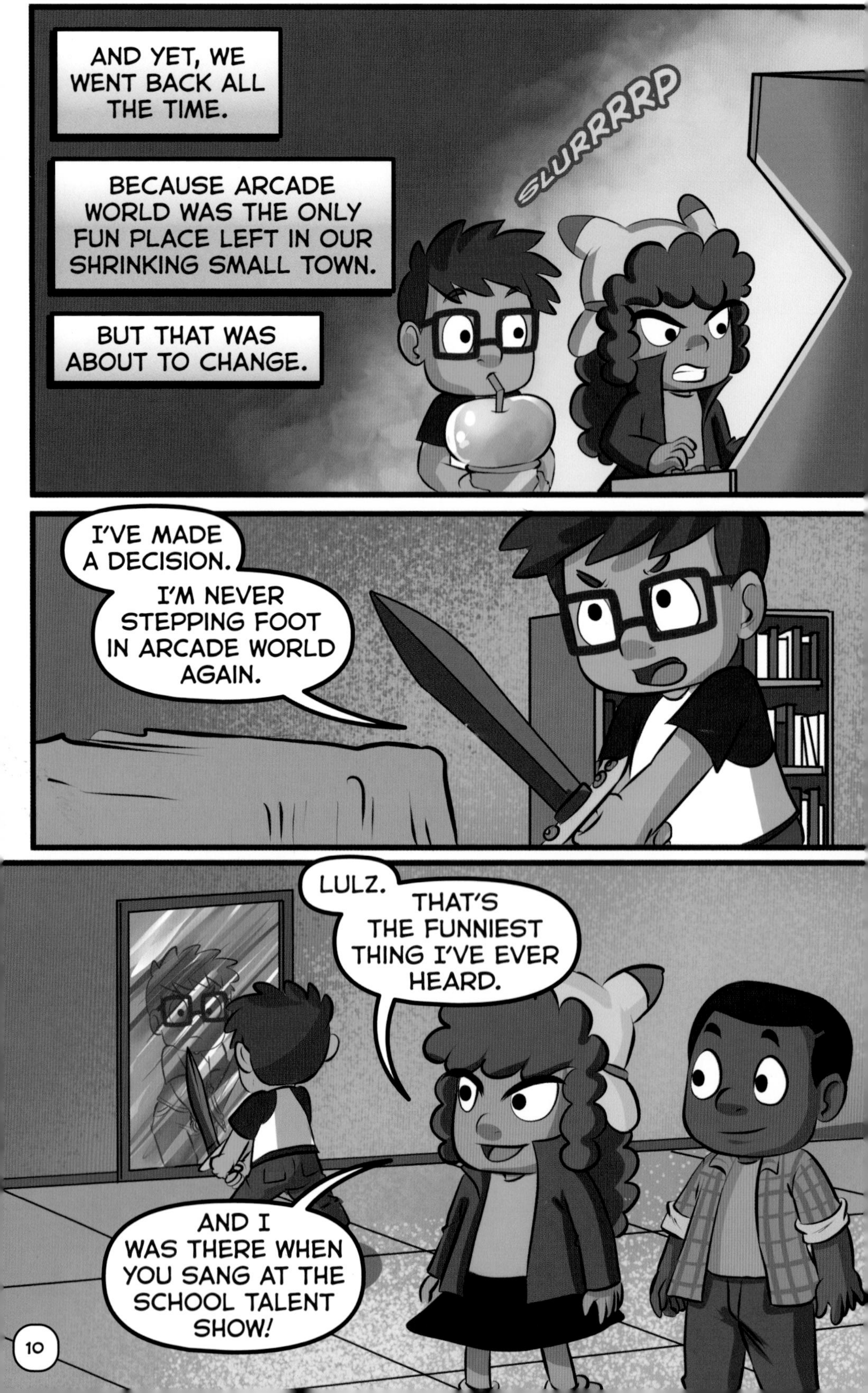
AND YET, WE WENT BACK ALL THE TIME.
BECAUSE ARCADE WORLD WAS THE ONLY FUN PLACE LEFT IN OUR SHRINKING SMALL TOWN.
BUT THAT WAS ABOUT TO CHANGE.
SLURRRRP
I'VE MADE A DECISION.
I'M NEVER STEPPING FOOT IN ARCADE WORLD AGAIN.
LULZ.
THAT'S THE FUNNIEST THING I'VE EVER HEARD.
AND I WAS THERE WHEN YOU SANG AT THE SCHOOL TALENT SHOW!

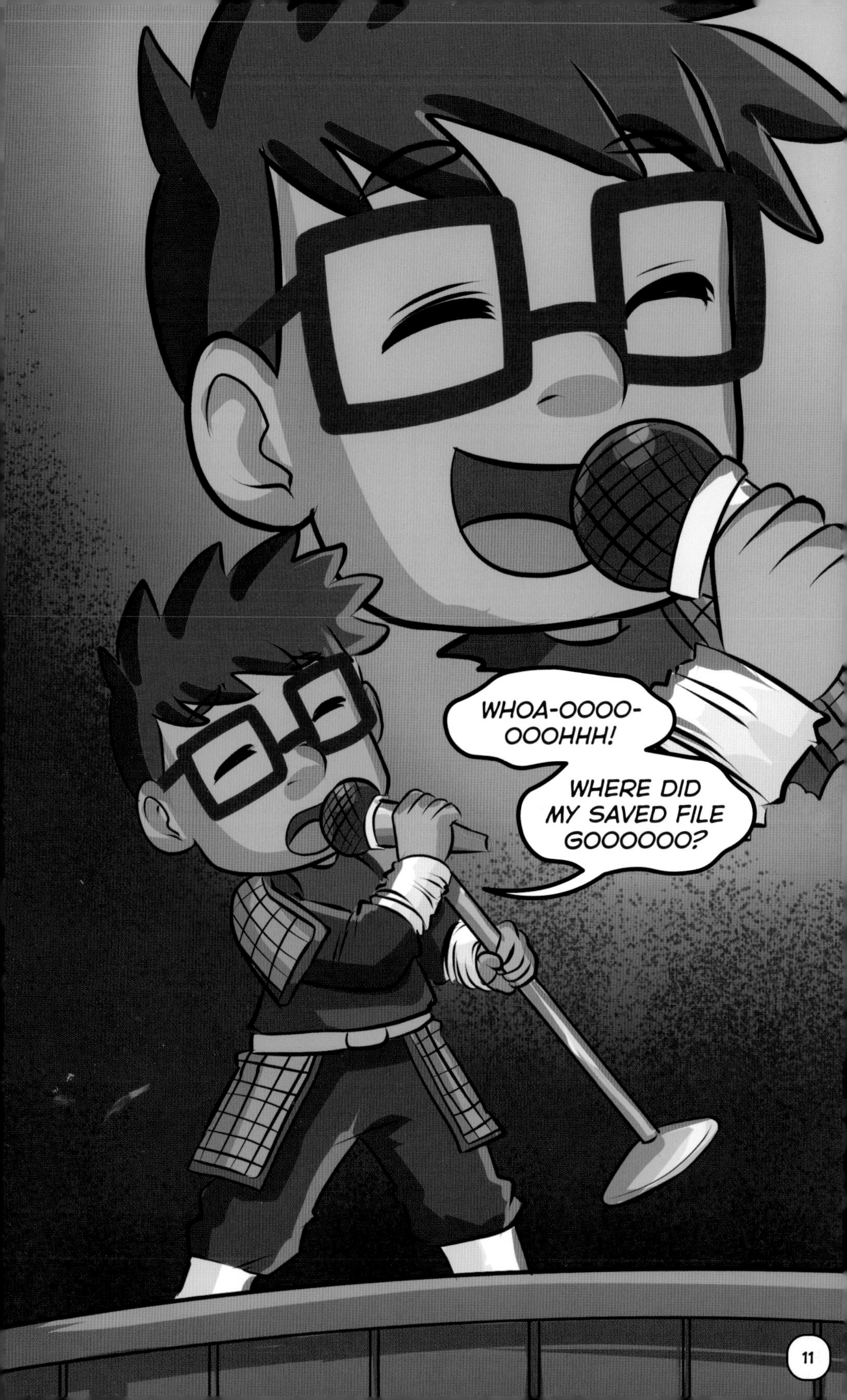
WHOA-OOOO-OOOHHH!
WHERE DID MY SAVED FILE GOOOOOO?

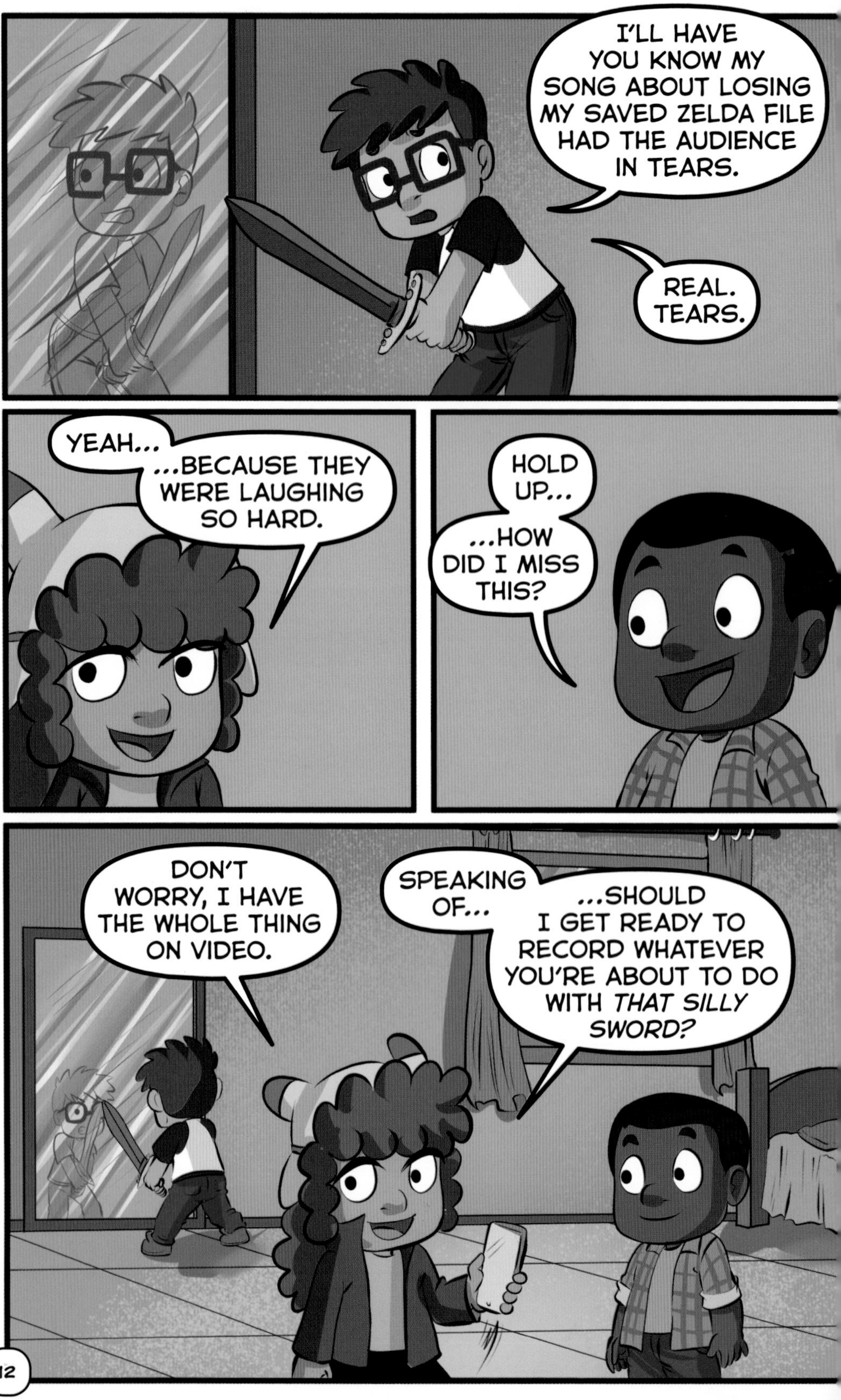
I'LL HAVE YOU KNOW MY SONG ABOUT LOSING MY SAVED ZELDA FILE HAD THE AUDIENCE IN TEARS.
REAL. TEARS.
YEAH...
...BECAUSE THEY WERE LAUGHING SO HARD.
HOLD UP...
...HOW DID I MISS THIS?
DON'T WORRY, I HAVE THE WHOLE THING ON VIDEO.
SPEAKING OF...
...SHOULD I GET READY TO RECORD WHATEVER YOU'RE ABOUT TO DO WITH *THAT SILLY SWORD?*

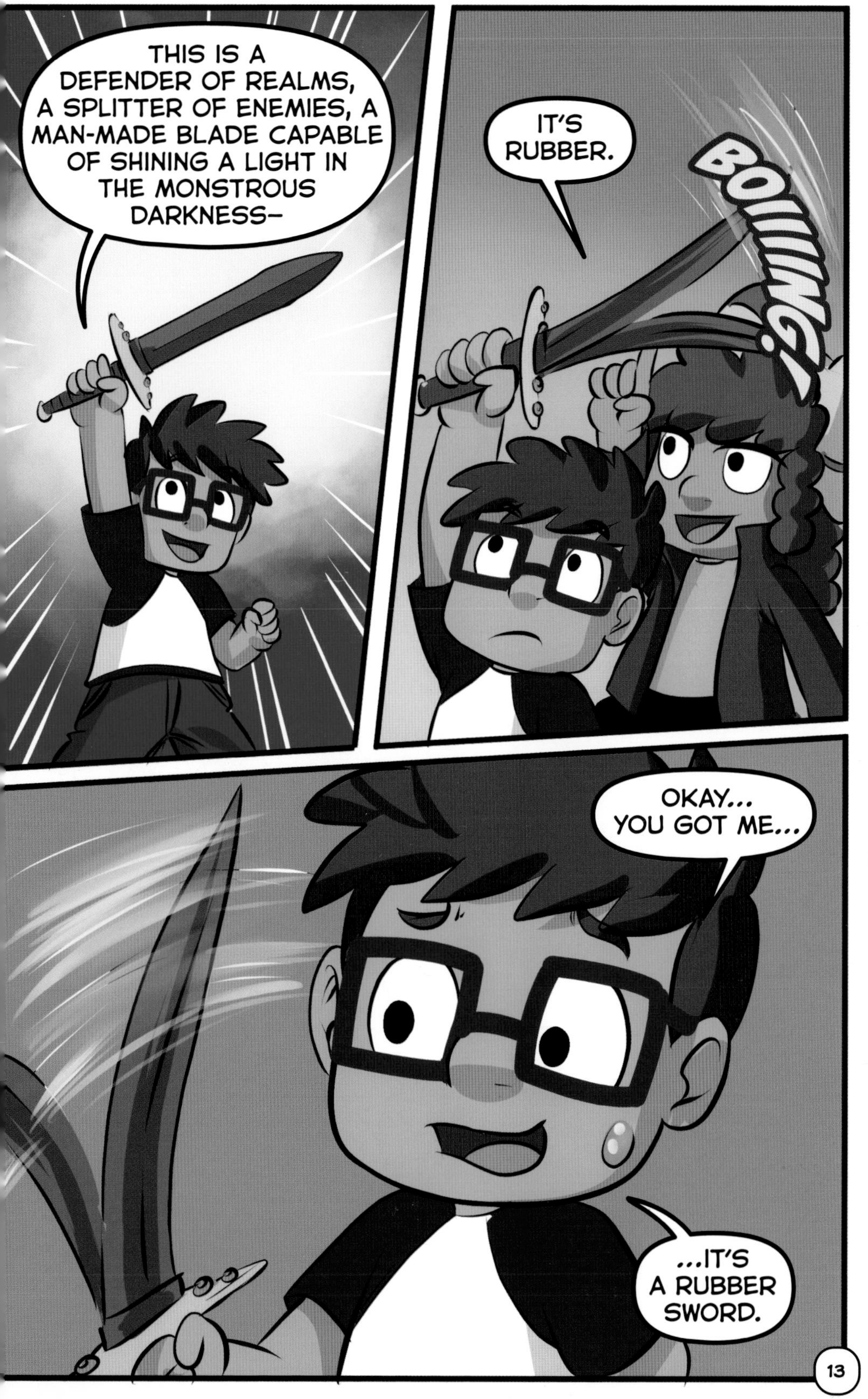
THIS IS A DEFENDER OF REALMS, A SPLITTER OF ENEMIES, A MAN-MADE BLADE CAPABLE OF SHINING A LIGHT IN THE MONSTROUS DARKNESS–
IT'S RUBBER.
BOIIING!
OKAY... YOU GOT ME...
...IT'S A RUBBER SWORD.

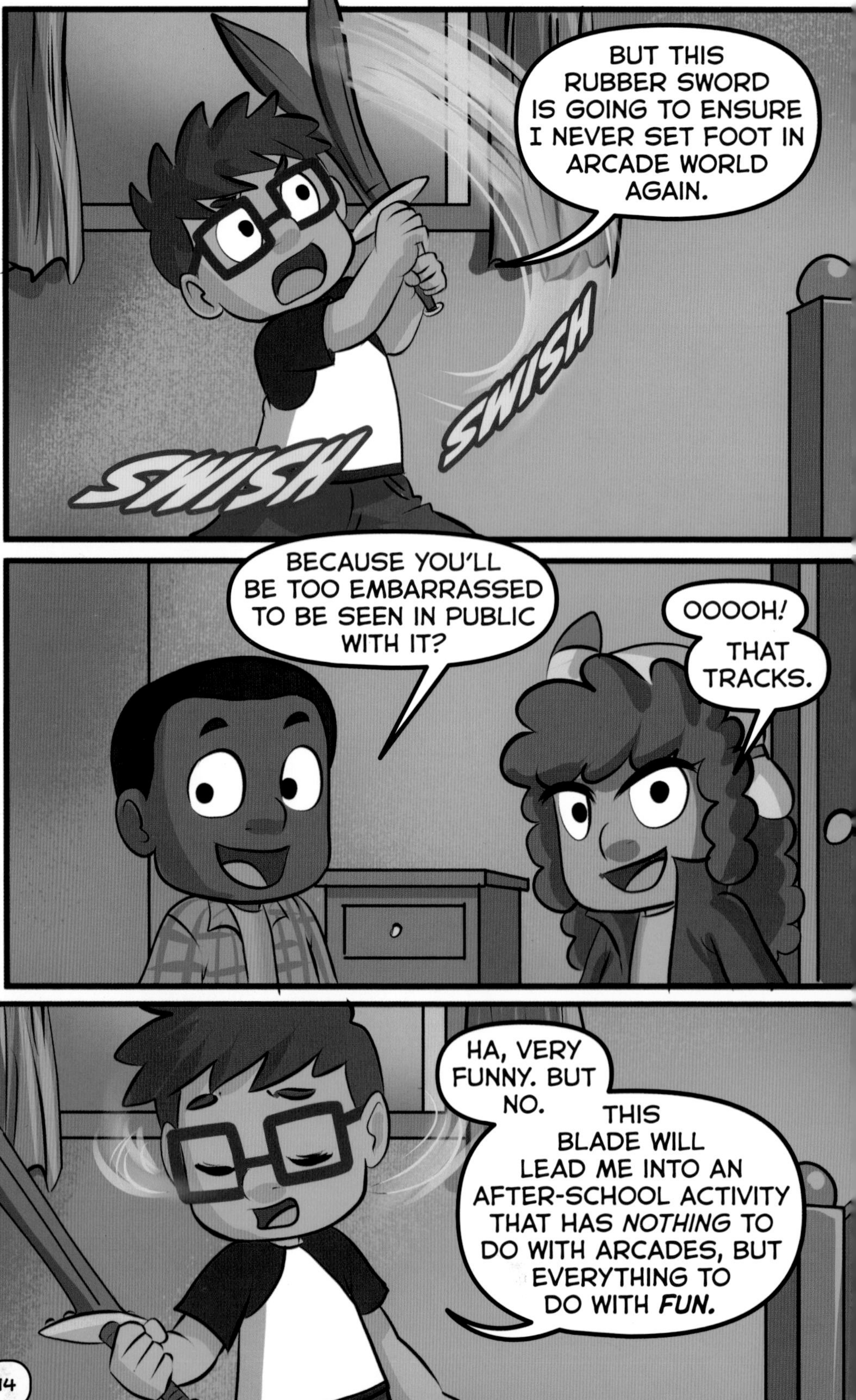
BUT THIS RUBBER SWORD IS GOING TO ENSURE I NEVER SET FOOT IN ARCADE WORLD AGAIN.
SWISH
SWISH
BECAUSE YOU'LL BE TOO EMBARRASSED TO BE SEEN IN PUBLIC WITH IT?
OOOOH! THAT TRACKS.
HA, VERY FUNNY. BUT NO.
THIS BLADE WILL LEAD ME INTO AN AFTER-SCHOOL ACTIVITY THAT HAS *NOTHING* TO DO WITH ARCADES, BUT EVERYTHING TO DO WITH ***FUN.***

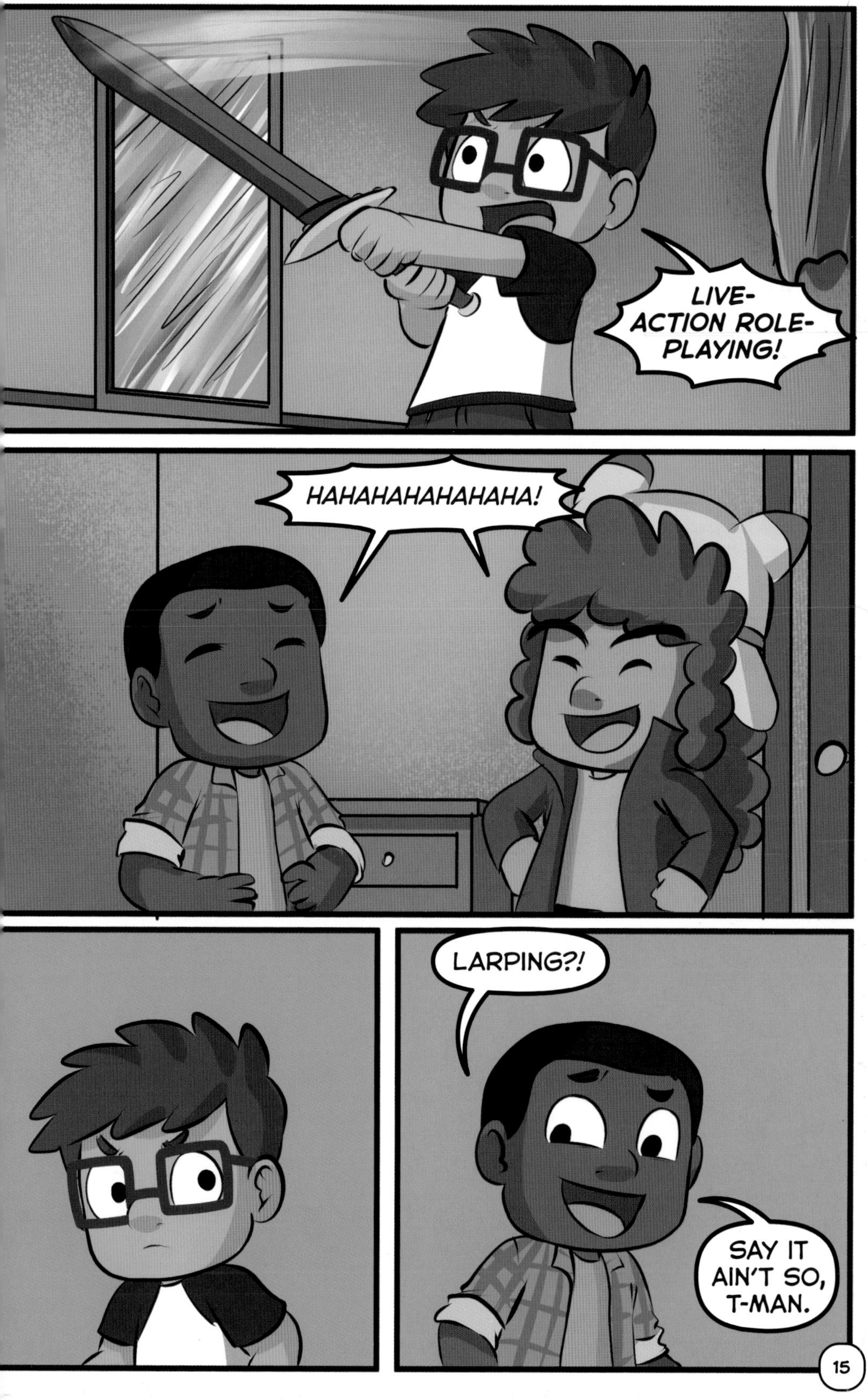
LIVE-ACTION ROLE-PLAYING!
HAHAHAHAHAHAHA!
LARPING?!
SAY IT AIN'T SO, T-MAN.

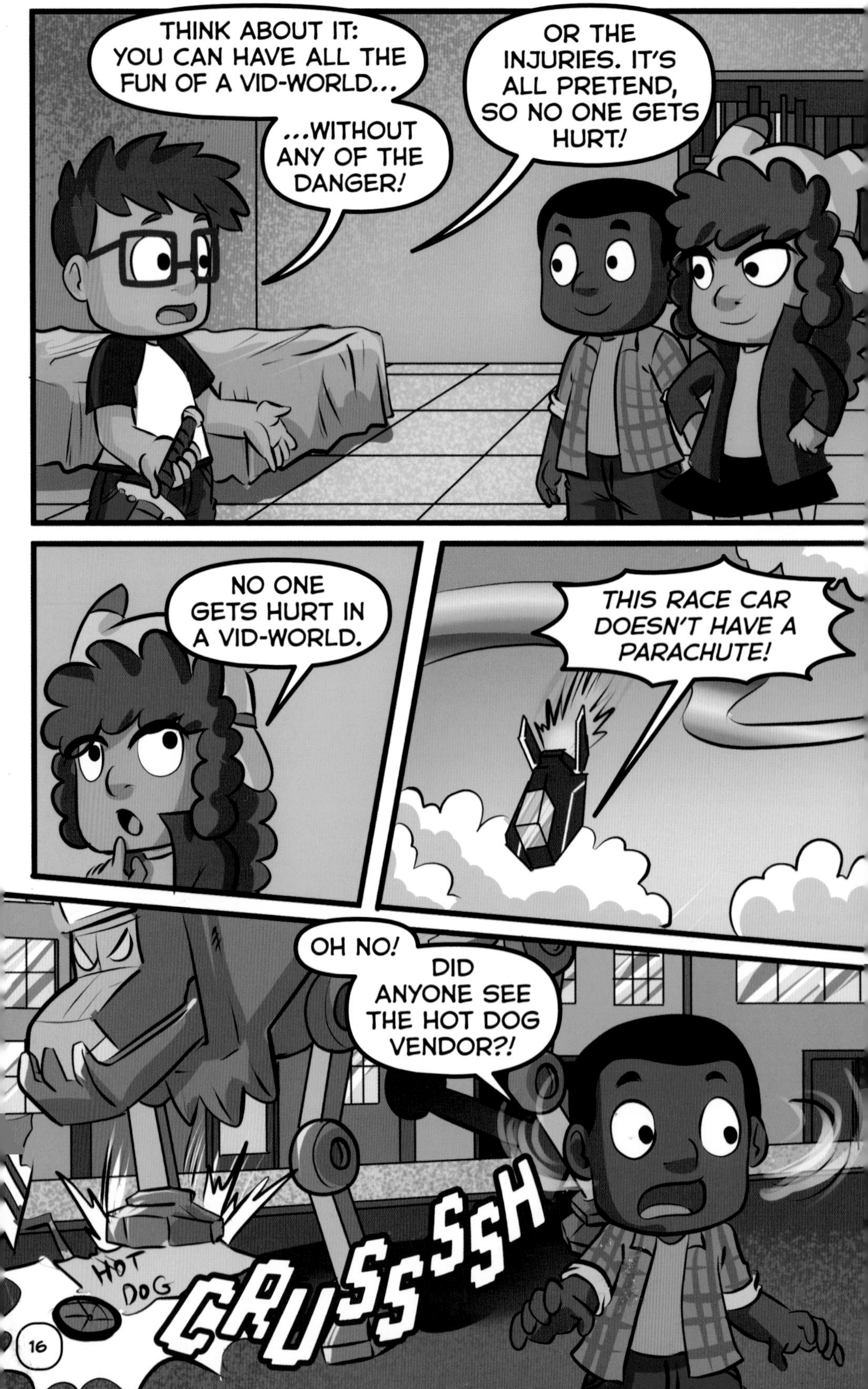
THINK ABOUT IT: YOU CAN HAVE ALL THE FUN OF A VID-WORLD...
...WITHOUT ANY OF THE DANGER!
OR THE INJURIES. IT'S ALL PRETEND, SO NO ONE GETS HURT!
NO ONE GETS HURT IN A VID-WORLD.
THIS RACE CAR DOESN'T HAVE A PARACHUTE!
OH NO!
DID ANYONE SEE THE HOT DOG VENDOR?!
HOT DOG
CRUSSSSSH

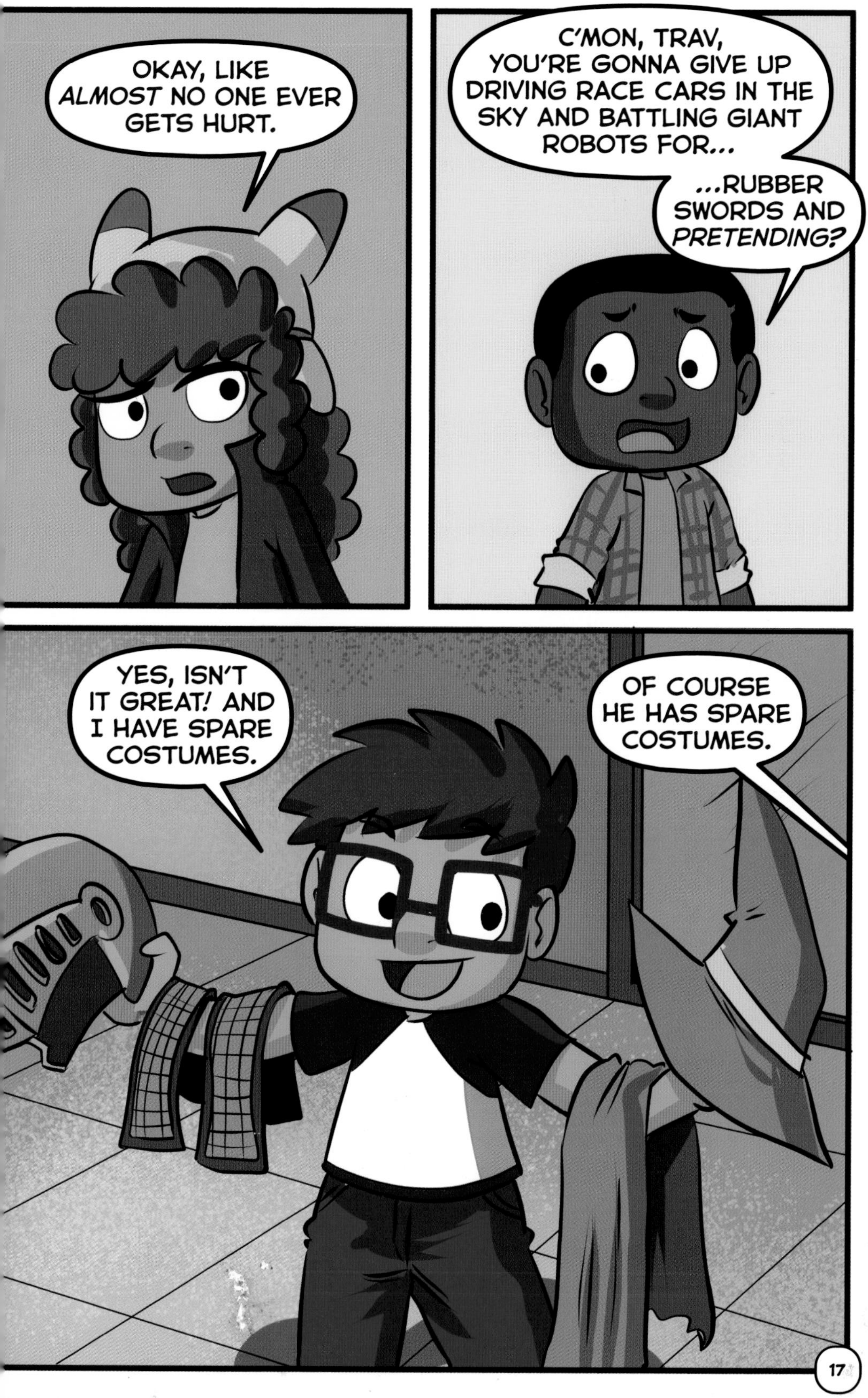
OKAY, LIKE *ALMOST* NO ONE EVER GETS HURT.
C'MON, TRAV, YOU'RE GONNA GIVE UP DRIVING RACE CARS IN THE SKY AND BATTLING GIANT ROBOTS FOR...
...RUBBER SWORDS AND *PRETENDING?*
YES, ISN'T IT GREAT! AND I HAVE SPARE COSTUMES.
OF COURSE HE HAS SPARE COSTUMES.

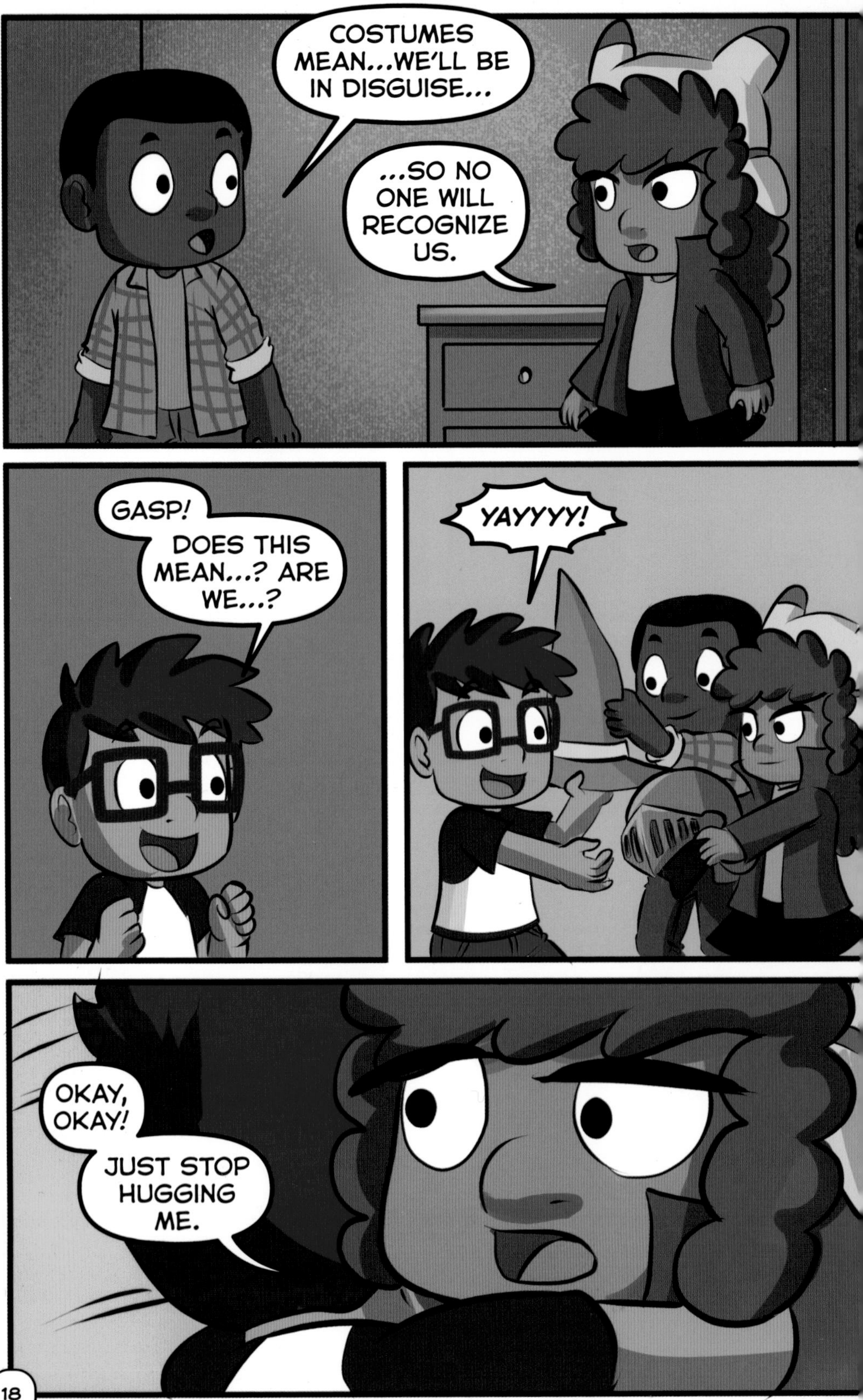
COSTUMES MEAN...WE'LL BE IN DISGUISE...
...SO NO ONE WILL RECOGNIZE US.
GASP!
DOES THIS MEAN...? ARE WE...?
YAYYYY!
OKAY, OKAY!
JUST STOP HUGGING ME.

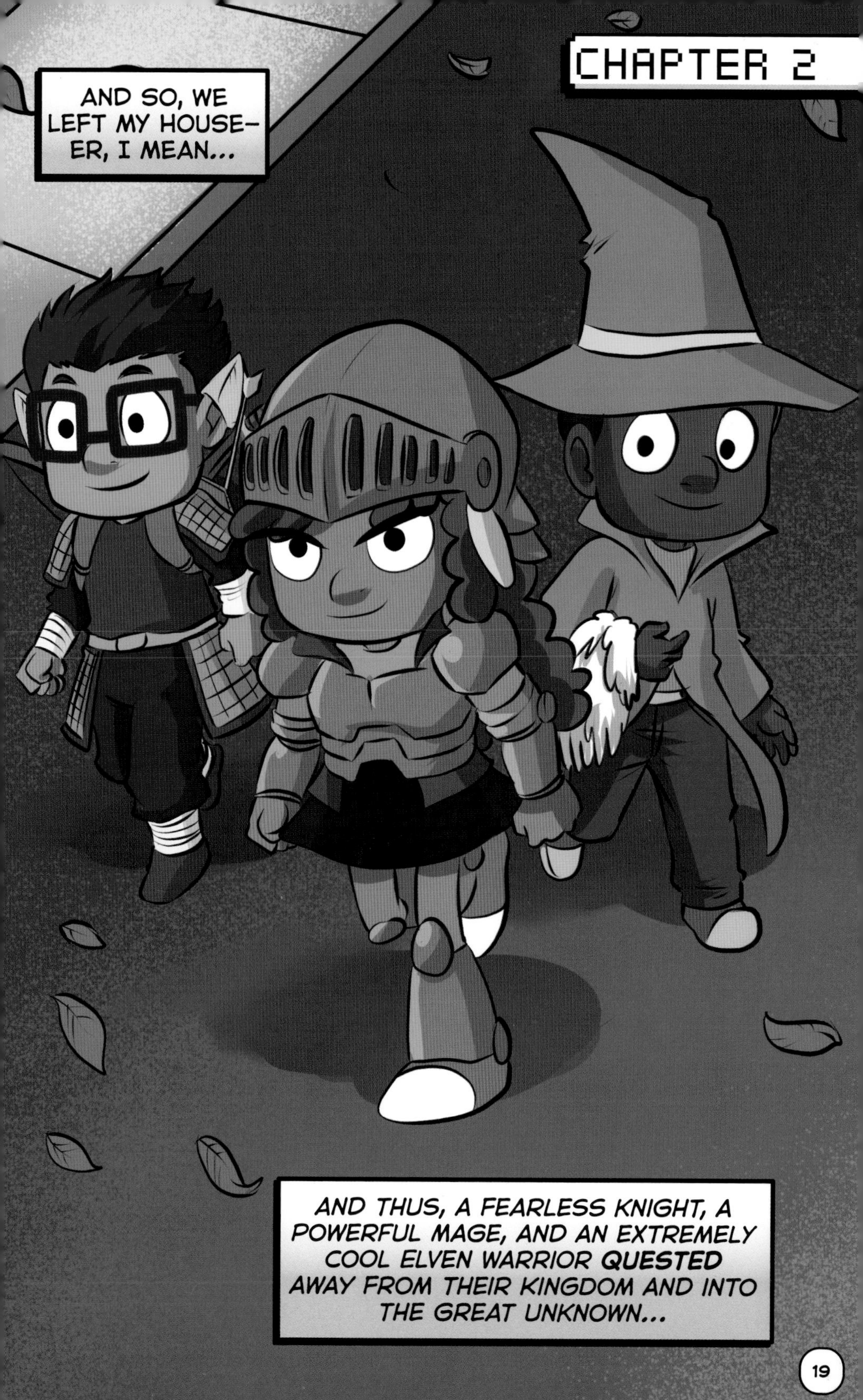
CHAPTER 2
AND SO, WE LEFT MY HOUSE–ER, I MEAN...
AND THUS, A FEARLESS KNIGHT, A POWERFUL MAGE, AND AN EXTREMELY COOL ELVEN WARRIOR **QUESTED** AWAY FROM THEIR KINGDOM AND INTO THE GREAT UNKNOWN...

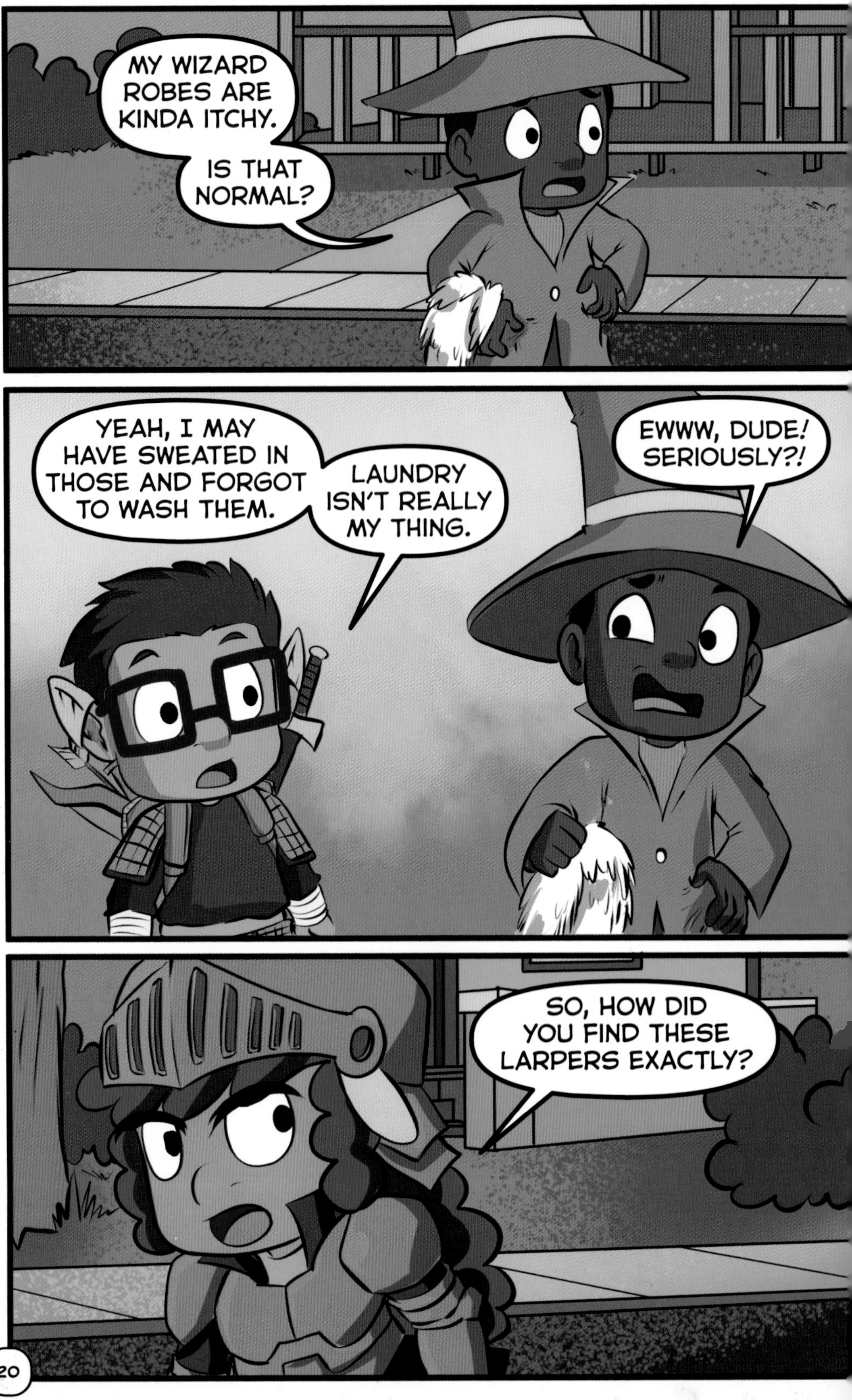
MY WIZARD ROBES ARE KINDA ITCHY.
IS THAT NORMAL?
YEAH, I MAY HAVE SWEATED IN THOSE AND FORGOT TO WASH THEM.
LAUNDRY ISN'T REALLY MY THING.
EWWW, DUDE! SERIOUSLY?!
SO, HOW DID YOU FIND THESE LARPERS EXACTLY?

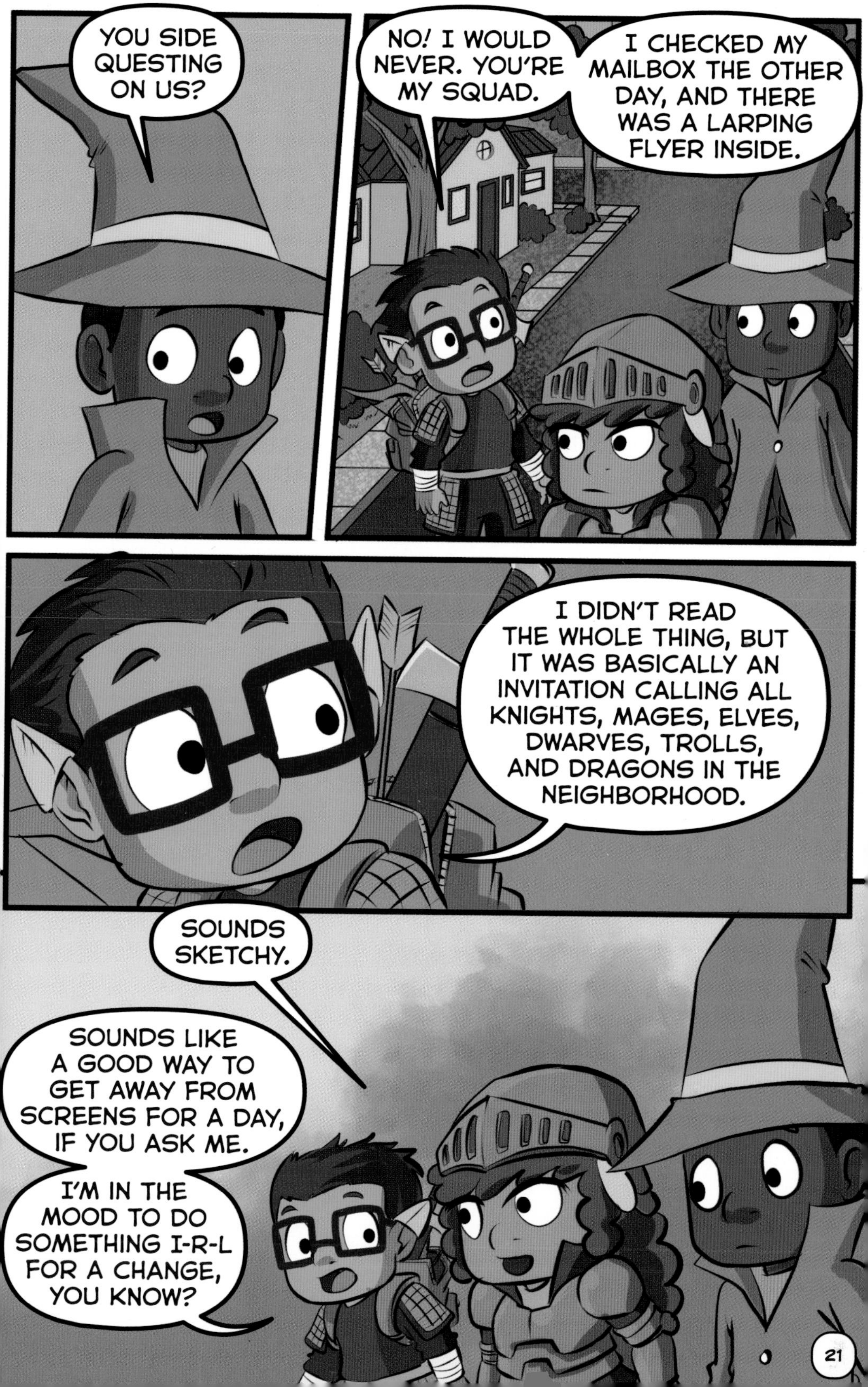
YOU SIDE QUESTING ON US?
NO! I WOULD NEVER. YOU'RE MY SQUAD.
I CHECKED MY MAILBOX THE OTHER DAY, AND THERE WAS A LARPING FLYER INSIDE.
I DIDN'T READ THE WHOLE THING, BUT IT WAS BASICALLY AN INVITATION CALLING ALL KNIGHTS, MAGES, ELVES, DWARVES, TROLLS, AND DRAGONS IN THE NEIGHBORHOOD.
SOUNDS SKETCHY.
SOUNDS LIKE A GOOD WAY TO GET AWAY FROM SCREENS FOR A DAY, IF YOU ASK ME.
I'M IN THE MOOD TO DO SOMETHING I-R-L FOR A CHANGE, YOU KNOW?

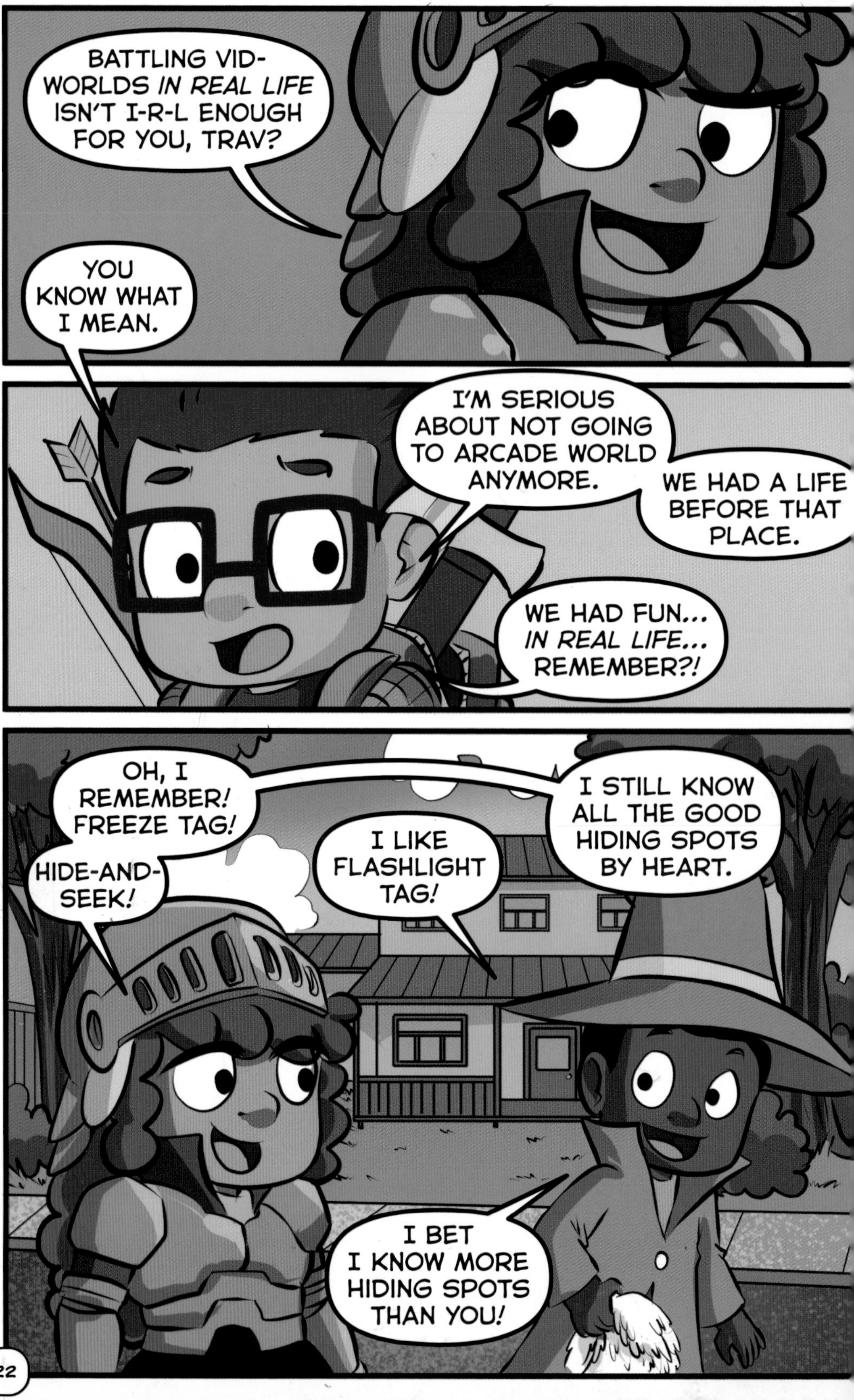
BATTLING VID-WORLDS *IN REAL LIFE* ISN'T I-R-L ENOUGH FOR YOU, TRAV?
YOU KNOW WHAT I MEAN.
I'M SERIOUS ABOUT NOT GOING TO ARCADE WORLD ANYMORE.
WE HAD A LIFE BEFORE THAT PLACE.
WE HAD FUN... *IN REAL LIFE...* REMEMBER?!
OH, I REMEMBER! FREEZE TAG!
HIDE-AND-SEEK!
I LIKE FLASHLIGHT TAG!
I STILL KNOW ALL THE GOOD HIDING SPOTS BY HEART.
I BET I KNOW MORE HIDING SPOTS THAN YOU!

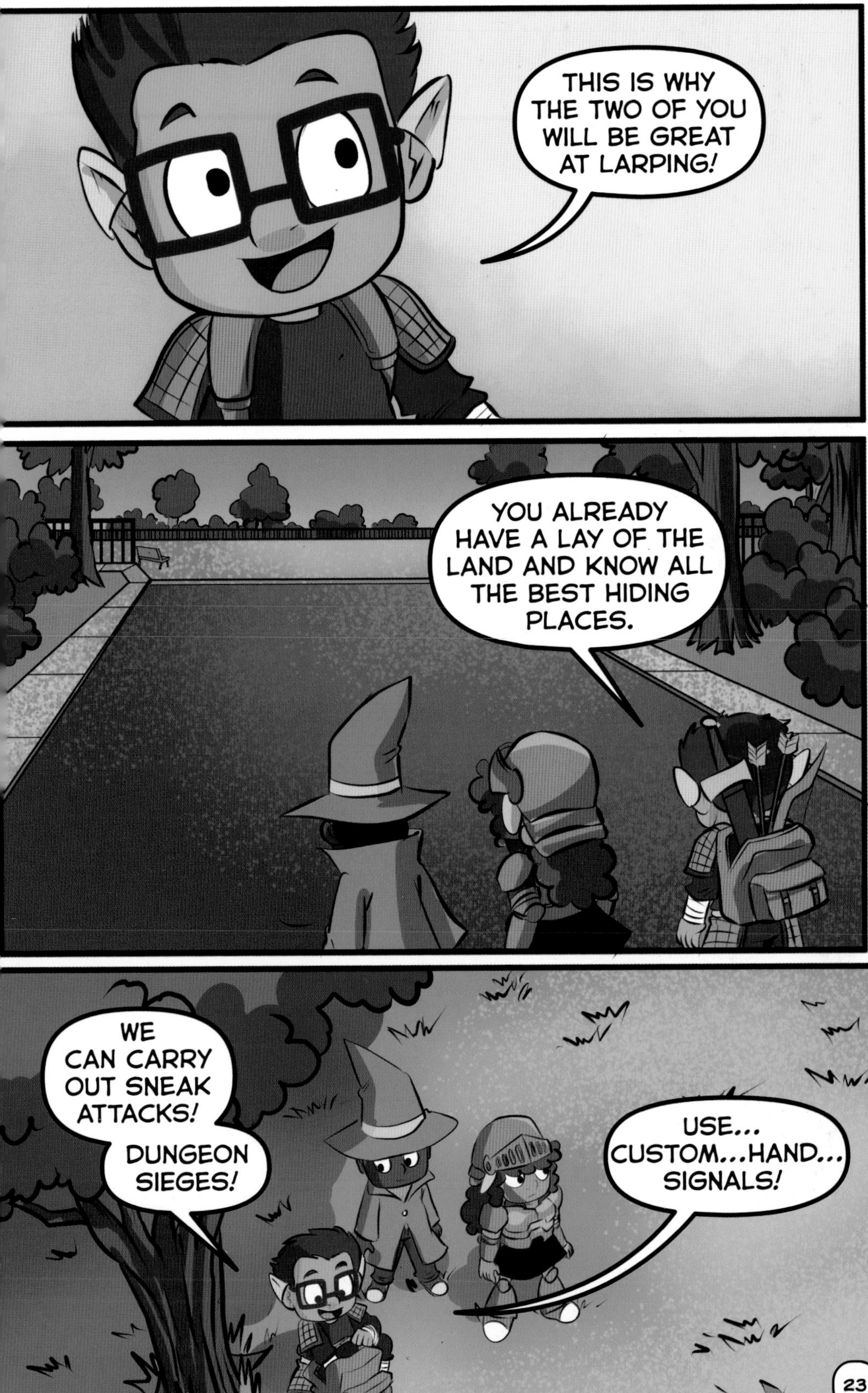
THIS IS WHY THE TWO OF YOU WILL BE GREAT AT LARPING!
YOU ALREADY HAVE A LAY OF THE LAND AND KNOW ALL THE BEST HIDING PLACES.
WE CAN CARRY OUT SNEAK ATTACKS!
DUNGEON SIEGES!
USE... CUSTOM...HAND... SIGNALS!

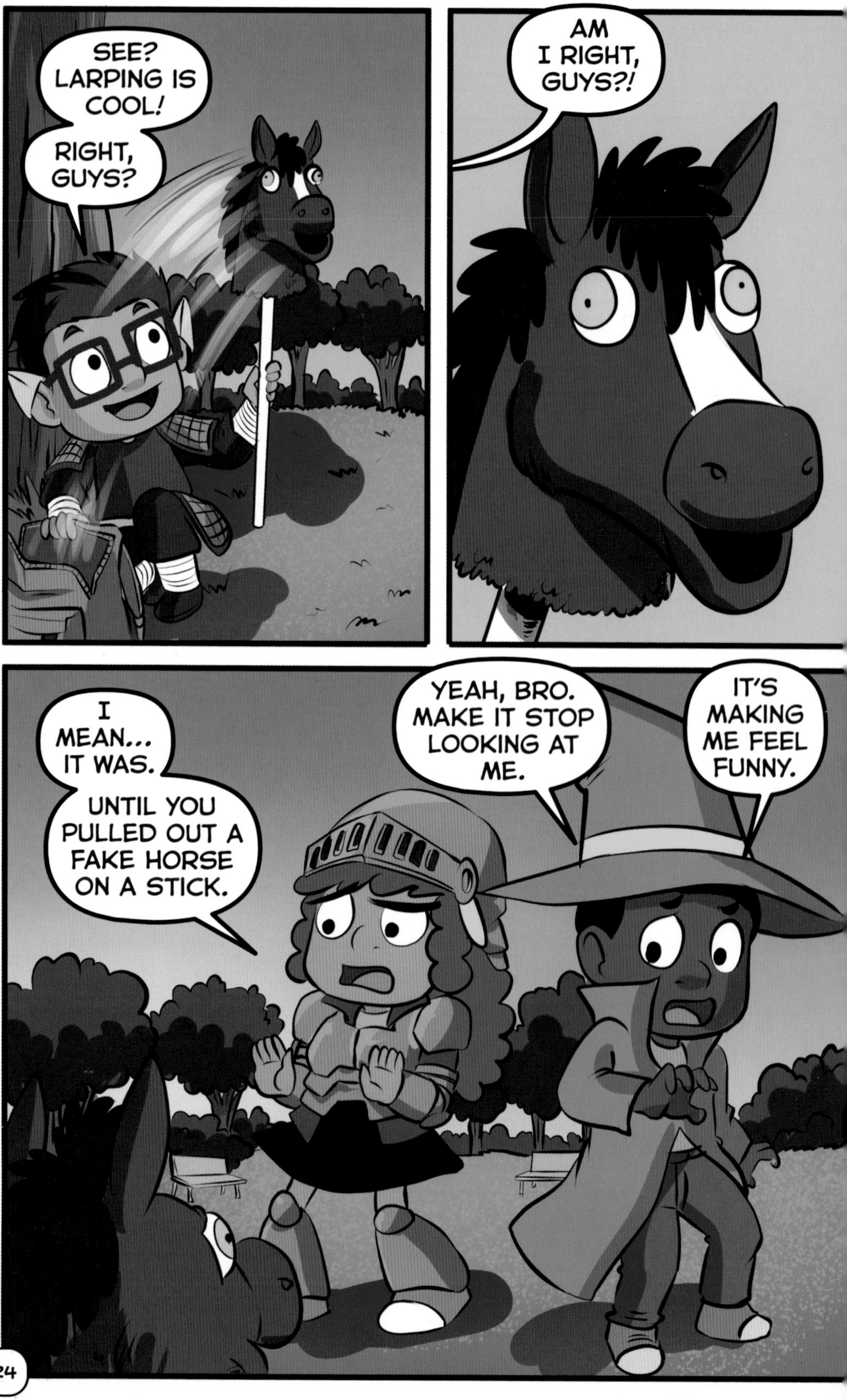
SEE? LARPING IS COOL!
RIGHT, GUYS?
AM I RIGHT, GUYS?!
I MEAN... IT WAS.
UNTIL YOU PULLED OUT A FAKE HORSE ON A STICK.
YEAH, BRO. MAKE IT STOP LOOKING AT ME.
IT'S MAKING ME FEEL FUNNY.

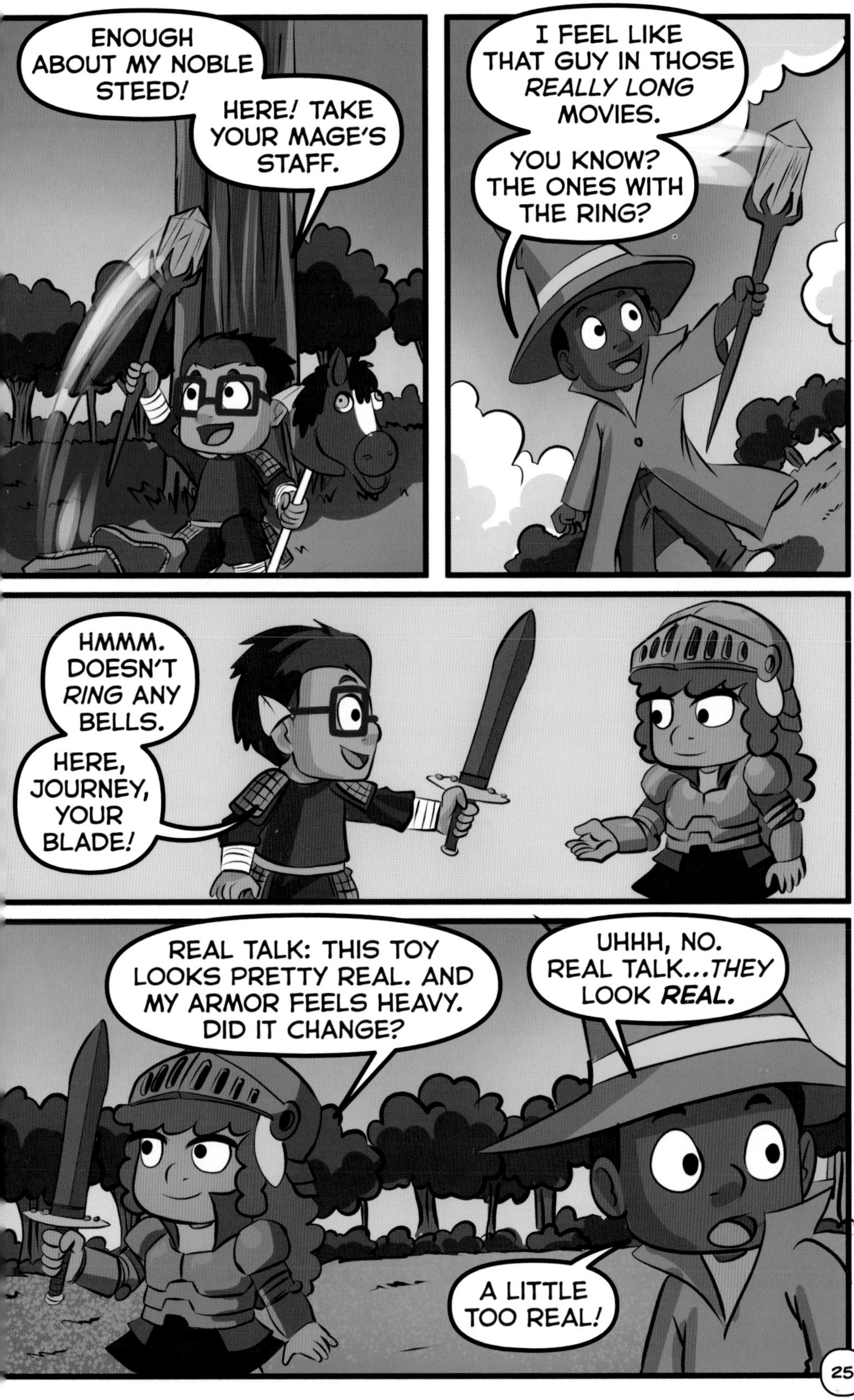
ENOUGH ABOUT MY NOBLE STEED!
HERE! TAKE YOUR MAGE'S STAFF.
I FEEL LIKE THAT GUY IN THOSE *REALLY LONG* MOVIES.
YOU KNOW? THE ONES WITH THE RING?
HMMM. DOESN'T *RING* ANY BELLS.
HERE, JOURNEY, YOUR BLADE!
REAL TALK: THIS TOY LOOKS PRETTY REAL. AND MY ARMOR FEELS HEAVY. DID IT CHANGE?
UHHH, NO. REAL TALK...*THEY* LOOK ***REAL.***
A LITTLE TOO REAL!

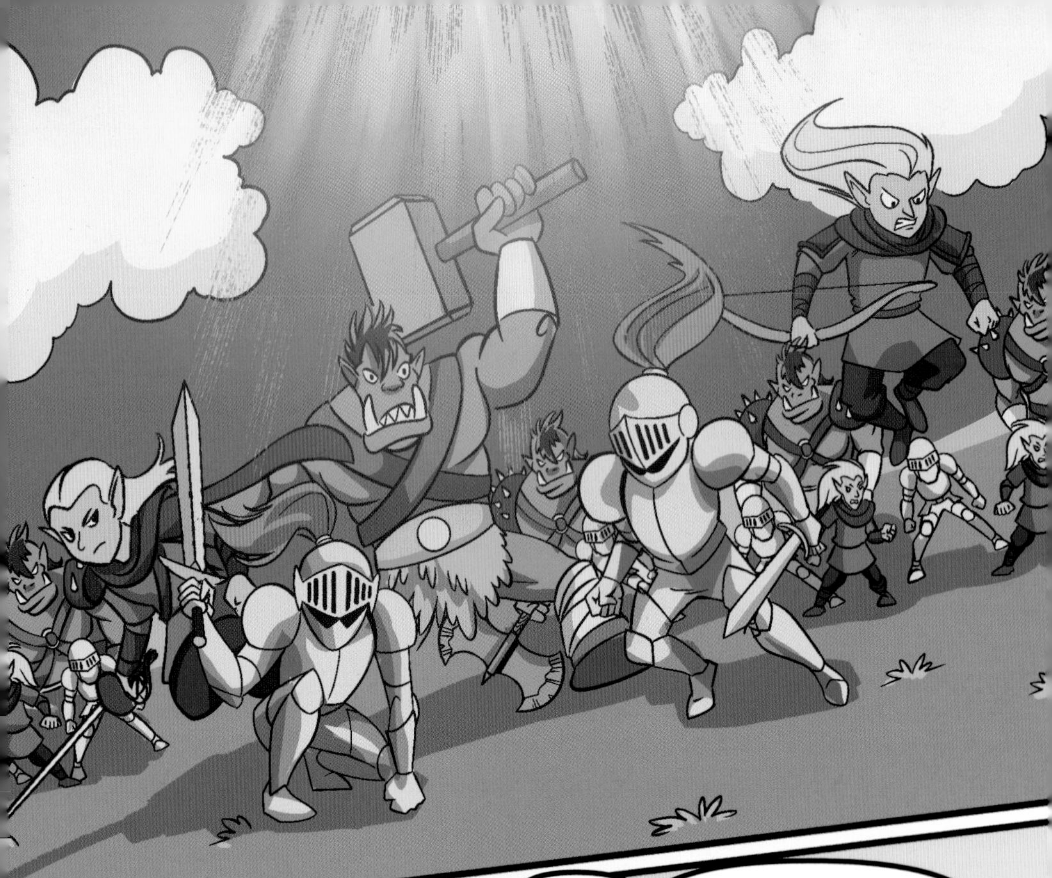

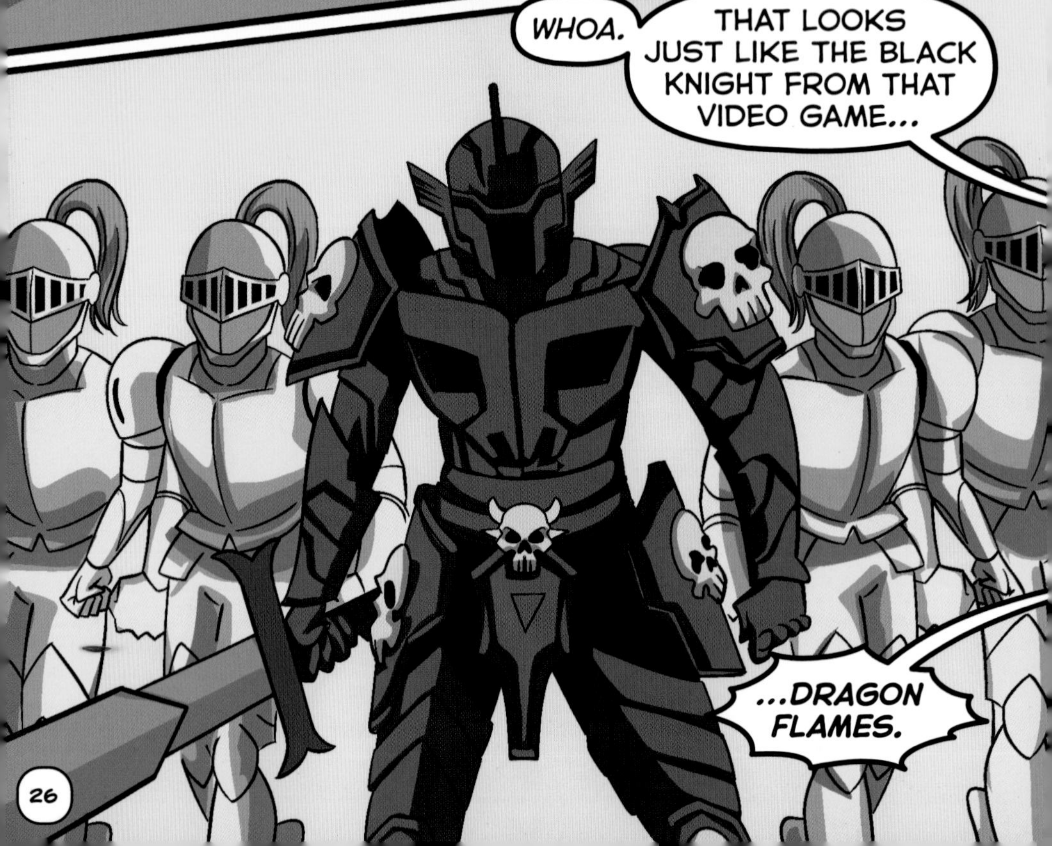
WHOA.
THAT LOOKS JUST LIKE THE BLACK KNIGHT FROM THAT VIDEO GAME...
...DRAGON FLAMES.

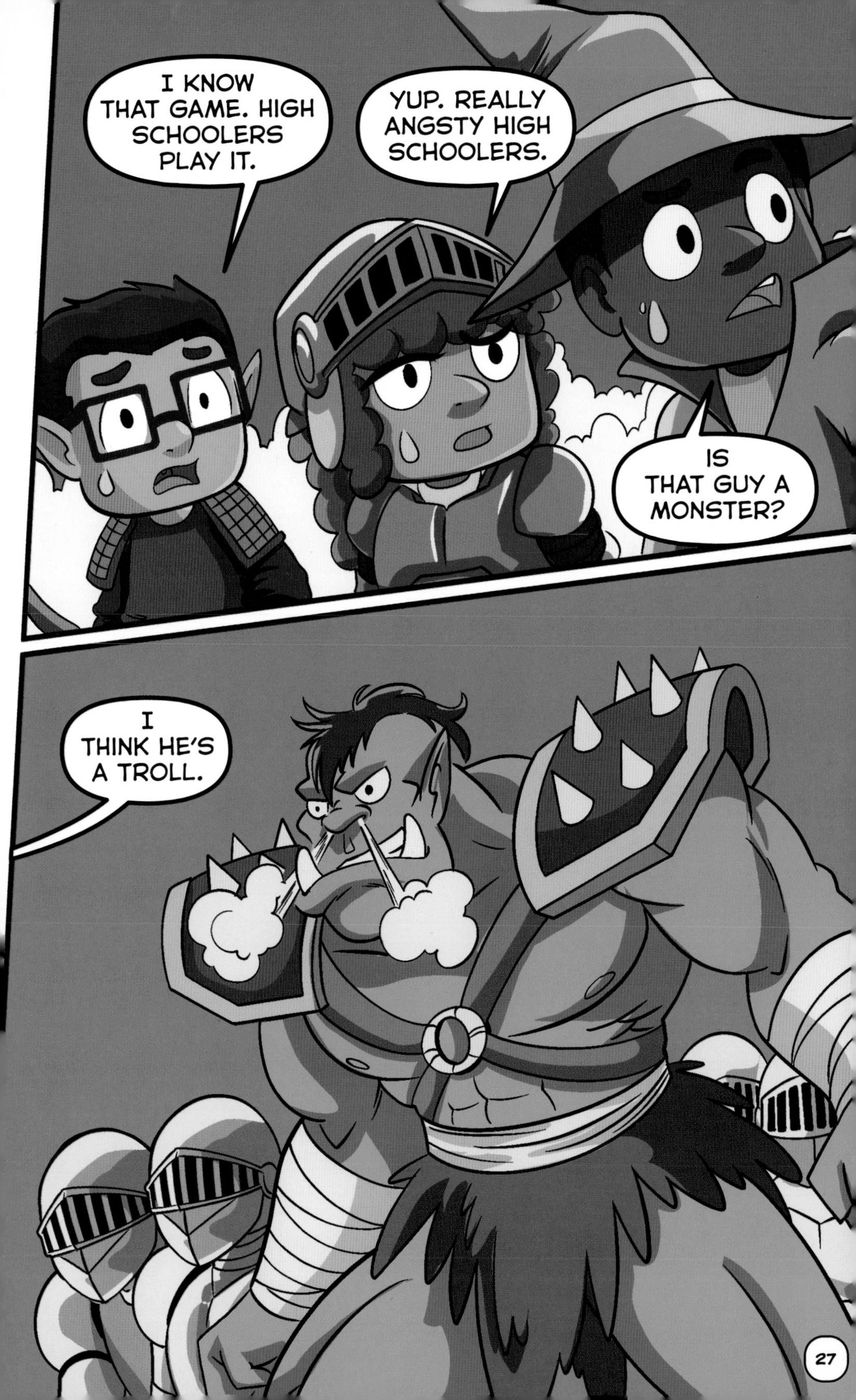

I KNOW THAT GAME. HIGH SCHOOLERS PLAY IT.
YUP. REALLY ANGSTY HIGH SCHOOLERS.
IS THAT GUY A MONSTER?
I THINK HE'S A TROLL.

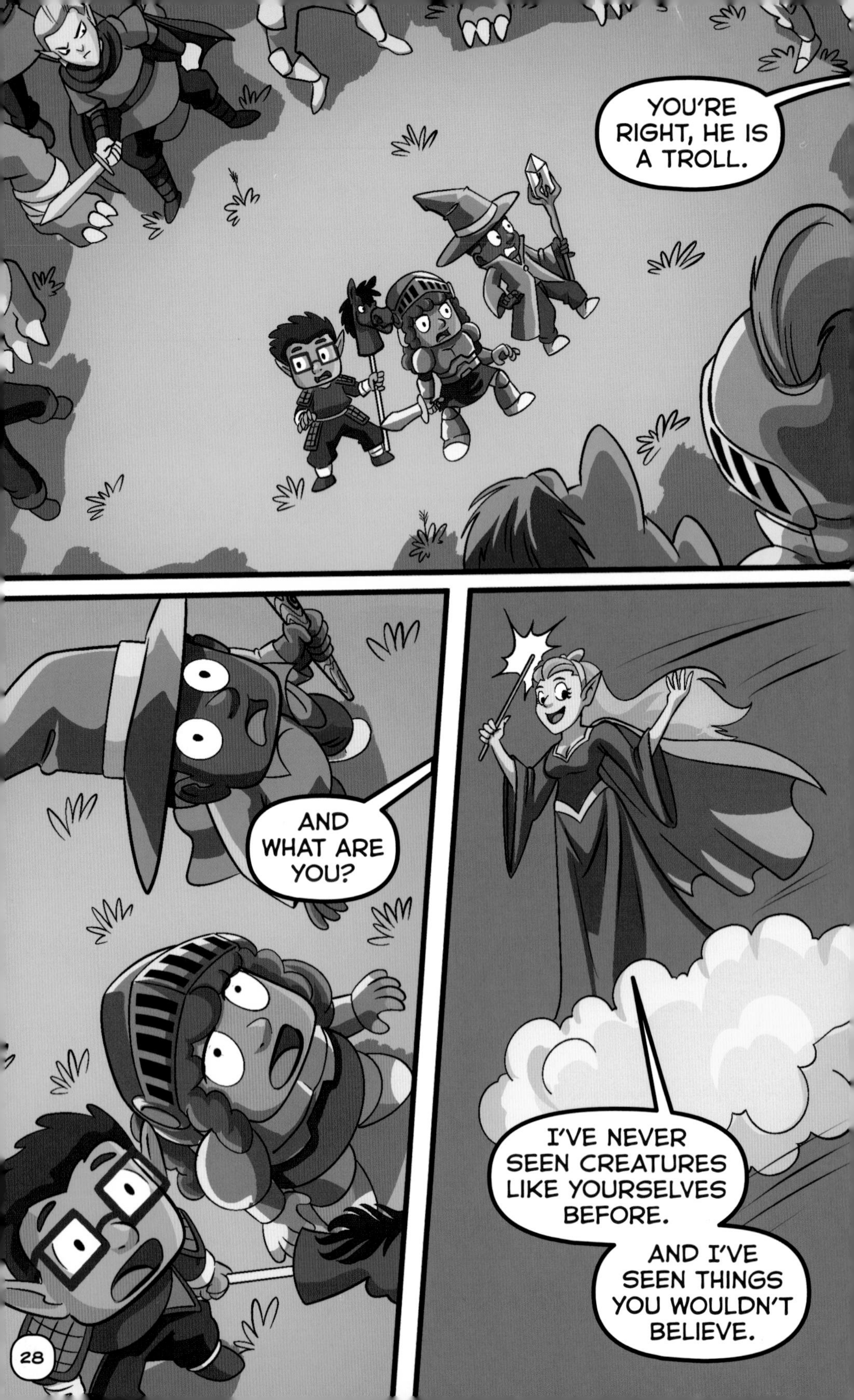
YOU'RE RIGHT, HE IS A TROLL.
AND WHAT ARE YOU?
I'VE NEVER SEEN CREATURES LIKE YOURSELVES BEFORE.
AND I'VE SEEN THINGS YOU WOULDN'T BELIEVE.

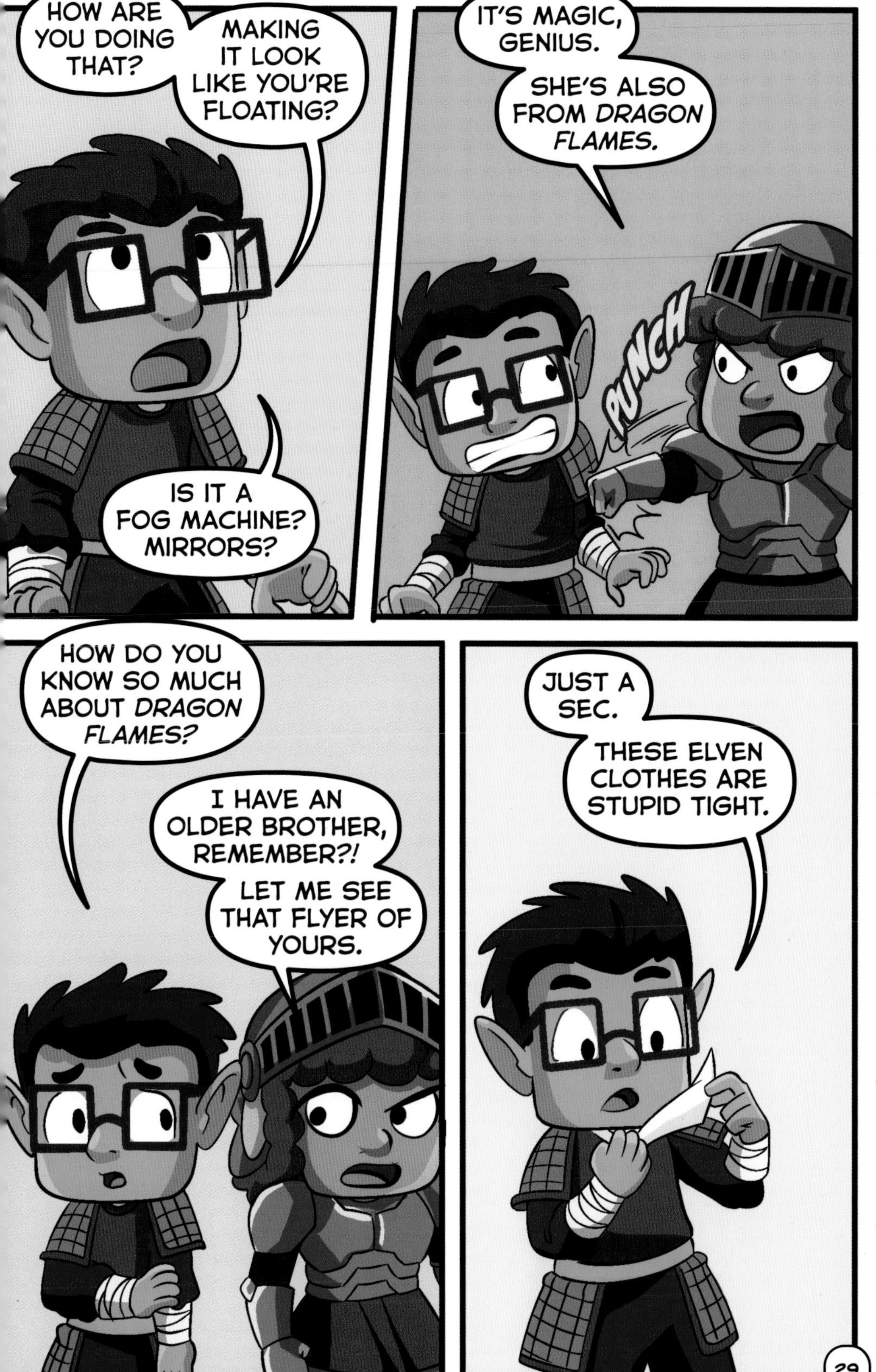
HOW ARE YOU DOING THAT?
MAKING IT LOOK LIKE YOU'RE FLOATING?
IS IT A FOG MACHINE? MIRRORS?
IT'S MAGIC, GENIUS.
SHE'S ALSO FROM *DRAGON FLAMES.*
PUNCH
HOW DO YOU KNOW SO MUCH ABOUT *DRAGON FLAMES?*
I HAVE AN OLDER BROTHER, REMEMBER?!
LET ME SEE THAT FLYER OF YOURS.
JUST A SEC.
THESE ELVEN CLOTHES ARE STUPID TIGHT.

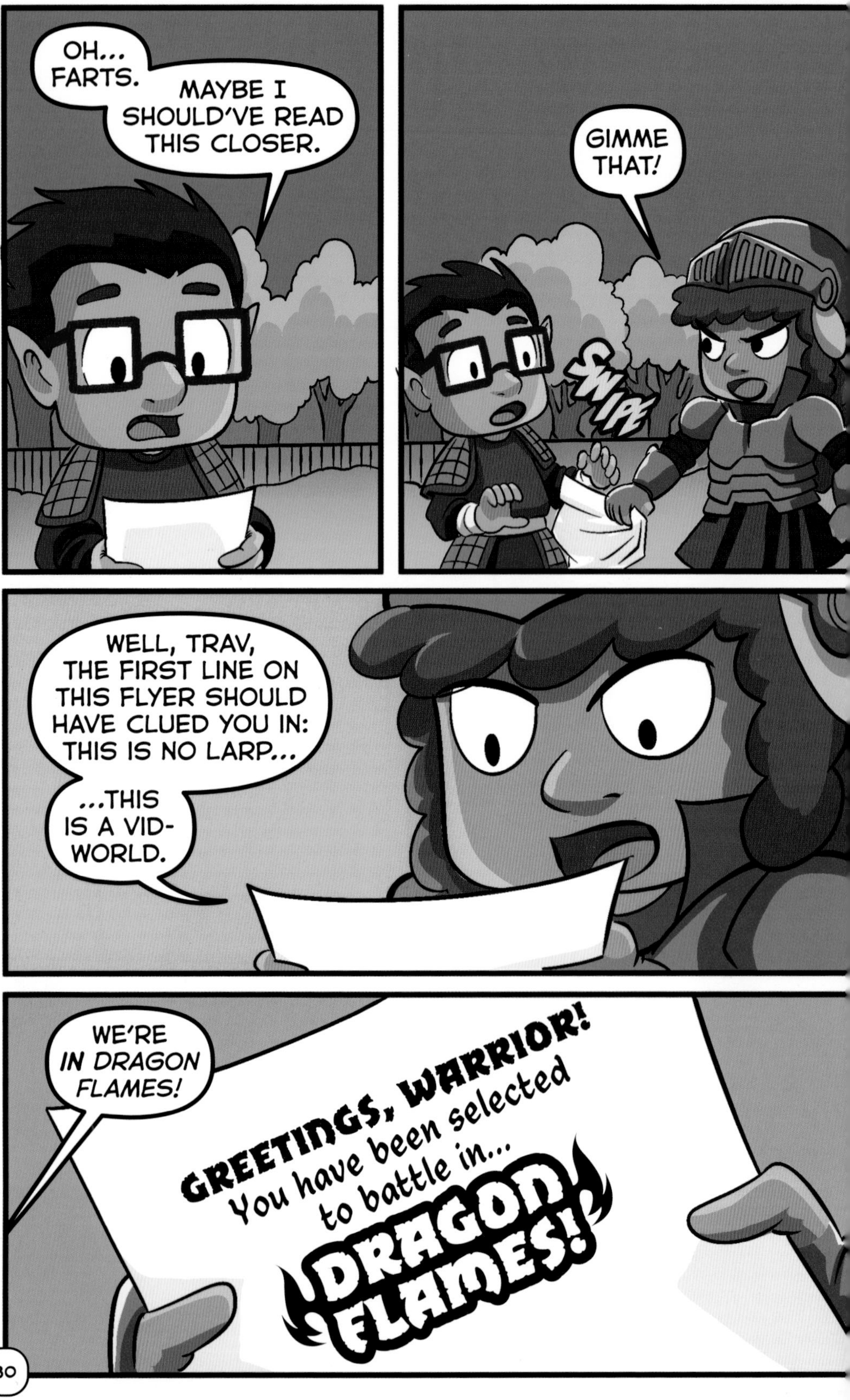
OH... FARTS.
MAYBE I SHOULD'VE READ THIS CLOSER.
GIMME THAT!
SWIPE
WELL, TRAV, THE FIRST LINE ON THIS FLYER SHOULD HAVE CLUED YOU IN: THIS IS NO LARP...
...THIS IS A VID-WORLD.
WE'RE *IN DRAGON FLAMES!*
GREETINGS, WARRIOR! You have been selected to battle in... DRAGON FLAMES!

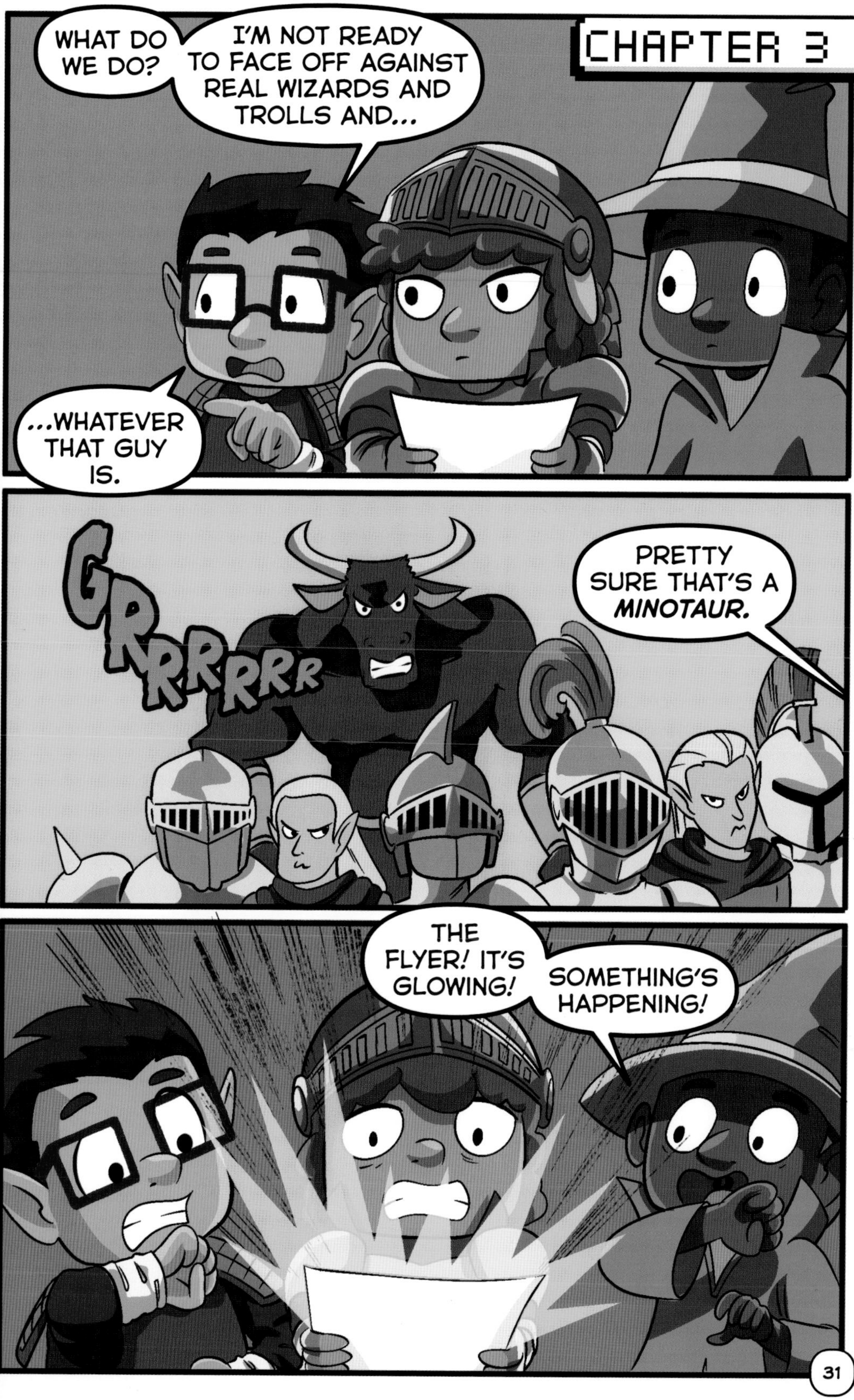
CHAPTER 3
WHAT DO WE DO?
I'M NOT READY TO FACE OFF AGAINST REAL WIZARDS AND TROLLS AND...
...WHATEVER THAT GUY IS.
GRRRRRR
PRETTY SURE THAT'S A *MINOTAUR.*
THE FLYER! IT'S GLOWING!
SOMETHING'S HAPPENING!

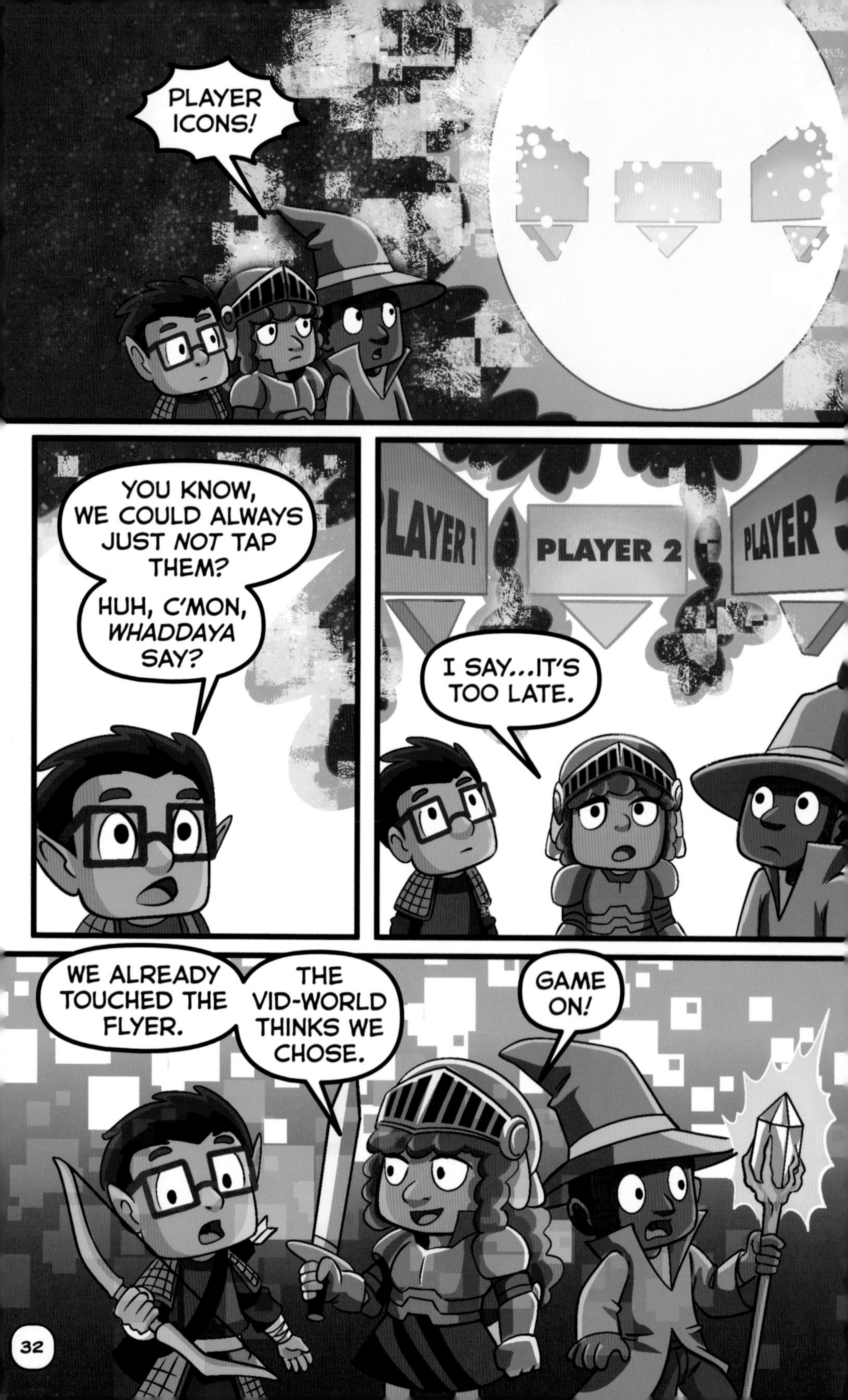
PLAYER ICONS!
YOU KNOW, WE COULD ALWAYS JUST NOT TAP THEM?
HUH, C'MON, WHADDAYA SAY?
PLAYER 2
I SAY...IT'S TOO LATE.
WE ALREADY TOUCHED THE FLYER.
THE VID-WORLD THINKS WE CHOSE.
GAME ON!

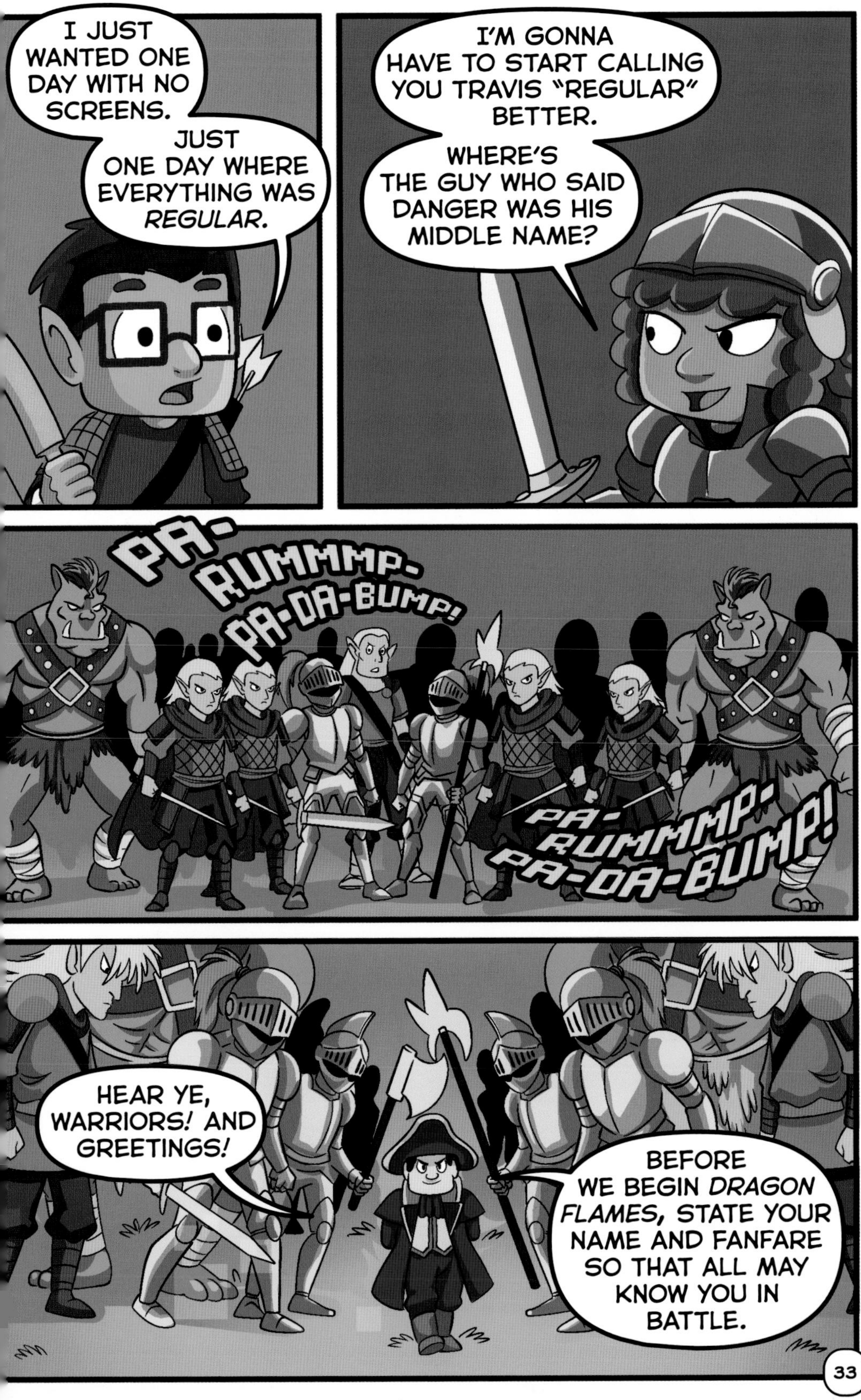

I JUST WANTED ONE DAY WITH NO SCREENS.
JUST ONE DAY WHERE EVERYTHING WAS *REGULAR*.
I'M GONNA HAVE TO START CALLING YOU TRAVIS "REGULAR" BETTER.
WHERE'S THE GUY WHO SAID DANGER WAS HIS MIDDLE NAME?
PA-RUMMMP-PA-DA-BUMP!
PA-RUMMMP-PA-DA-BUMP!
HEAR YE, WARRIORS! AND GREETINGS!
BEFORE WE BEGIN *DRAGON FLAMES*, STATE YOUR NAME AND FANFARE SO THAT ALL MAY KNOW YOU IN BATTLE.

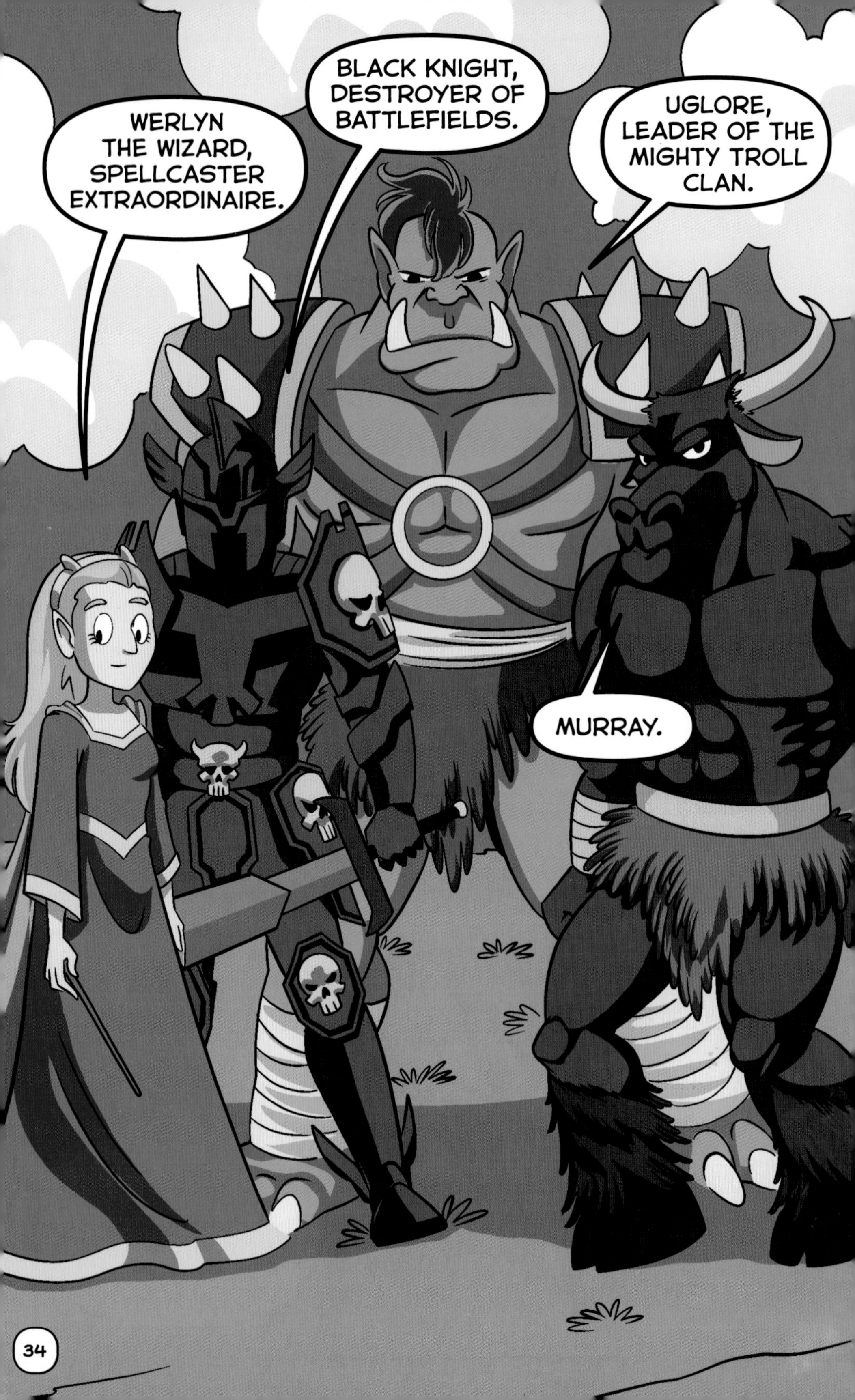
WERLYN THE WIZARD, SPELLCASTER EXTRAORDINAIRE.
BLACK KNIGHT, DESTROYER OF BATTLEFIELDS.
UGLORE, LEADER OF THE MIGHTY TROLL CLAN.
MURRAY.

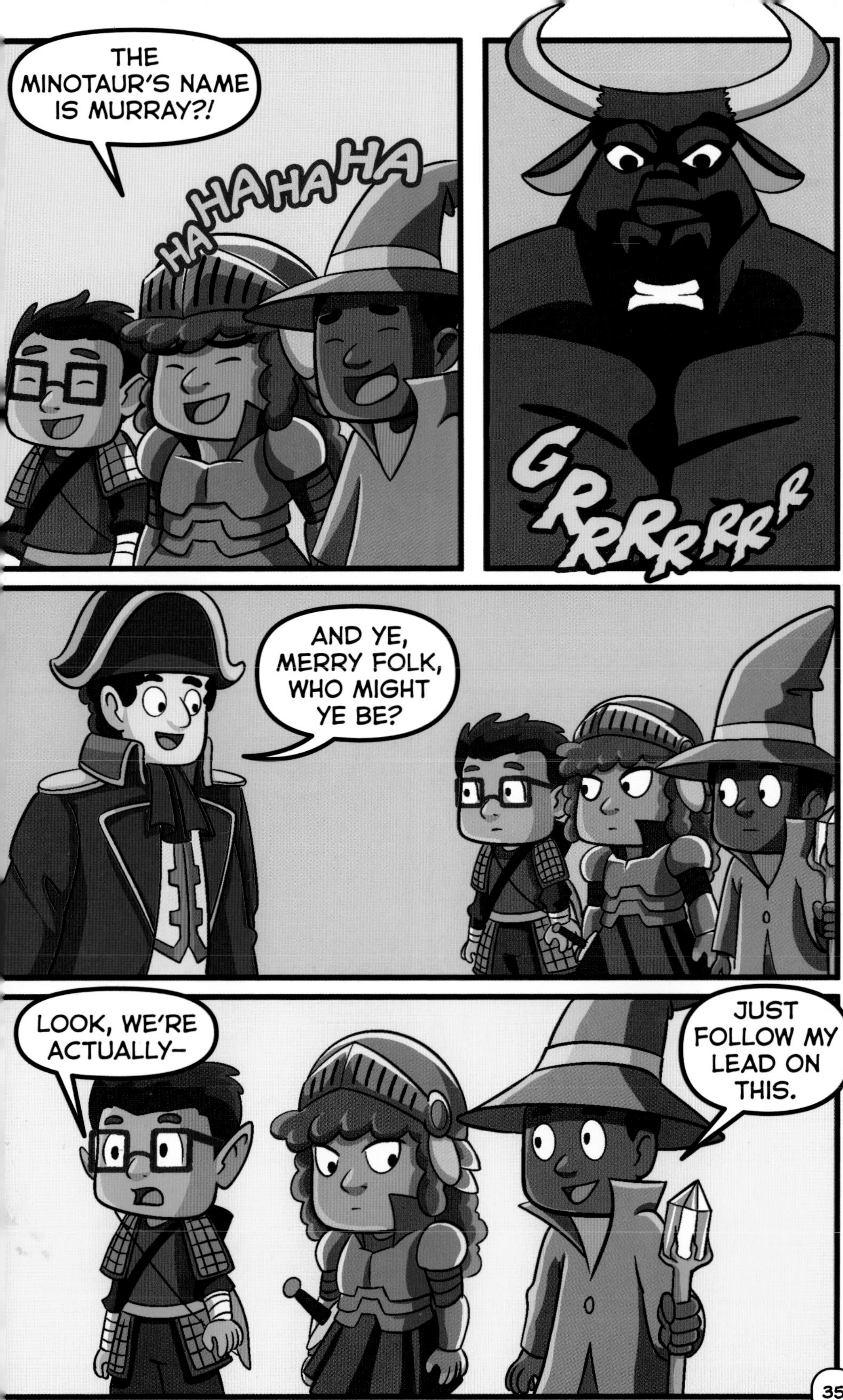
THE MINOTAUR'S NAME IS MURRAY?!
HAHAHAHAHA
GRRRRRRR
AND YE, MERRY FOLK, WHO MIGHT YE BE?
LOOK, WE'RE ACTUALLY–
JUST FOLLOW MY LEAD ON THIS.

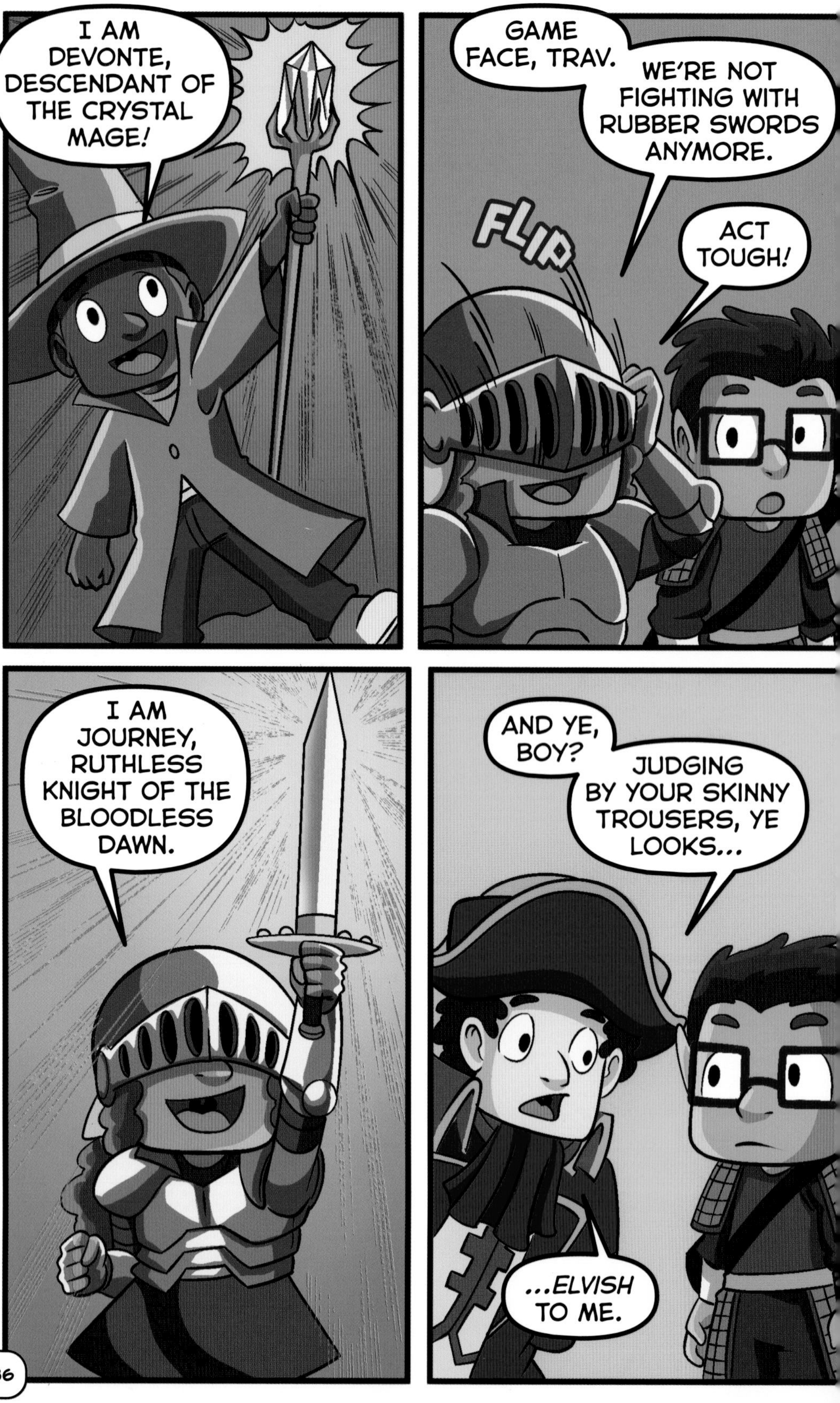
I AM DEVONTE, DESCENDANT OF THE CRYSTAL MAGE!
GAME FACE, TRAV.
WE'RE NOT FIGHTING WITH RUBBER SWORDS ANYMORE.
FLIP
ACT TOUGH!
I AM JOURNEY, RUTHLESS KNIGHT OF THE BLOODLESS DAWN.
AND YE, BOY?
JUDGING BY YOUR SKINNY TROUSERS, YE LOOKS...
...ELVISH TO ME.

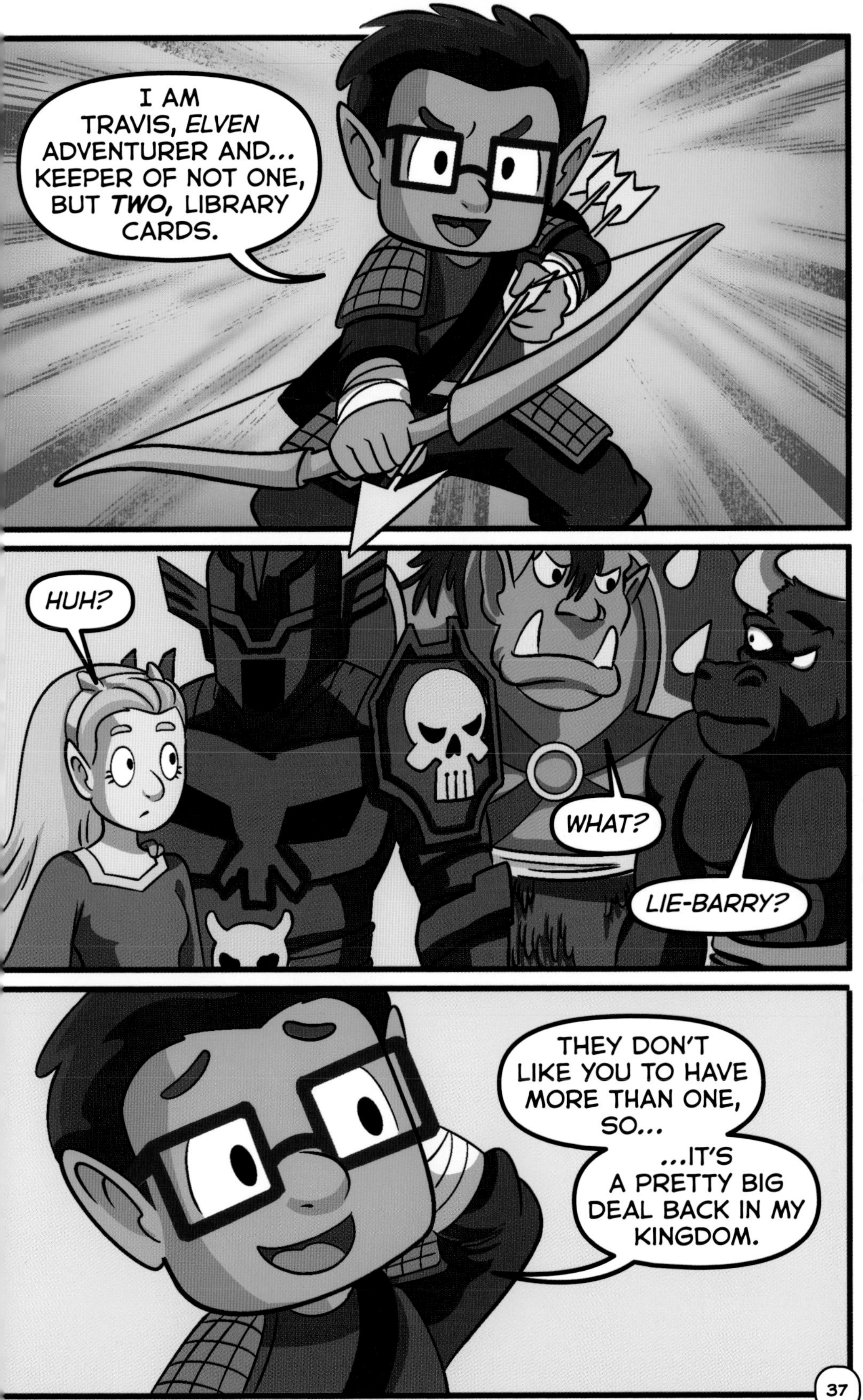
I AM TRAVIS, *ELVEN* ADVENTURER AND... KEEPER OF NOT ONE, BUT ***TWO,*** LIBRARY CARDS.
HUH?
WHAT?
LIE-BARRY?
THEY DON'T LIKE YOU TO HAVE MORE THAN ONE, SO...
...IT'S A PRETTY BIG DEAL BACK IN MY KINGDOM.

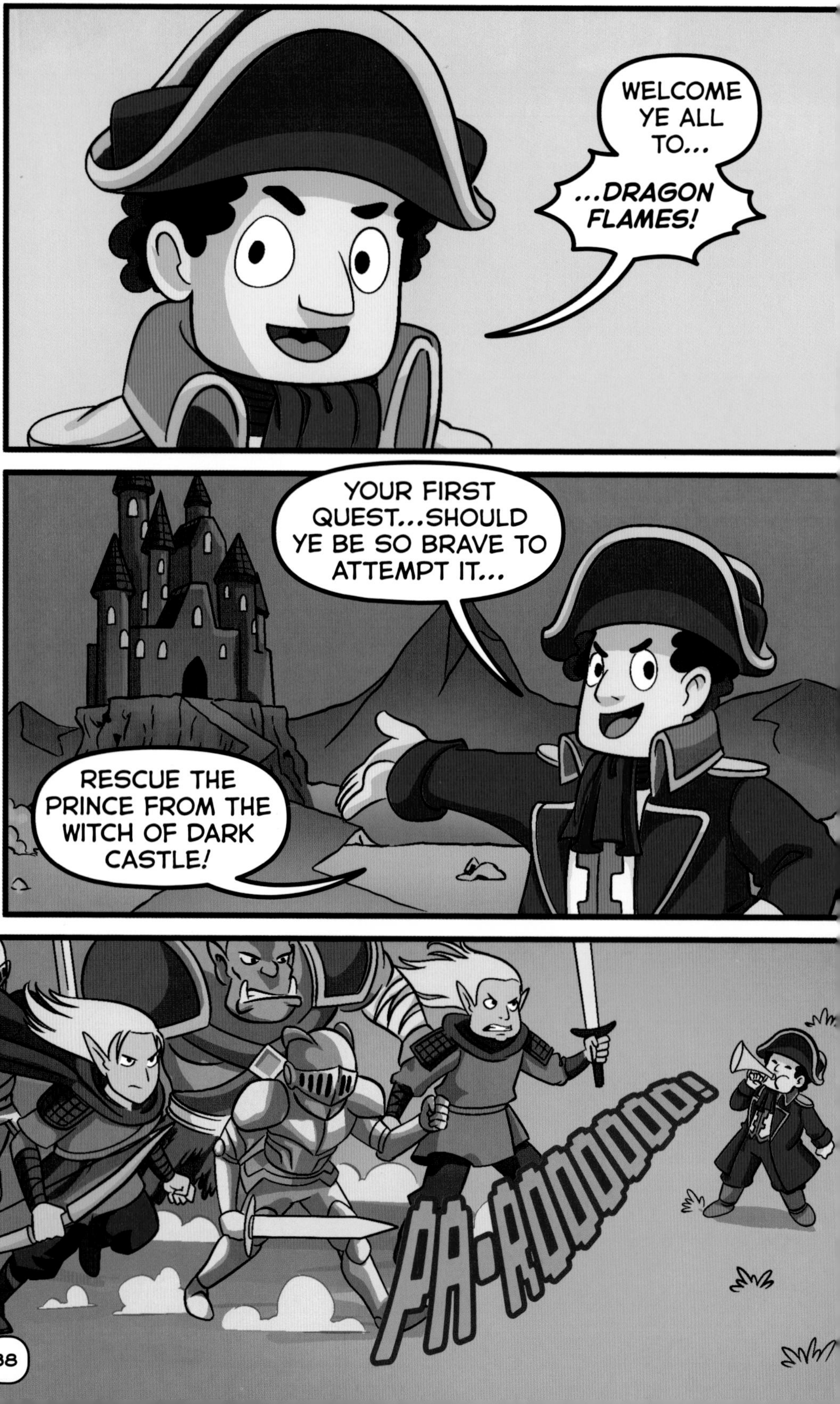
WELCOME YE ALL TO...
...DRAGON FLAMES!
YOUR FIRST QUEST...SHOULD YE BE SO BRAVE TO ATTEMPT IT...
RESCUE THE PRINCE FROM THE WITCH OF DARK CASTLE!
PA-ROOOOOO!

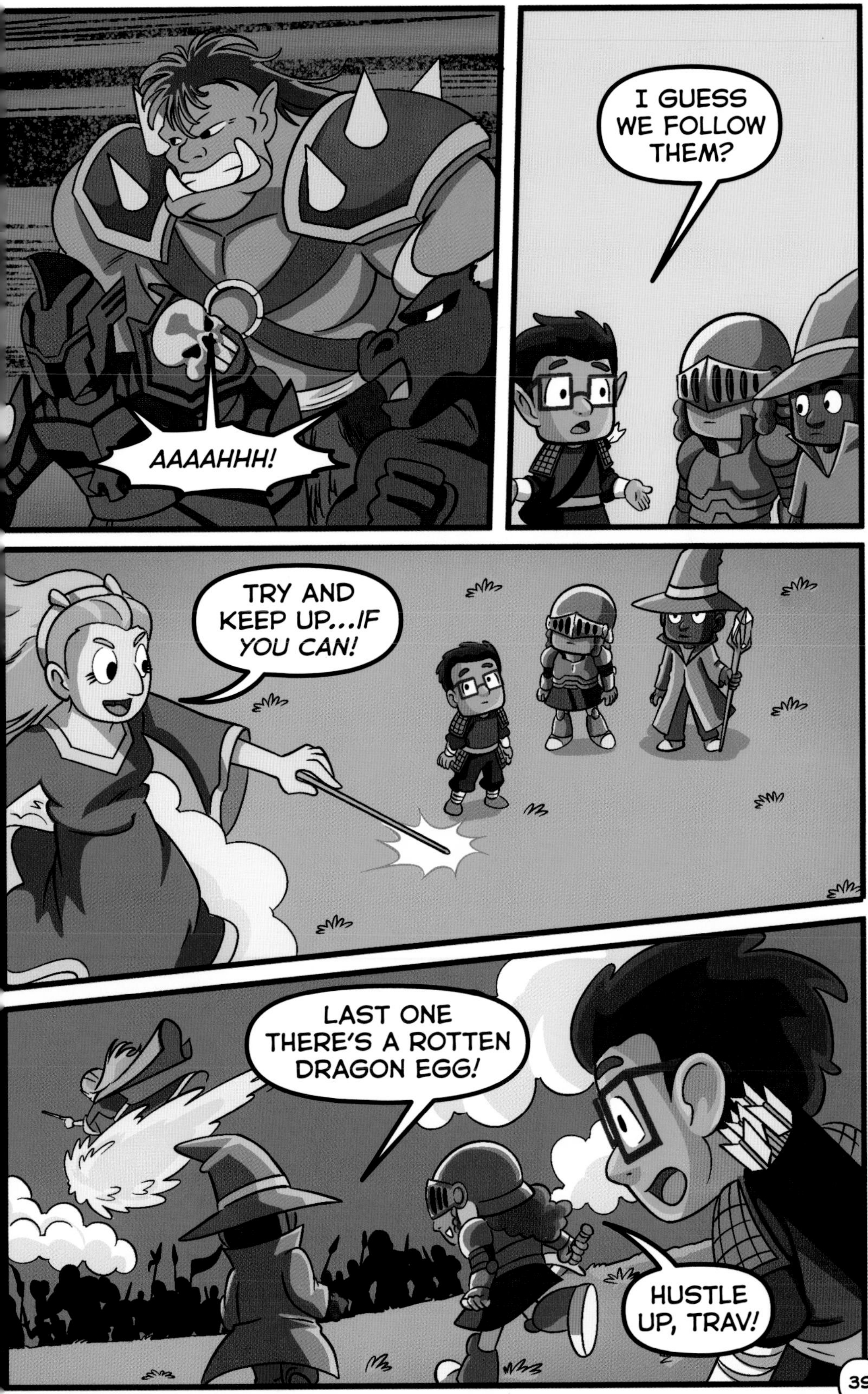

AAAAHHH!
I GUESS WE FOLLOW THEM?
TRY AND KEEP UP...IF YOU CAN!
LAST ONE THERE'S A ROTTEN DRAGON EGG!
HUSTLE UP, TRAV!

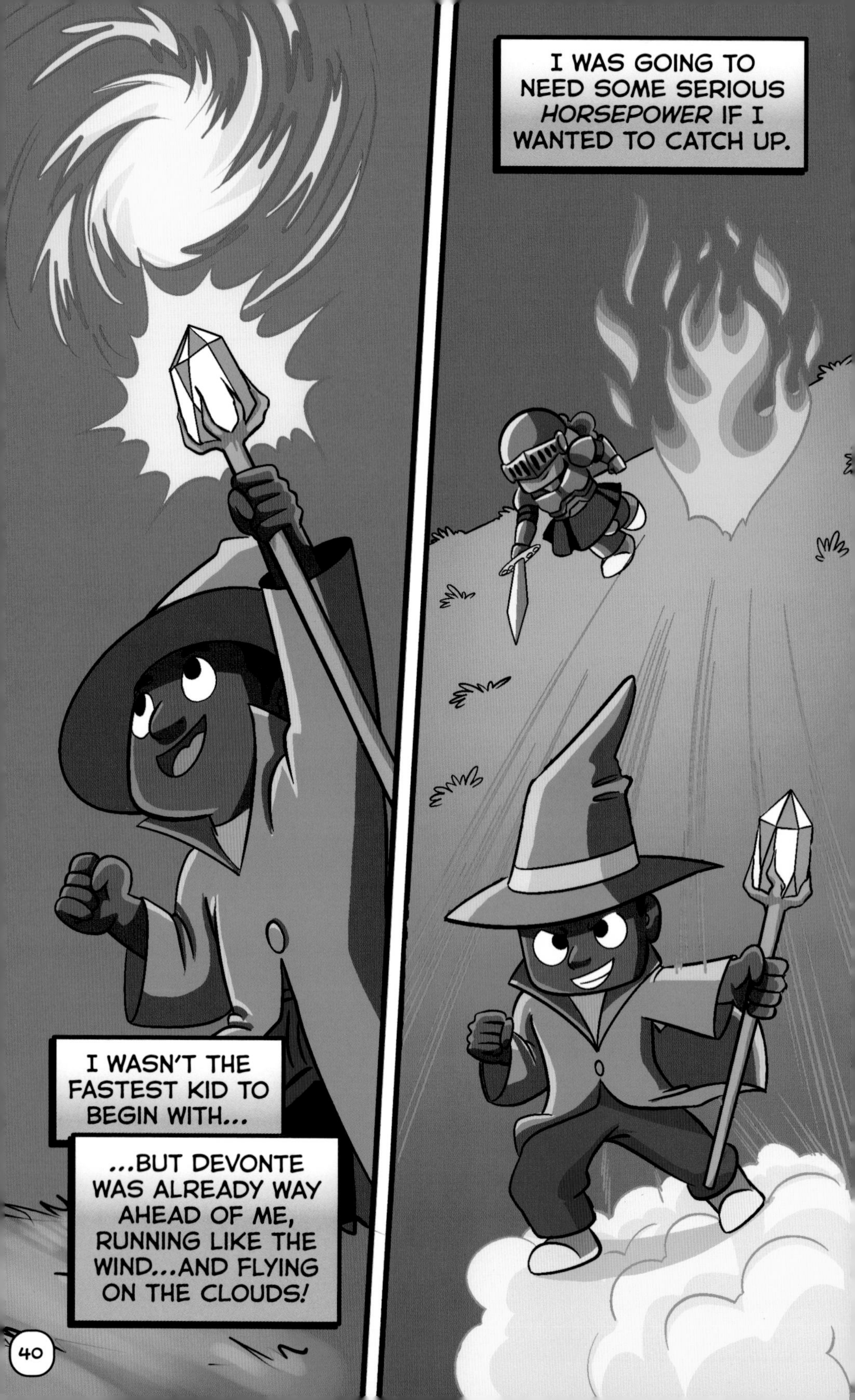
I WASN'T THE FASTEST KID TO BEGIN WITH...
...BUT DEVONTE WAS ALREADY WAY AHEAD OF ME, RUNNING LIKE THE WIND...AND FLYING ON THE CLOUDS!
I WAS GOING TO NEED SOME SERIOUS *HORSEPOWER* IF I WANTED TO CATCH UP.

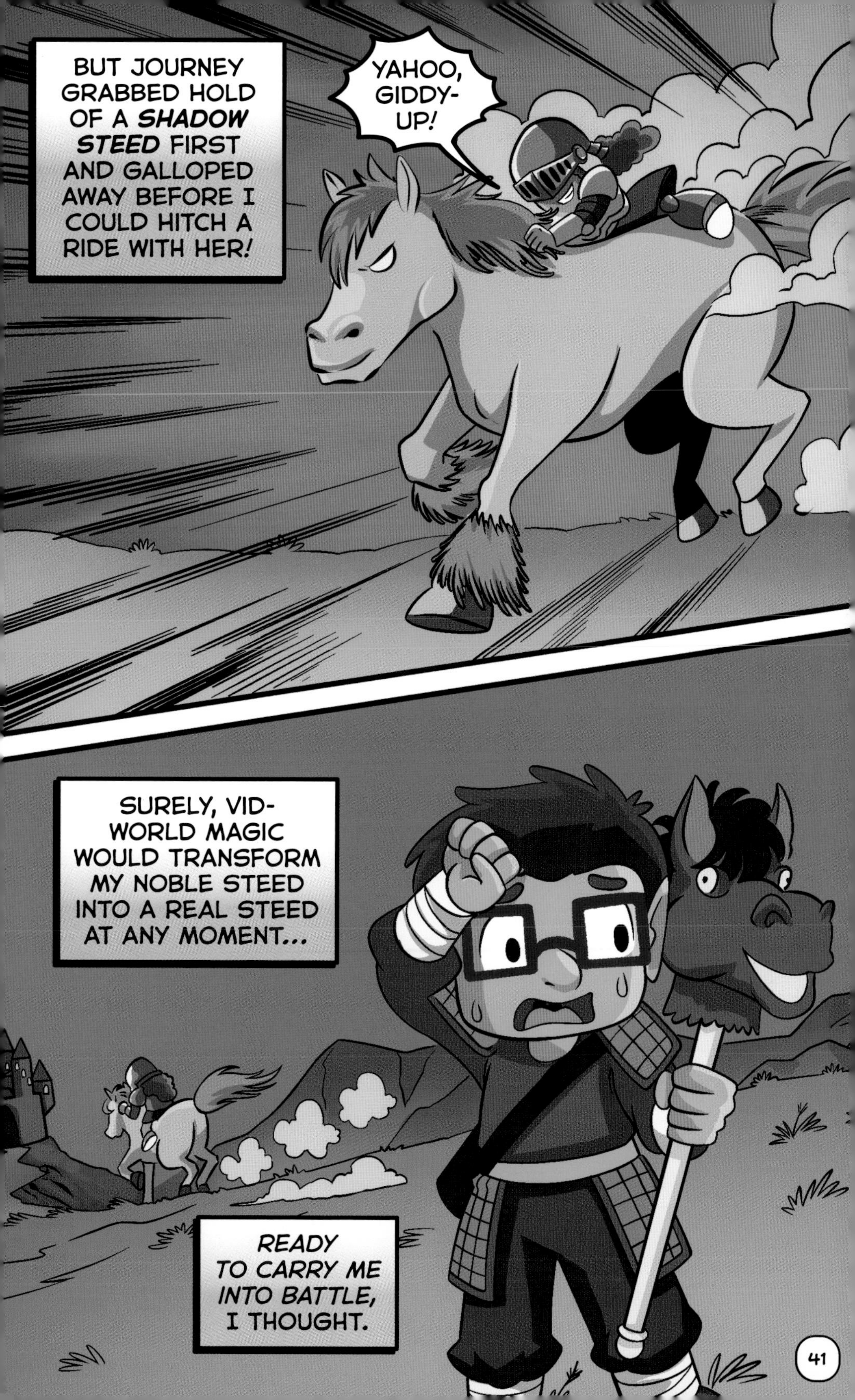
BUT JOURNEY GRABBED HOLD OF A *SHADOW STEED* FIRST AND GALLOPED AWAY BEFORE I COULD HITCH A RIDE WITH HER!
YAHOO, GIDDY-UP!
SURELY, VID-WORLD MAGIC WOULD TRANSFORM MY NOBLE STEED INTO A REAL STEED AT ANY MOMENT...
READY TO CARRY ME INTO BATTLE, I THOUGHT.

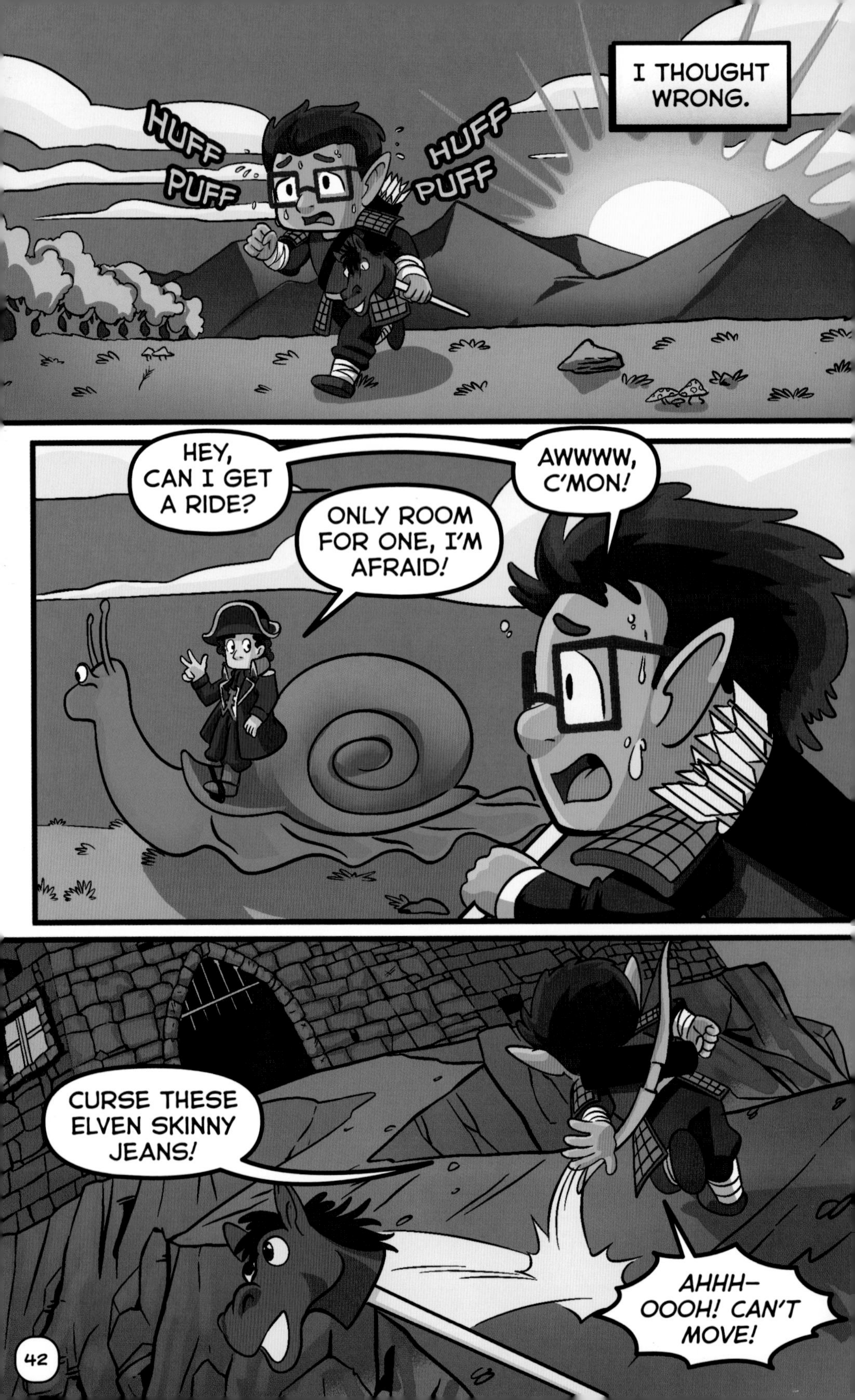
I THOUGHT WRONG.
HUFF PUFF
HUFF PUFF
HEY, CAN I GET A RIDE?
ONLY ROOM FOR ONE, I'M AFRAID!
AWWWW, C'MON!
CURSE THESE ELVEN SKINNY JEANS!
AHHH—OOOH! CAN'T MOVE!

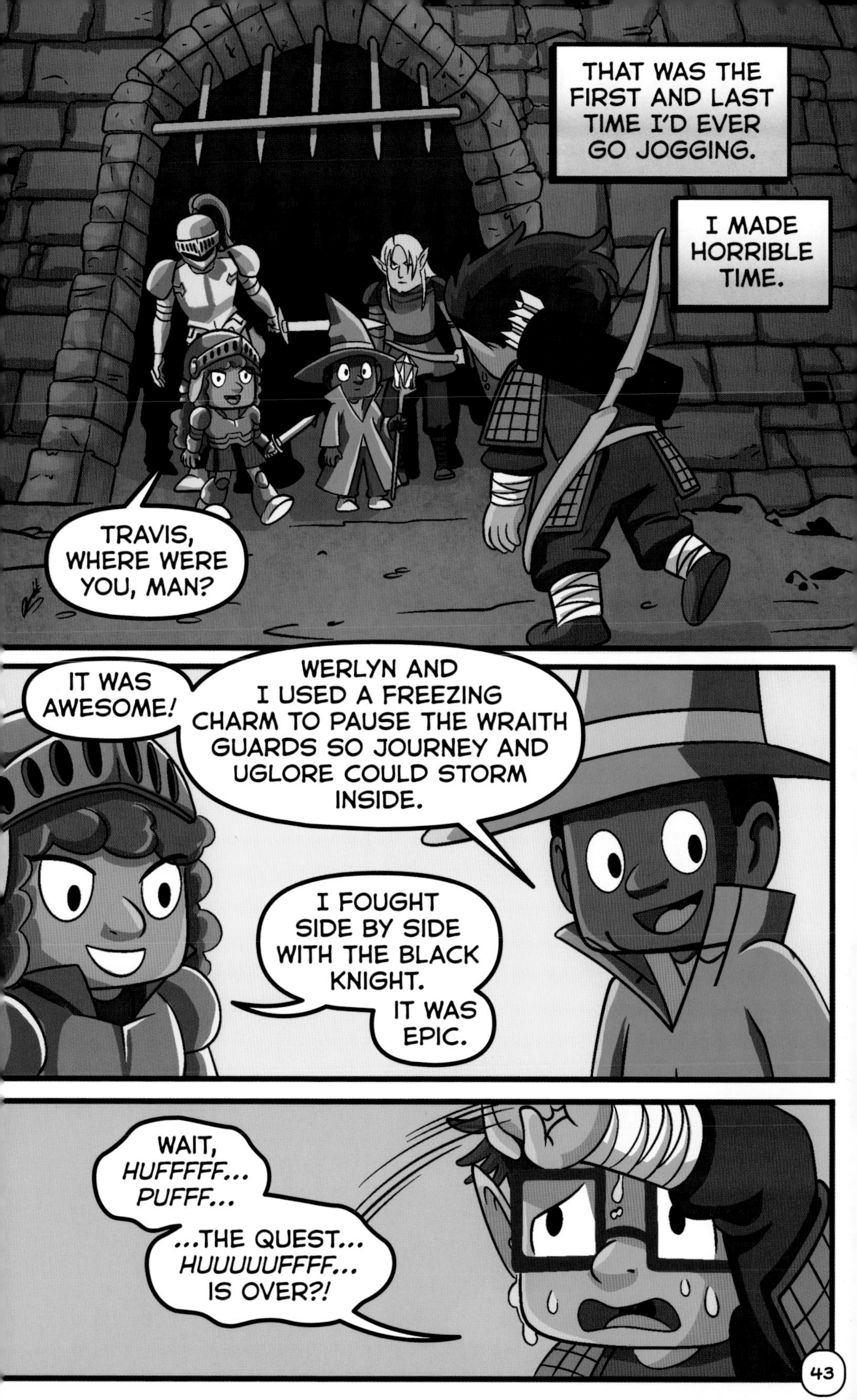
THAT WAS THE FIRST AND LAST TIME I'D EVER GO JOGGING.
I MADE HORRIBLE TIME.
TRAVIS, WHERE WERE YOU, MAN?
IT WAS AWESOME!
WERLYN AND I USED A FREEZING CHARM TO PAUSE THE WRAITH GUARDS SO JOURNEY AND UGLORE COULD STORM INSIDE.
I FOUGHT SIDE BY SIDE WITH THE BLACK KNIGHT.
IT WAS EPIC.
WAIT, *HUFFFFF... PUFFF...*
...THE QUEST... *HUUUUUFFFF...* IS OVER?!

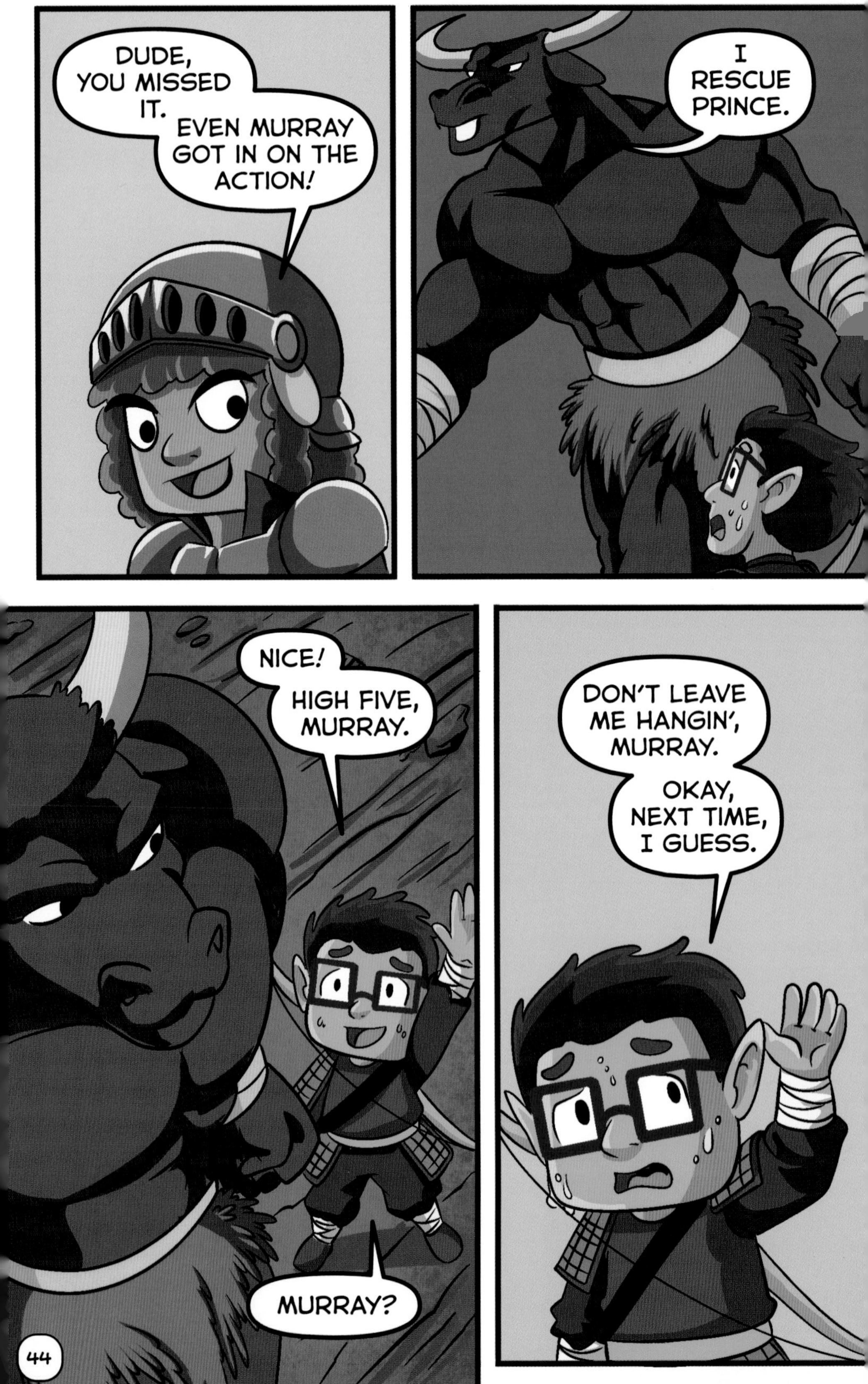
DUDE, YOU MISSED IT.
EVEN MURRAY GOT IN ON THE ACTION!
I RESCUE PRINCE.
NICE!
HIGH FIVE, MURRAY.
MURRAY?
DON'T LEAVE ME HANGIN', MURRAY.
OKAY, NEXT TIME, I GUESS.

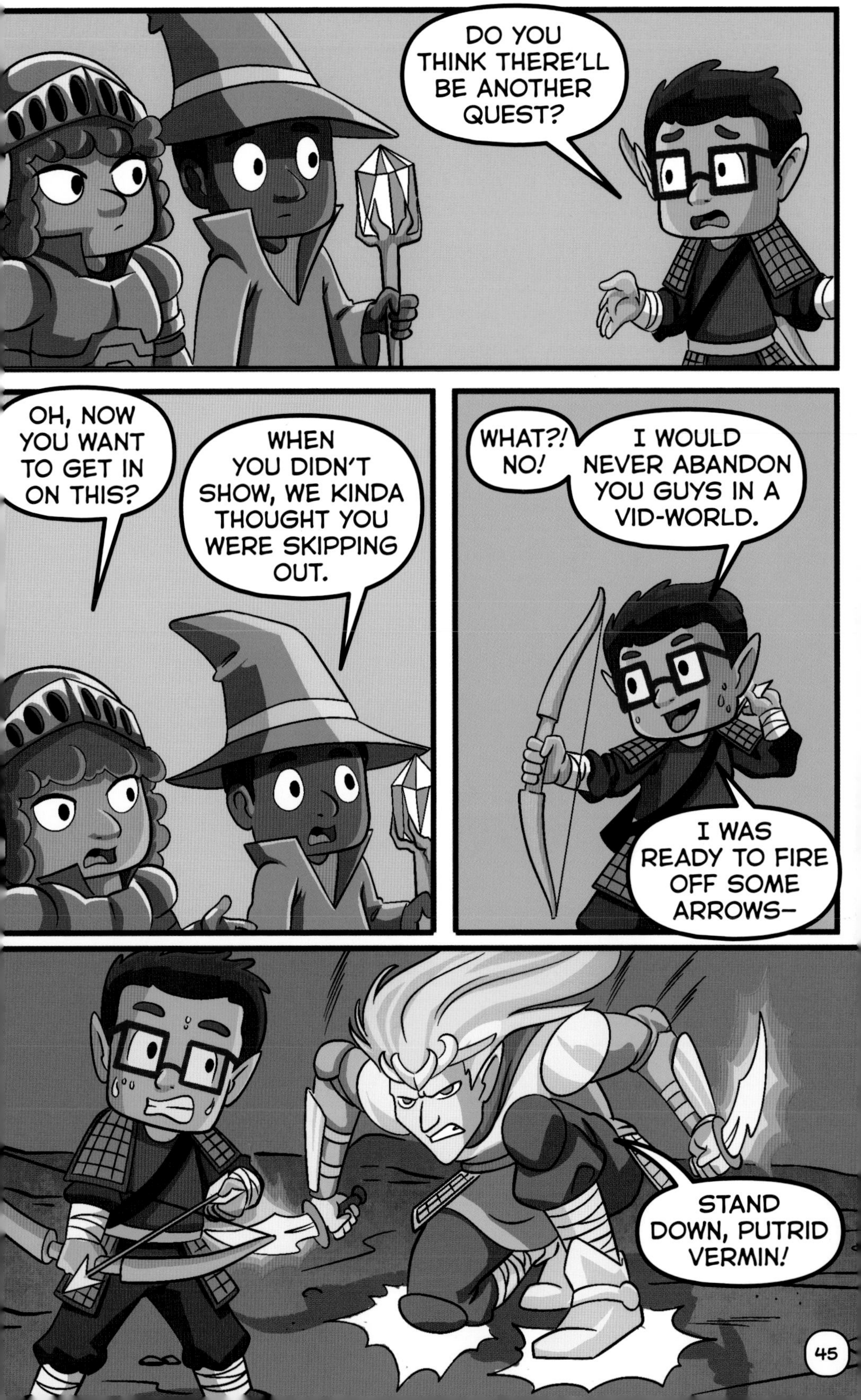
DO YOU THINK THERE'LL BE ANOTHER QUEST?
OH, NOW YOU WANT TO GET IN ON THIS?
WHEN YOU DIDN'T SHOW, WE KINDA THOUGHT YOU WERE SKIPPING OUT.
WHAT?! NO!
I WOULD NEVER ABANDON YOU GUYS IN A VID-WORLD.
I WAS READY TO FIRE OFF SOME ARROWS–
STAND DOWN, PUTRID VERMIN!

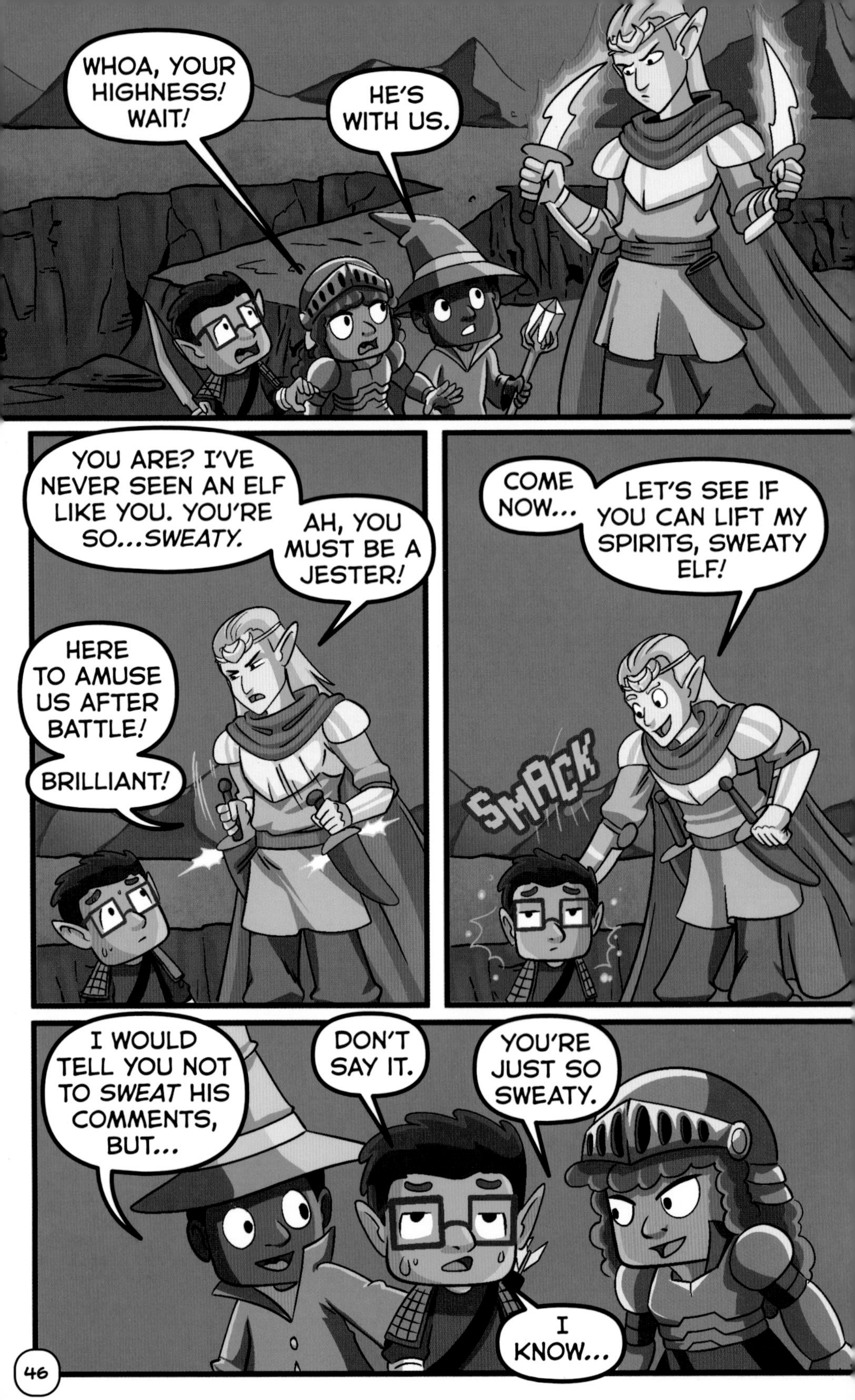

WHOA, YOUR HIGHNESS! WAIT!
HE'S WITH US.
YOU ARE? I'VE NEVER SEEN AN ELF LIKE YOU. YOU'RE SO...*SWEATY.*
AH, YOU MUST BE A JESTER!
HERE TO AMUSE US AFTER BATTLE!
BRILLIANT!
COME NOW...
LET'S SEE IF YOU CAN LIFT MY SPIRITS, SWEATY ELF!
SMACK
I WOULD TELL YOU NOT TO *SWEAT* HIS COMMENTS, BUT...
DON'T SAY IT.
YOU'RE JUST SO SWEATY.
I KNOW...

CHAPTER 4

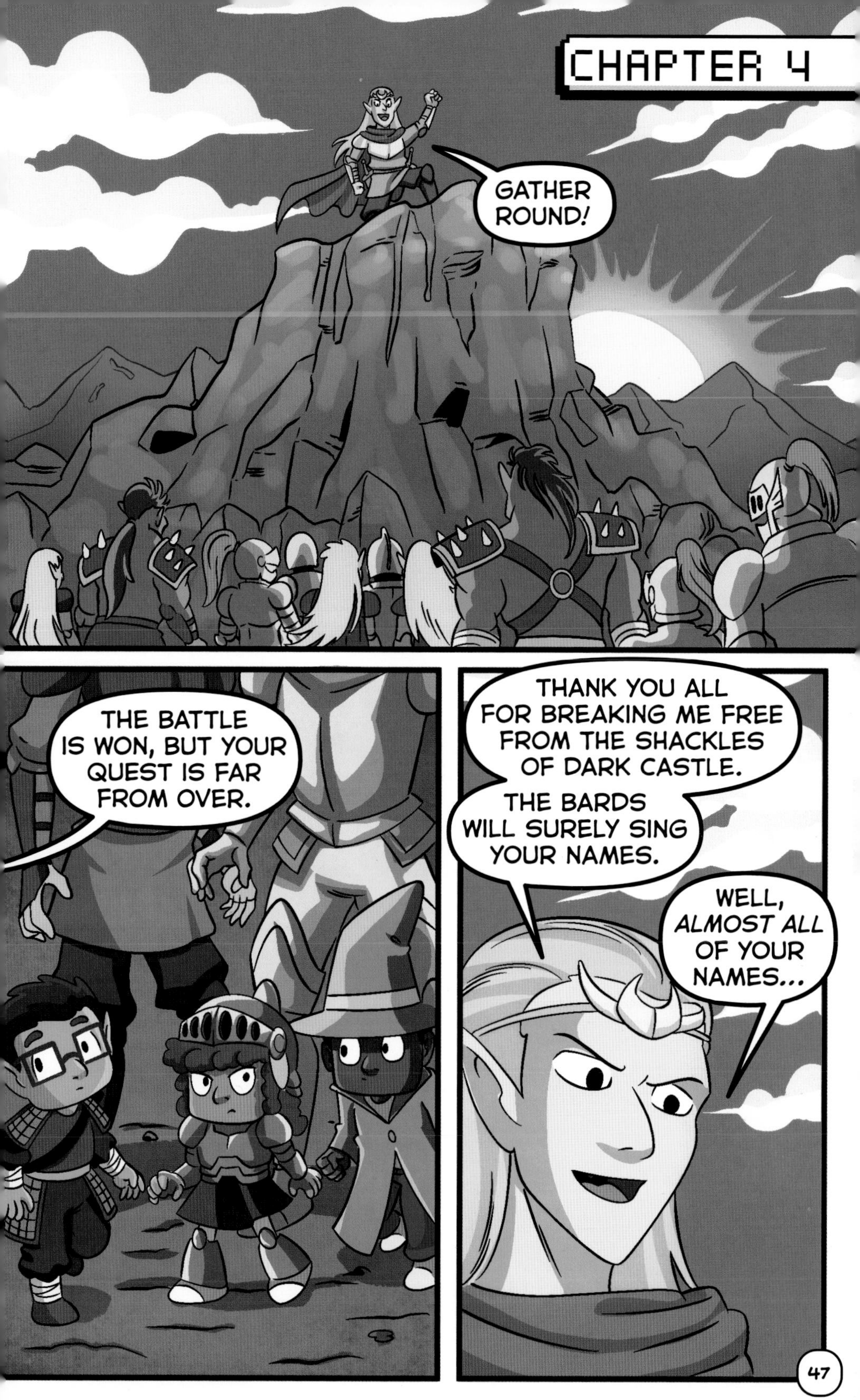
GATHER ROUND!
THE BATTLE IS WON, BUT YOUR QUEST IS FAR FROM OVER.
THANK YOU ALL FOR BREAKING ME FREE FROM THE SHACKLES OF DARK CASTLE.
THE BARDS WILL SURELY SING YOUR NAMES.
WELL, *ALMOST ALL* OF YOUR NAMES...

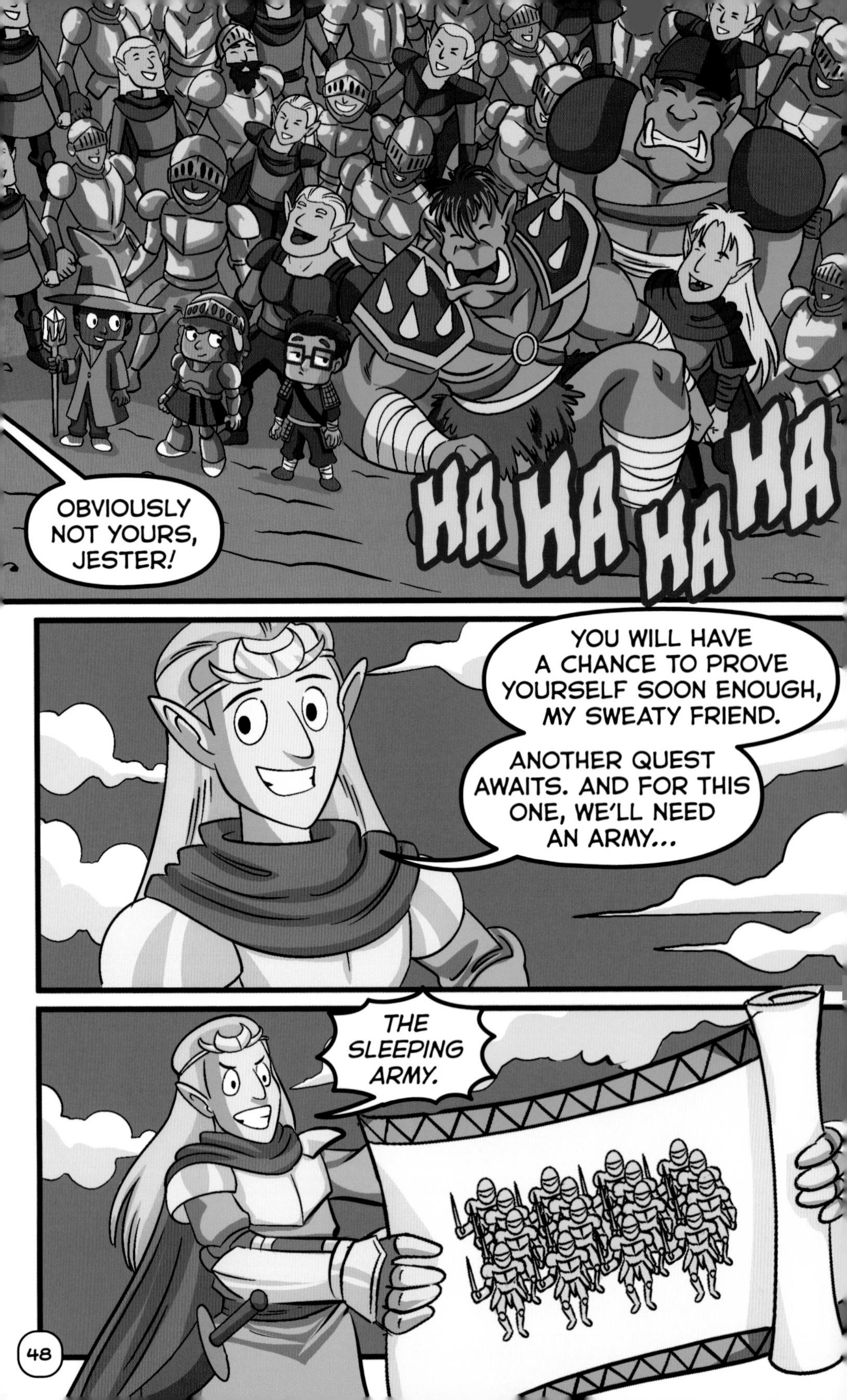
OBVIOUSLY NOT YOURS, JESTER!
HA HA HA HA
YOU WILL HAVE A CHANCE TO PROVE YOURSELF SOON ENOUGH, MY SWEATY FRIEND.
ANOTHER QUEST AWAITS. AND FOR THIS ONE, WE'LL NEED AN ARMY...
THE SLEEPING ARMY.

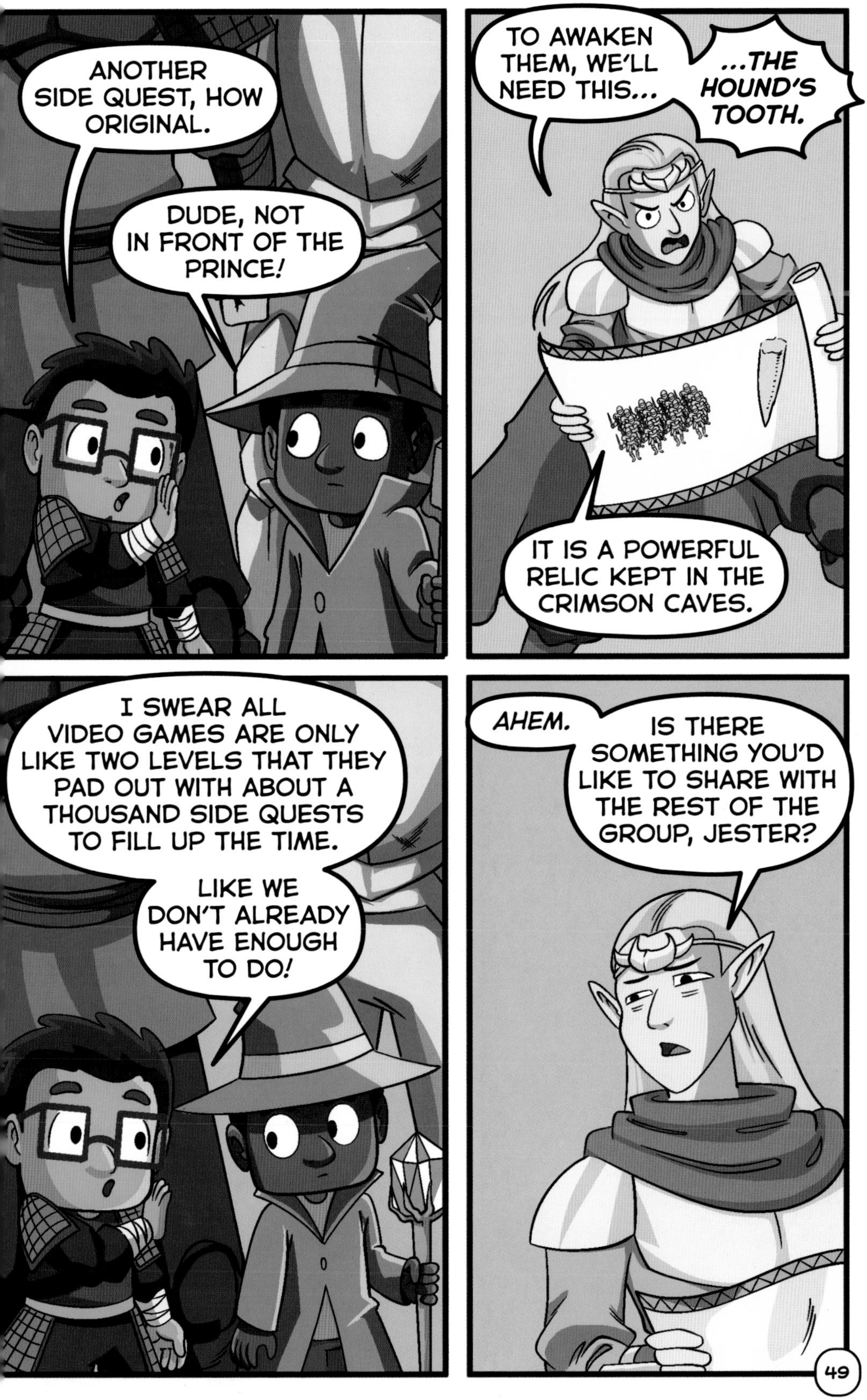
ANOTHER SIDE QUEST, HOW ORIGINAL.
DUDE, NOT IN FRONT OF THE PRINCE!
TO AWAKEN THEM, WE'LL NEED THIS...
...THE HOUND'S TOOTH.
IT IS A POWERFUL RELIC KEPT IN THE CRIMSON CAVES.
I SWEAR ALL VIDEO GAMES ARE ONLY LIKE TWO LEVELS THAT THEY PAD OUT WITH ABOUT A THOUSAND SIDE QUESTS TO FILL UP THE TIME.
LIKE WE DON'T ALREADY HAVE ENOUGH TO DO!
AHEM.
IS THERE SOMETHING YOU'D LIKE TO SHARE WITH THE REST OF THE GROUP, JESTER?

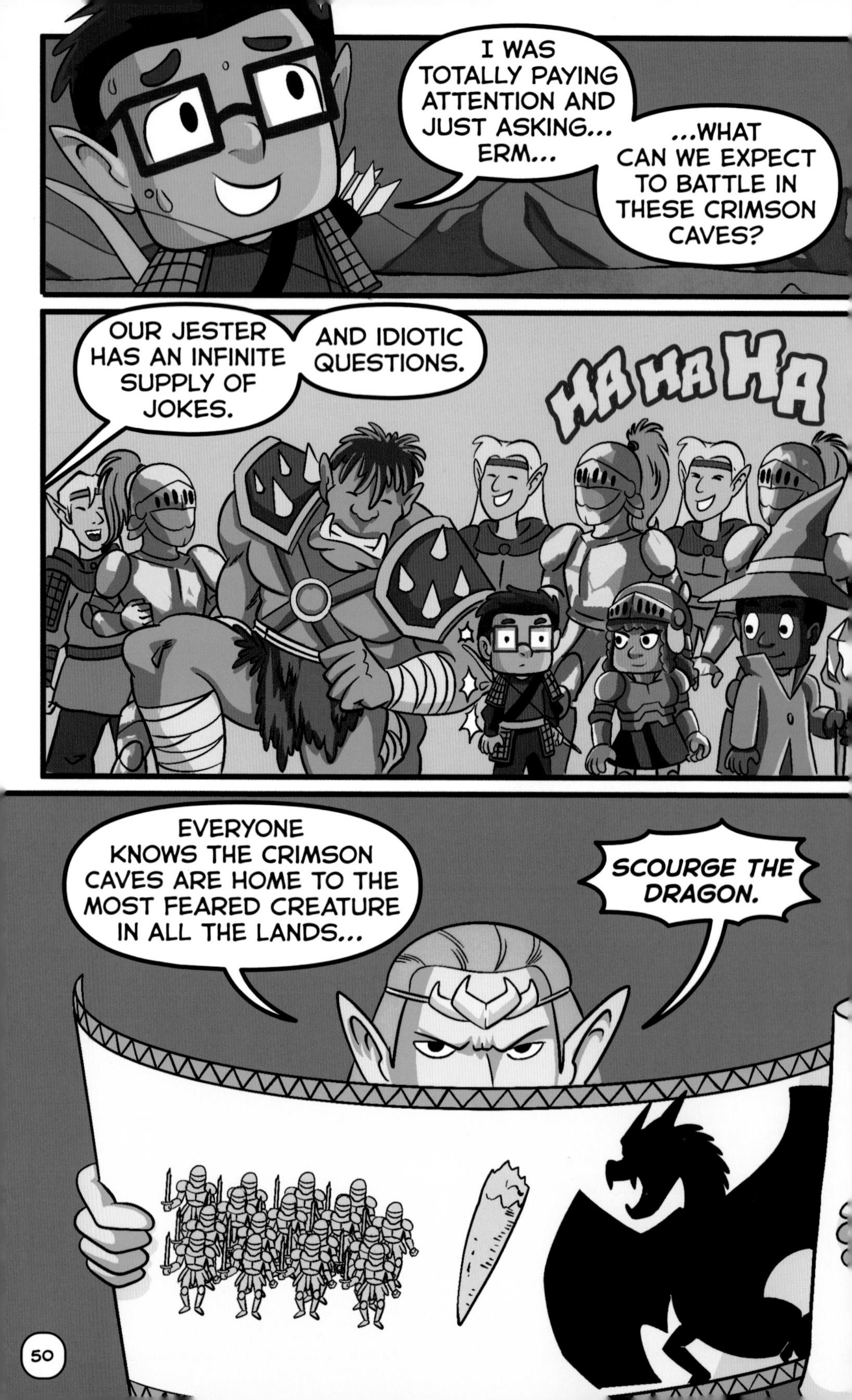
I WAS TOTALLY PAYING ATTENTION AND JUST ASKING... ERM...
...WHAT CAN WE EXPECT TO BATTLE IN THESE CRIMSON CAVES?
OUR JESTER HAS AN INFINITE SUPPLY OF JOKES.
AND IDIOTIC QUESTIONS.
HA HA HA
EVERYONE KNOWS THE CRIMSON CAVES ARE HOME TO THE MOST FEARED CREATURE IN ALL THE LANDS...
SCOURGE THE DRAGON.

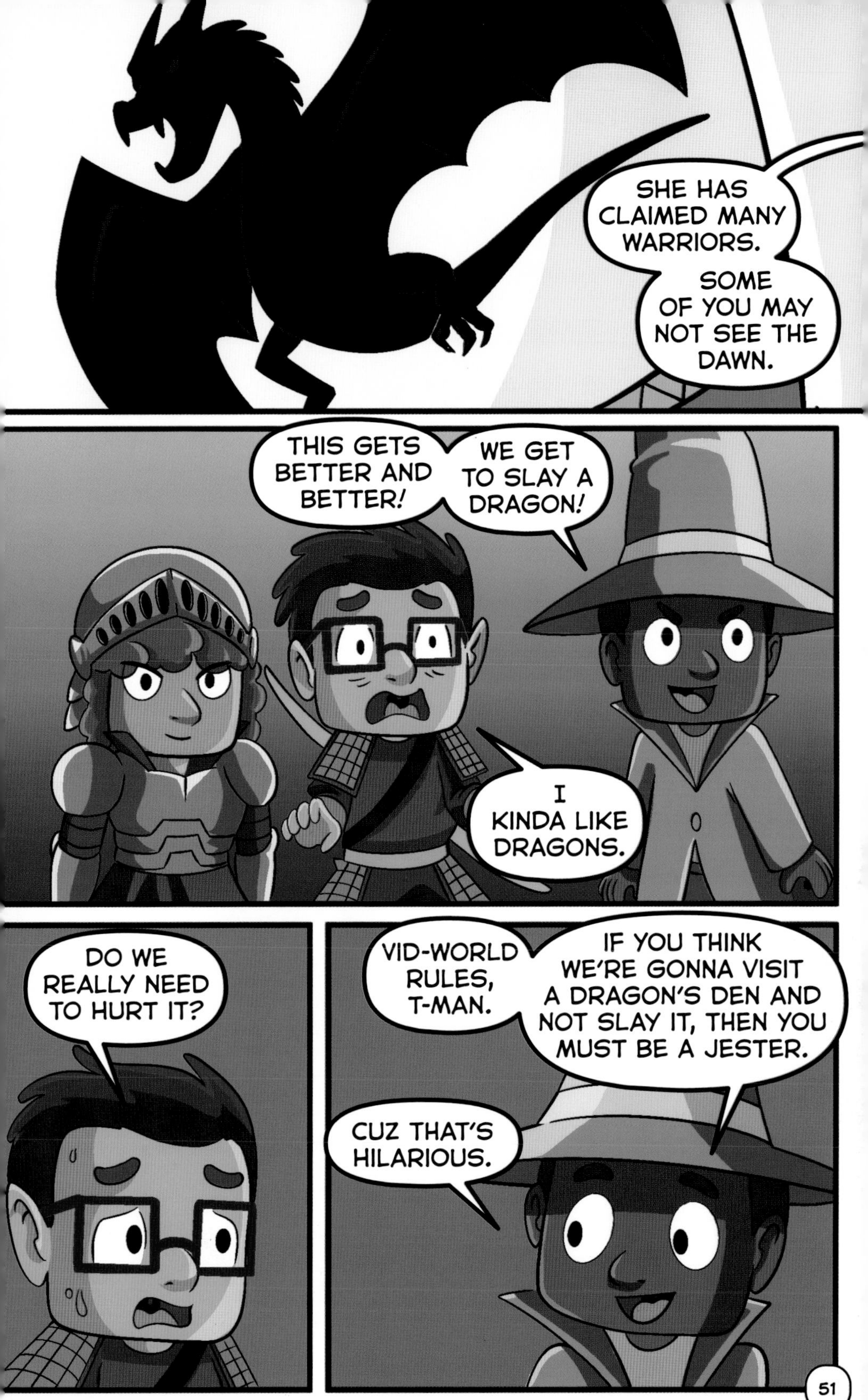
SHE HAS CLAIMED MANY WARRIORS.
SOME OF YOU MAY NOT SEE THE DAWN.
THIS GETS BETTER AND BETTER!
WE GET TO SLAY A DRAGON!
I KINDA LIKE DRAGONS.
DO WE REALLY NEED TO HURT IT?
VID-WORLD RULES, T-MAN.
IF YOU THINK WE'RE GONNA VISIT A DRAGON'S DEN AND NOT SLAY IT, THEN YOU MUST BE A JESTER.
CUZ THAT'S HILARIOUS.

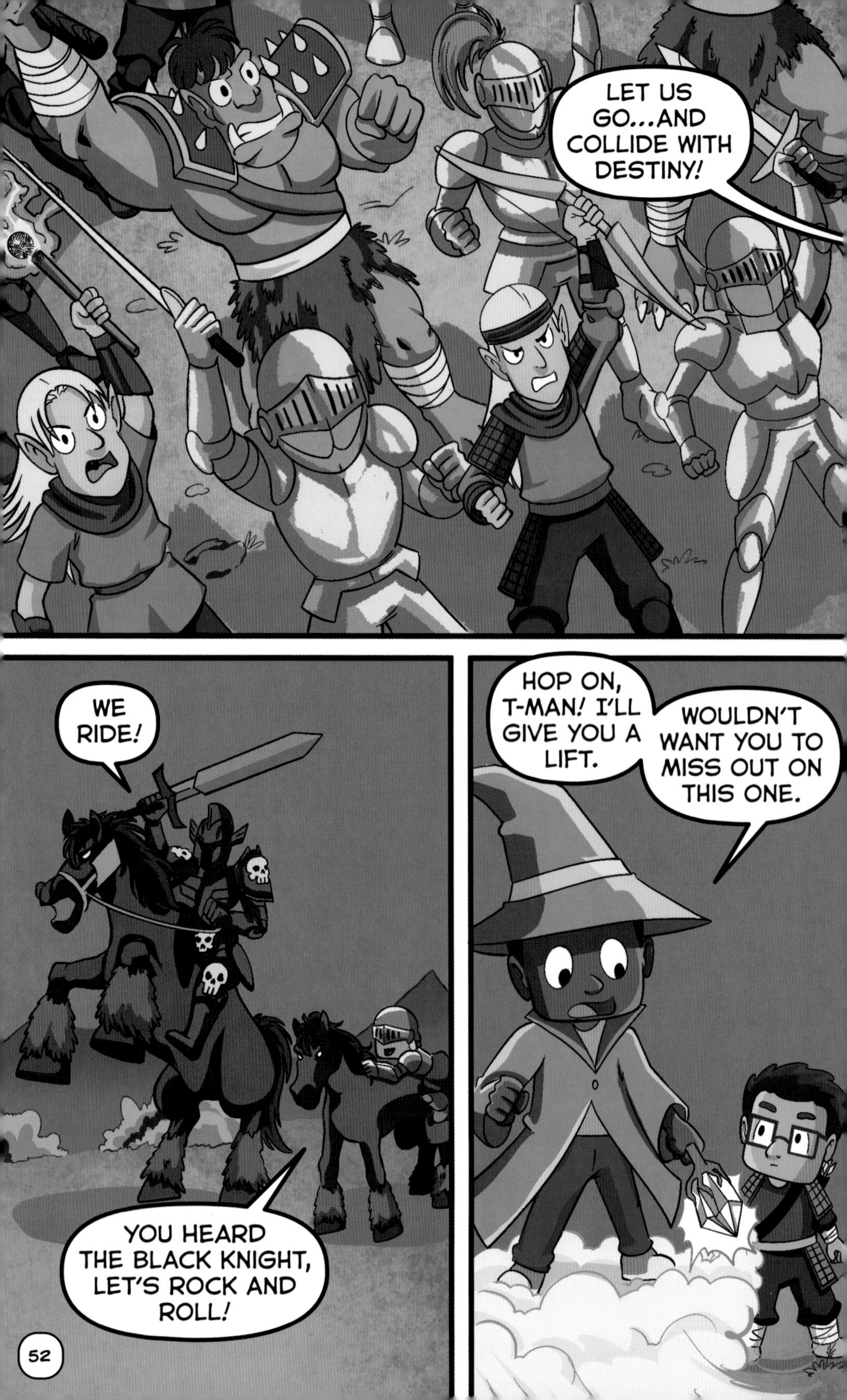
LET US GO...AND COLLIDE WITH DESTINY!
WE RIDE!
YOU HEARD THE BLACK KNIGHT, LET'S ROCK AND ROLL!
HOP ON, T-MAN! I'LL GIVE YOU A LIFT.
WOULDN'T WANT YOU TO MISS OUT ON THIS ONE.

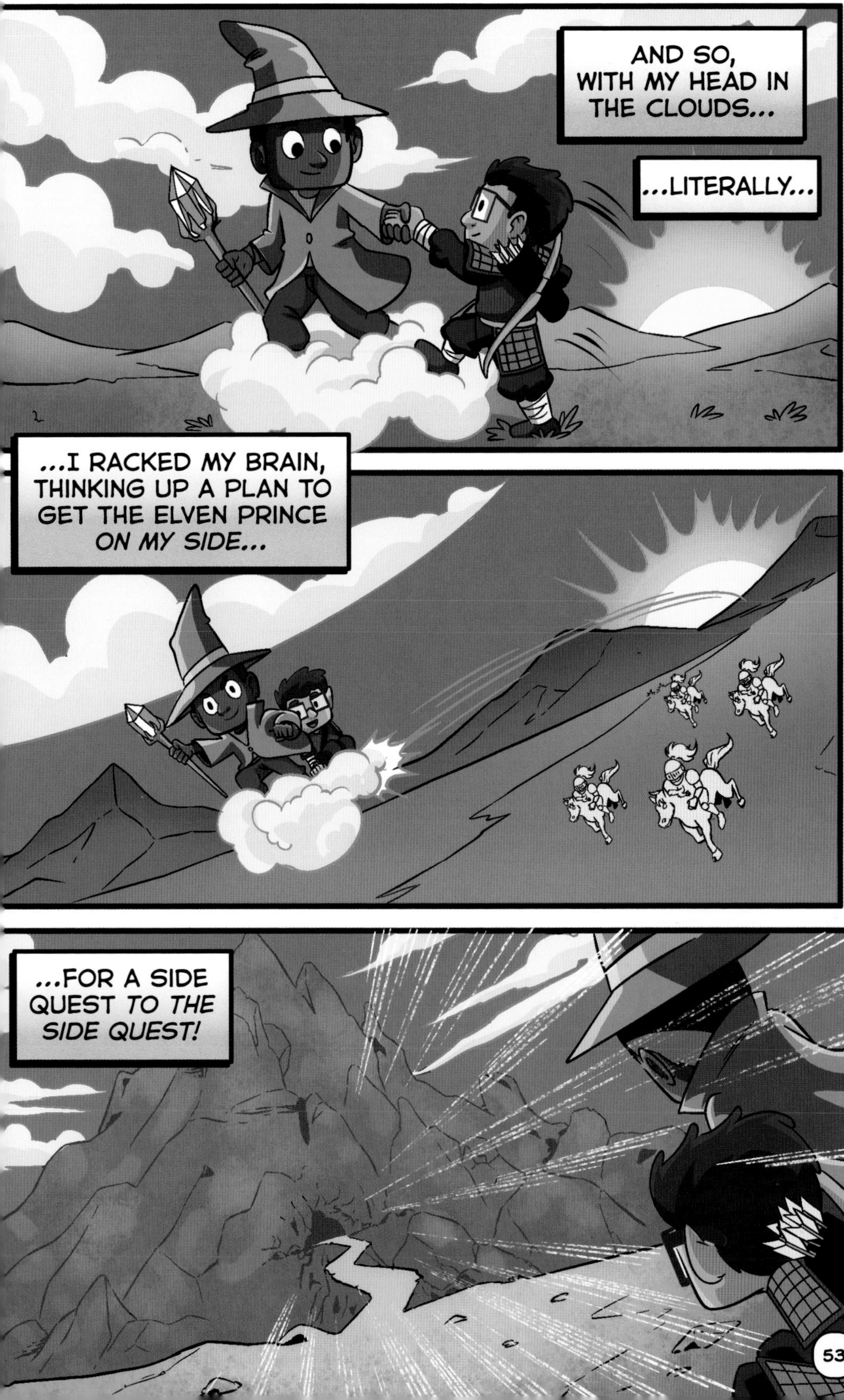
AND SO, WITH MY HEAD IN THE CLOUDS...
...LITERALLY...
...I RACKED MY BRAIN, THINKING UP A PLAN TO GET THE ELVEN PRINCE *ON MY SIDE*...
...FOR A SIDE QUEST *TO THE SIDE QUEST!*

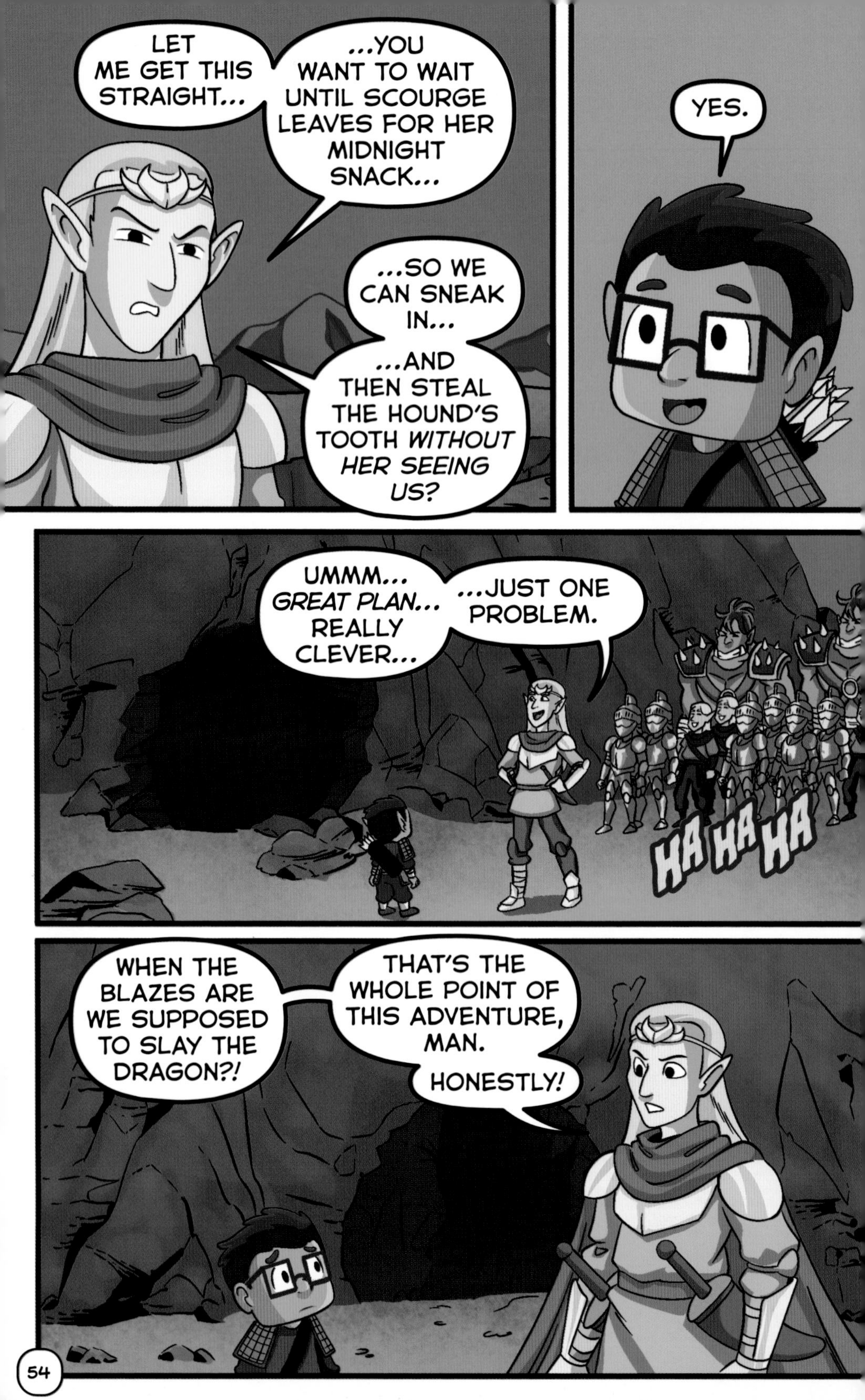
LET ME GET THIS STRAIGHT...
...YOU WANT TO WAIT UNTIL SCOURGE LEAVES FOR HER MIDNIGHT SNACK...
...SO WE CAN SNEAK IN...
...AND THEN STEAL THE HOUND'S TOOTH *WITHOUT HER SEEING* US?
YES.
UMMM... *GREAT PLAN...* REALLY CLEVER...
...JUST ONE PROBLEM.
HA HA HA
WHEN THE BLAZES ARE WE SUPPOSED TO SLAY THE DRAGON?!
THAT'S THE WHOLE POINT OF THIS ADVENTURE, MAN.
HONESTLY!

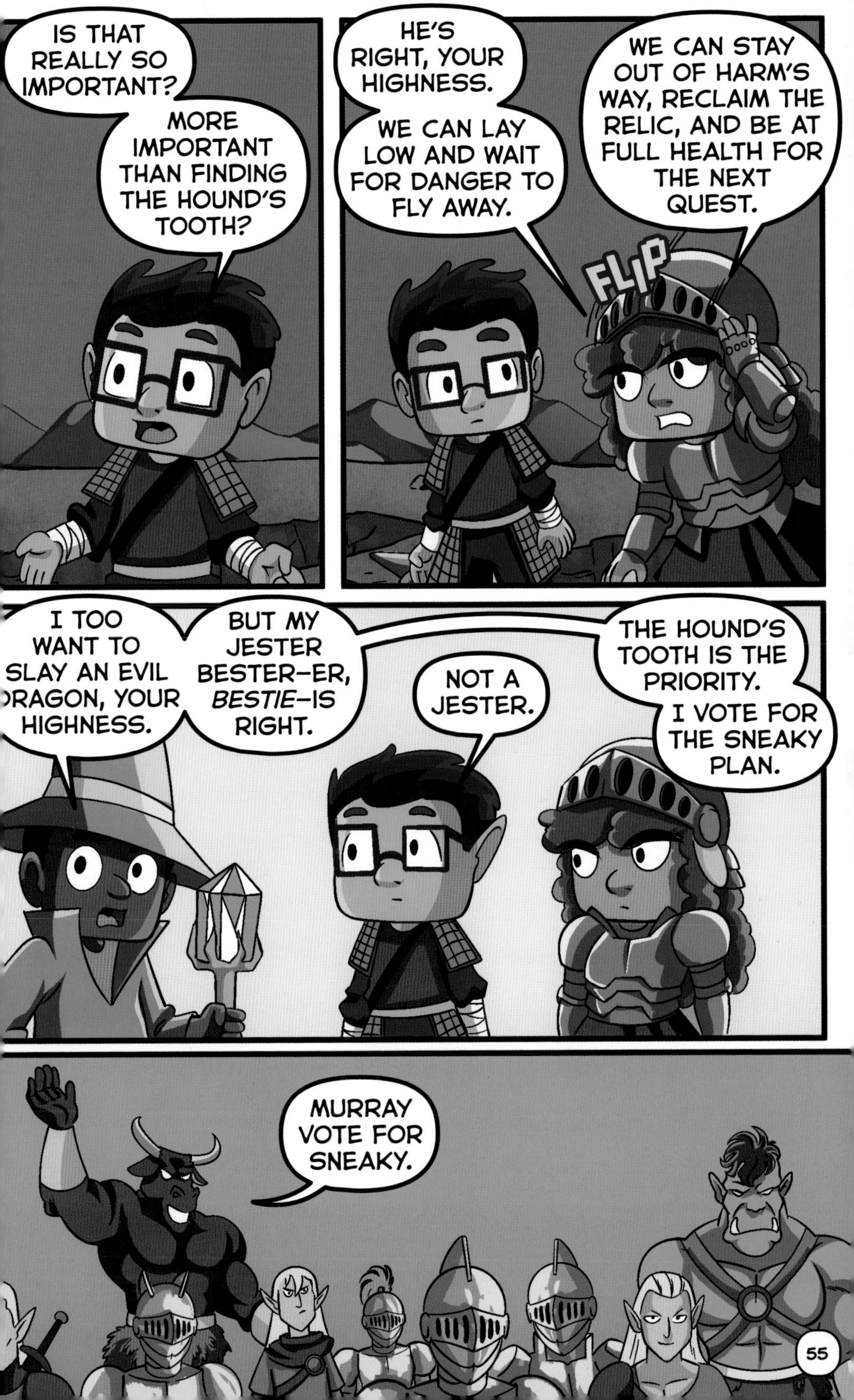
IS THAT REALLY SO IMPORTANT?
MORE IMPORTANT THAN FINDING THE HOUND'S TOOTH?
HE'S RIGHT, YOUR HIGHNESS.
WE CAN LAY LOW AND WAIT FOR DANGER TO FLY AWAY.
WE CAN STAY OUT OF HARM'S WAY, RECLAIM THE RELIC, AND BE AT FULL HEALTH FOR THE NEXT QUEST.
FLIP
I TOO WANT TO SLAY AN EVIL DRAGON, YOUR HIGHNESS.
BUT MY JESTER BESTER—ER, *BESTIE*—IS RIGHT.
NOT A JESTER.
THE HOUND'S TOOTH IS THE PRIORITY.
I VOTE FOR THE SNEAKY PLAN.
MURRAY VOTE FOR SNEAKY.

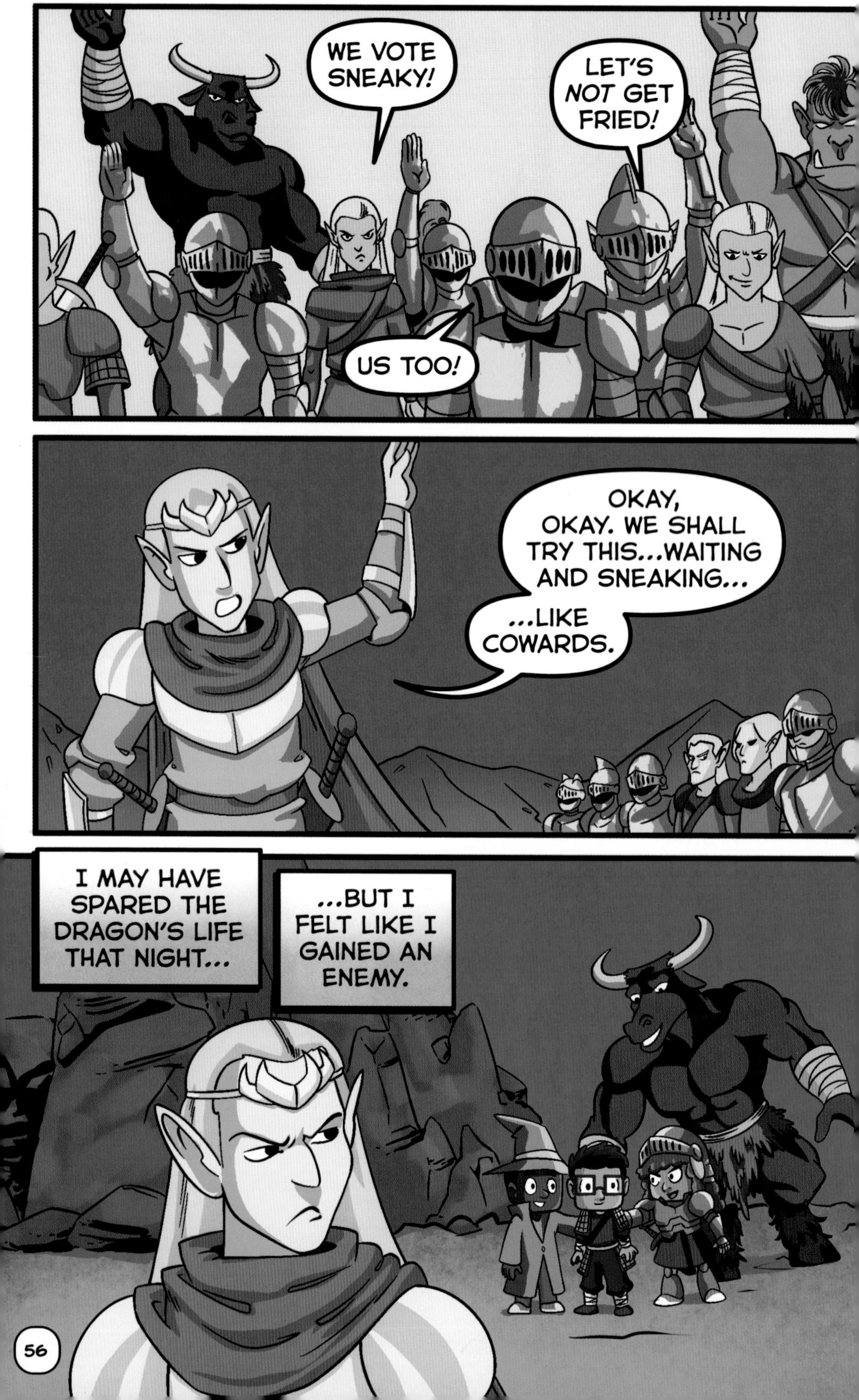
WE VOTE SNEAKY!
LET'S NOT GET FRIED!
US TOO!
OKAY, OKAY. WE SHALL TRY THIS...WAITING AND SNEAKING...
...LIKE COWARDS.
I MAY HAVE SPARED THE DRAGON'S LIFE THAT NIGHT...
...BUT I FELT LIKE I GAINED AN ENEMY.

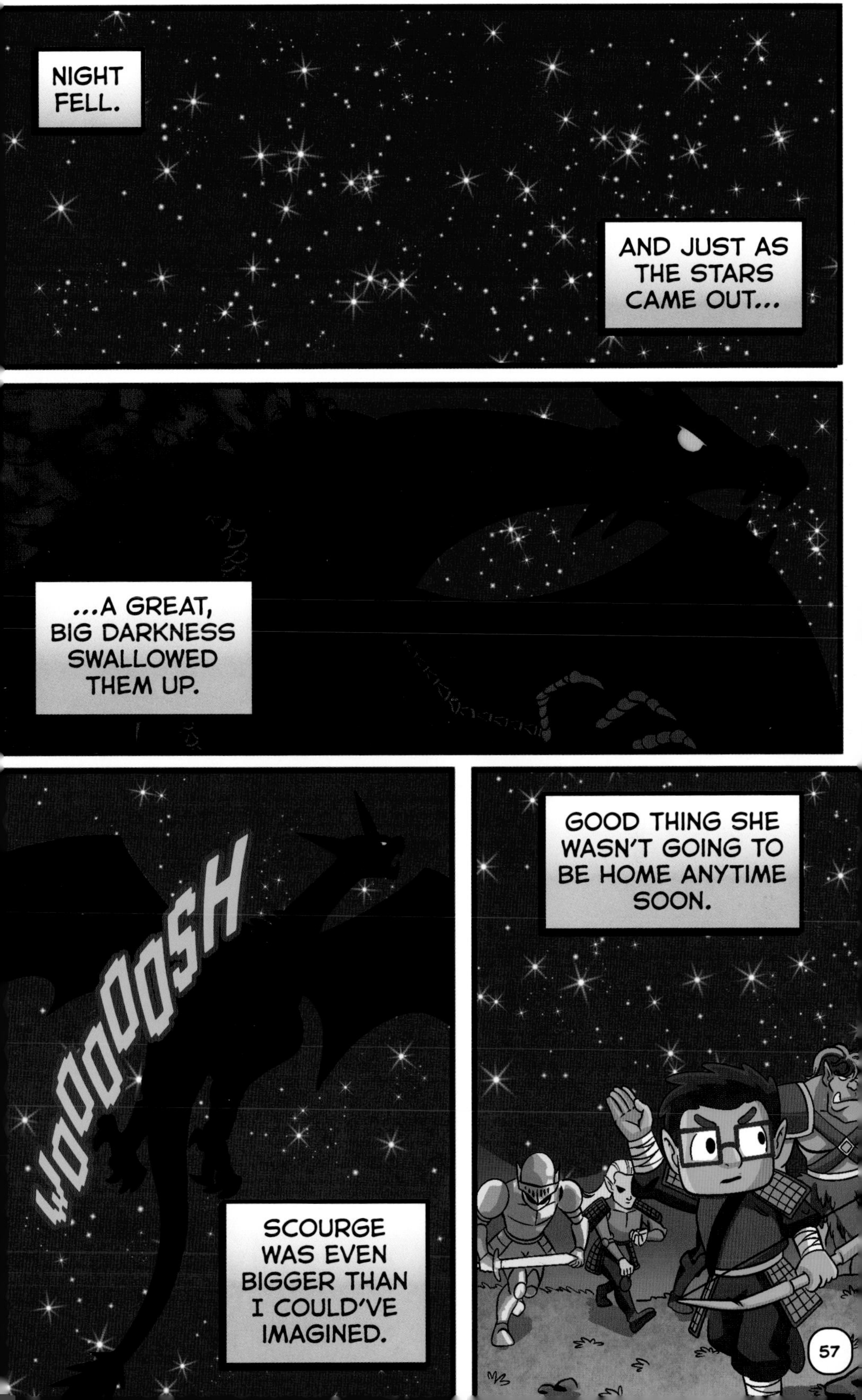
NIGHT FELL.
AND JUST AS THE STARS CAME OUT...
...A GREAT, BIG DARKNESS SWALLOWED THEM UP.
WOOOOOSH
SCOURGE WAS EVEN BIGGER THAN I COULD'VE IMAGINED.
GOOD THING SHE WASN'T GOING TO BE HOME ANYTIME SOON.

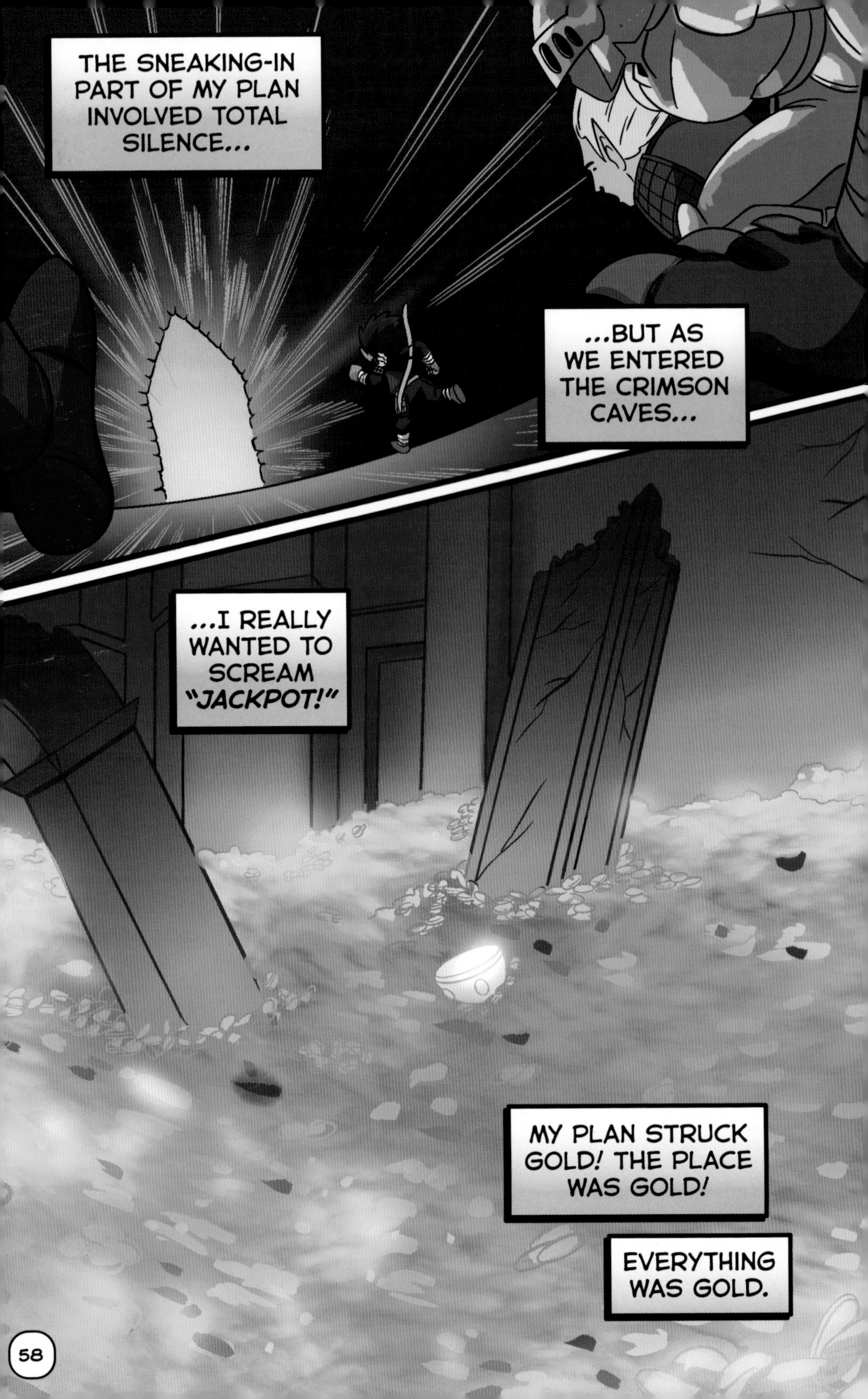
THE SNEAKING-IN PART OF MY PLAN INVOLVED TOTAL SILENCE...
...BUT AS WE ENTERED THE CRIMSON CAVES...
...I REALLY WANTED TO SCREAM "JACKPOT!"
MY PLAN STRUCK GOLD! THE PLACE WAS GOLD!
EVERYTHING WAS GOLD.

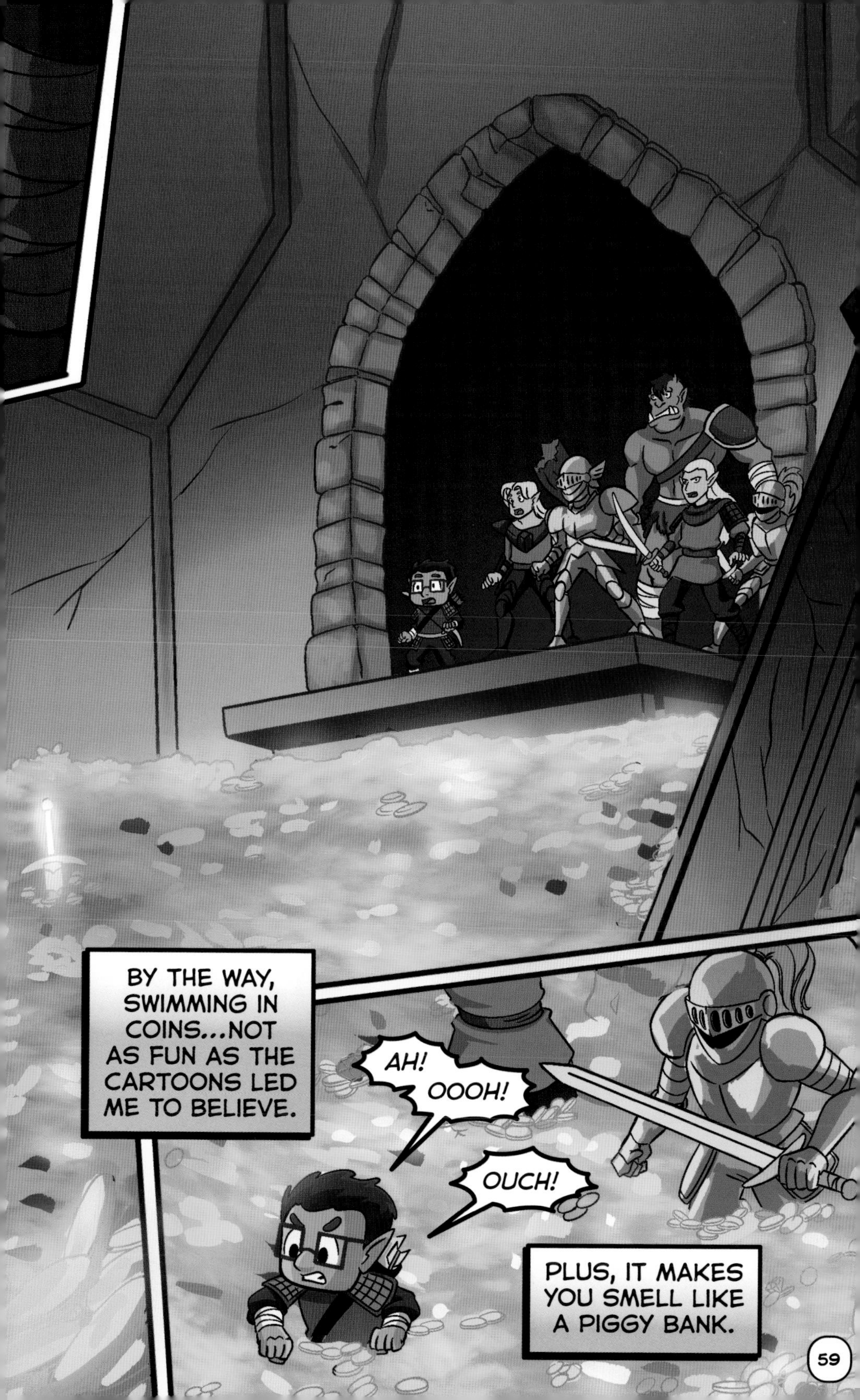

BY THE WAY, SWIMMING IN COINS...NOT AS FUN AS THE CARTOONS LED ME TO BELIEVE.
AH!
OOOH!
OUCH!
PLUS, IT MAKES YOU SMELL LIKE A PIGGY BANK.

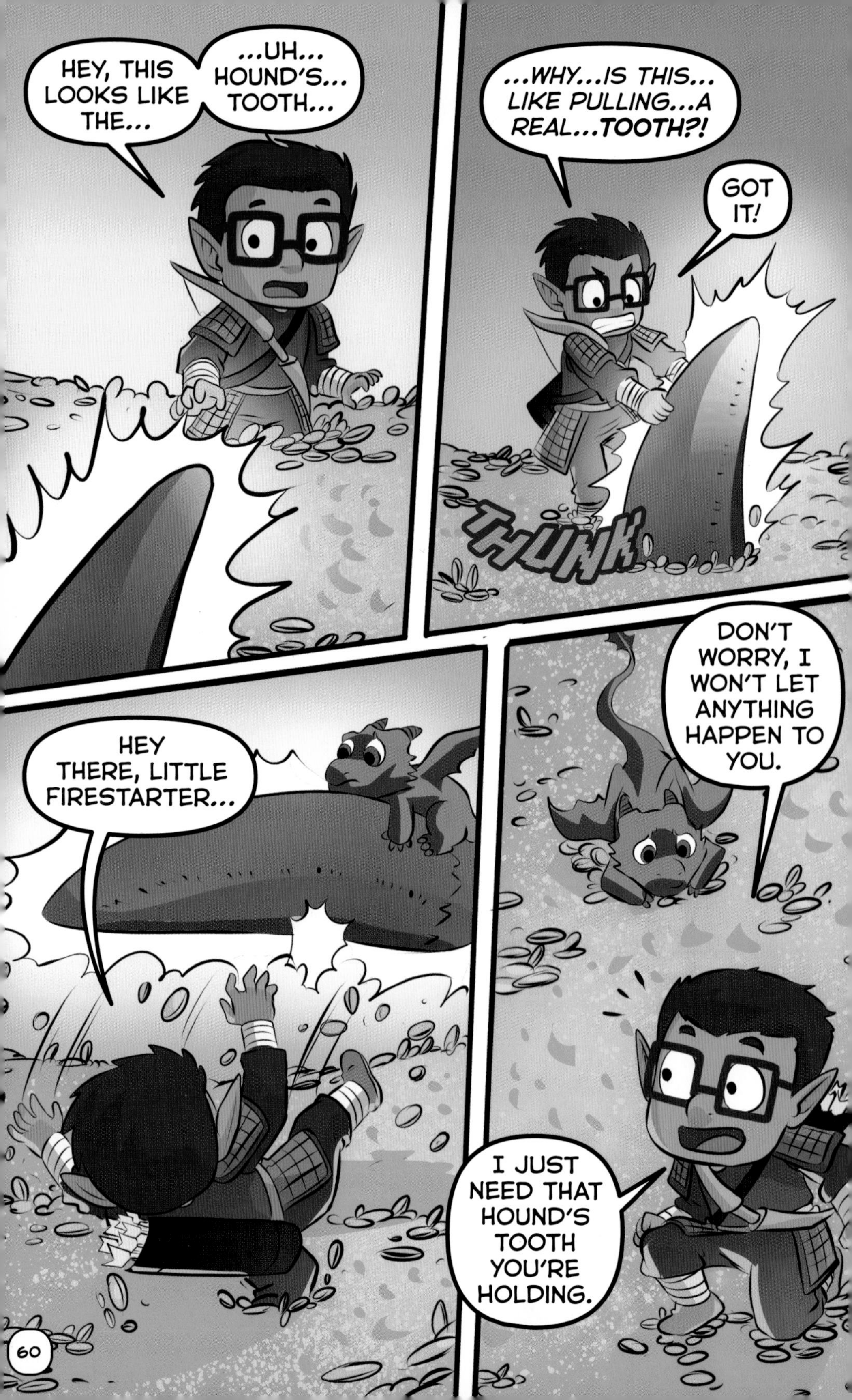
HEY, THIS LOOKS LIKE THE...
...UH... HOUND'S... TOOTH...
...WHY...IS THIS... LIKE PULLING...A REAL...TOOTH?!
GOT IT!
THUNK
HEY THERE, LITTLE FIRESTARTER...
DON'T WORRY, I WON'T LET ANYTHING HAPPEN TO YOU.
I JUST NEED THAT HOUND'S TOOTH YOU'RE HOLDING.

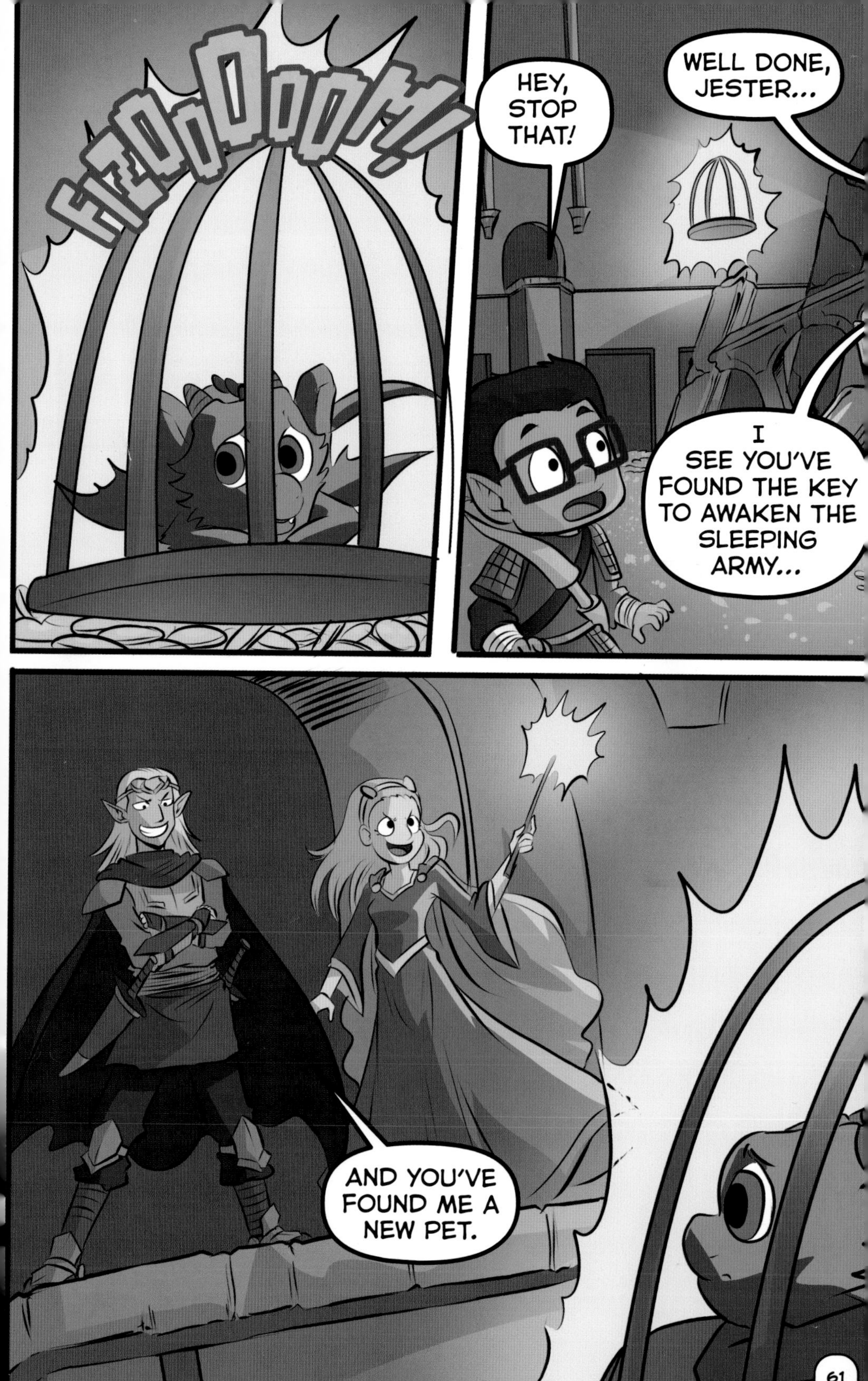
FIZOOOOOOM!!
HEY, STOP THAT!
WELL DONE, JESTER...
I SEE YOU'VE FOUND THE KEY TO AWAKEN THE SLEEPING ARMY...
AND YOU'VE FOUND ME A NEW PET.

CHAPTER 5

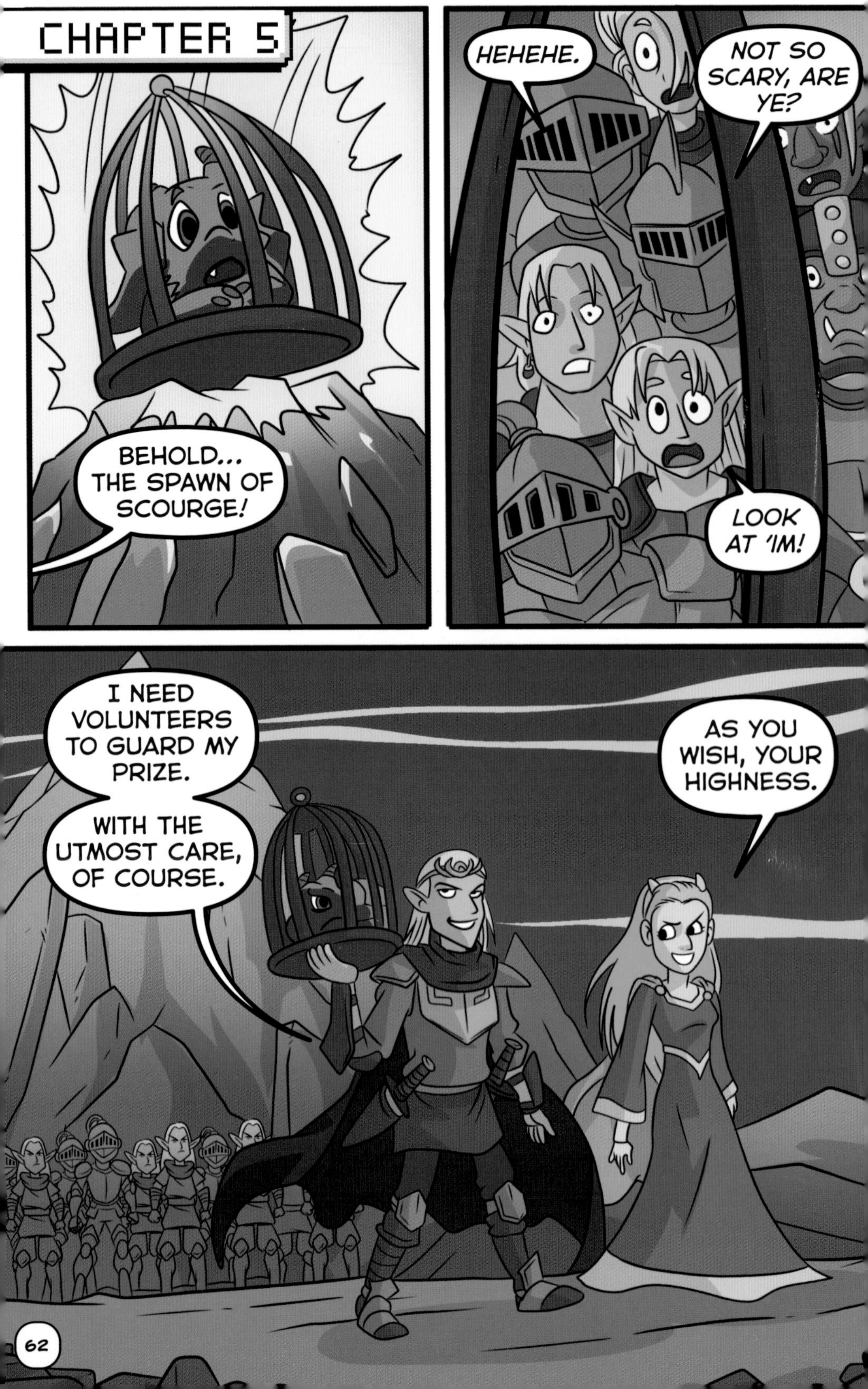
BEHOLD... THE SPAWN OF SCOURGE!
HEHEHE.
NOT SO SCARY, ARE YE?
LOOK AT 'IM!
I NEED VOLUNTEERS TO GUARD MY PRIZE.
WITH THE UTMOST CARE, OF COURSE.
AS YOU WISH, YOUR HIGHNESS.

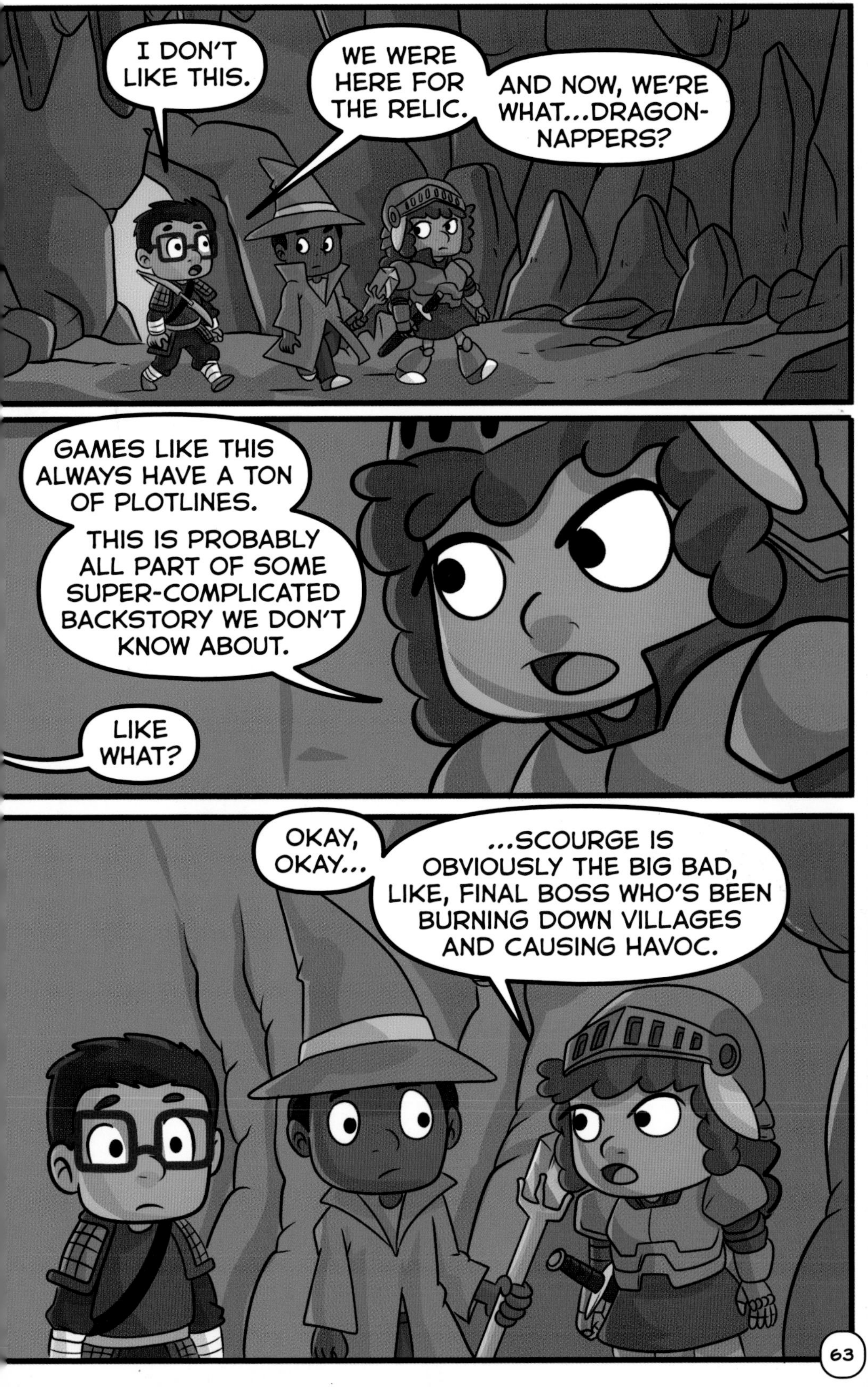
I DON'T LIKE THIS.
WE WERE HERE FOR THE RELIC.
AND NOW, WE'RE WHAT...DRAGON-NAPPERS?
GAMES LIKE THIS ALWAYS HAVE A TON OF PLOTLINES.
THIS IS PROBABLY ALL PART OF SOME SUPER-COMPLICATED BACKSTORY WE DON'T KNOW ABOUT.
LIKE WHAT?
OKAY, OKAY...
...SCOURGE IS OBVIOUSLY THE BIG BAD, LIKE, FINAL BOSS WHO'S BEEN BURNING DOWN VILLAGES AND CAUSING HAVOC.

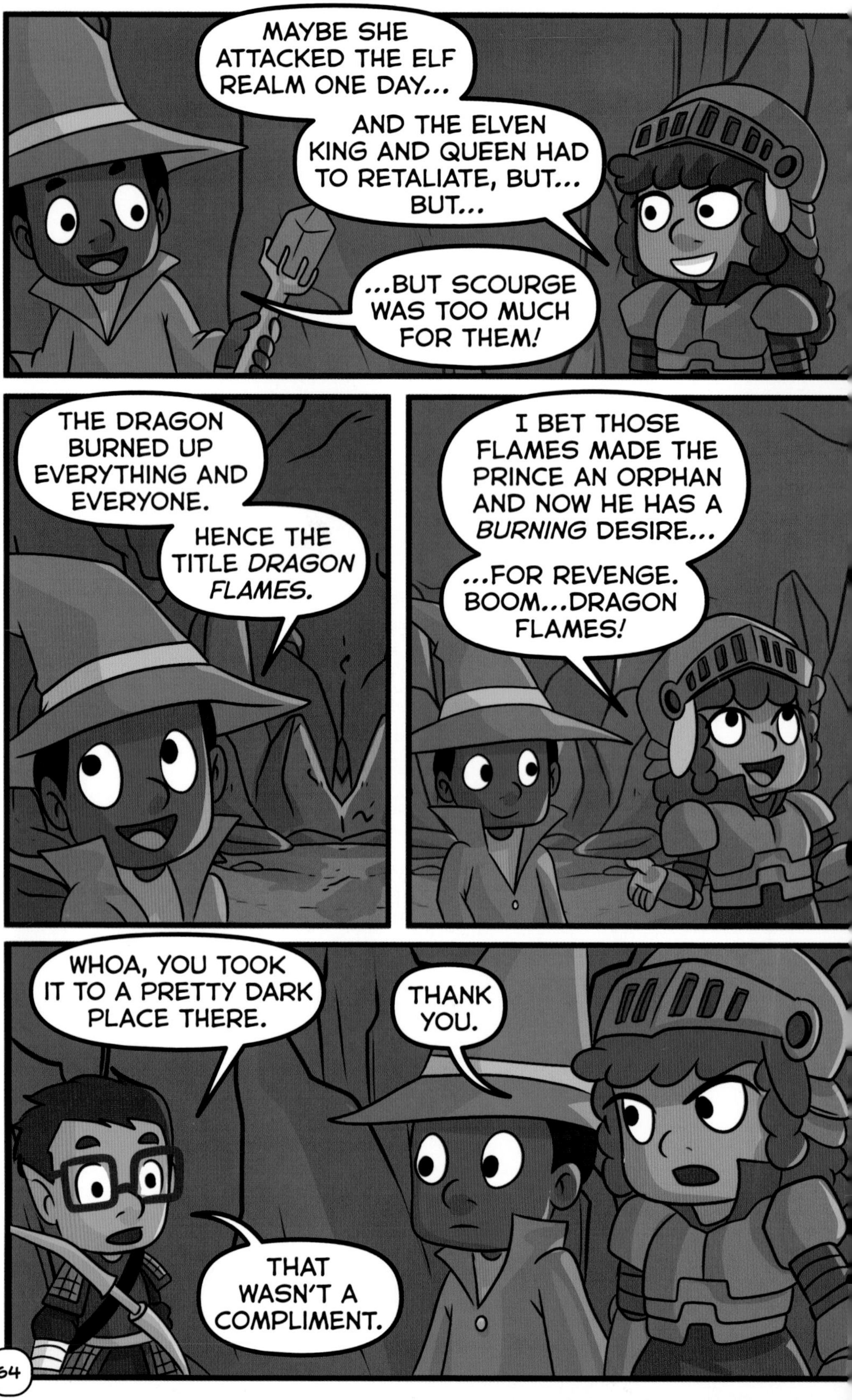
MAYBE SHE ATTACKED THE ELF REALM ONE DAY...
AND THE ELVEN KING AND QUEEN HAD TO RETALIATE, BUT... BUT...
...BUT SCOURGE WAS TOO MUCH FOR THEM!
THE DRAGON BURNED UP EVERYTHING AND EVERYONE.
HENCE THE TITLE *DRAGON FLAMES.*
I BET THOSE FLAMES MADE THE PRINCE AN ORPHAN AND NOW HE HAS A *BURNING* DESIRE...
...FOR REVENGE. BOOM...DRAGON FLAMES!
WHOA, YOU TOOK IT TO A PRETTY DARK PLACE THERE.
THANK YOU.
THAT WASN'T A COMPLIMENT.

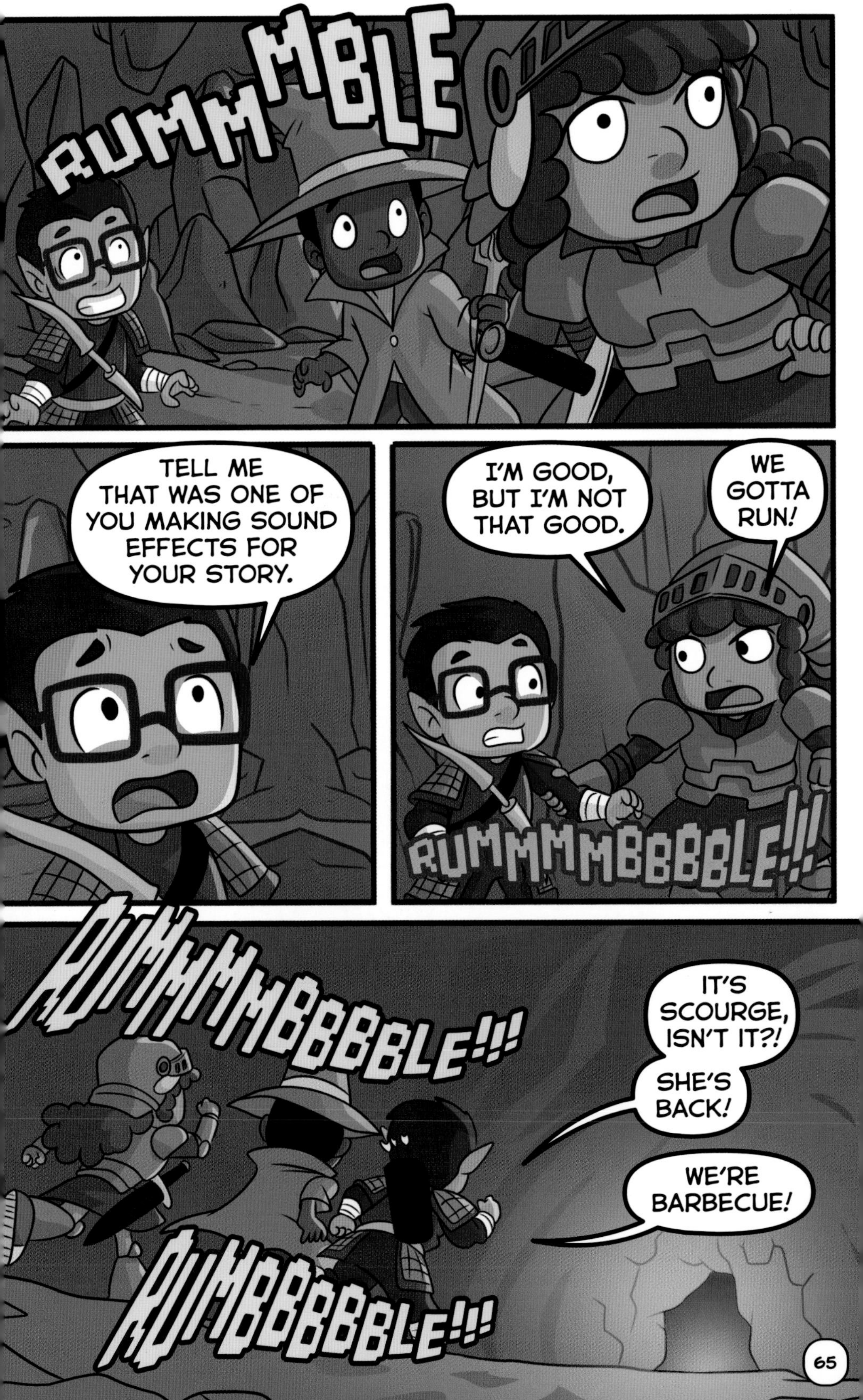
RUMMMBLE
TELL ME THAT WAS ONE OF YOU MAKING SOUND EFFECTS FOR YOUR STORY.
I'M GOOD, BUT I'M NOT THAT GOOD.
WE GOTTA RUN!
RUMMMMBBBBLE!!!
RUMMMMBBBBLE!!!
IT'S SCOURGE, ISN'T IT?!
SHE'S BACK!
WE'RE BARBECUE!
RUMBBBBBLE!!!

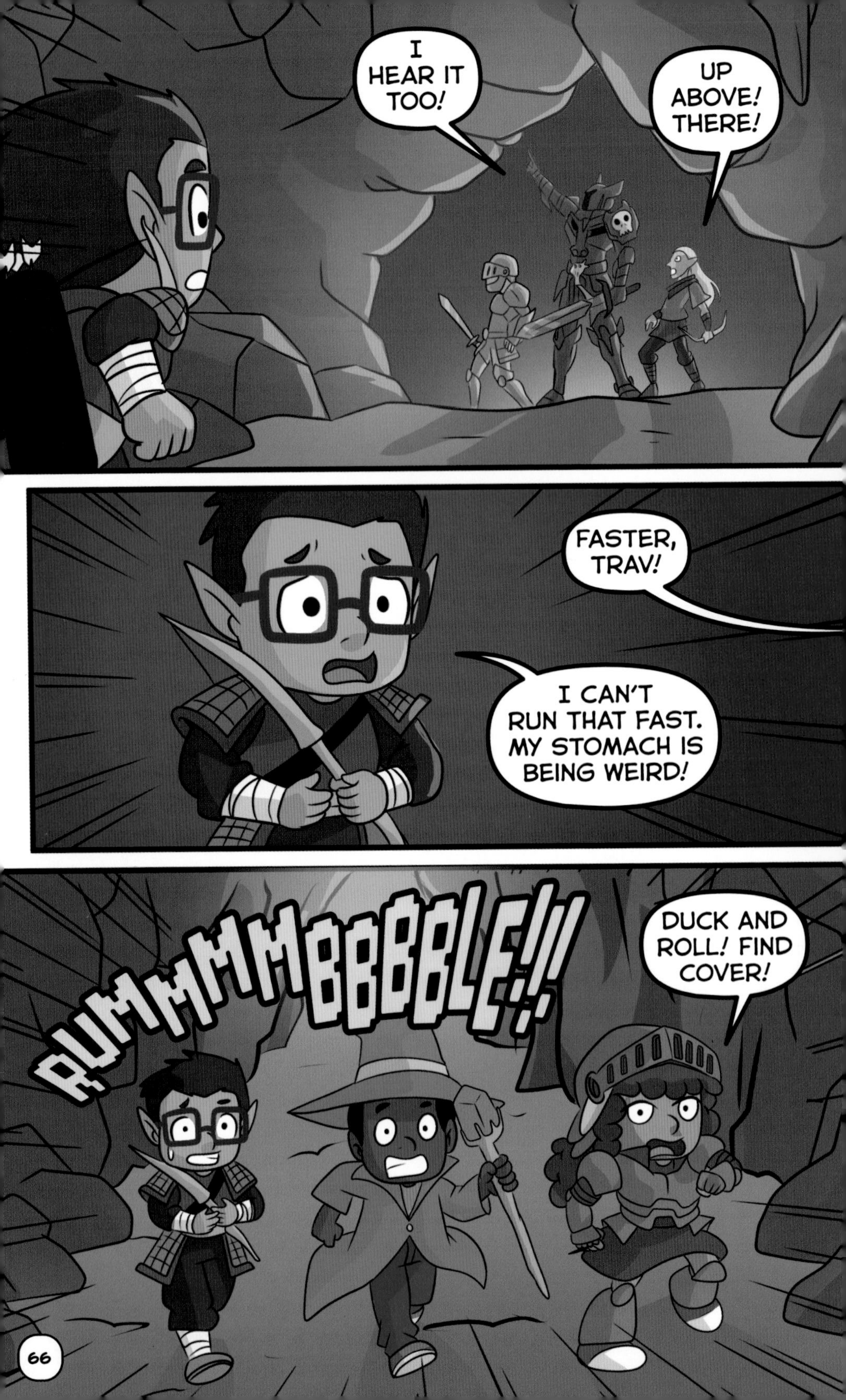
I HEAR IT TOO!
UP ABOVE! THERE!
FASTER, TRAV!
I CAN'T RUN THAT FAST. MY STOMACH IS BEING WEIRD!
RUMMMMBBBBLE!!!
DUCK AND ROLL! FIND COVER!

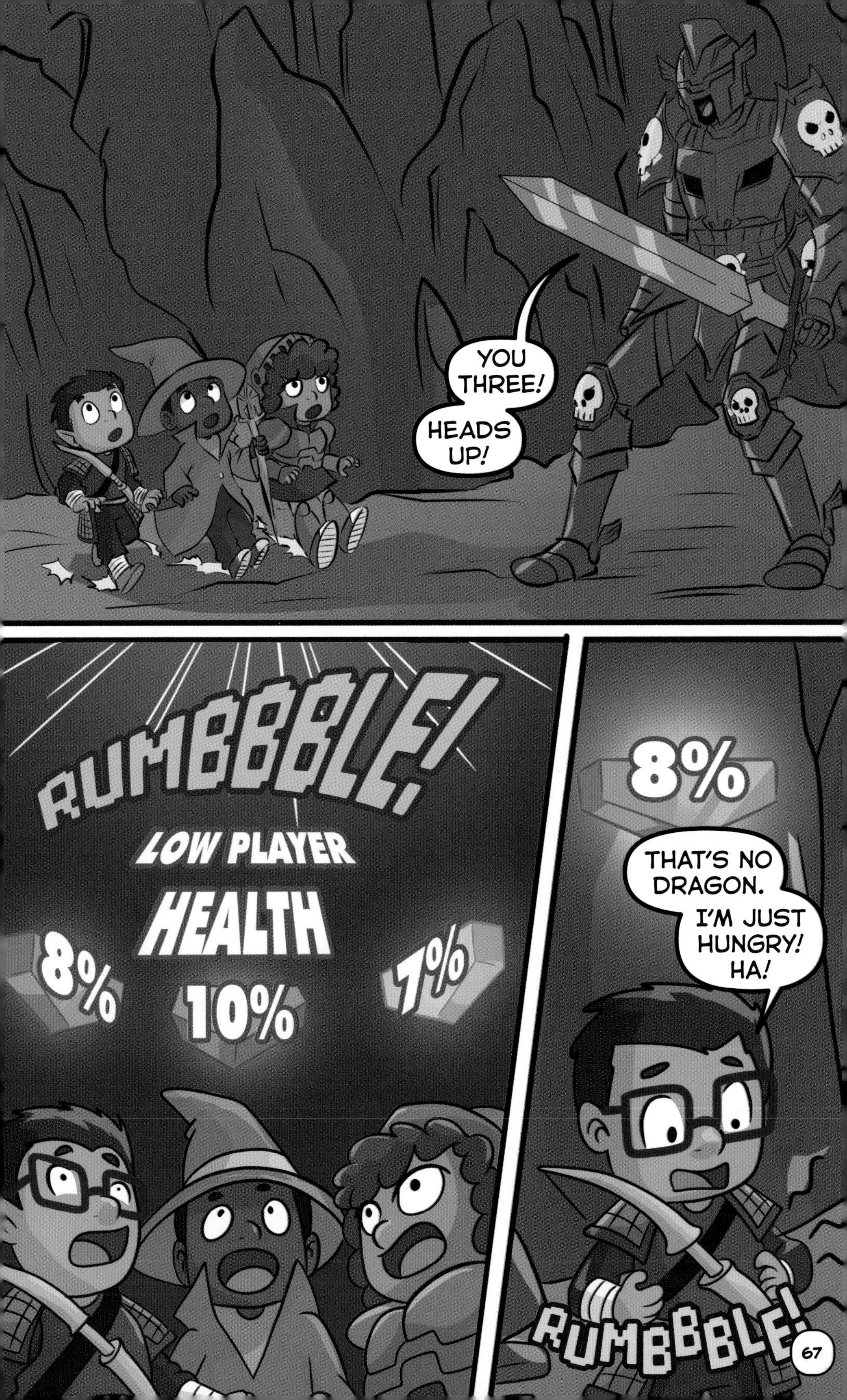
YOU THREE!
HEADS UP!
RUMBBBLE!
LOW PLAYER HEALTH
8%
10%
7%
8%
THAT'S NO DRAGON.
I'M JUST HUNGRY! HA!
RUMBBBLE!

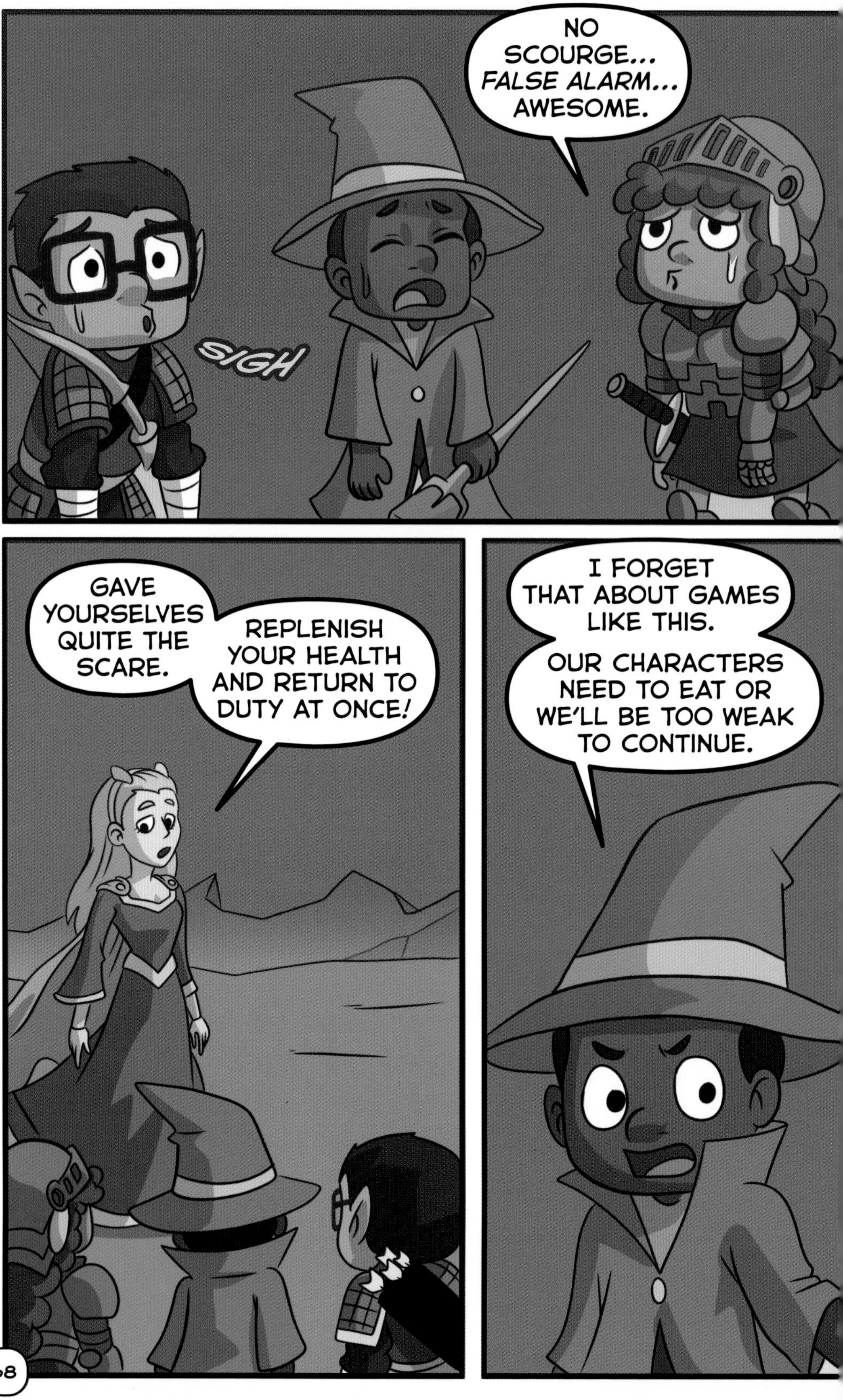
NO SCOURGE... FALSE ALARM... AWESOME.
SIGH
GAVE YOURSELVES QUITE THE SCARE.
REPLENISH YOUR HEALTH AND RETURN TO DUTY AT ONCE!
I FORGET THAT ABOUT GAMES LIKE THIS.
OUR CHARACTERS NEED TO EAT OR WE'LL BE TOO WEAK TO CONTINUE.

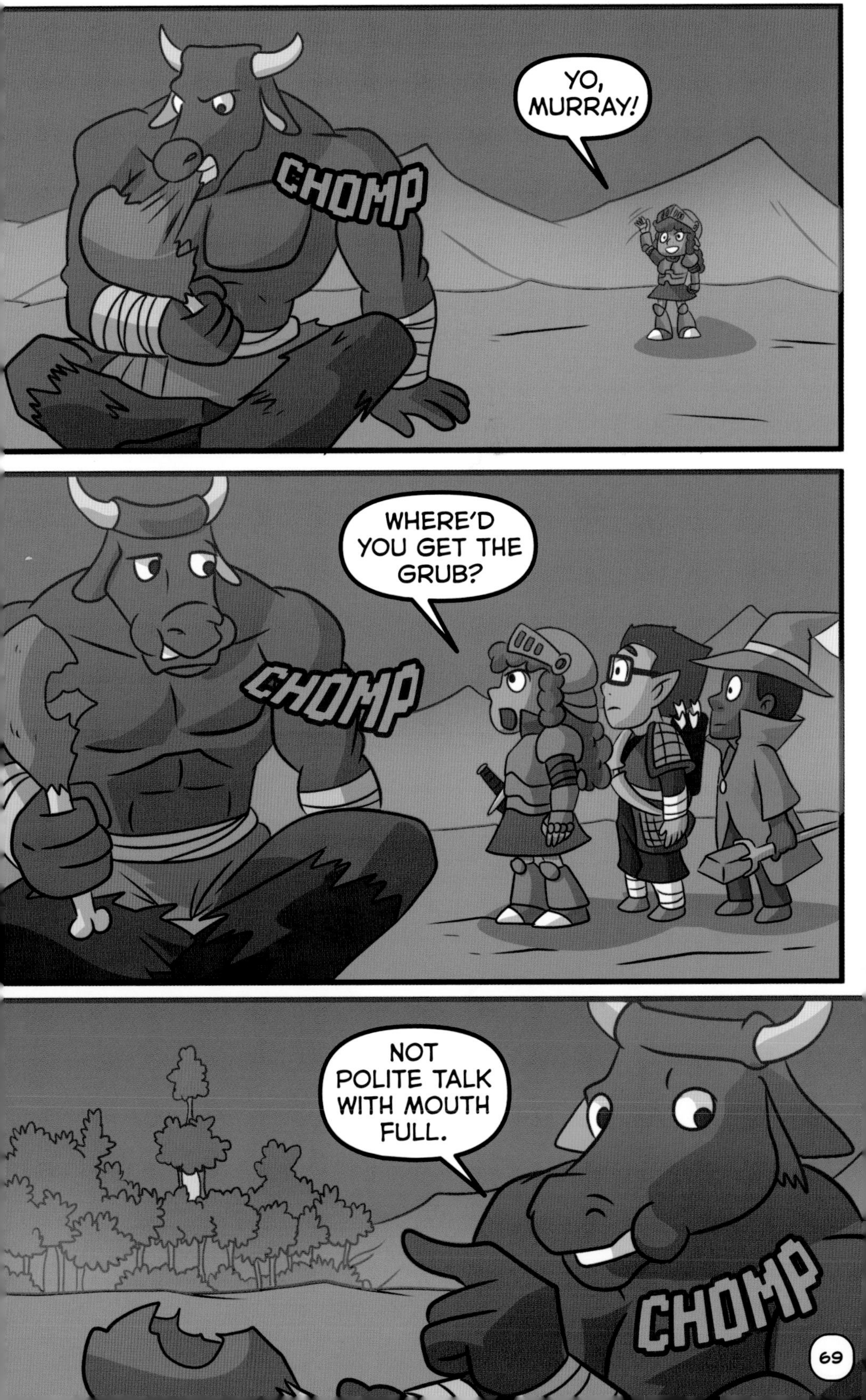
CHOMP
YO, MURRAY!
WHERE'D YOU GET THE GRUB?
CHOMP
NOT POLITE TALK WITH MOUTH FULL.
CHOMP

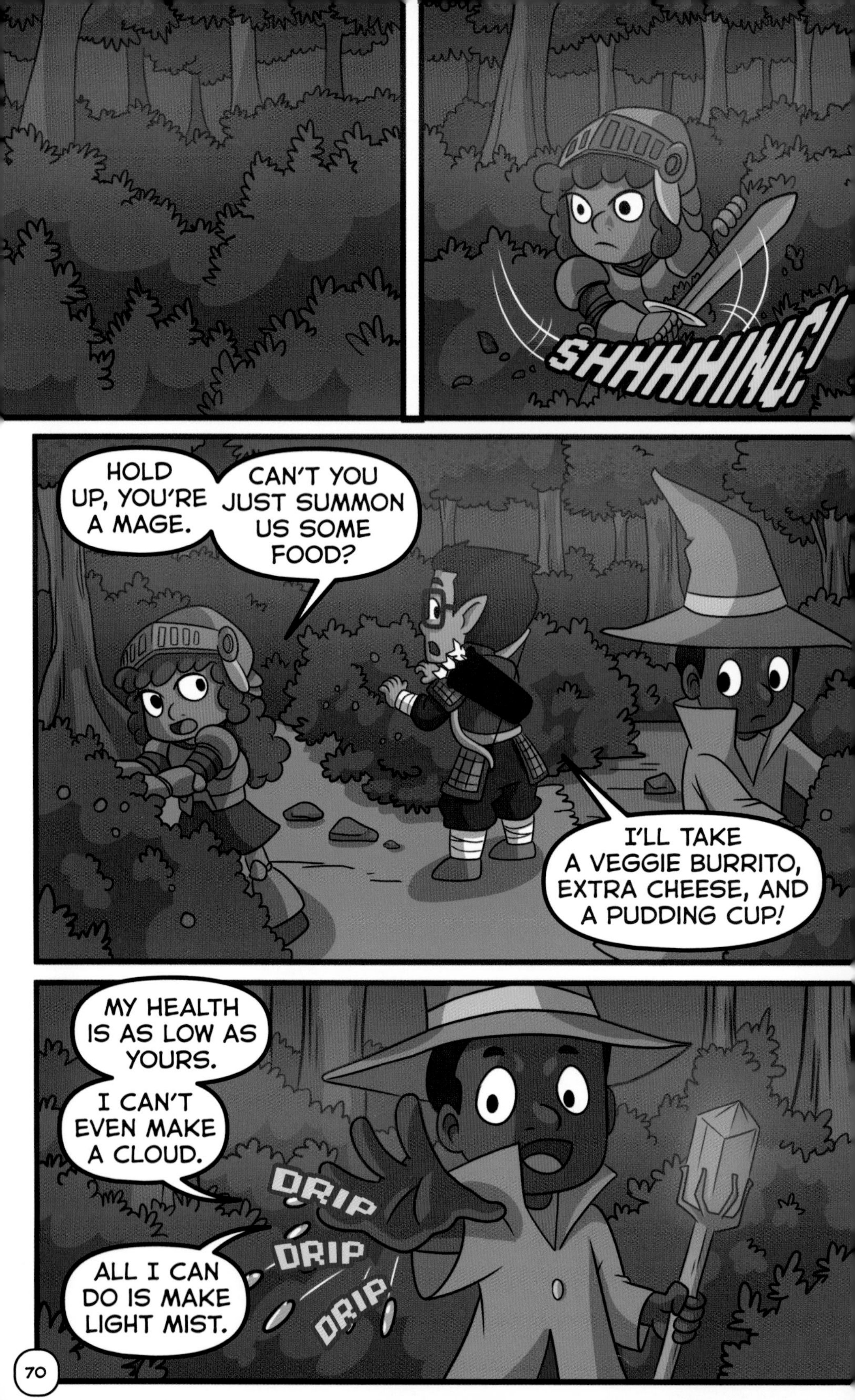
SHHHHING!
HOLD UP, YOU'RE A MAGE.
CAN'T YOU JUST SUMMON US SOME FOOD?
I'LL TAKE A VEGGIE BURRITO, EXTRA CHEESE, AND A PUDDING CUP!
MY HEALTH IS AS LOW AS YOURS.
I CAN'T EVEN MAKE A CLOUD.
DRIP
DRIP
DRIP
ALL I CAN DO IS MAKE LIGHT MIST.

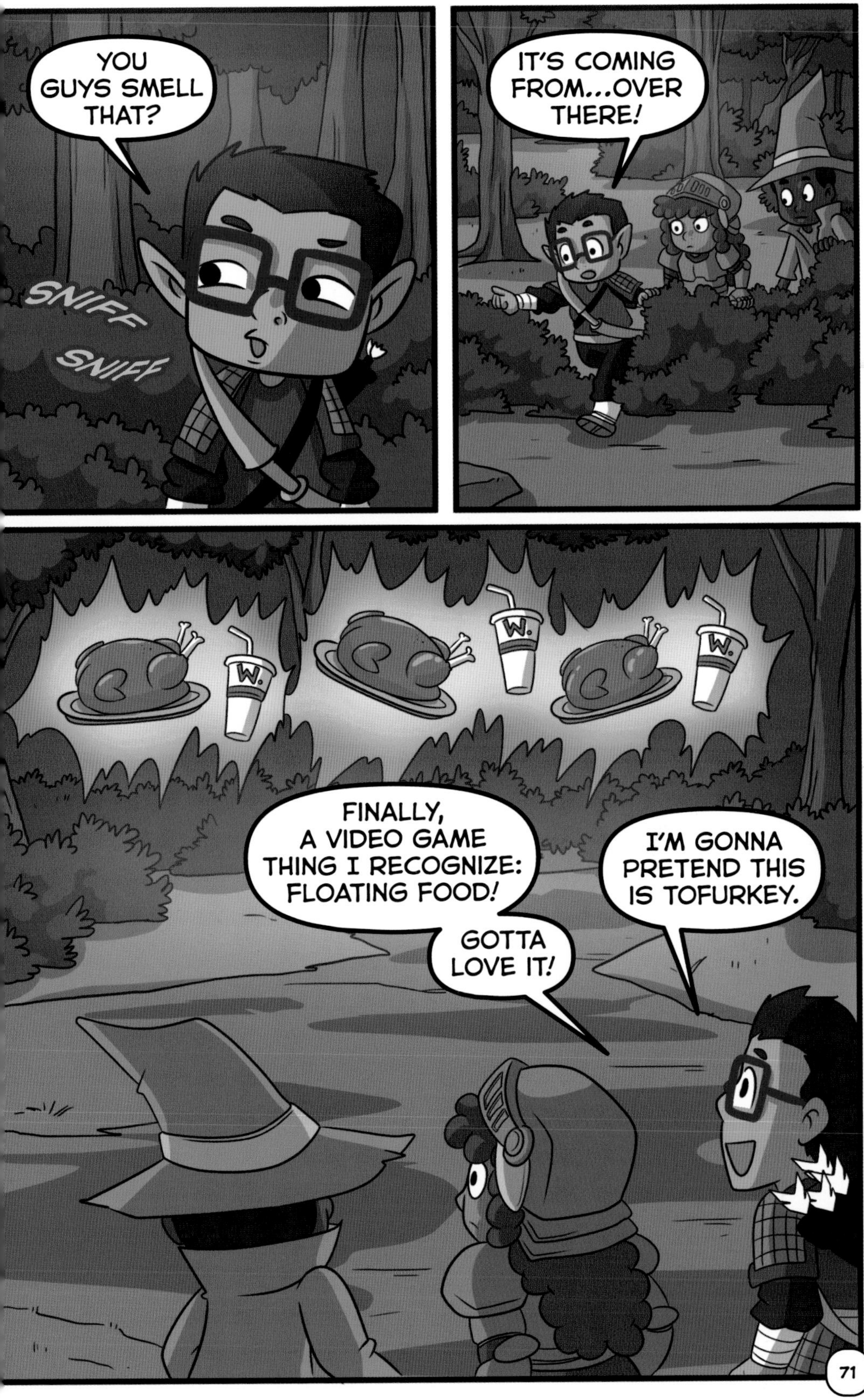
YOU GUYS SMELL THAT?
SNIFF
SNIFF
IT'S COMING FROM...OVER THERE!
FINALLY, A VIDEO GAME THING I RECOGNIZE: FLOATING FOOD!
GOTTA LOVE IT!
I'M GONNA PRETEND THIS IS TOFURKEY.

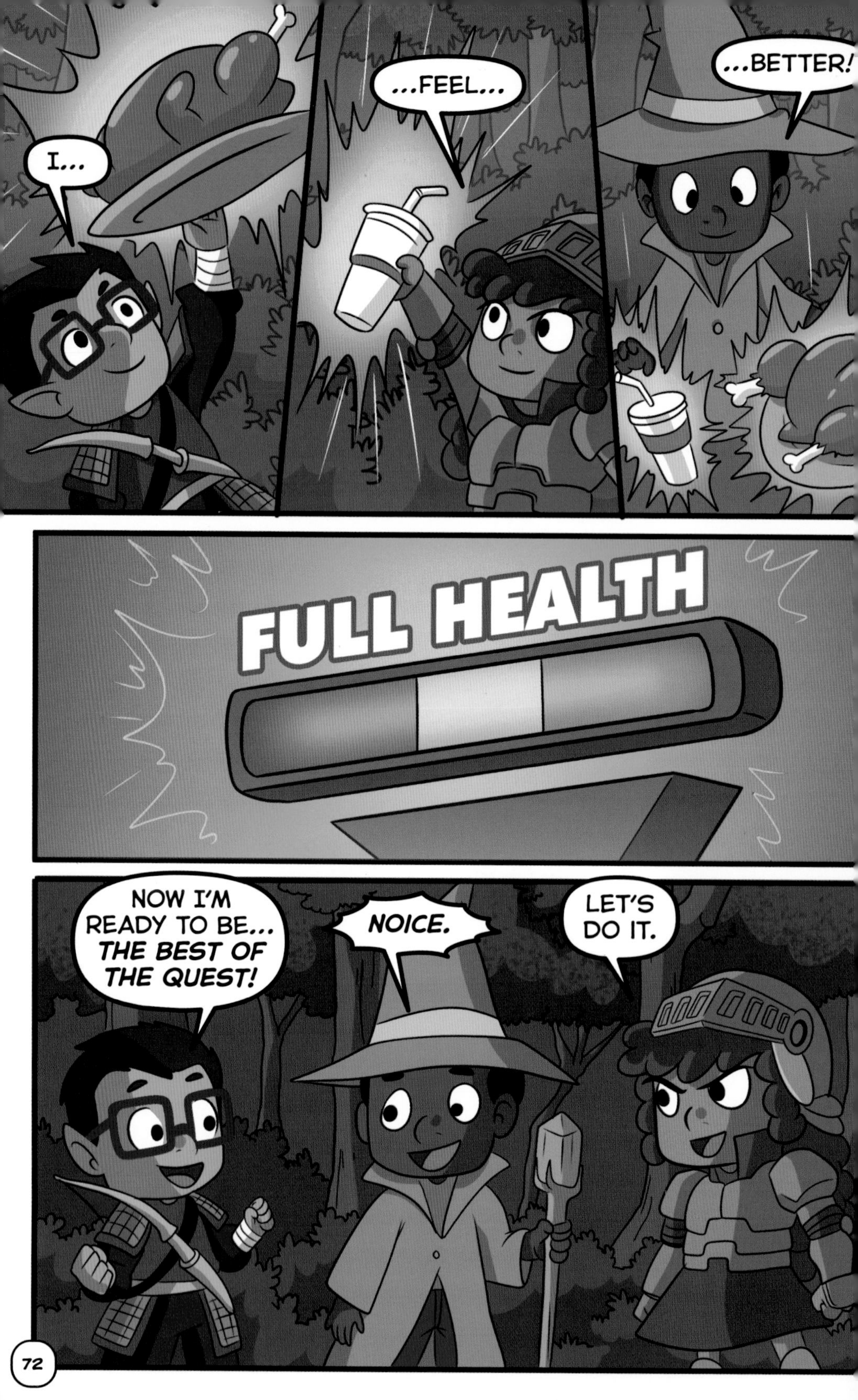
I...
...FEEL...
...BETTER!
FULL HEALTH
NOW I'M READY TO BE... *THE BEST OF THE QUEST!*
NOICE.
LET'S DO IT.

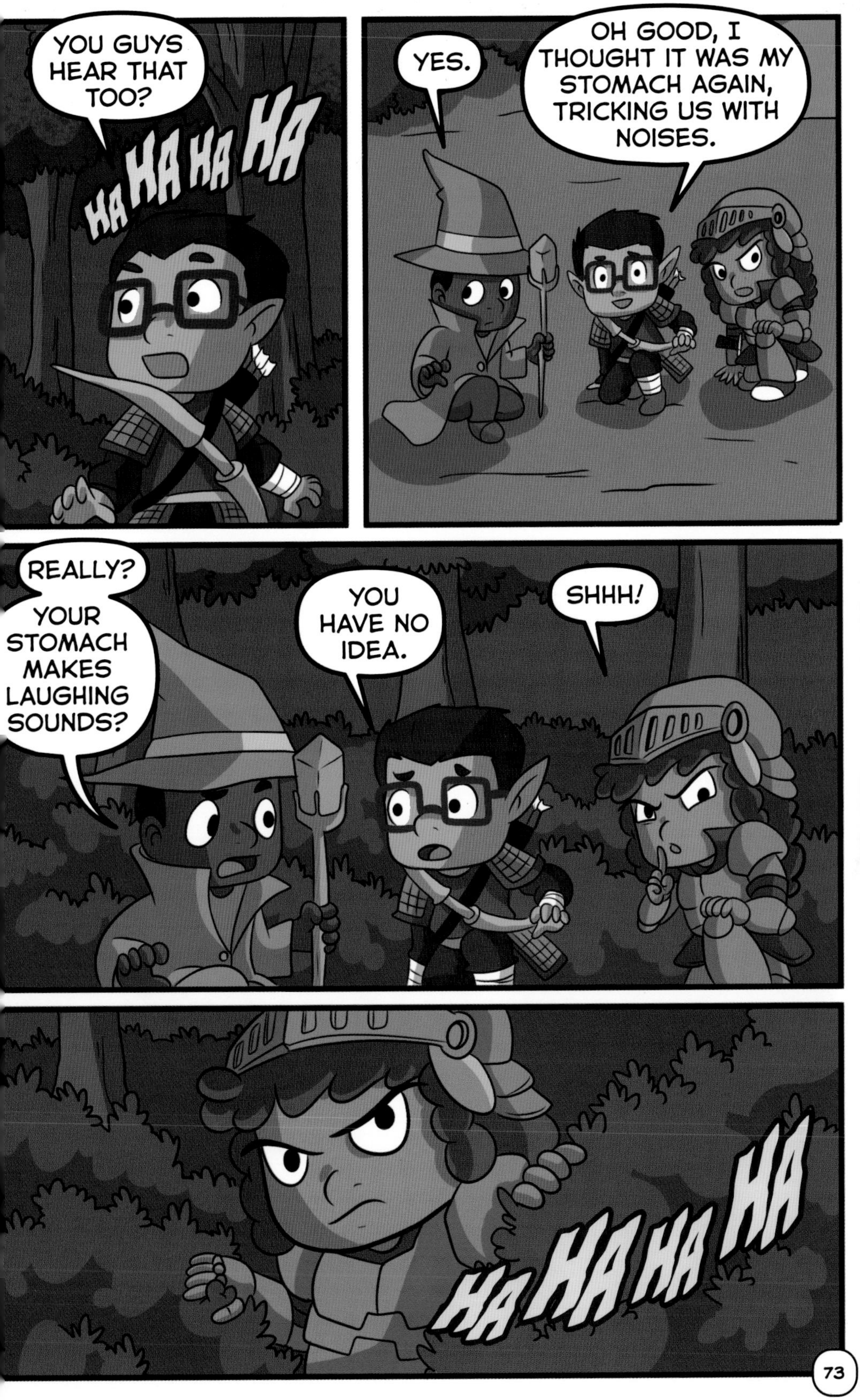
YOU GUYS HEAR THAT TOO?
HA HA HA HA
YES.
OH GOOD, I THOUGHT IT WAS MY STOMACH AGAIN, TRICKING US WITH NOISES.
REALLY? YOUR STOMACH MAKES LAUGHING SOUNDS?
YOU HAVE NO IDEA.
SHHH!
HA HA HA HA HA

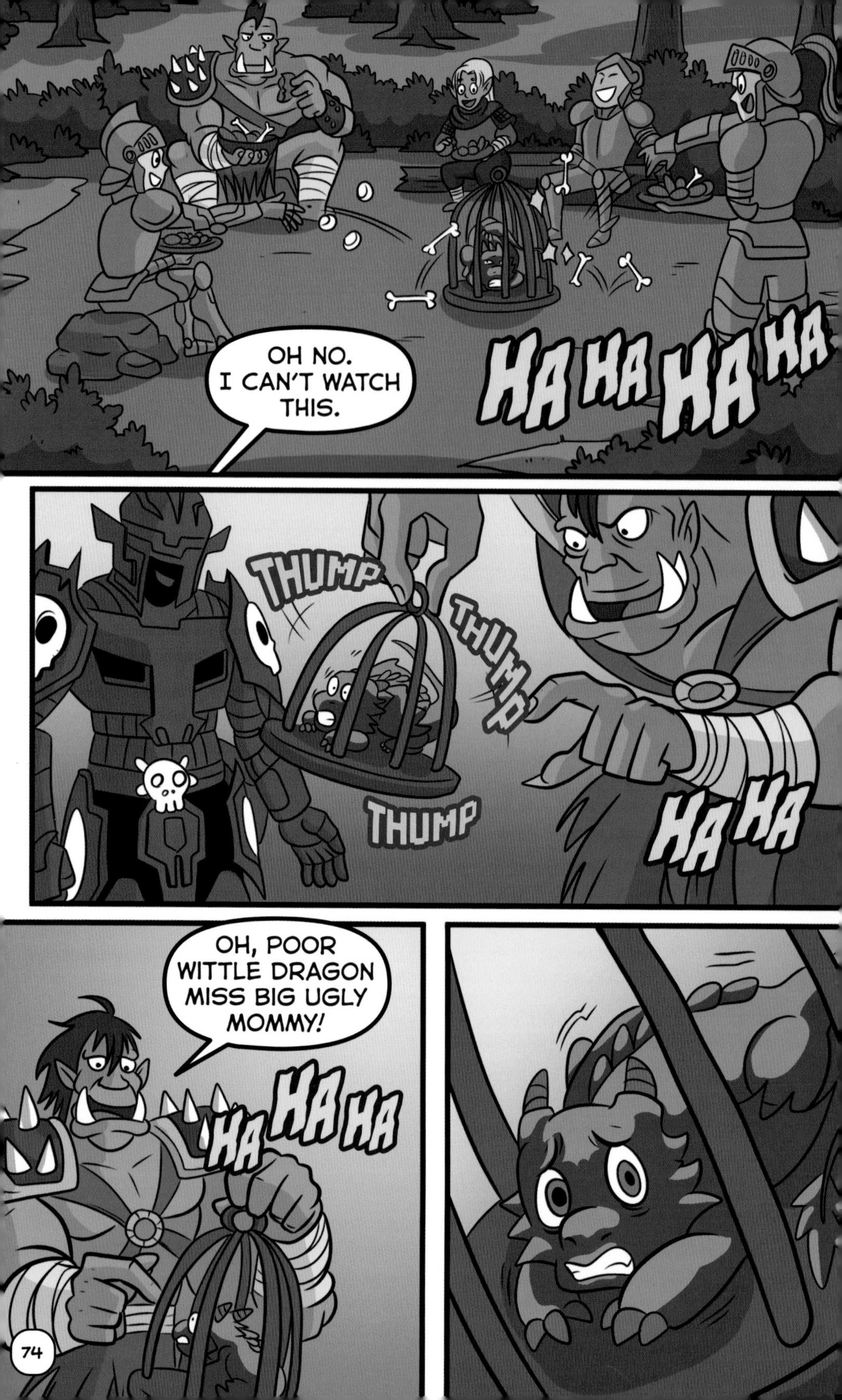
OH NO.
I CAN'T WATCH
THIS.
HA HA HA HA
THUMP
THUMP
THUMP
HA HA
OH, POOR
WITTLE DRAGON
MISS BIG UGLY
MOMMY!
HA HA HA

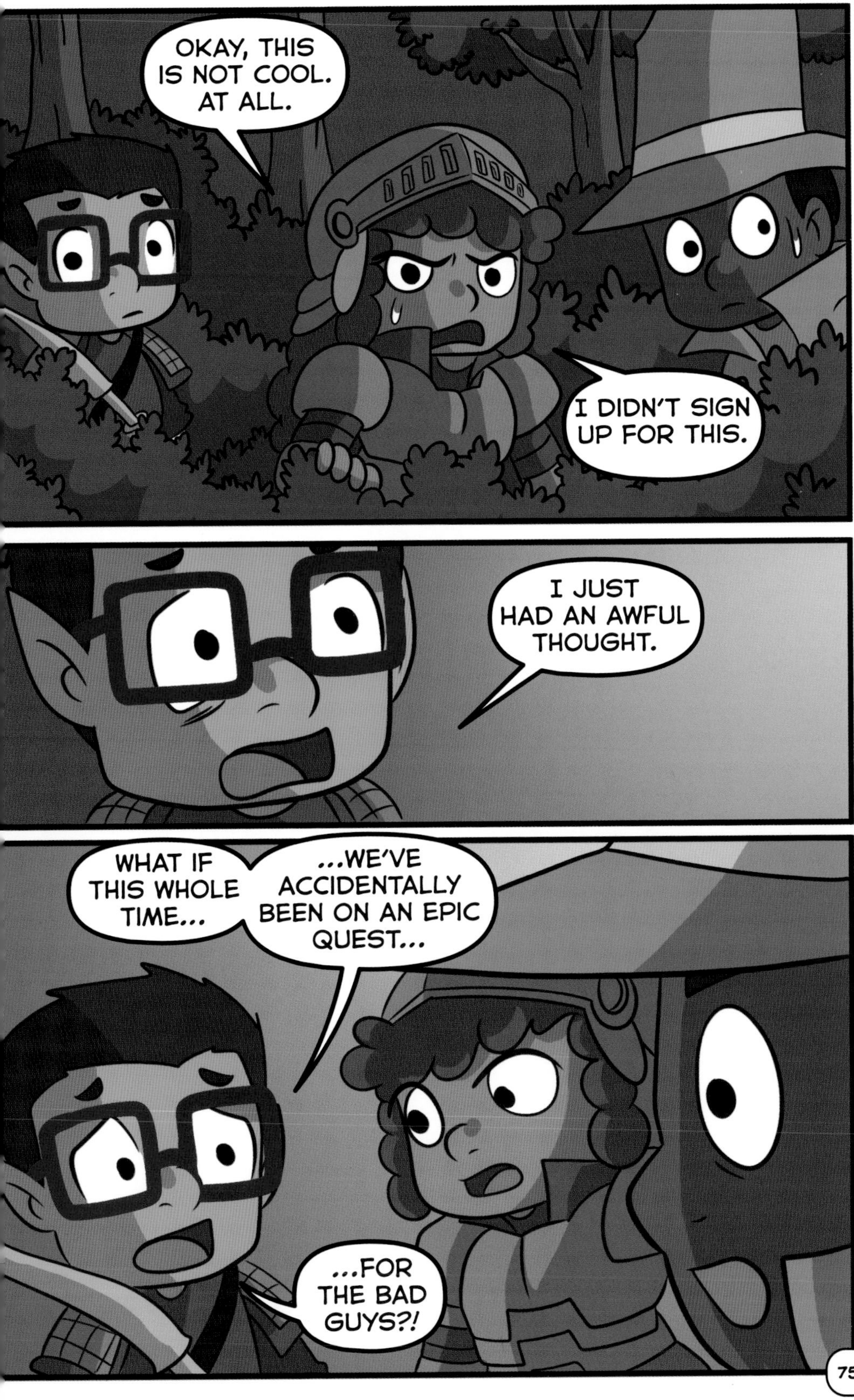
OKAY, THIS IS NOT COOL. AT ALL.
I DIDN'T SIGN UP FOR THIS.
I JUST HAD AN AWFUL THOUGHT.
WHAT IF THIS WHOLE TIME...
...WE'VE ACCIDENTALLY BEEN ON AN EPIC QUEST...
...FOR THE BAD GUYS?!

CHAPTER 6

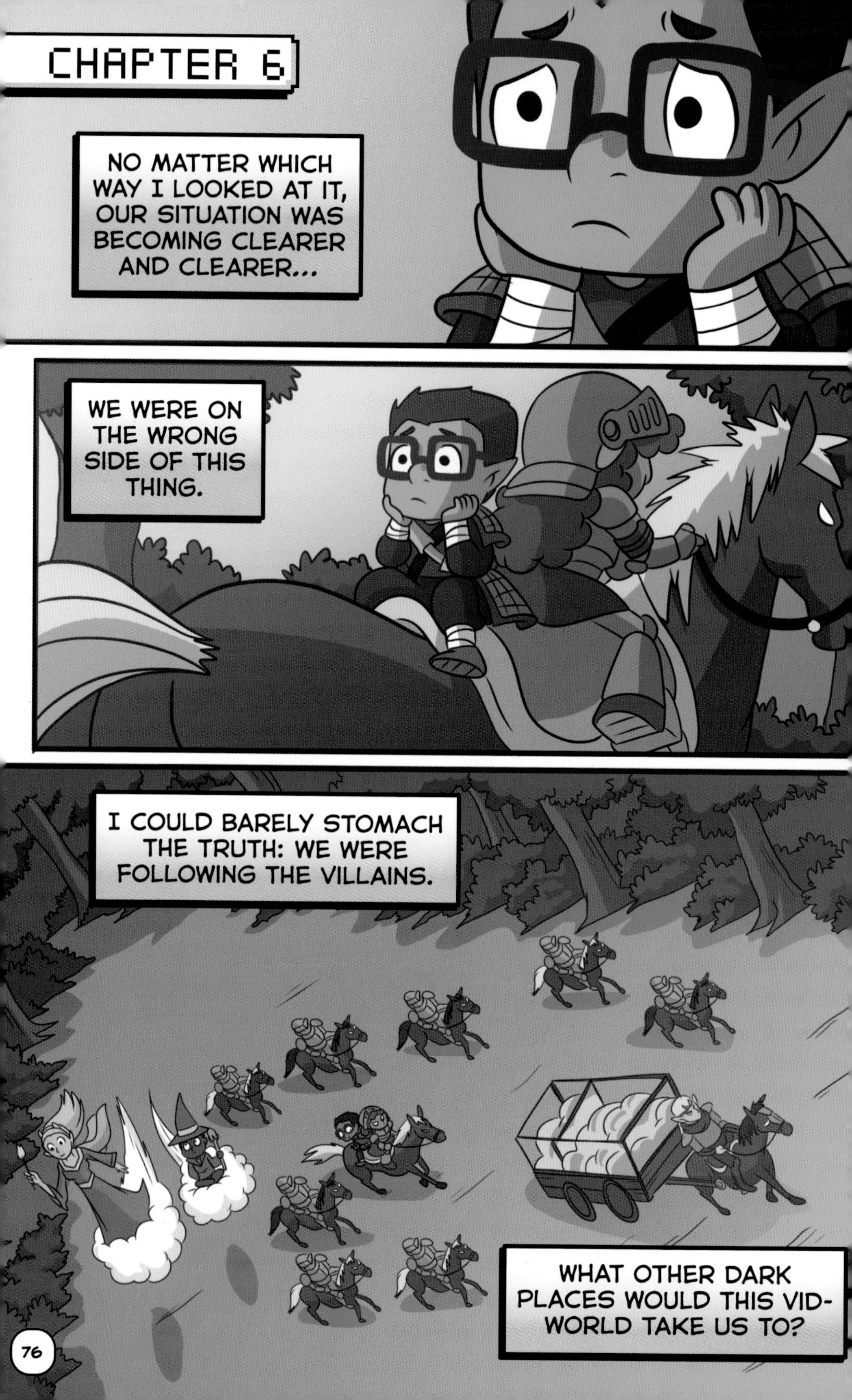
NO MATTER WHICH WAY I LOOKED AT IT, OUR SITUATION WAS BECOMING CLEARER AND CLEARER...
WE WERE ON THE WRONG SIDE OF THIS THING.
I COULD BARELY STOMACH THE TRUTH: WE WERE FOLLOWING THE VILLAINS.
WHAT OTHER DARK PLACES WOULD THIS VID-WORLD TAKE US TO?

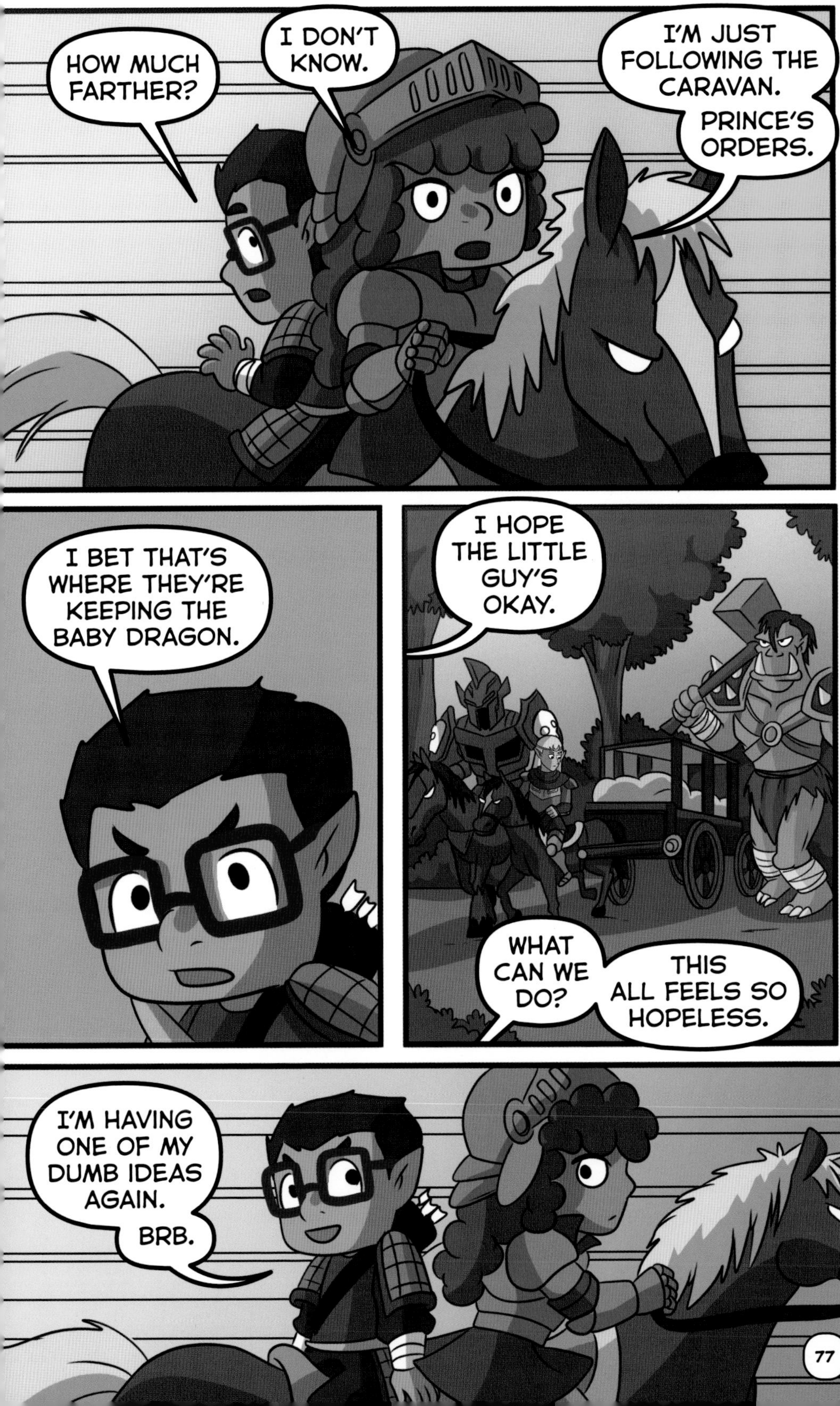
HOW MUCH FARTHER?
I DON'T KNOW.
I'M JUST FOLLOWING THE CARAVAN.
PRINCE'S ORDERS.
I BET THAT'S WHERE THEY'RE KEEPING THE BABY DRAGON.
I HOPE THE LITTLE GUY'S OKAY.
WHAT CAN WE DO?
THIS ALL FEELS SO HOPELESS.
I'M HAVING ONE OF MY DUMB IDEAS AGAIN.
BRB.

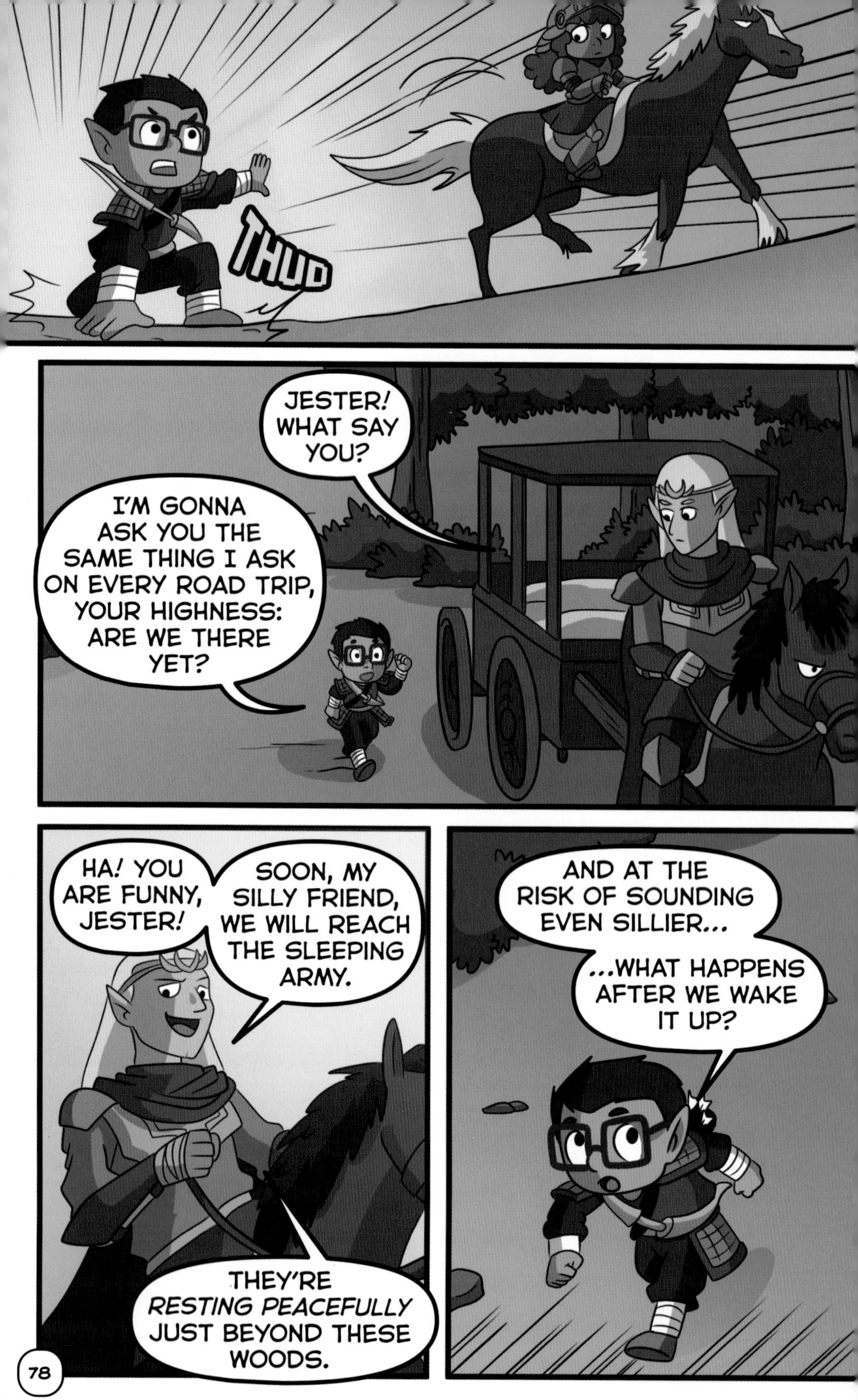
THUD
JESTER! WHAT SAY YOU?
I'M GONNA ASK YOU THE SAME THING I ASK ON EVERY ROAD TRIP, YOUR HIGHNESS: ARE WE THERE YET?
HA! YOU ARE FUNNY, JESTER!
SOON, MY SILLY FRIEND, WE WILL REACH THE SLEEPING ARMY.
THEY'RE *RESTING PEACEFULLY* JUST BEYOND THESE WOODS.
AND AT THE RISK OF SOUNDING EVEN SILLIER...
...WHAT HAPPENS AFTER WE WAKE IT UP?

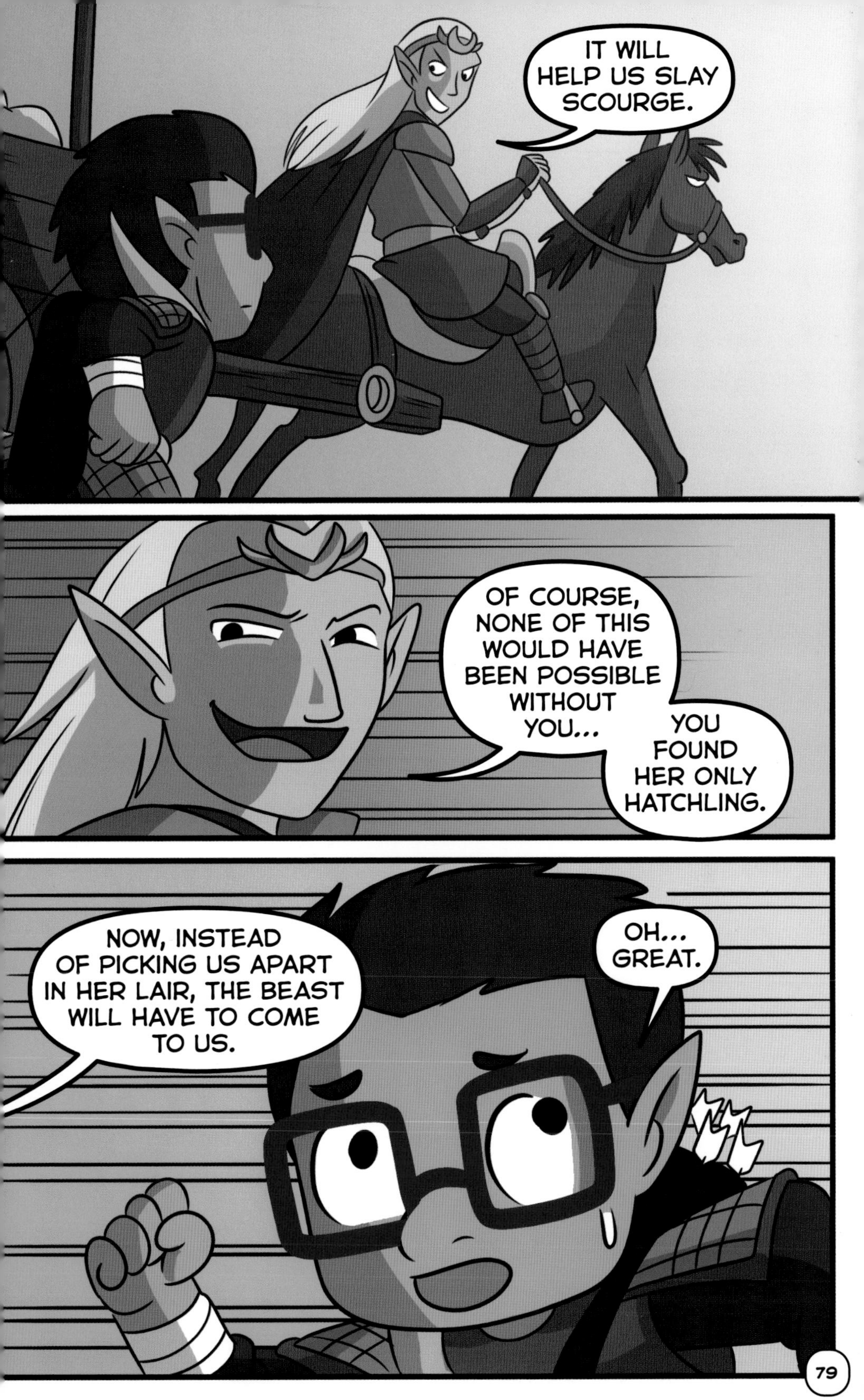
IT WILL HELP US SLAY SCOURGE.
OF COURSE, NONE OF THIS WOULD HAVE BEEN POSSIBLE WITHOUT YOU...
YOU FOUND HER ONLY HATCHLING.
NOW, INSTEAD OF PICKING US APART IN HER LAIR, THE BEAST WILL HAVE TO COME TO US.
OH... GREAT.

ONE MORE THING...BACK AT DARK CASTLE...

...THE WITCH WHO HAD YOU IMPRISONED...

...WOULD YOU DESCRIBE HER AS *EVIL*?

I WOULD DESCRIBE HER MANY WAYS: WITCH, QUEEN, *MOTHER.*

SHE WAS YOUR MOM?!

OH YES. SHE LOVES DRAGONS AND THINKS WE CAN LIVE IN HARMONY.

I DISAGREED.

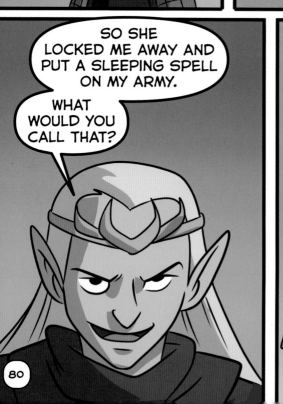

SO SHE LOCKED ME AWAY AND PUT A SLEEPING SPELL ON MY ARMY.

WHAT WOULD YOU CALL THAT?

AWWWWK-WARD!

OKAY...I'VE ASKED ENOUGH QUESTIONS FOR ONE HORSE RIDE.

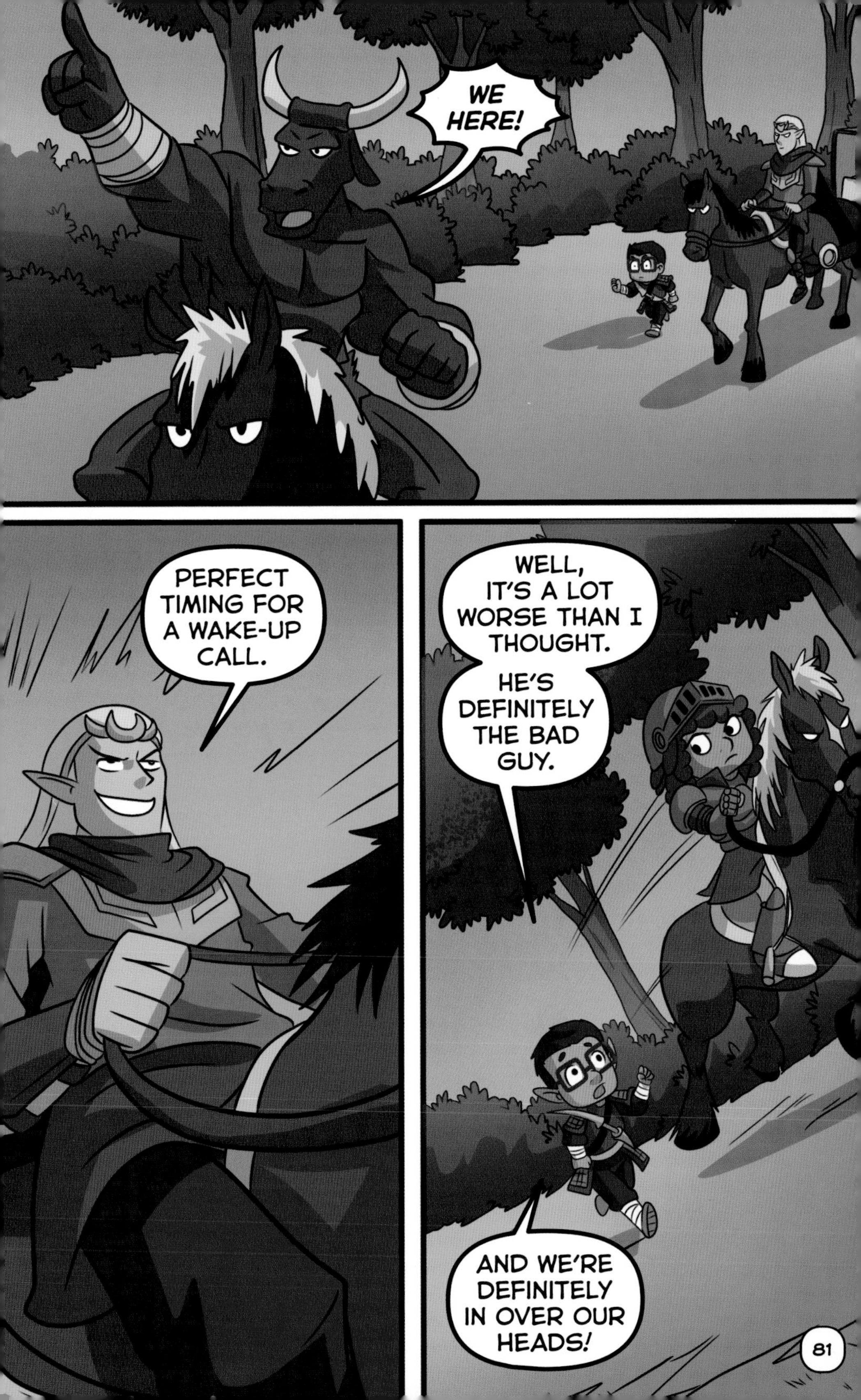

WE HERE!
PERFECT TIMING FOR A WAKE-UP CALL.
WELL, IT'S A LOT WORSE THAN I THOUGHT.
HE'S DEFINITELY THE BAD GUY.
AND WE'RE DEFINITELY IN OVER OUR HEADS!

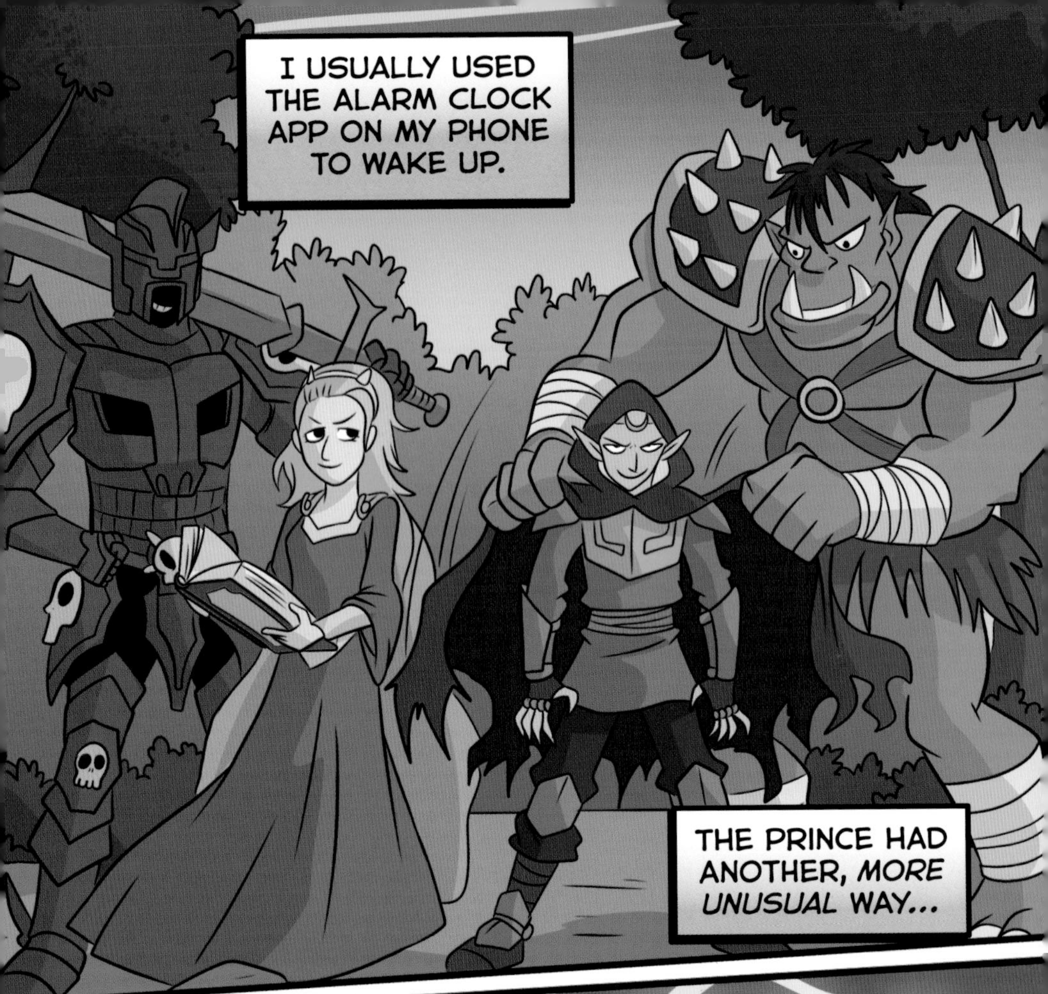
I USUALLY USED THE ALARM CLOCK APP ON MY PHONE TO WAKE UP.
THE PRINCE HAD ANOTHER, *MORE UNUSUAL* WAY...

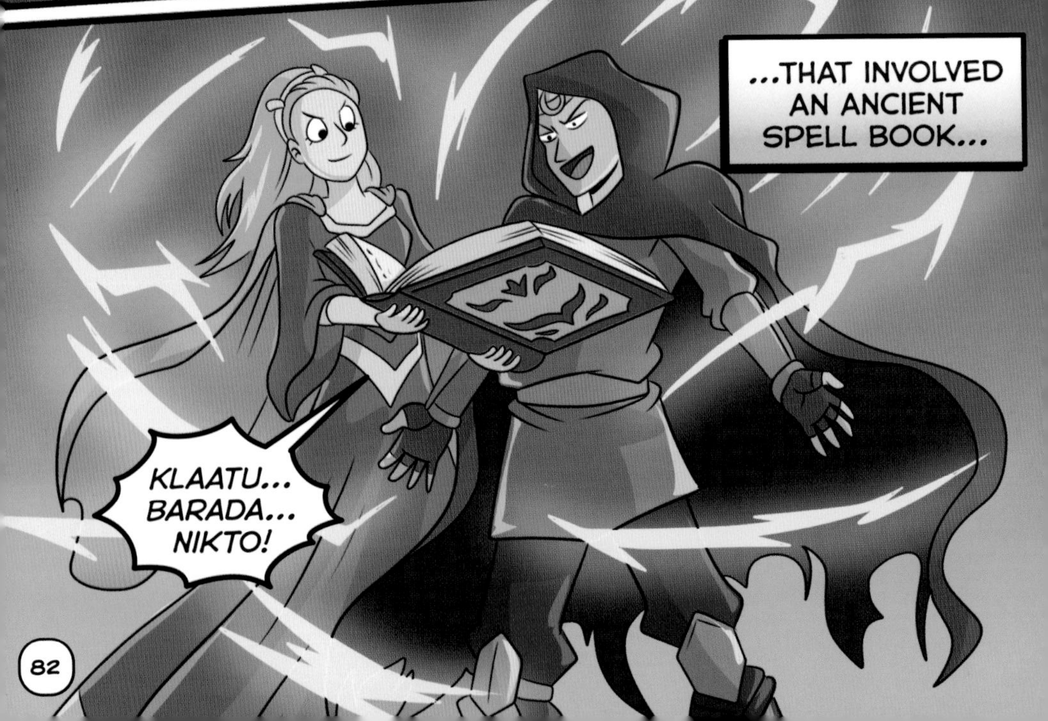
...THAT INVOLVED AN ANCIENT SPELL BOOK...
KLAATU... BARADA... NIKTO!

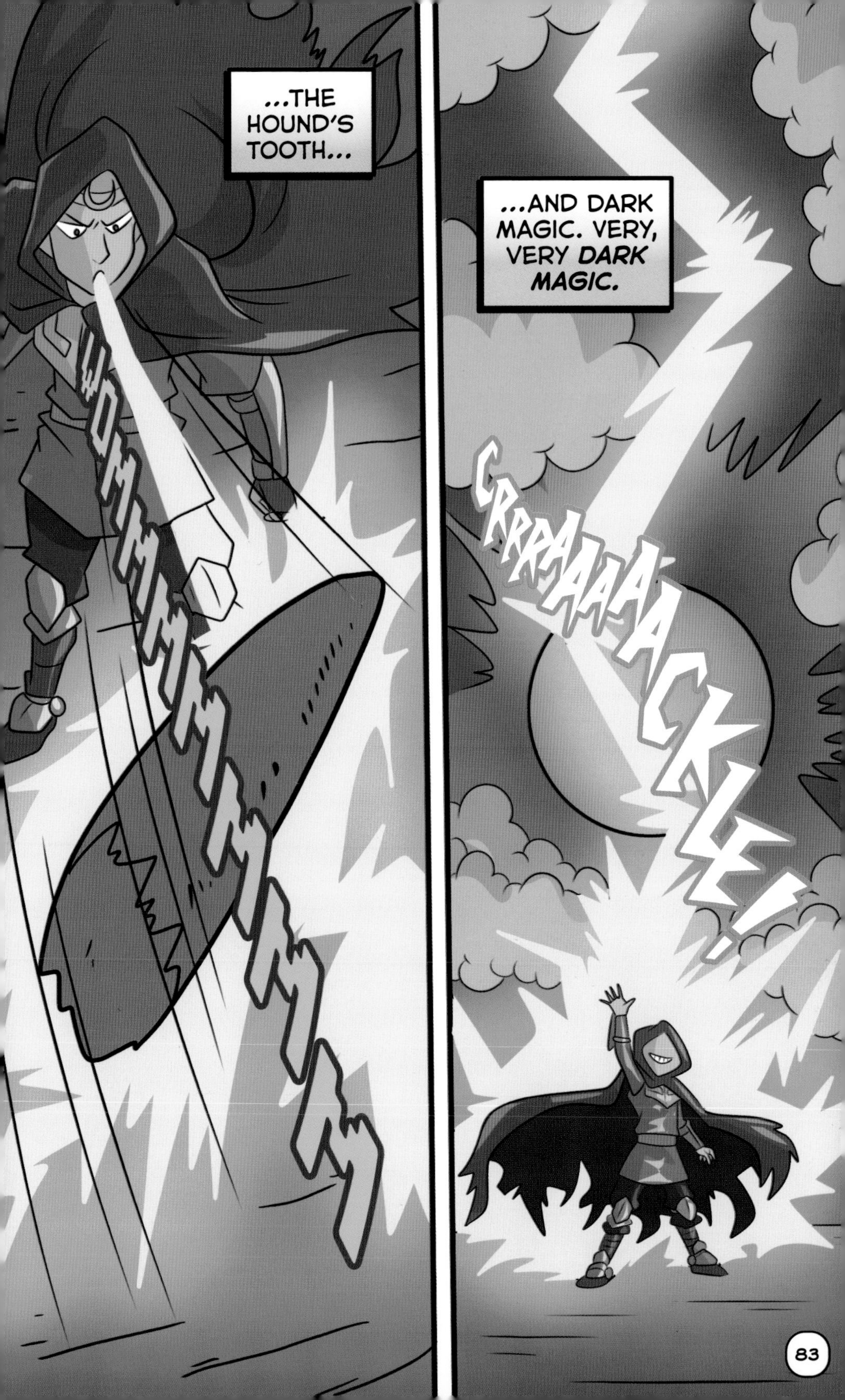
...THE HOUND'S TOOTH...
WOMMMMMMMMMM
...AND DARK MAGIC. VERY, VERY *DARK MAGIC.*
CRRRAAAAACKLE!

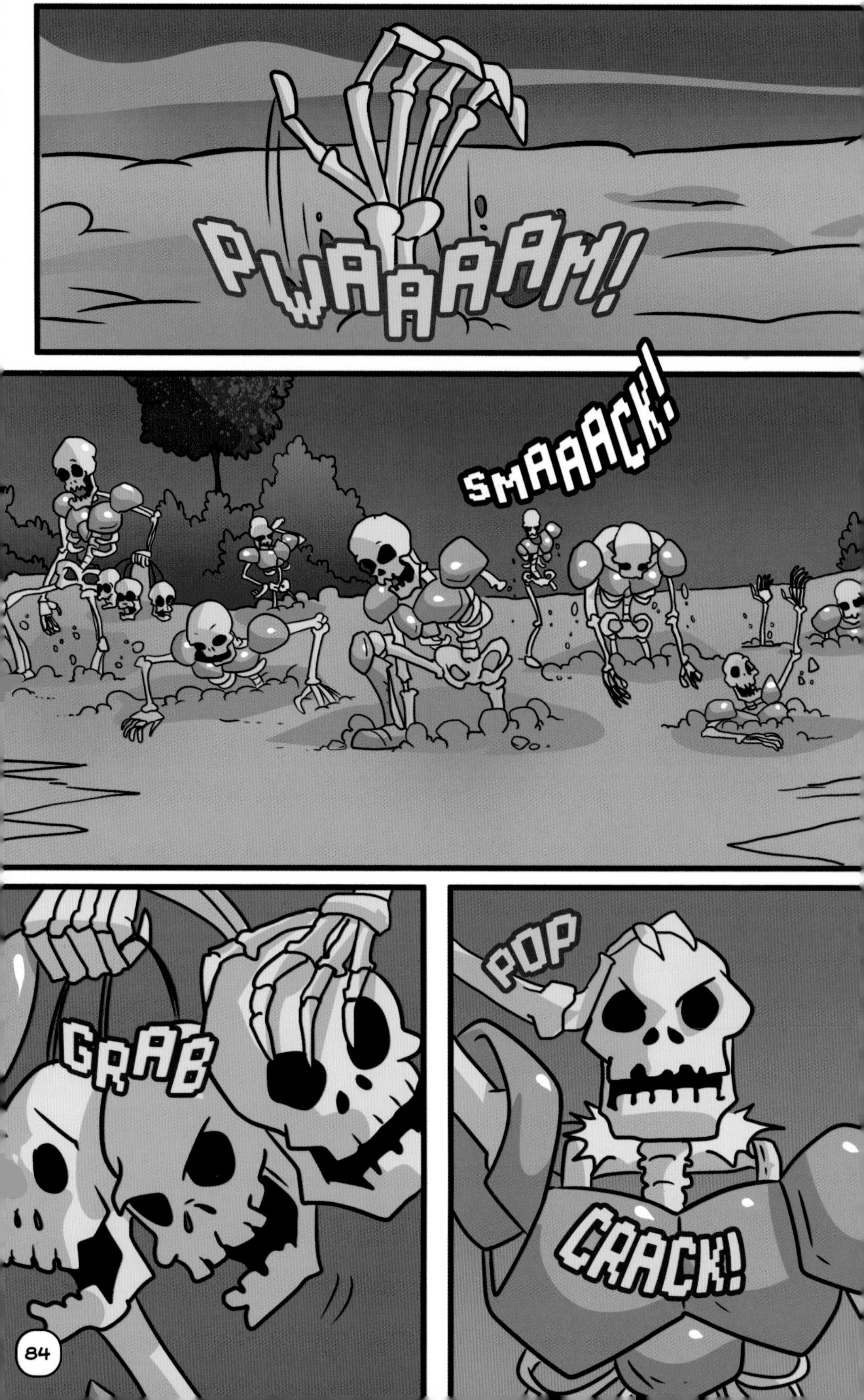
PWAAAAM!
SMAAACK!
GRAB
POP
CRACK!

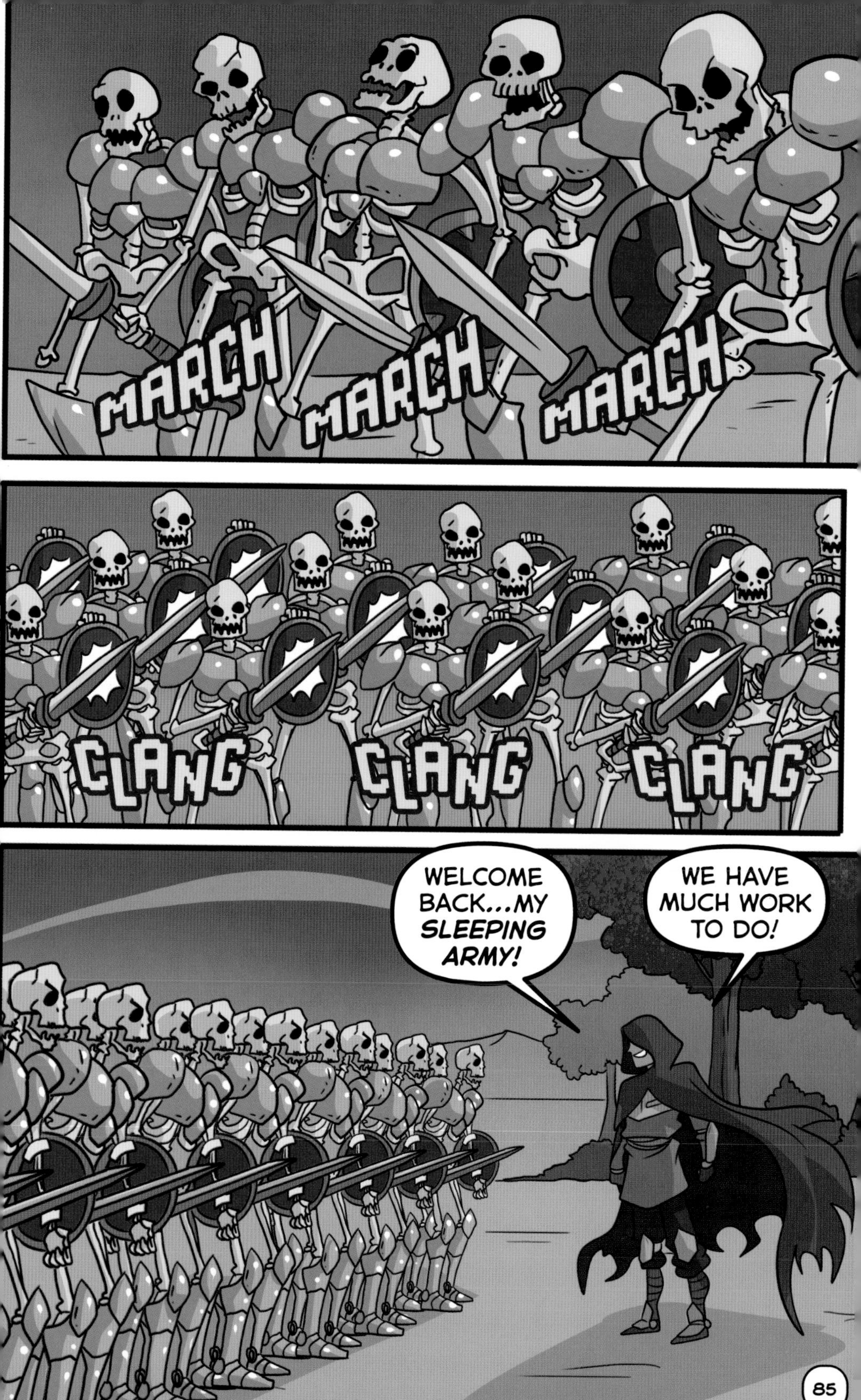
MARCH MARCH MARCH
CLANG CLANG CLANG
WELCOME BACK...MY SLEEPING ARMY!
WE HAVE MUCH WORK TO DO!

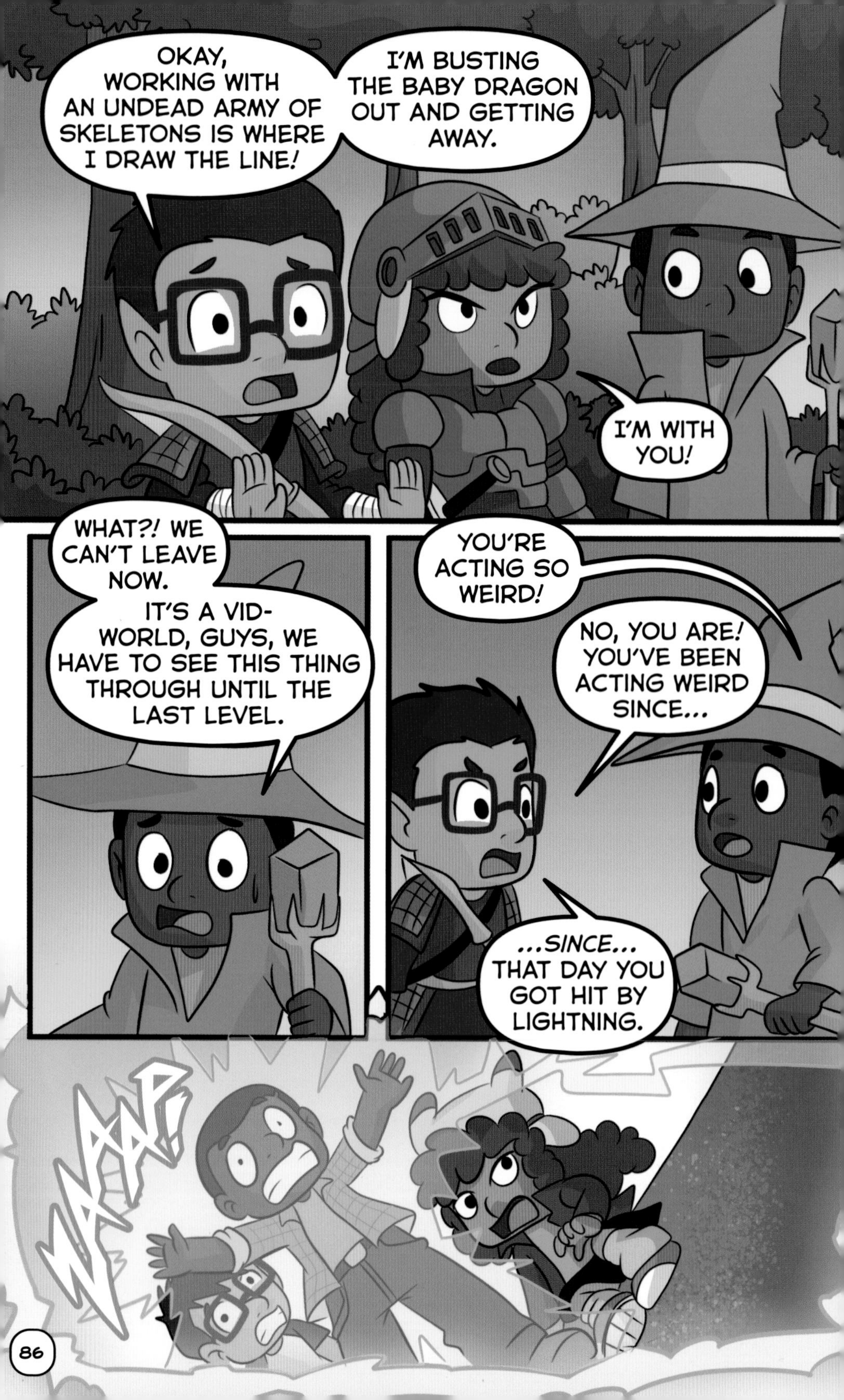
OKAY, WORKING WITH AN UNDEAD ARMY OF SKELETONS IS WHERE I DRAW THE LINE!
I'M BUSTING THE BABY DRAGON OUT AND GETTING AWAY.
I'M WITH YOU!
WHAT?! WE CAN'T LEAVE NOW.
IT'S A VID-WORLD, GUYS, WE HAVE TO SEE THIS THING THROUGH UNTIL THE LAST LEVEL.
YOU'RE ACTING SO WEIRD!
NO, YOU ARE! YOU'VE BEEN ACTING WEIRD SINCE...
...SINCE... THAT DAY YOU GOT HIT BY LIGHTNING.
ZAP!

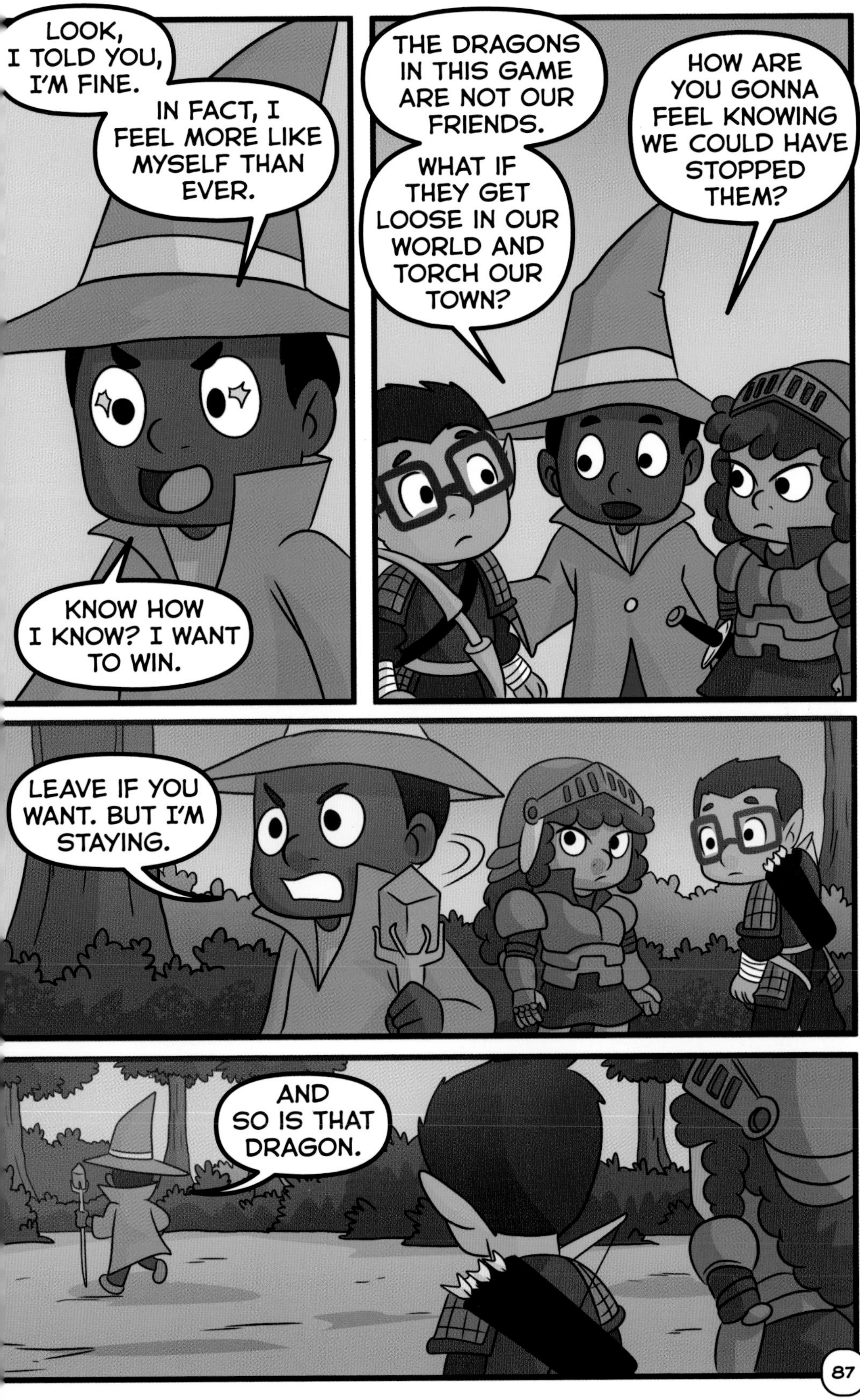
LOOK, I TOLD YOU, I'M FINE.
IN FACT, I FEEL MORE LIKE MYSELF THAN EVER.
KNOW HOW I KNOW? I WANT TO WIN.
THE DRAGONS IN THIS GAME ARE NOT OUR FRIENDS.
WHAT IF THEY GET LOOSE IN OUR WORLD AND TORCH OUR TOWN?
HOW ARE YOU GONNA FEEL KNOWING WE COULD HAVE STOPPED THEM?
LEAVE IF YOU WANT. BUT I'M STAYING.
AND SO IS THAT DRAGON.

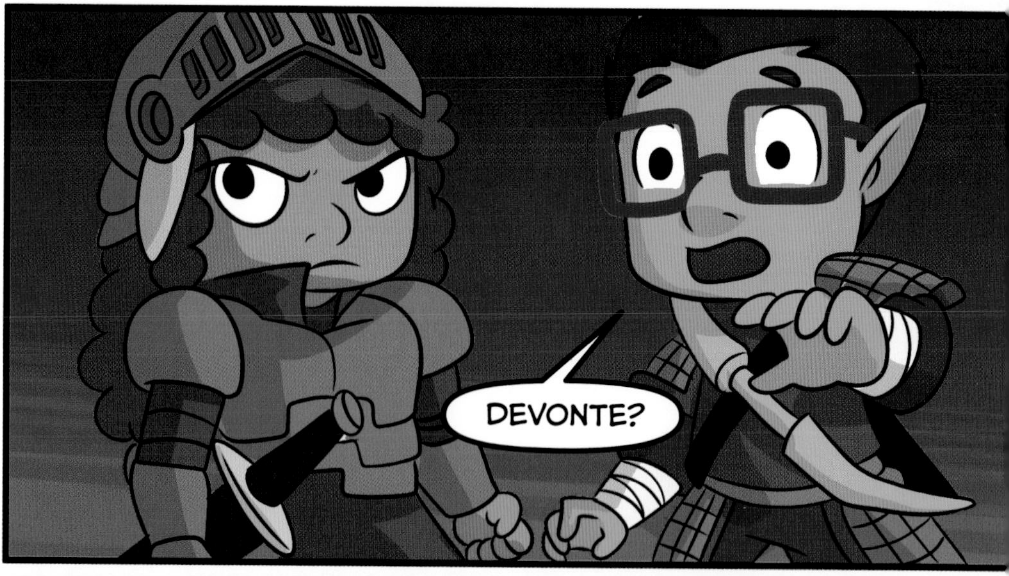
DEVONTE?

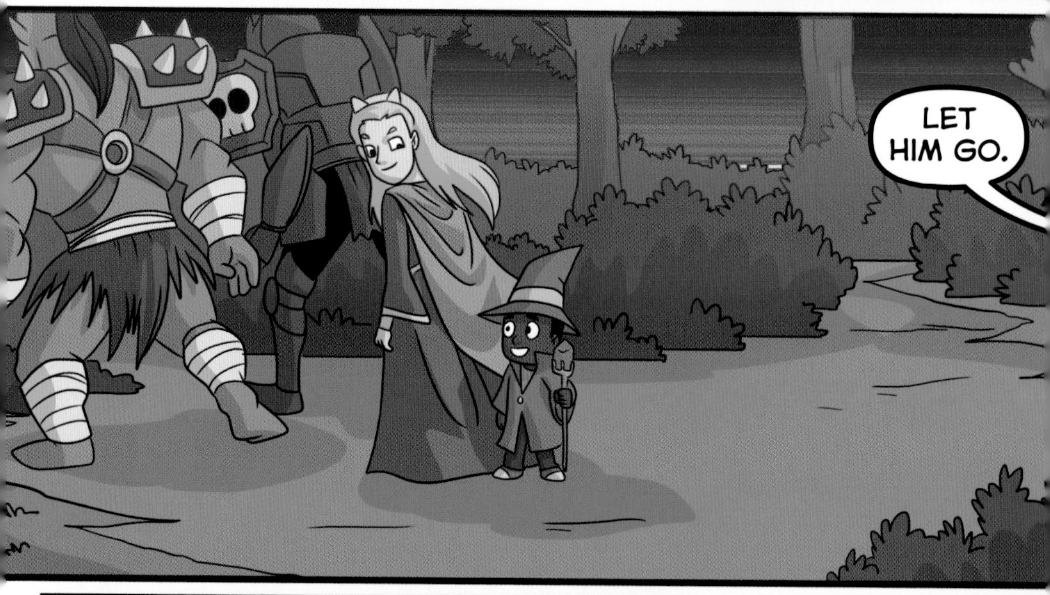
LET HIM GO.

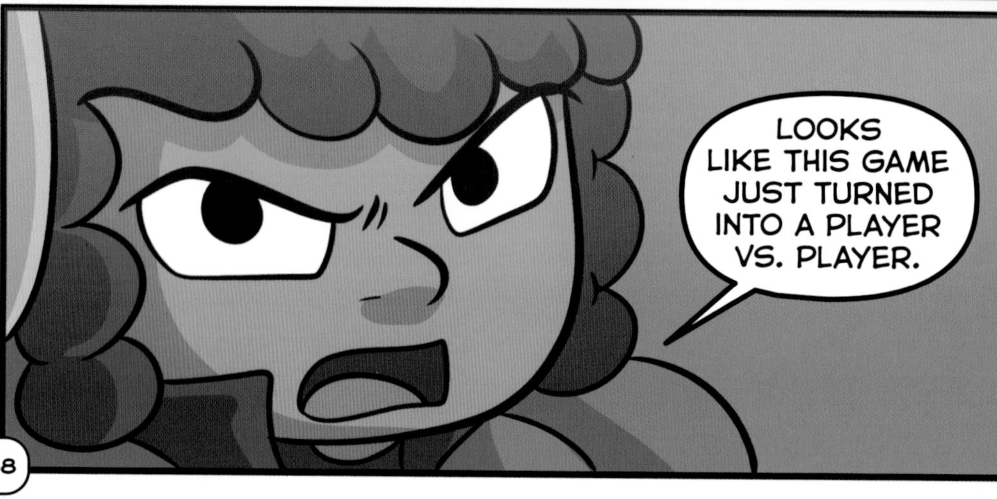
LOOKS LIKE THIS GAME JUST TURNED INTO A PLAYER VS. PLAYER.

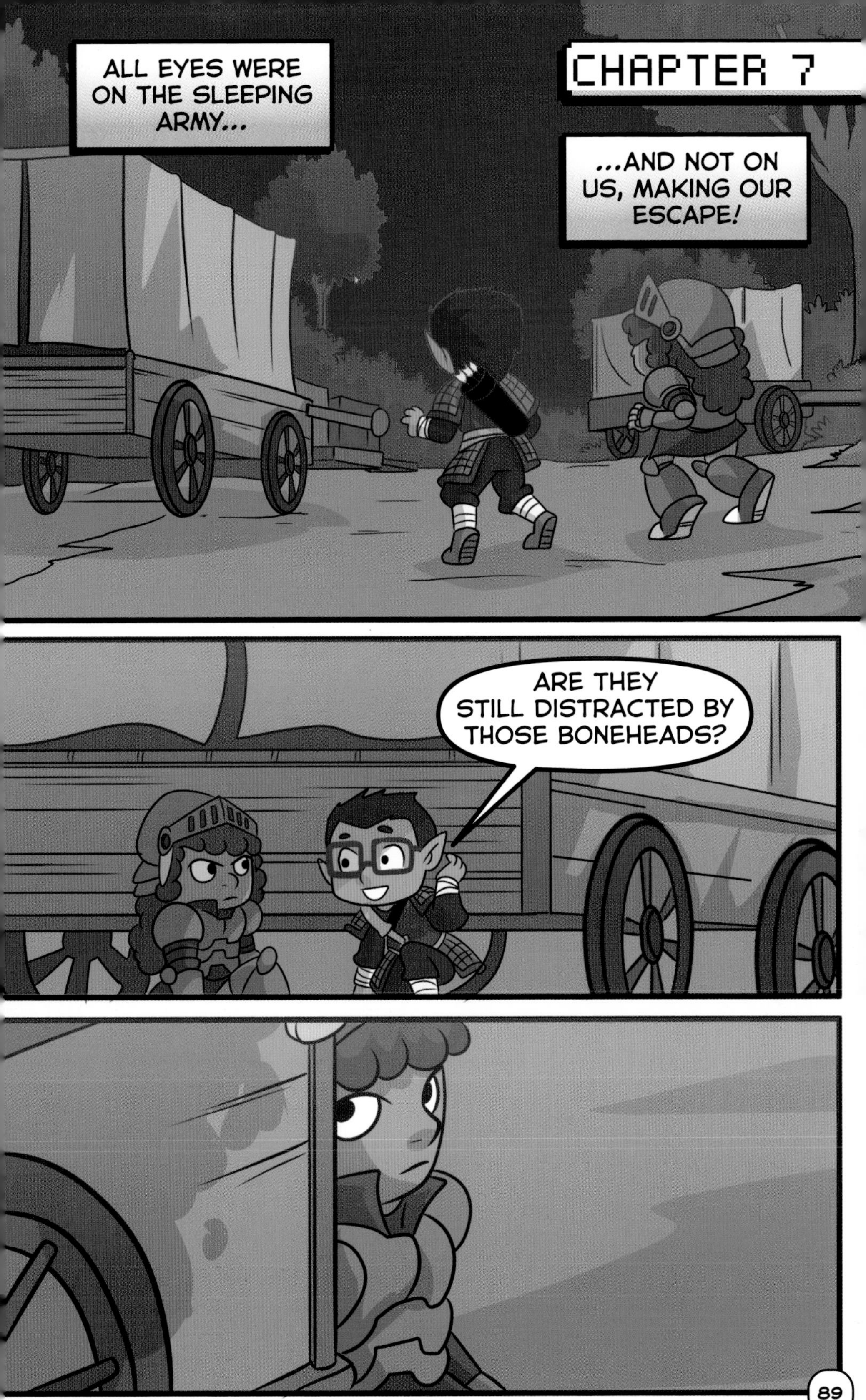
ALL EYES WERE ON THE SLEEPING ARMY...
CHAPTER 7
...AND NOT ON US, MAKING OUR ESCAPE!
ARE THEY STILL DISTRACTED BY THOSE BONEHEADS?

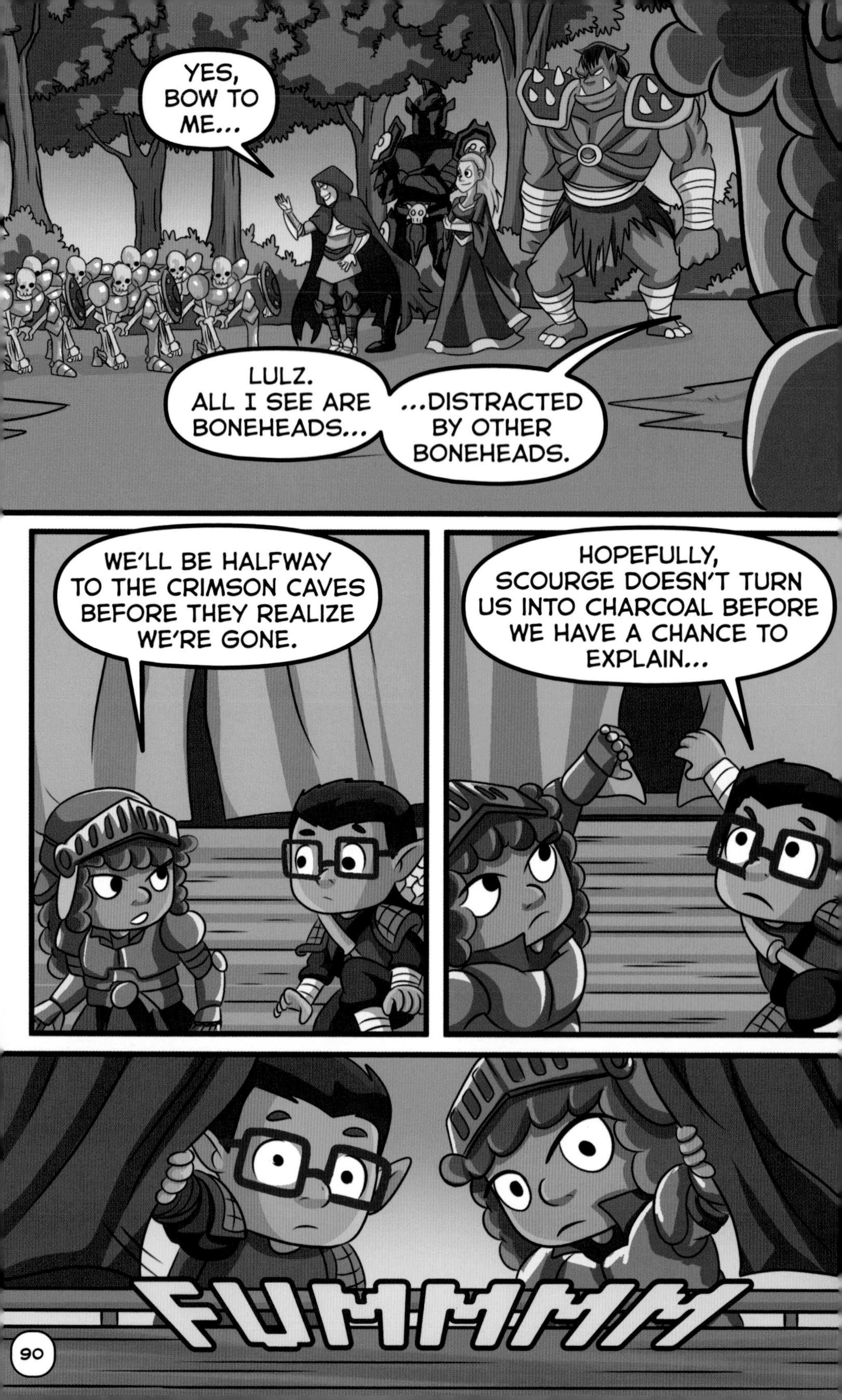
YES, BOW TO ME...
LULZ. ALL I SEE ARE BONEHEADS...
...DISTRACTED BY OTHER BONEHEADS.
WE'LL BE HALFWAY TO THE CRIMSON CAVES BEFORE THEY REALIZE WE'RE GONE.
HOPEFULLY, SCOURGE DOESN'T TURN US INTO CHARCOAL BEFORE WE HAVE A CHANCE TO EXPLAIN...
FUMMMM

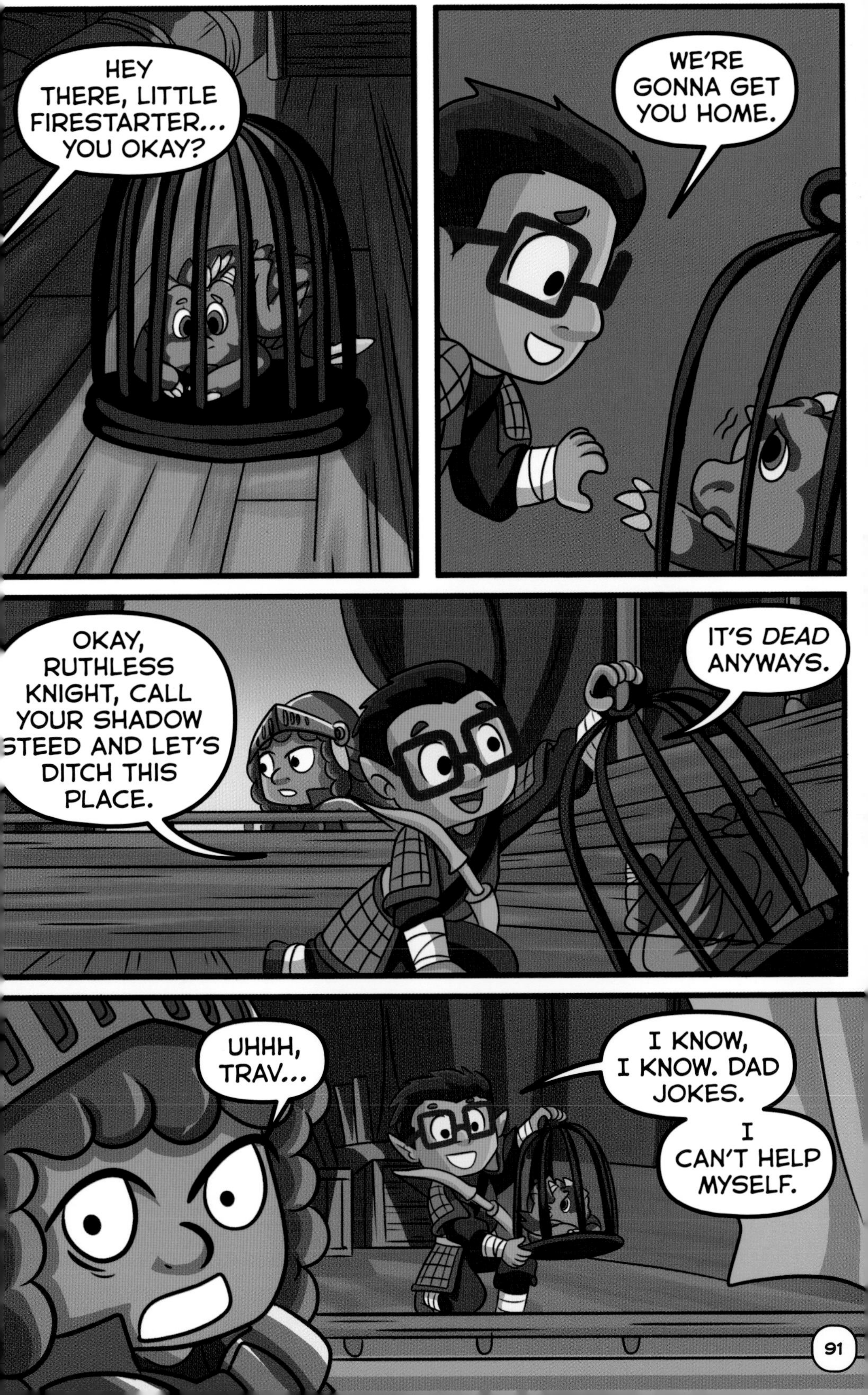

HEY THERE, LITTLE FIRESTARTER... YOU OKAY?
WE'RE GONNA GET YOU HOME.
OKAY, RUTHLESS KNIGHT, CALL YOUR SHADOW STEED AND LET'S DITCH THIS PLACE.
IT'S *DEAD* ANYWAYS.
UHHH, TRAV...
I KNOW, I KNOW. DAD JOKES.
I CAN'T HELP MYSELF.

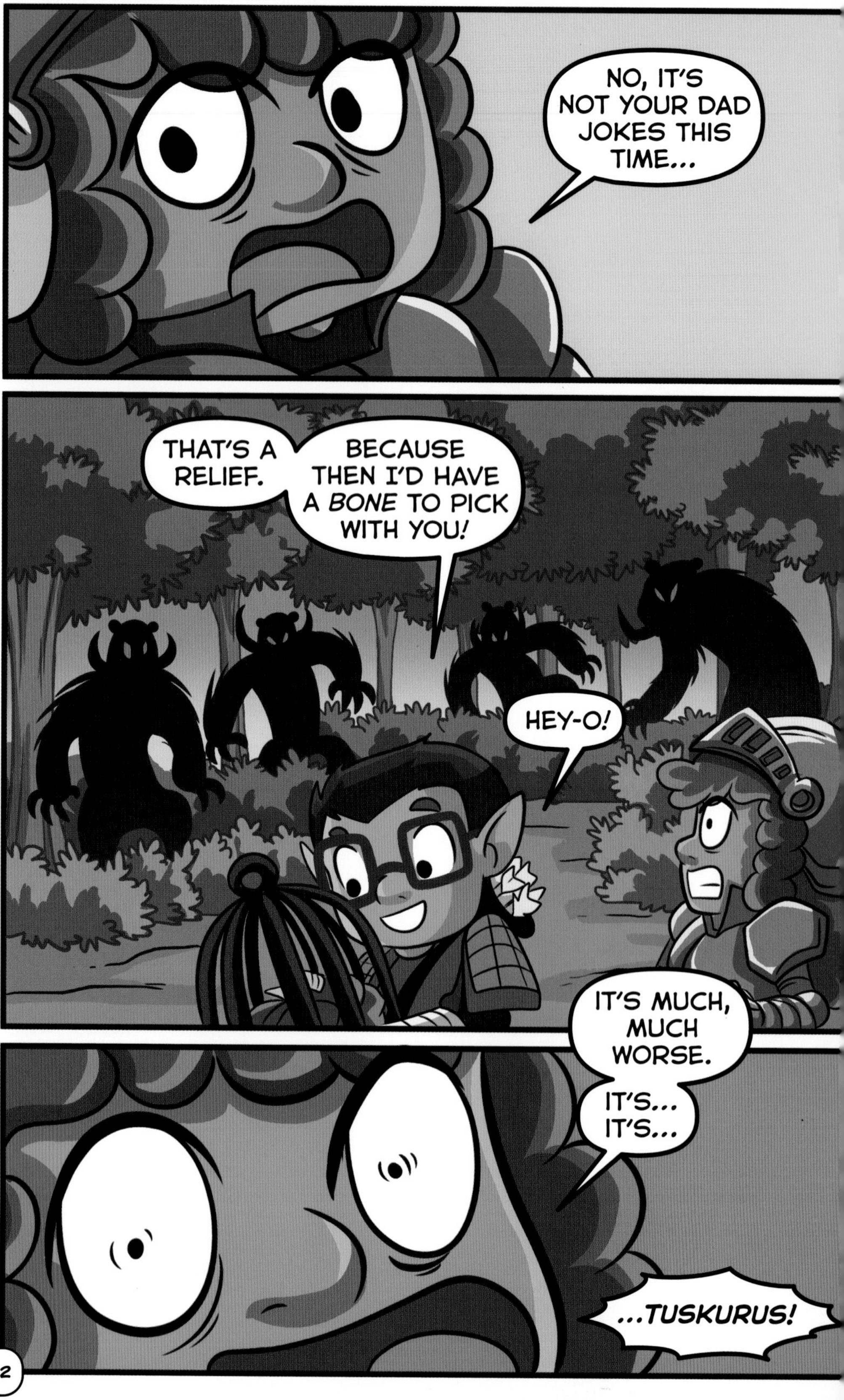

NO, IT'S NOT YOUR DAD JOKES THIS TIME...
THAT'S A RELIEF.
BECAUSE THEN I'D HAVE A *BONE* TO PICK WITH YOU!
HEY-O!
IT'S MUCH, MUCH WORSE.
IT'S... IT'S...
...TUSKURUS!

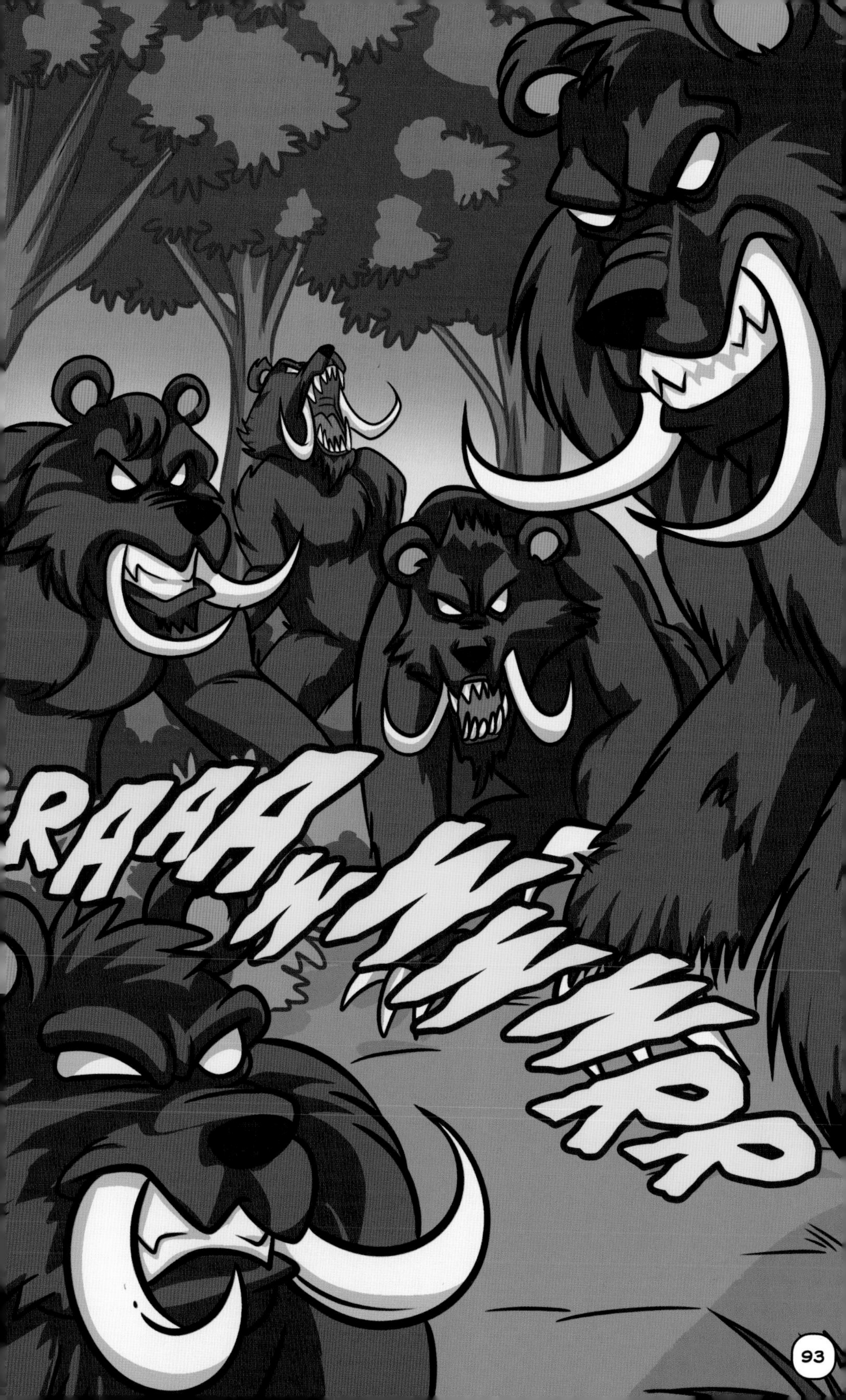
RAAAWWWWRR

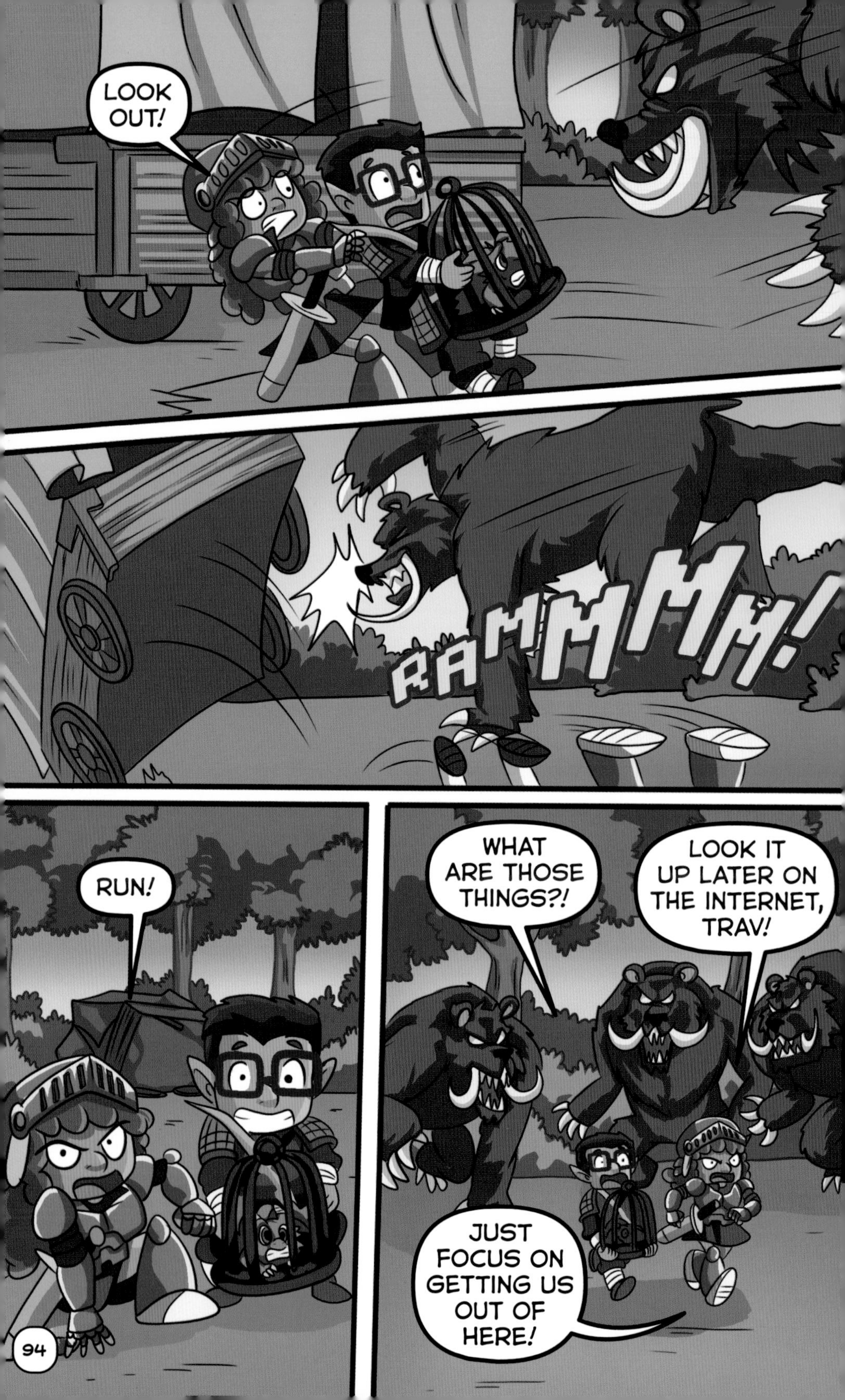
LOOK OUT!
RAMMMMM!
RUN!
WHAT ARE THOSE THINGS?!
LOOK IT UP LATER ON THE INTERNET, TRAV!
JUST FOCUS ON GETTING US OUT OF HERE!

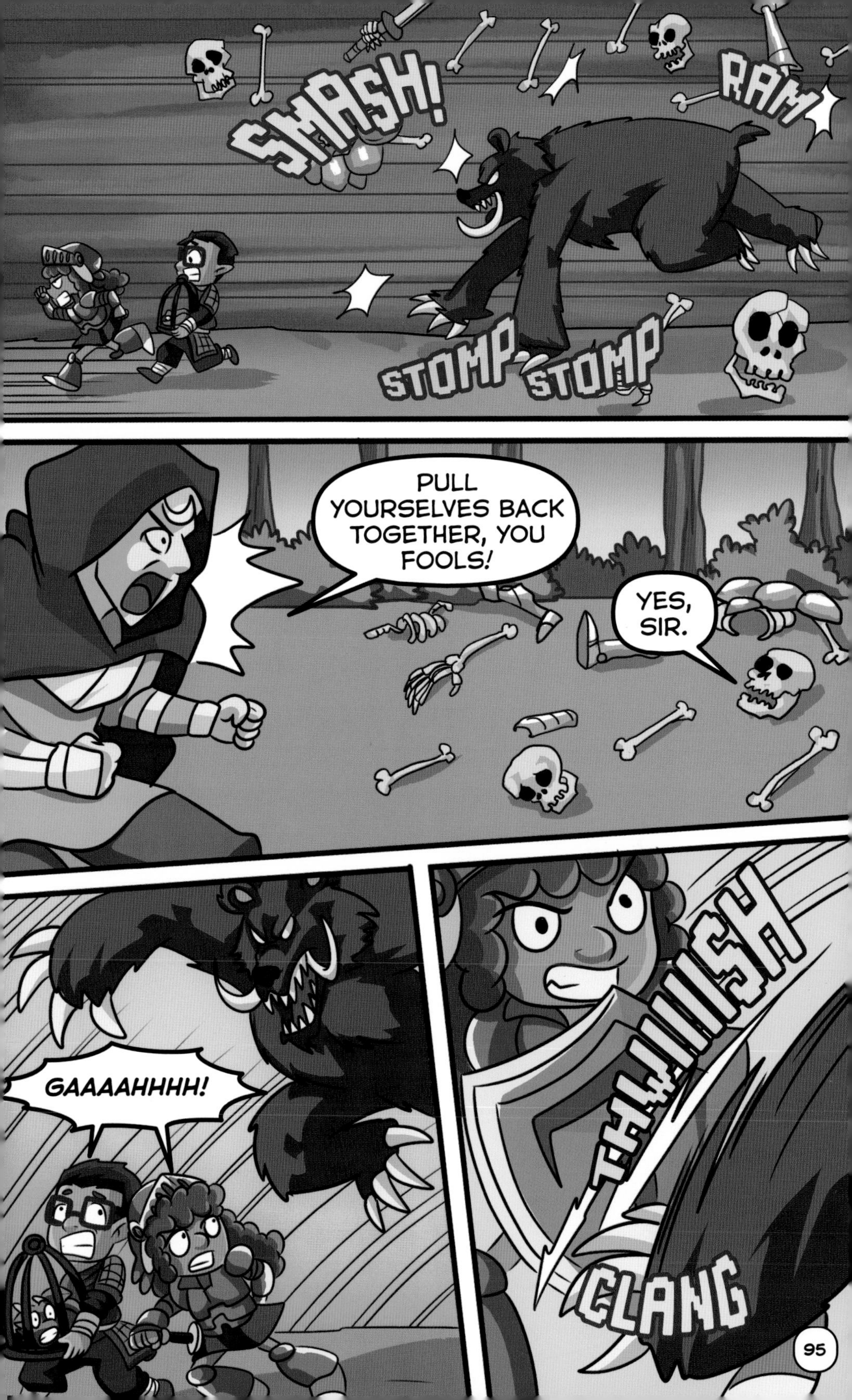
SMASH!
RAM
STOMP
STOMP
PULL YOURSELVES BACK TOGETHER, YOU FOOLS!
YES, SIR.
GAAAAHHHH!
THWHISH
CLANG

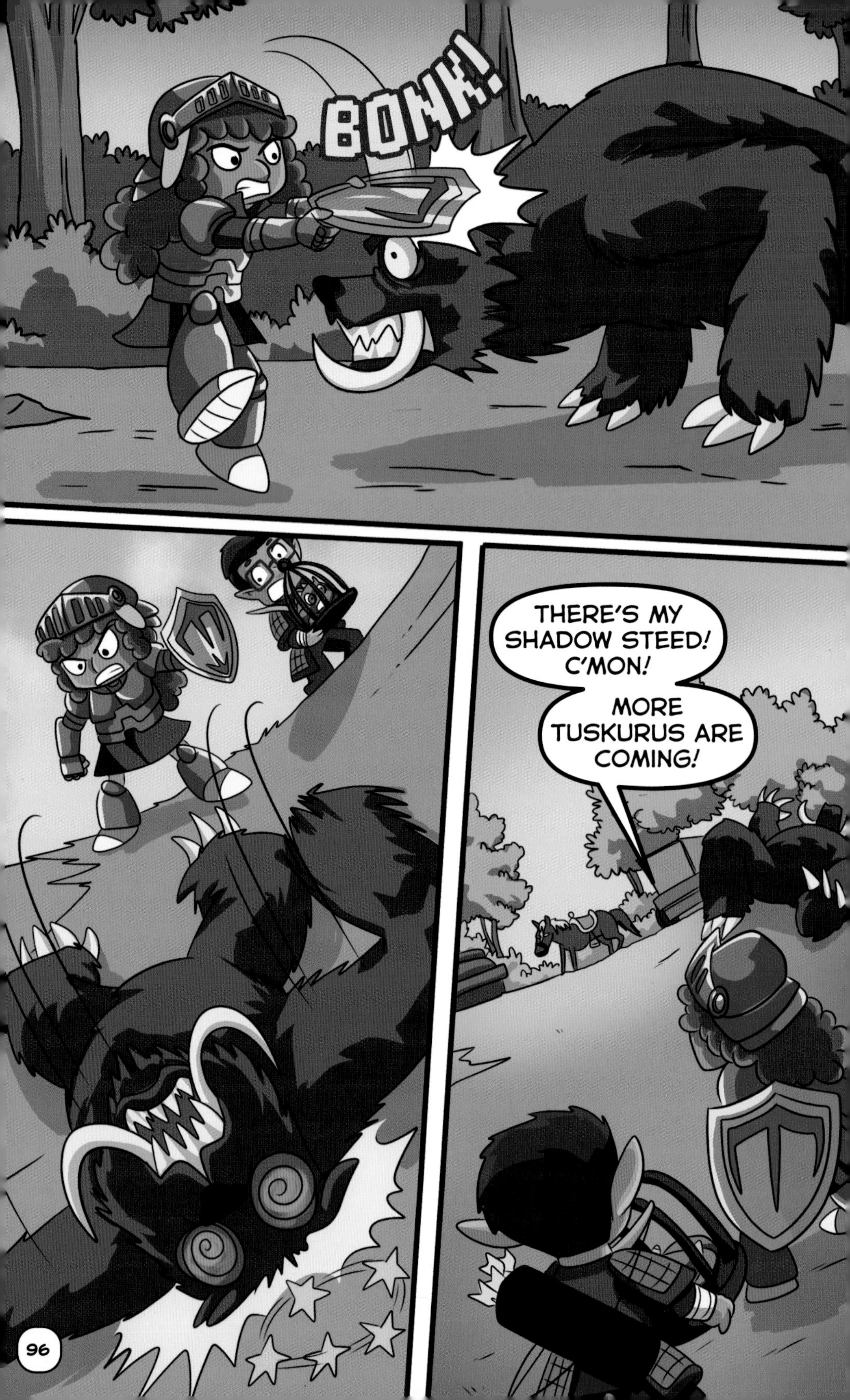
BONK!
THERE'S MY SHADOW STEED! C'MON!
MORE TUSKURUS ARE COMING!

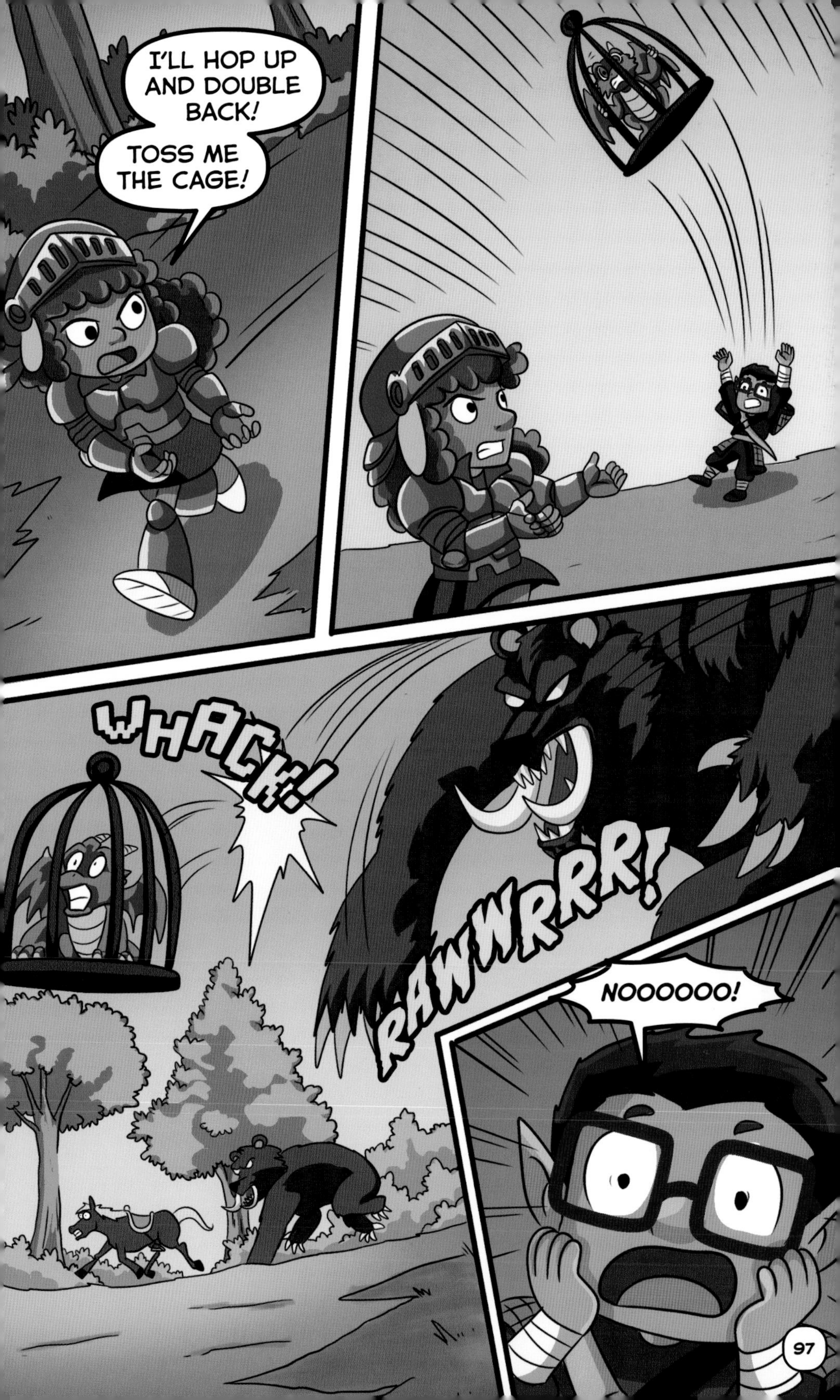
I'LL HOP UP AND DOUBLE BACK!
TOSS ME THE CAGE!
WHACK!!
RAWWRRR!
NOOOOOO!

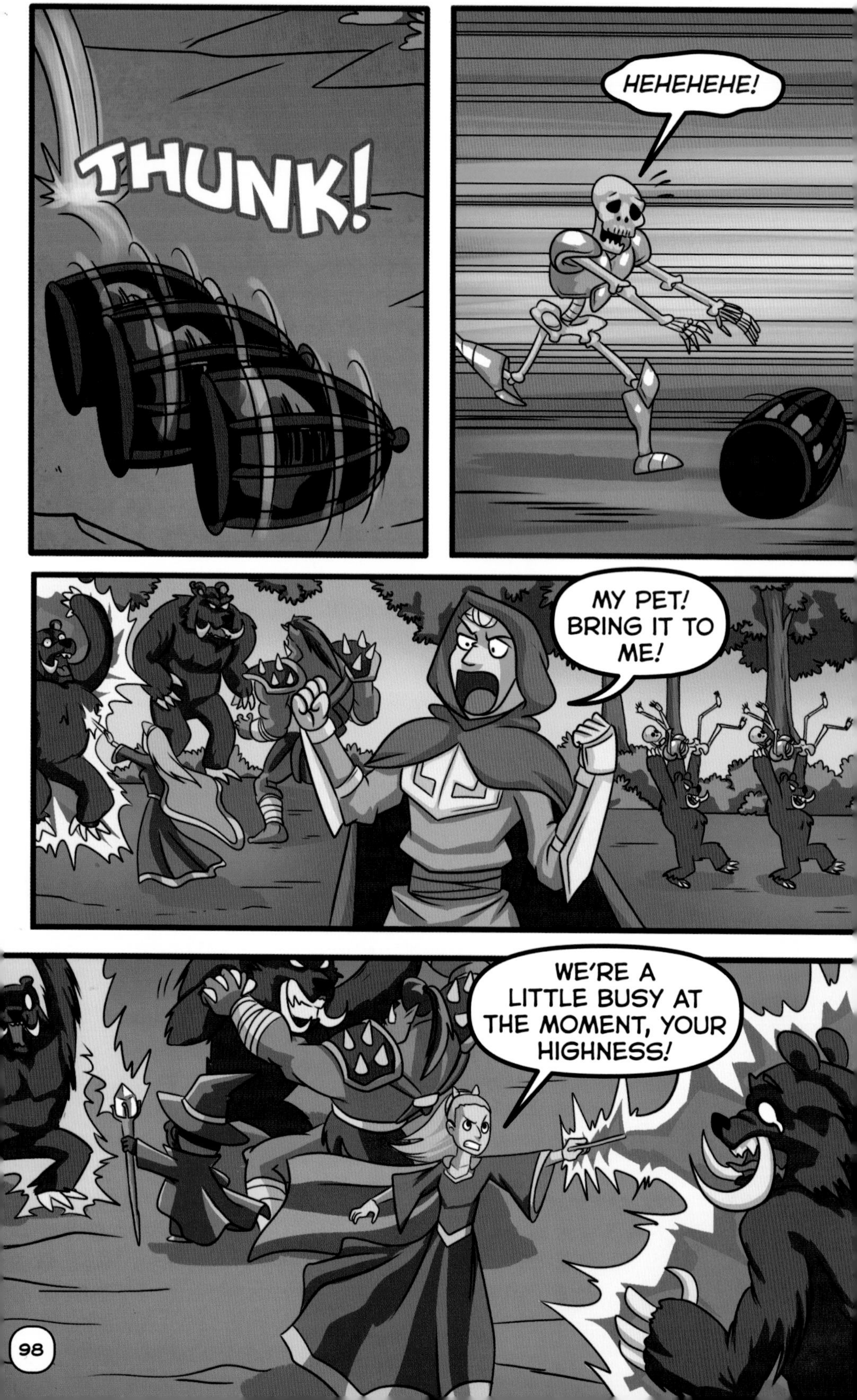
THUNK!
HEHEHEHE!
MY PET! BRING IT TO ME!
WE'RE A LITTLE BUSY AT THE MOMENT, YOUR HIGHNESS!

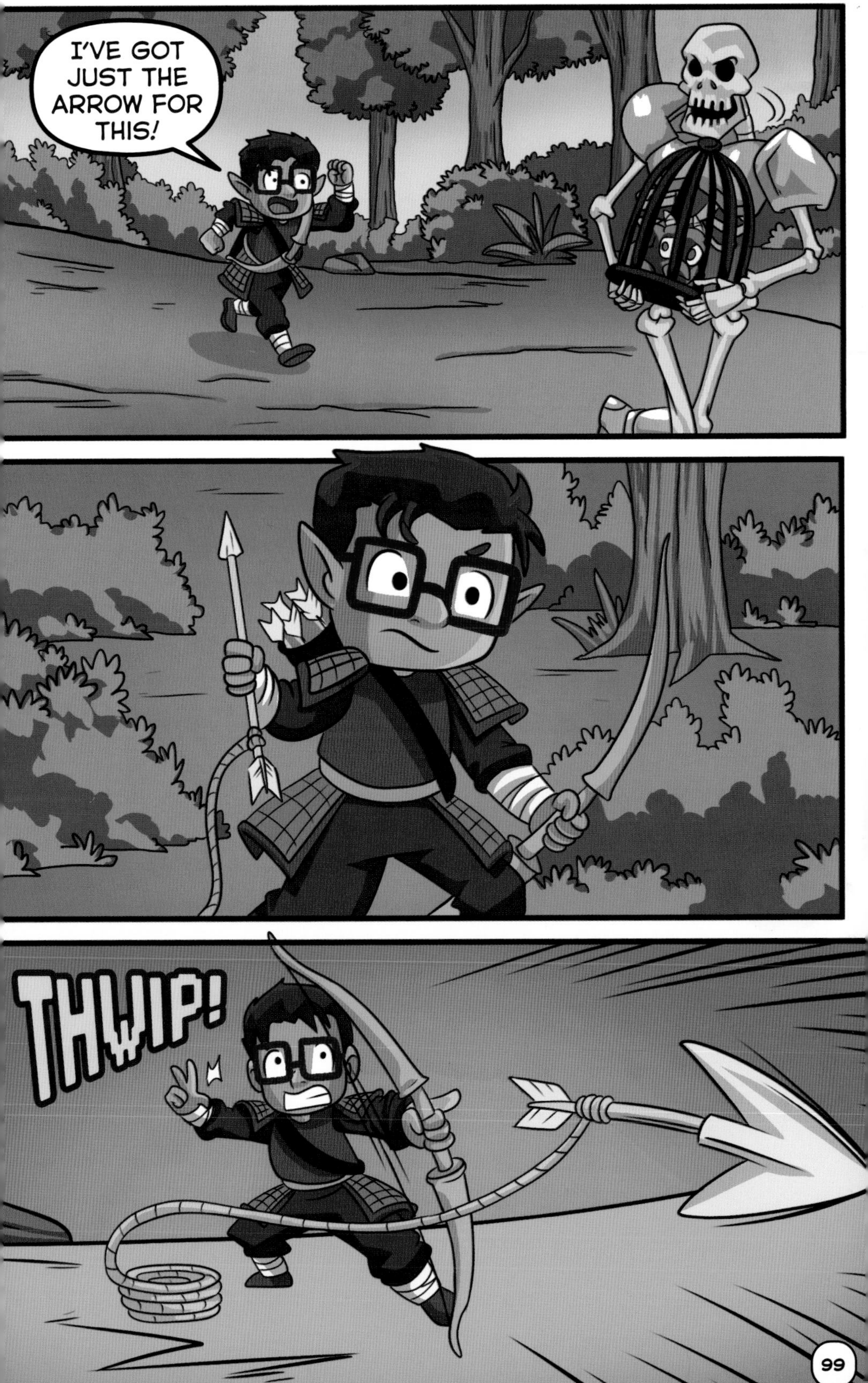
I'VE GOT JUST THE ARROW FOR THIS!
THWIP!

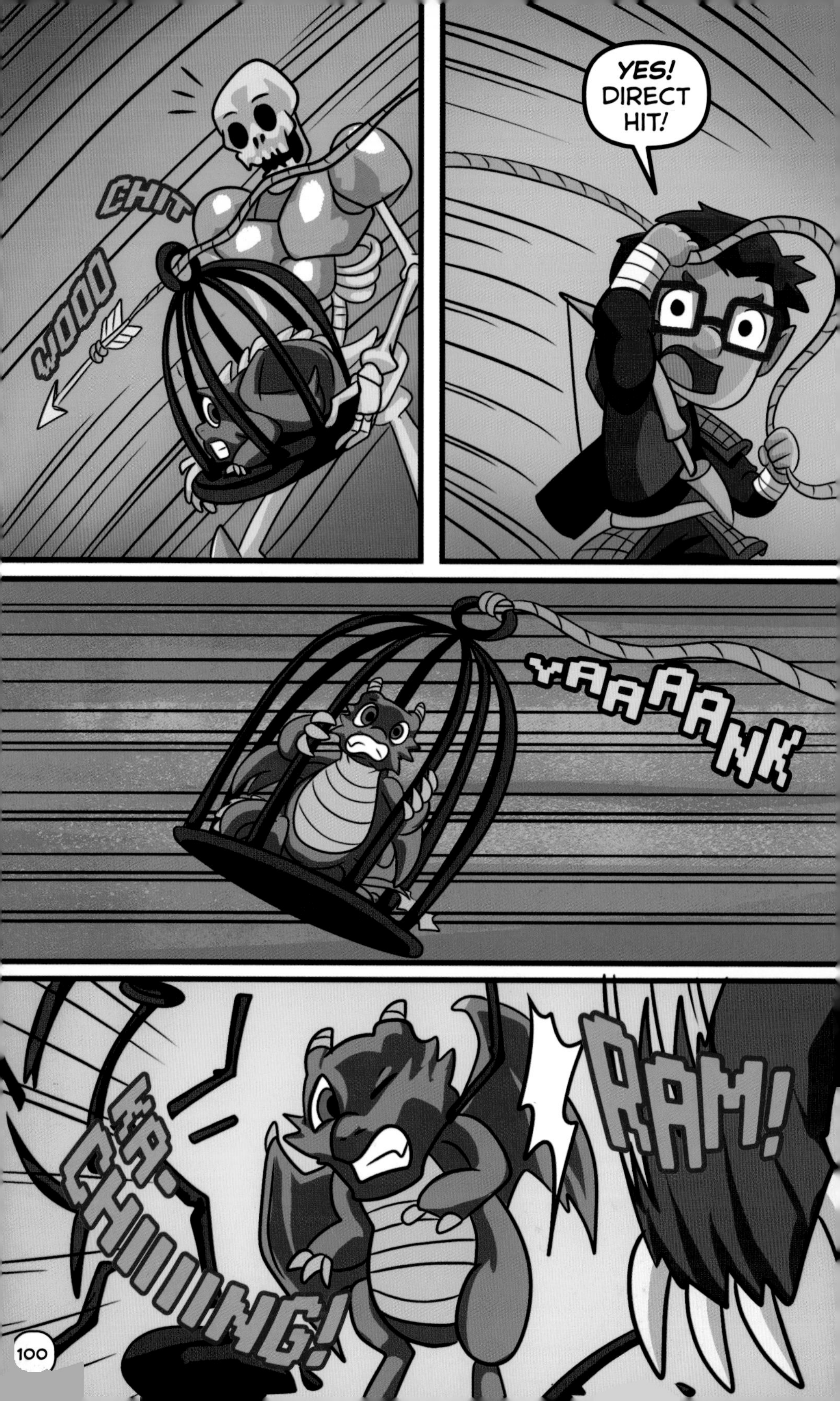
CHIT
WOOO
YES! DIRECT HIT!
YAAAAANK
KA-CHIIIING!
RAM!

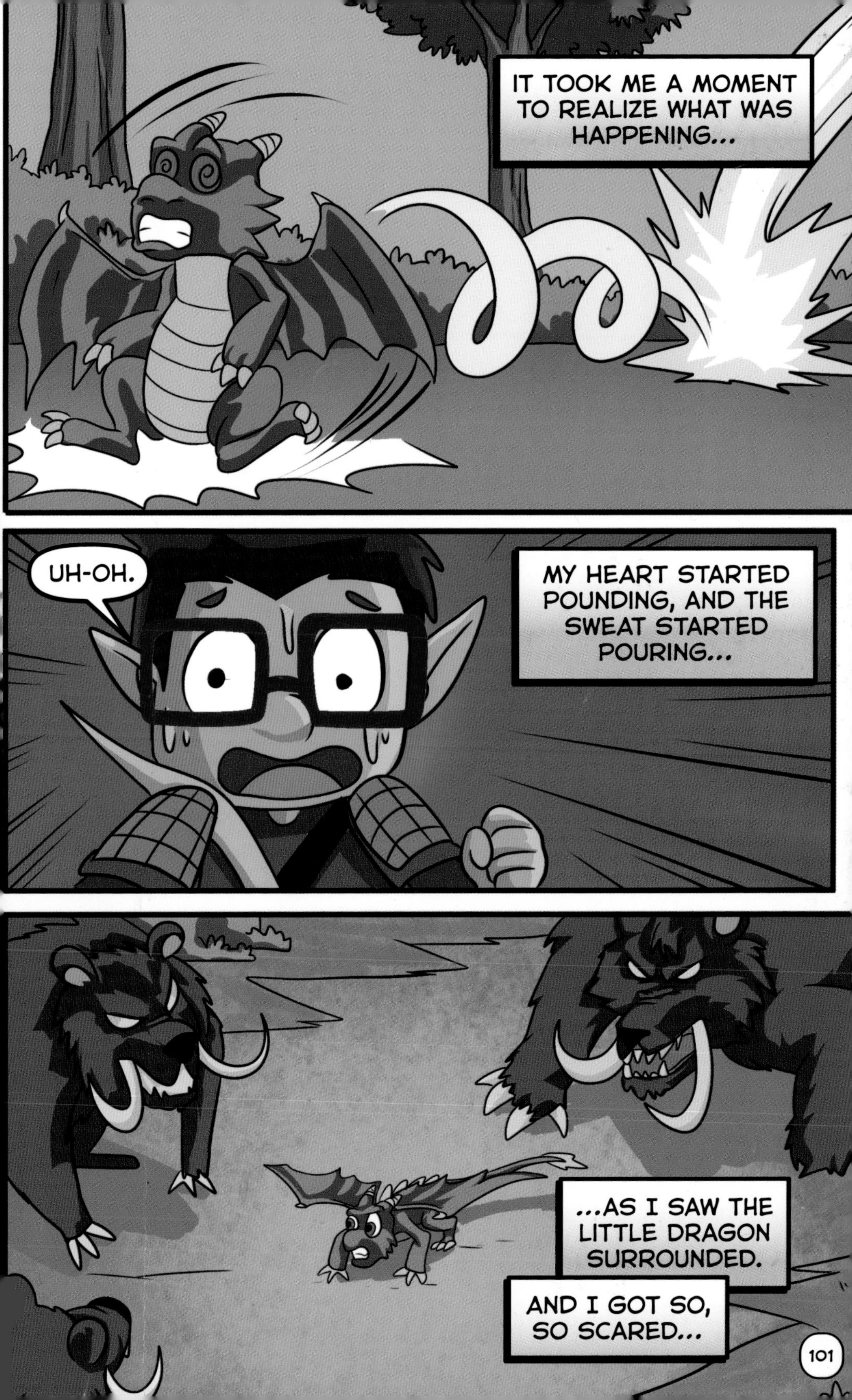

IT TOOK ME A MOMENT TO REALIZE WHAT WAS HAPPENING...
UH-OH.
MY HEART STARTED POUNDING, AND THE SWEAT STARTED POURING...
...AS I SAW THE LITTLE DRAGON SURROUNDED.
AND I GOT SO, SO SCARED...

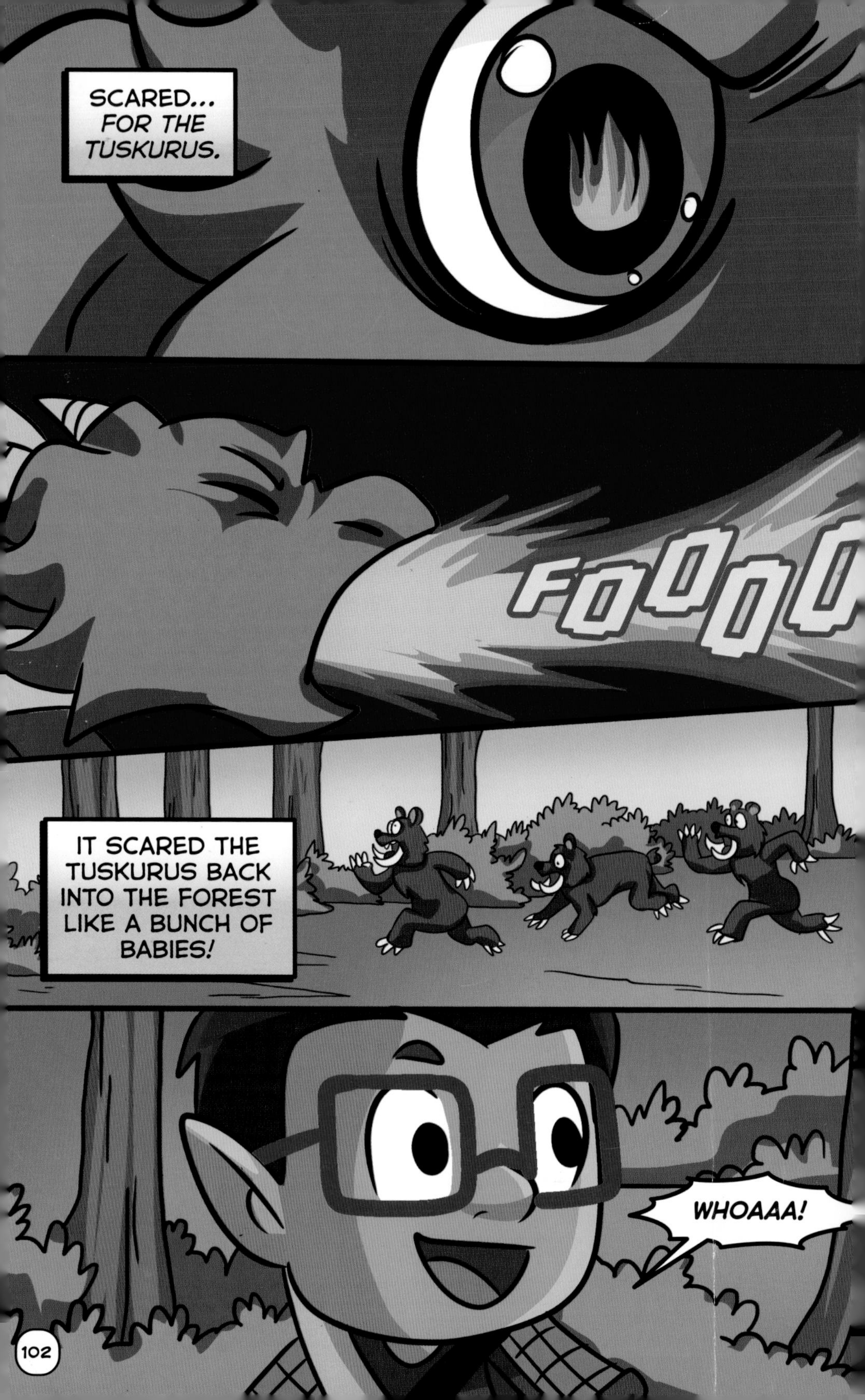
SCARED... FOR THE TUSKURUS.
FOOOO
IT SCARED THE TUSKURUS BACK INTO THE FOREST LIKE A BUNCH OF BABIES!
WHOAAA!

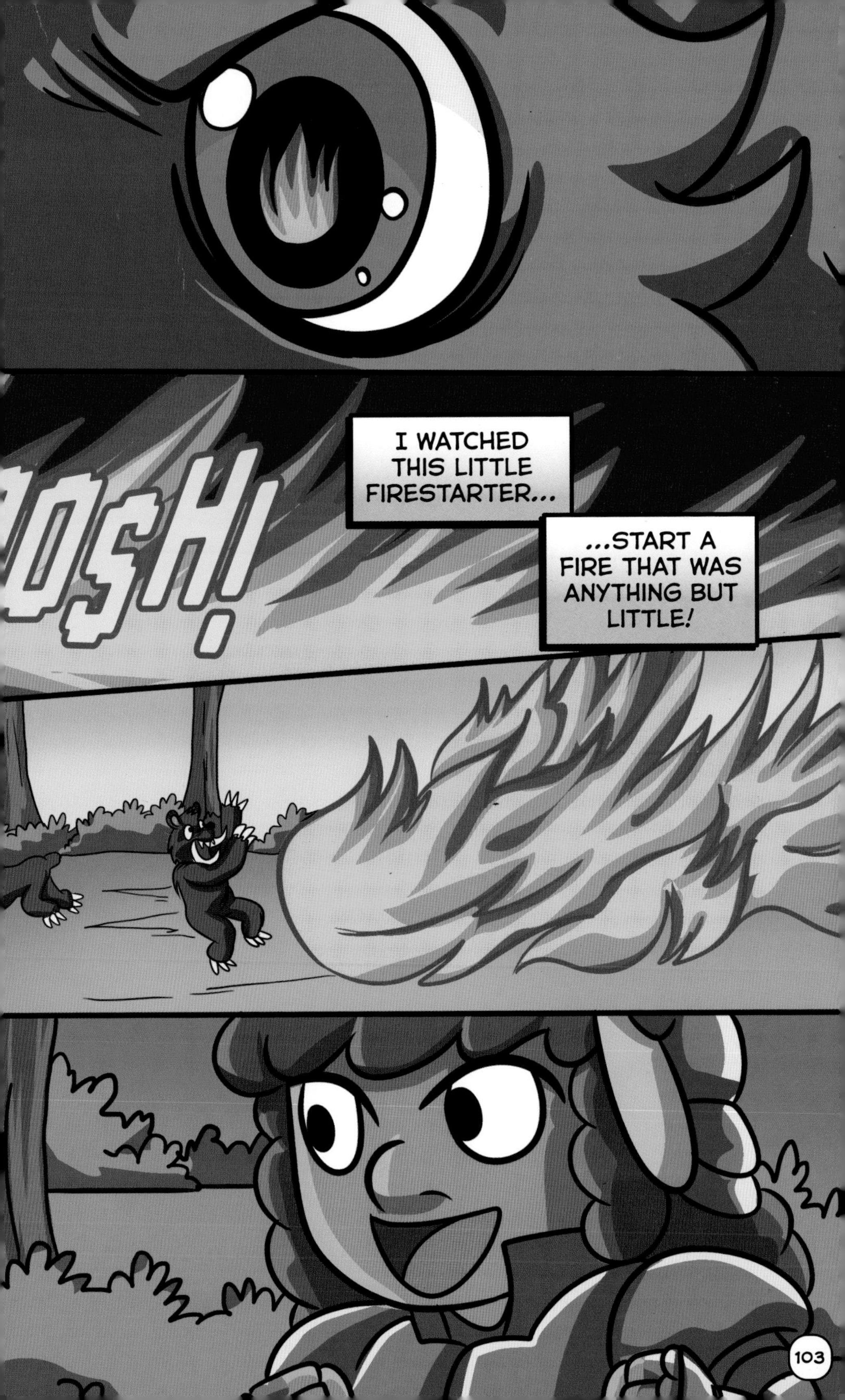
OSH!
I WATCHED THIS LITTLE FIRESTARTER...
...START A FIRE THAT WAS ANYTHING BUT LITTLE!

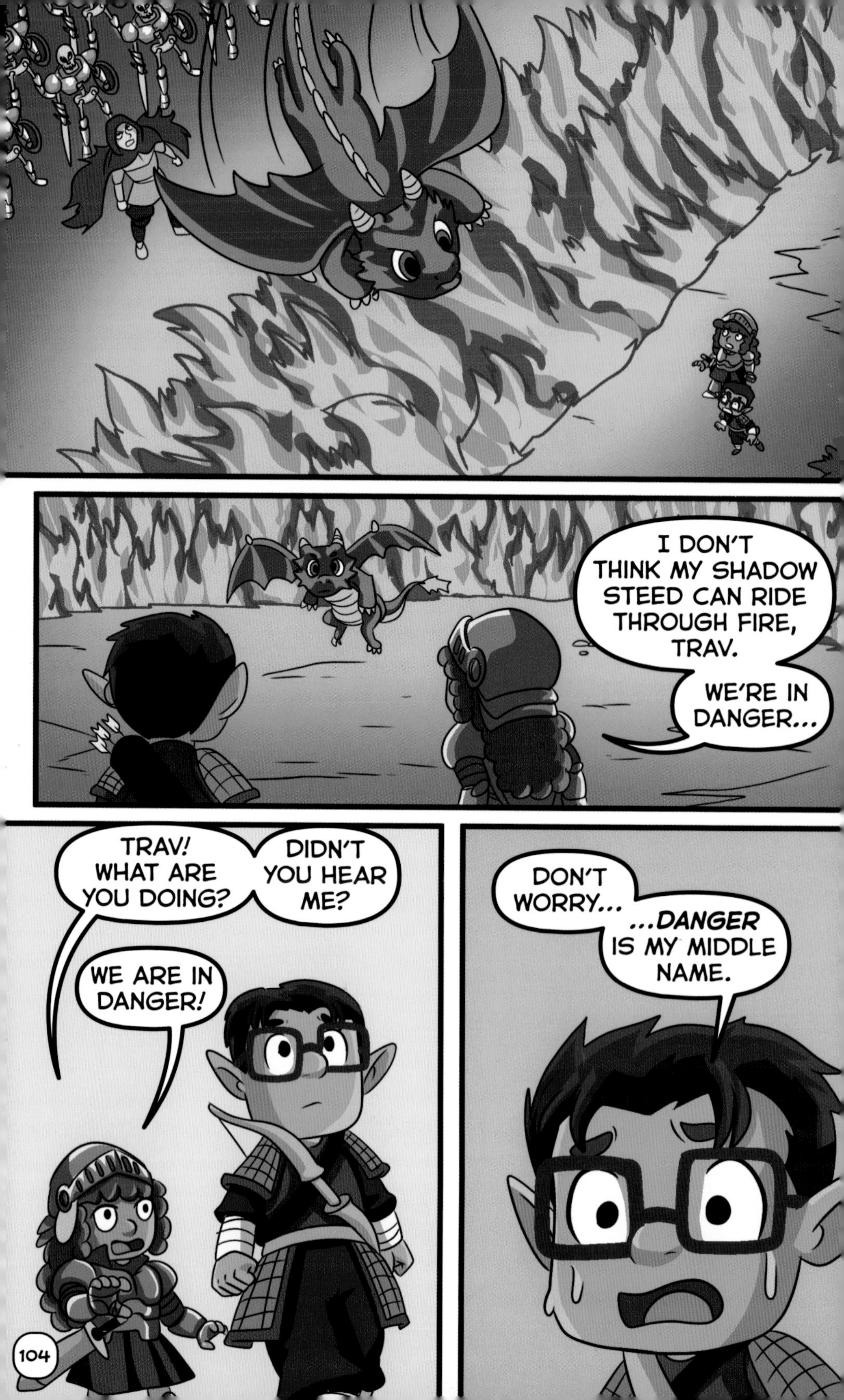
I DON'T THINK MY SHADOW STEED CAN RIDE THROUGH FIRE, TRAV.
WE'RE IN DANGER...
TRAV! WHAT ARE YOU DOING?
DIDN'T YOU HEAR ME?
WE ARE IN DANGER!
DON'T WORRY...
...*DANGER* IS MY MIDDLE NAME.

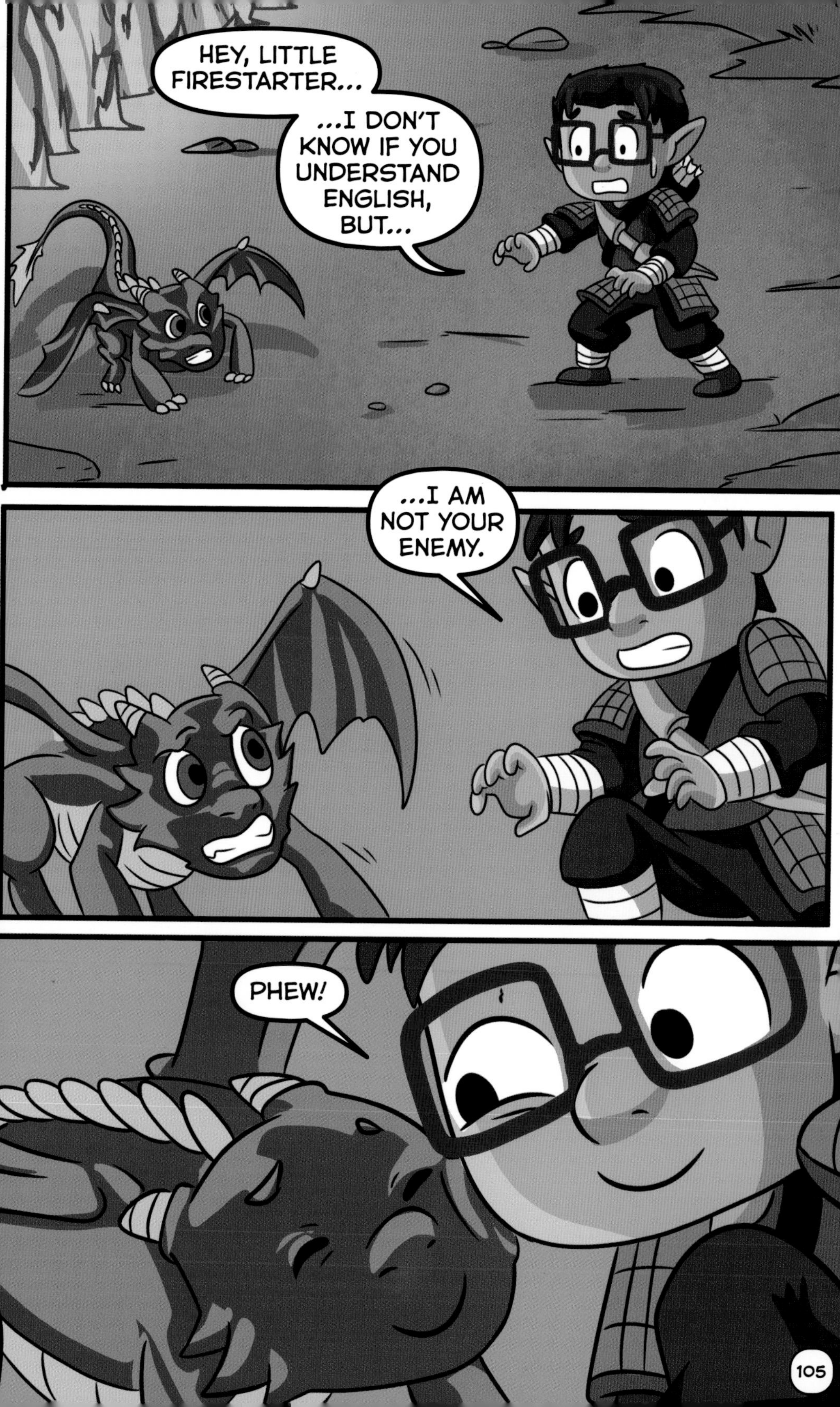
HEY, LITTLE FIRESTARTER...
...I DON'T KNOW IF YOU UNDERSTAND ENGLISH, BUT...
...I AM NOT YOUR ENEMY.
PHEW!

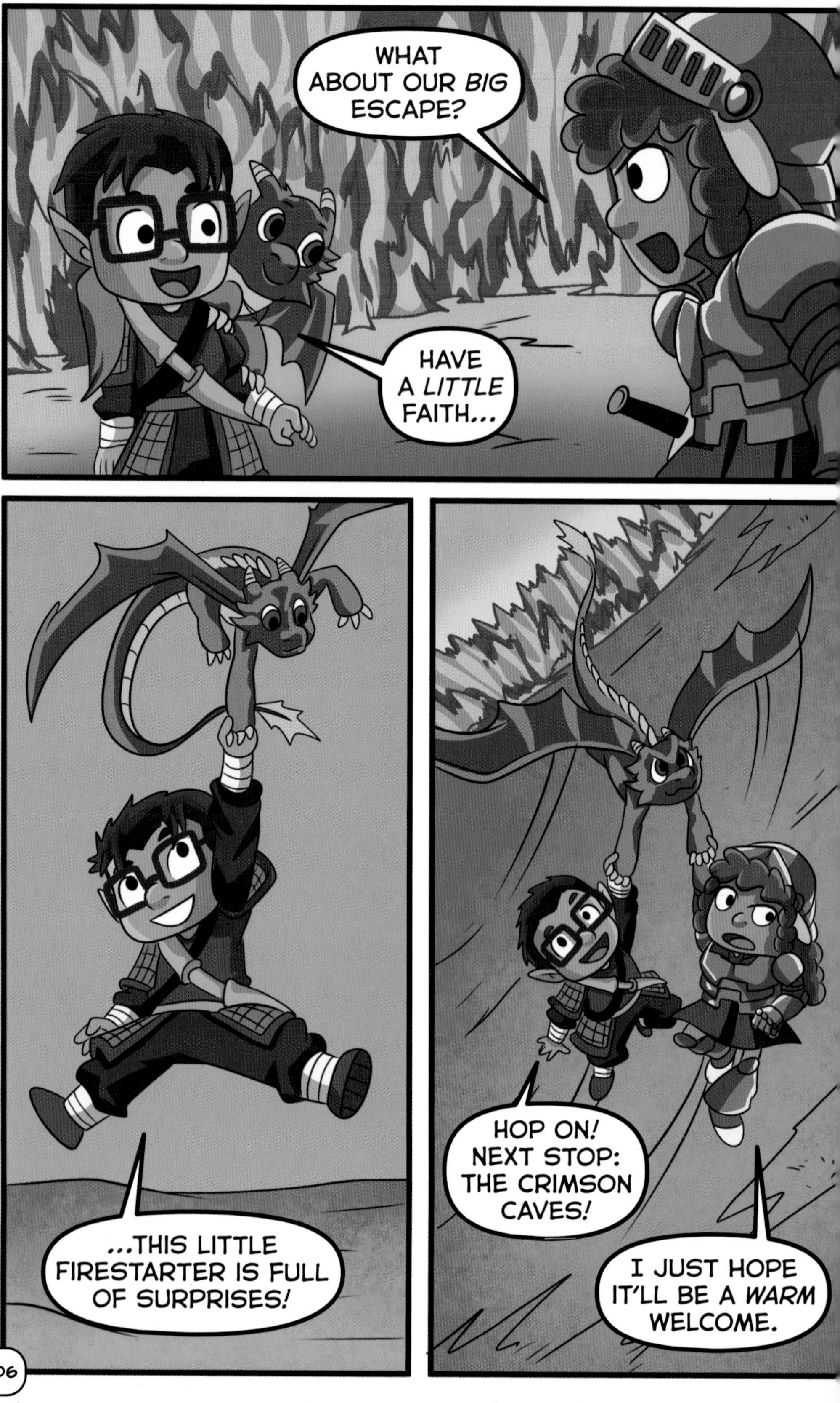
WHAT ABOUT OUR *BIG* ESCAPE?
HAVE A *LITTLE* FAITH...
...THIS LITTLE FIRESTARTER IS FULL OF SURPRISES!
HOP ON! NEXT STOP: THE CRIMSON CAVES!
I JUST HOPE IT'LL BE A *WARM* WELCOME.

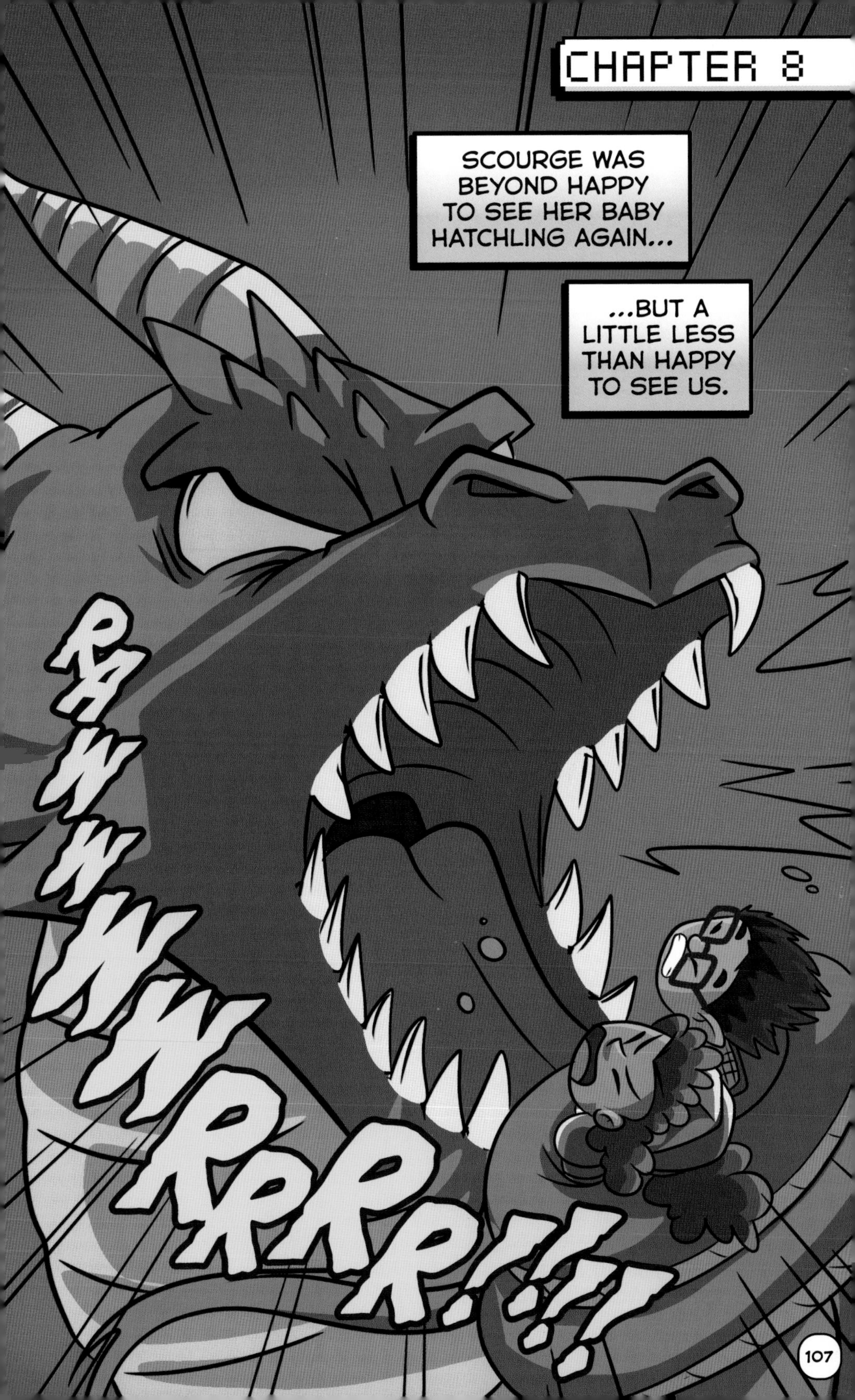
CHAPTER 8
SCOURGE WAS BEYOND HAPPY TO SEE HER BABY HATCHLING AGAIN...
...BUT A LITTLE LESS THAN HAPPY TO SEE US.
RAWWWWRRRR!!!!

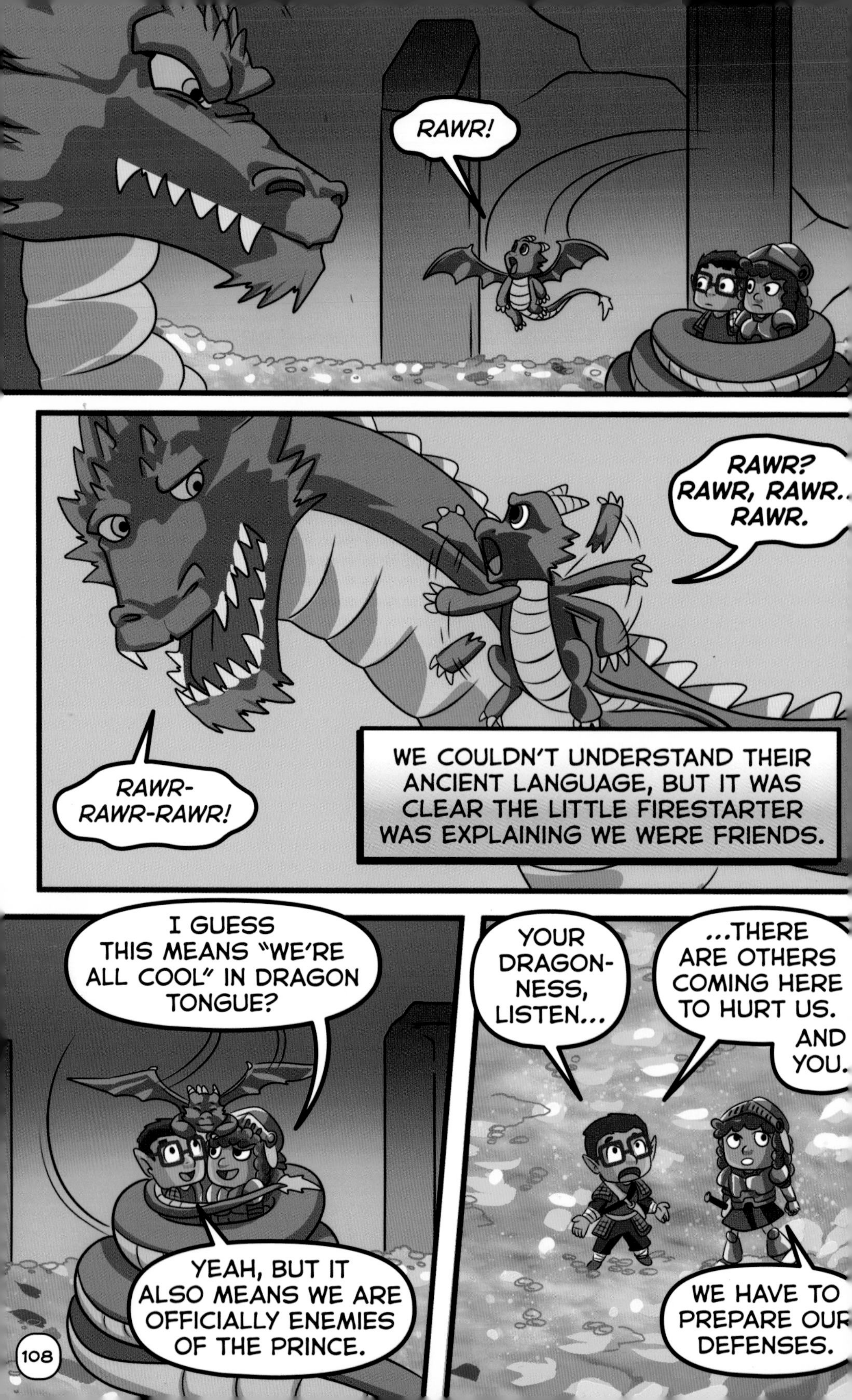
RAWR!
RAWR? RAWR, RAWR... RAWR.
RAWR-RAWR-RAWR!
WE COULDN'T UNDERSTAND THEIR ANCIENT LANGUAGE, BUT IT WAS CLEAR THE LITTLE FIRESTARTER WAS EXPLAINING WE WERE FRIENDS.
I GUESS THIS MEANS "WE'RE ALL COOL" IN DRAGON TONGUE?
YEAH, BUT IT ALSO MEANS WE ARE OFFICIALLY ENEMIES OF THE PRINCE.
YOUR DRAGON-NESS, LISTEN...
...THERE ARE OTHERS COMING HERE TO HURT US. AND YOU.
WE HAVE TO PREPARE OUR DEFENSES.

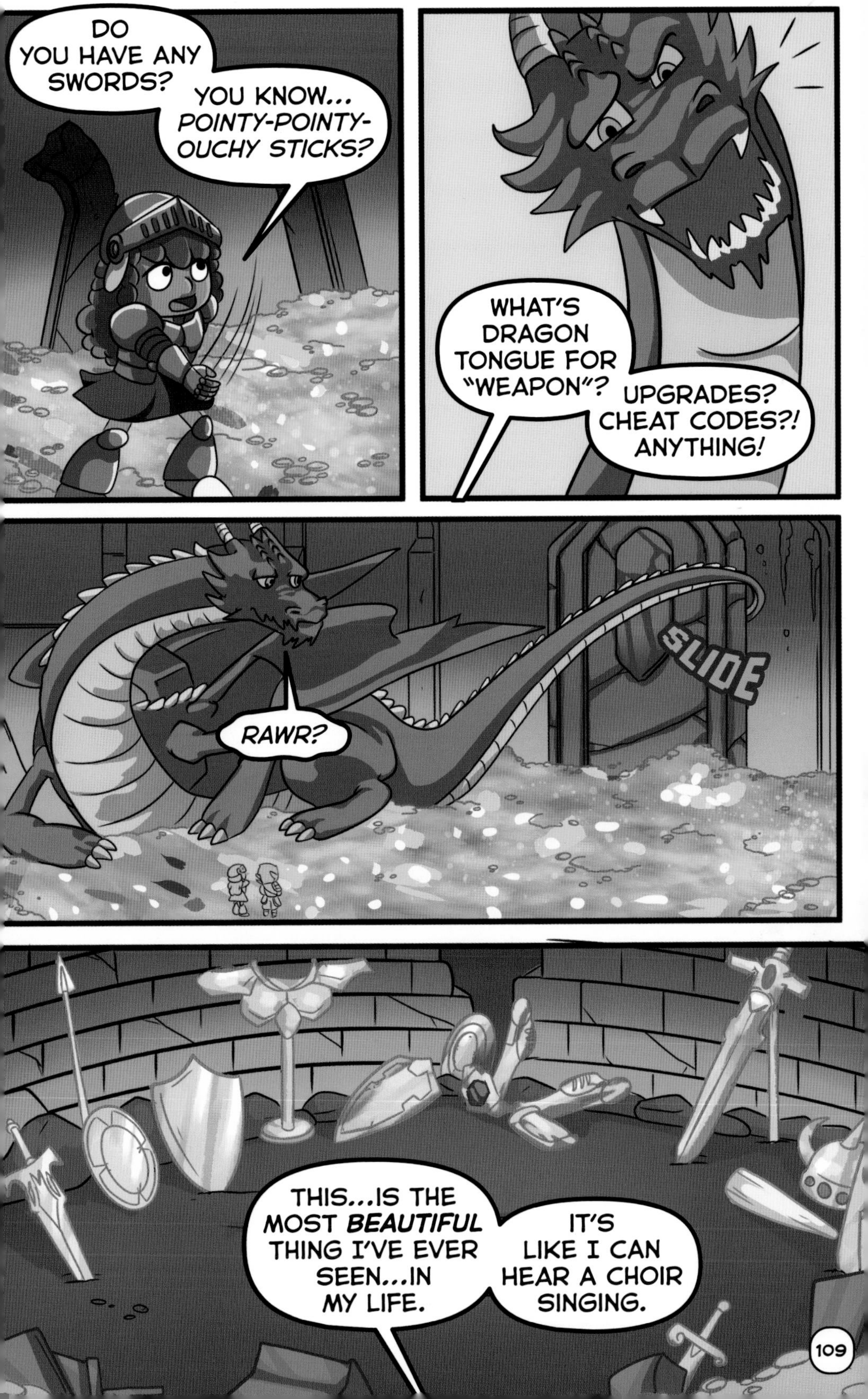
DO YOU HAVE ANY SWORDS?
YOU KNOW... POINTY-POINTY-OUCHY STICKS?
WHAT'S DRAGON TONGUE FOR "WEAPON"?
UPGRADES? CHEAT CODES?! ANYTHING!
SLIDE
RAWR?
THIS...IS THE MOST *BEAUTIFUL* THING I'VE EVER SEEN...IN MY LIFE.
IT'S LIKE I CAN HEAR A CHOIR SINGING.

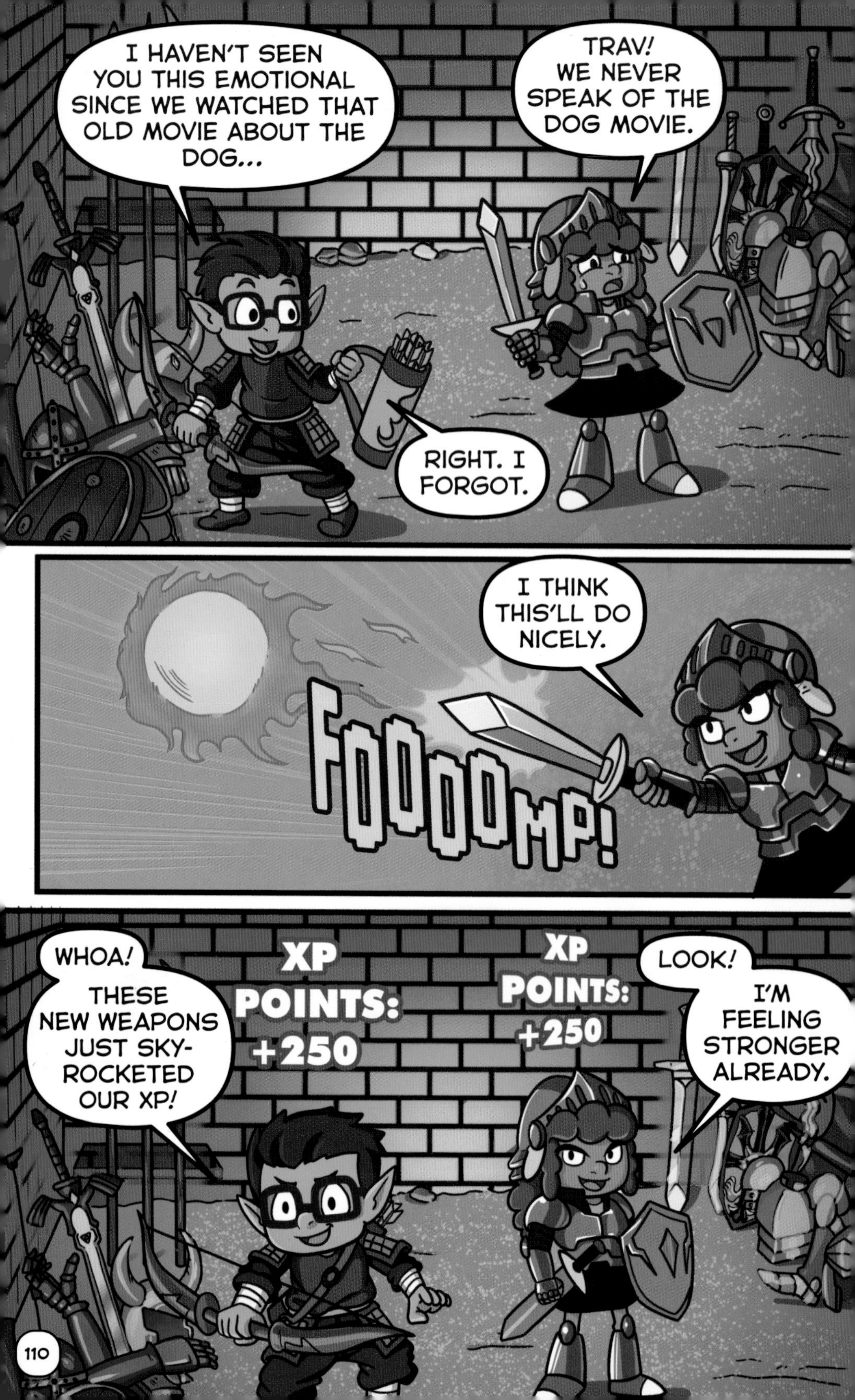
I HAVEN'T SEEN YOU THIS EMOTIONAL SINCE WE WATCHED THAT OLD MOVIE ABOUT THE DOG...
TRAV! WE NEVER SPEAK OF THE DOG MOVIE.
RIGHT. I FORGOT.
I THINK THIS'LL DO NICELY.
FOOOOMP!
WHOA! THESE NEW WEAPONS JUST SKY-ROCKETED OUR XP!
XP POINTS: +250
XP POINTS: +250
LOOK! I'M FEELING STRONGER ALREADY.

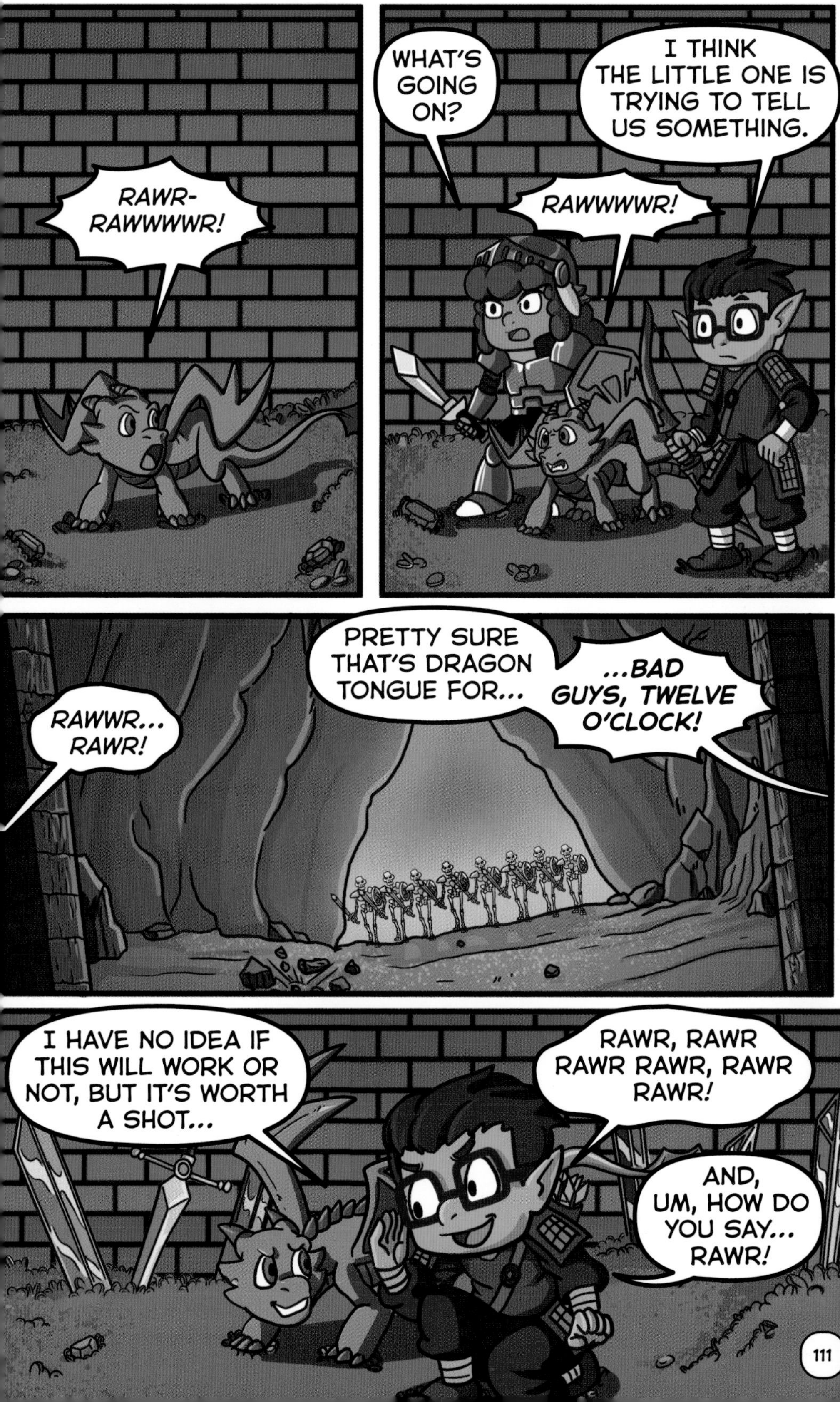
RAWR-
RAWWWWR!
WHAT'S GOING ON?
I THINK THE LITTLE ONE IS TRYING TO TELL US SOMETHING.
RAWWWWR!
RAWWR... RAWR!
PRETTY SURE THAT'S DRAGON TONGUE FOR...
...BAD GUYS, TWELVE O'CLOCK!
I HAVE NO IDEA IF THIS WILL WORK OR NOT, BUT IT'S WORTH A SHOT...
RAWR, RAWR RAWR RAWR, RAWR RAWR!
AND, UM, HOW DO YOU SAY... RAWR!

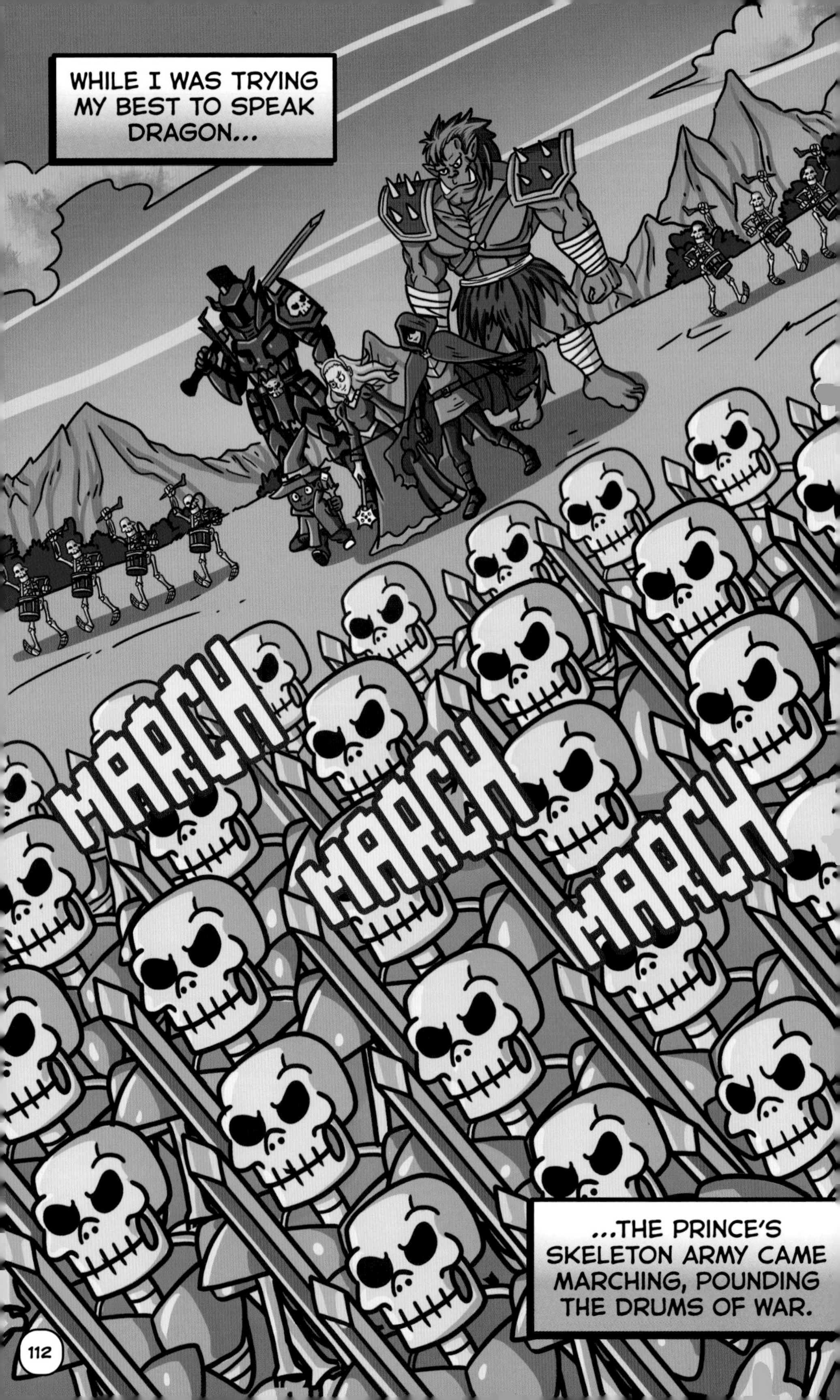
WHILE I WAS TRYING MY BEST TO SPEAK DRAGON...
MARCH
MARCH
MARCH
...THE PRINCE'S SKELETON ARMY CAME MARCHING, POUNDING THE DRUMS OF WAR.

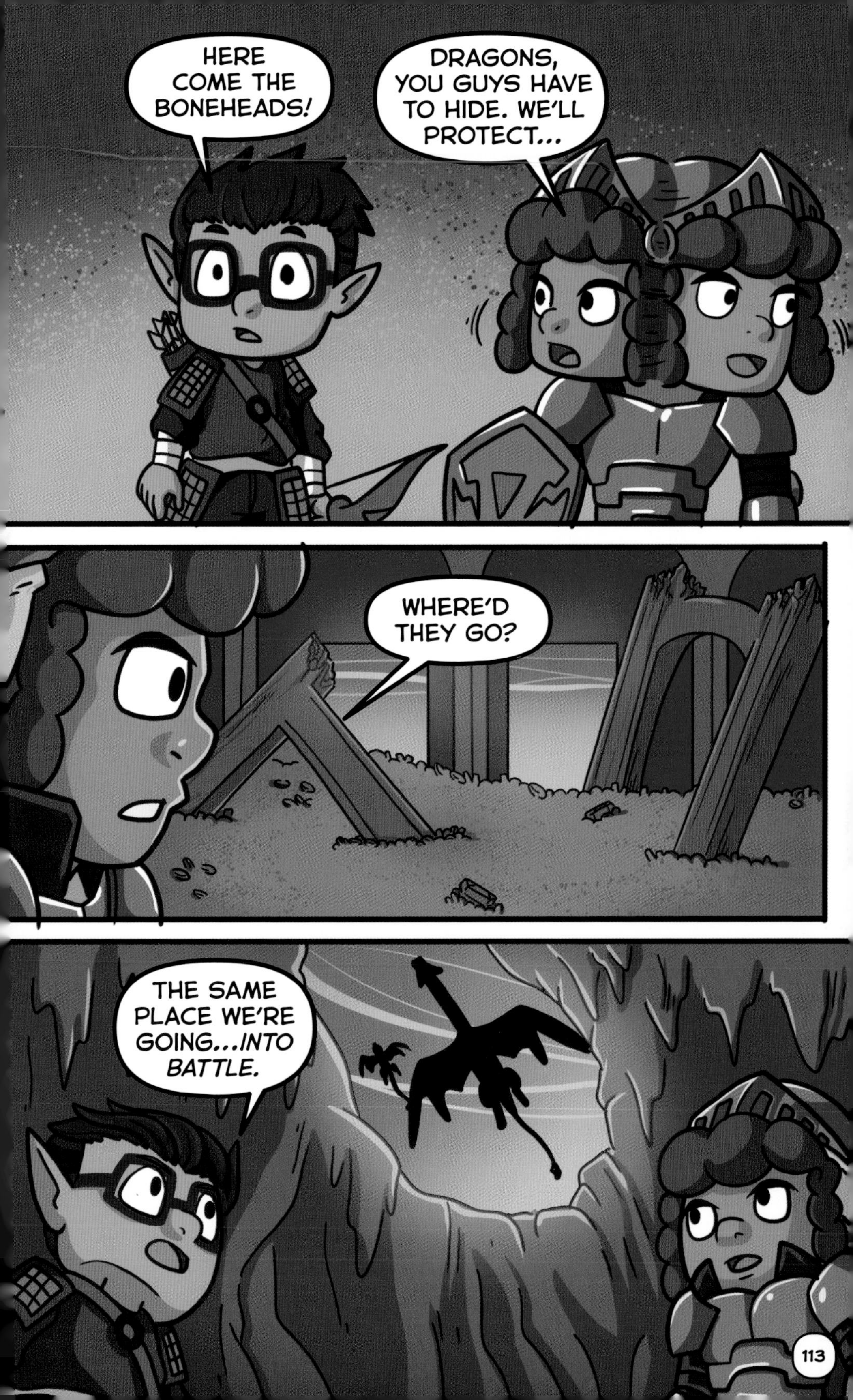
HERE COME THE BONEHEADS!
DRAGONS, YOU GUYS HAVE TO HIDE. WE'LL PROTECT...
WHERE'D THEY GO?
THE SAME PLACE WE'RE GOING...*INTO BATTLE.*

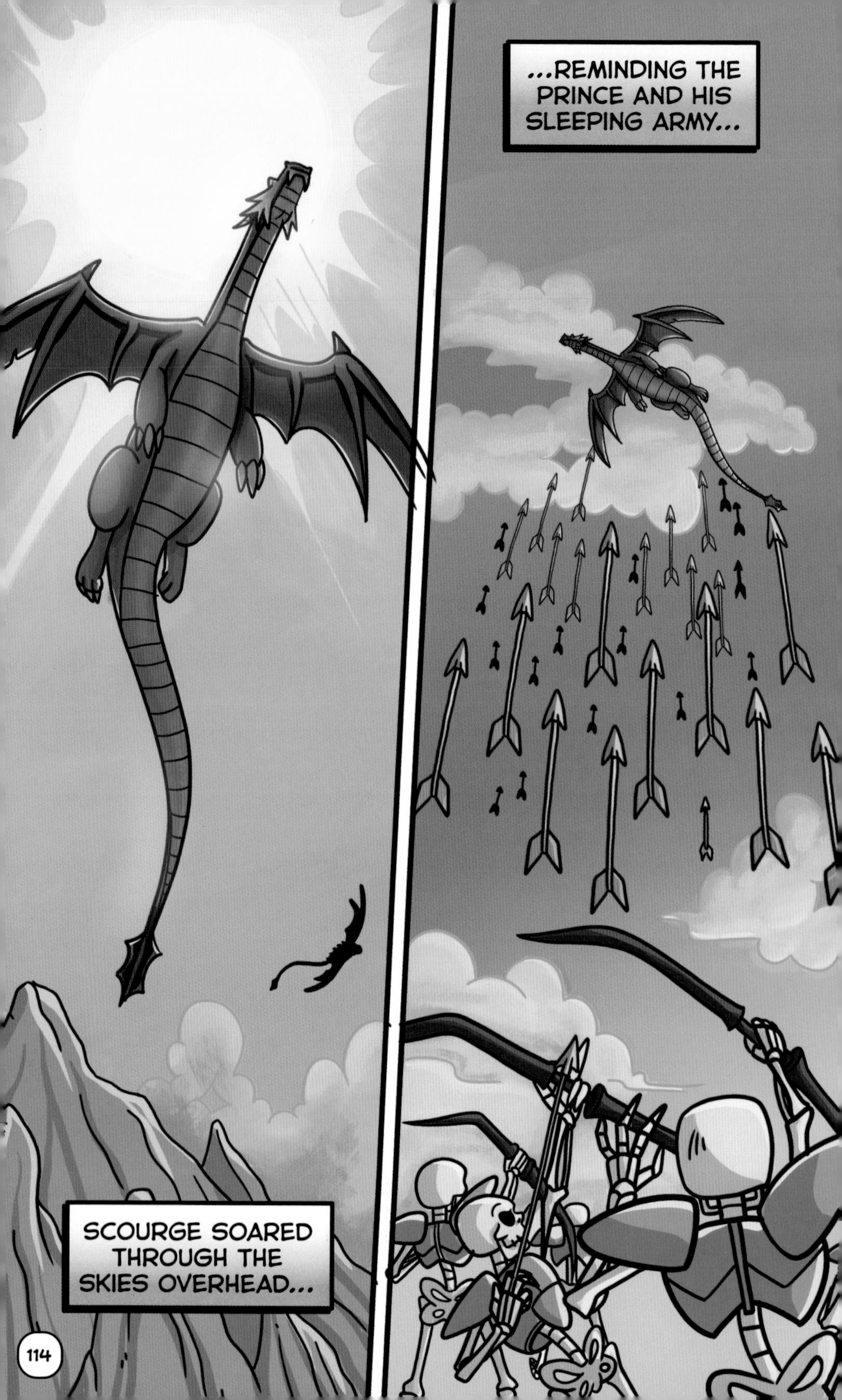
SCOURGE SOARED THROUGH THE SKIES OVERHEAD...
...REMINDING THE PRINCE AND HIS SLEEPING ARMY...

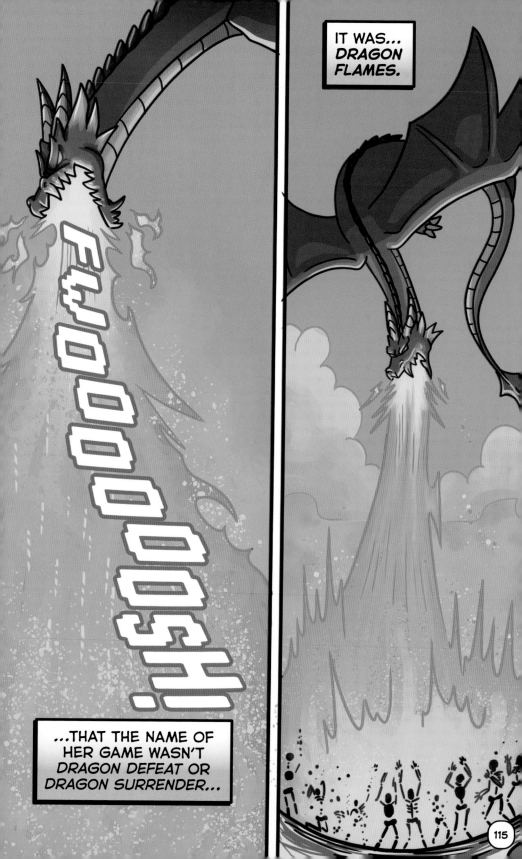

IT WAS...
DRAGON
FLAMES.

FWOOOOOOSH!

...THAT THE NAME OF
HER GAME WASN'T
DRAGON DEFEAT OR
DRAGON SURRENDER...

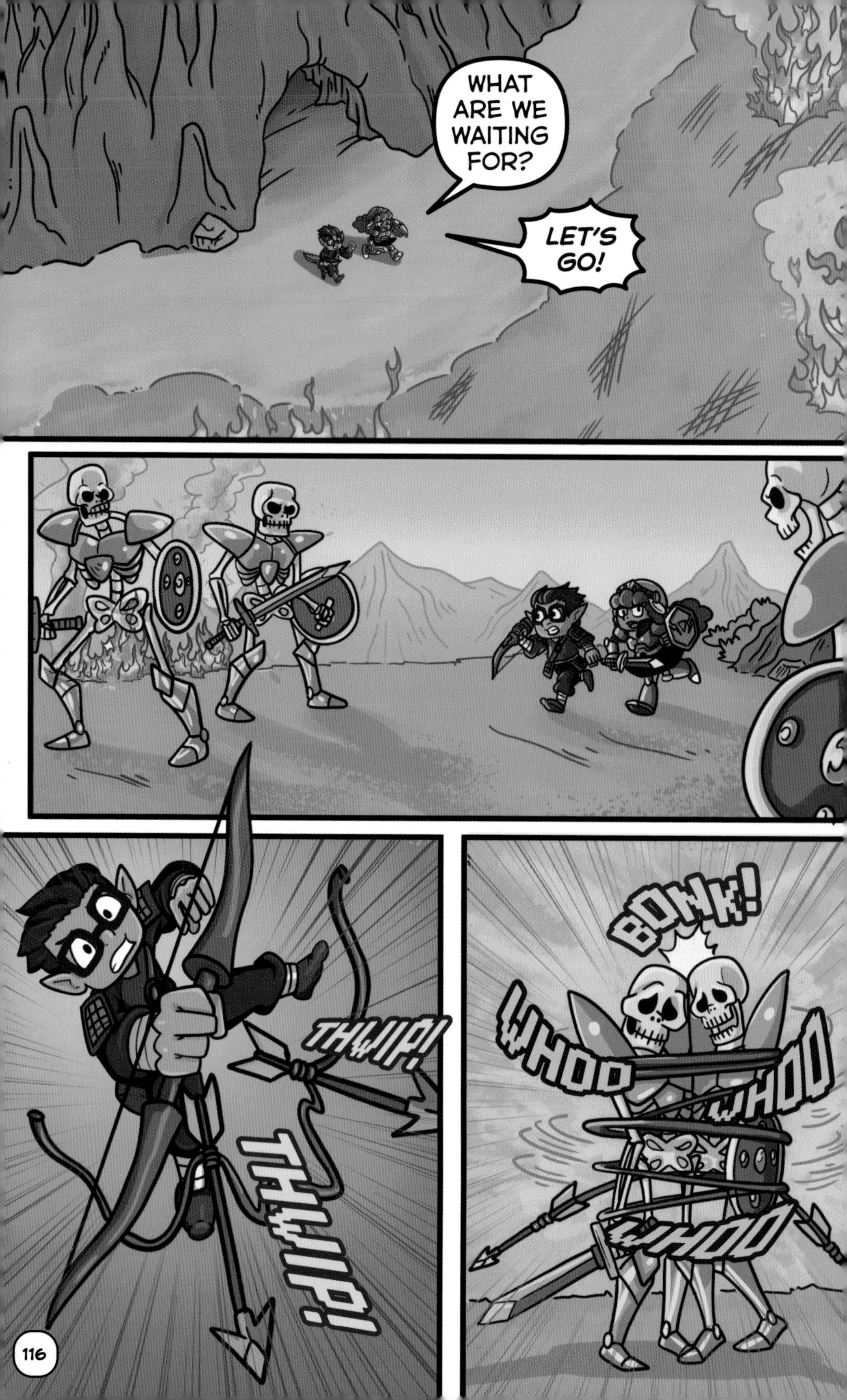
WHAT ARE WE WAITING FOR?
LET'S GO!
THWIP!
THWIP!
BONK!
WHOO
WHOO
WHOO

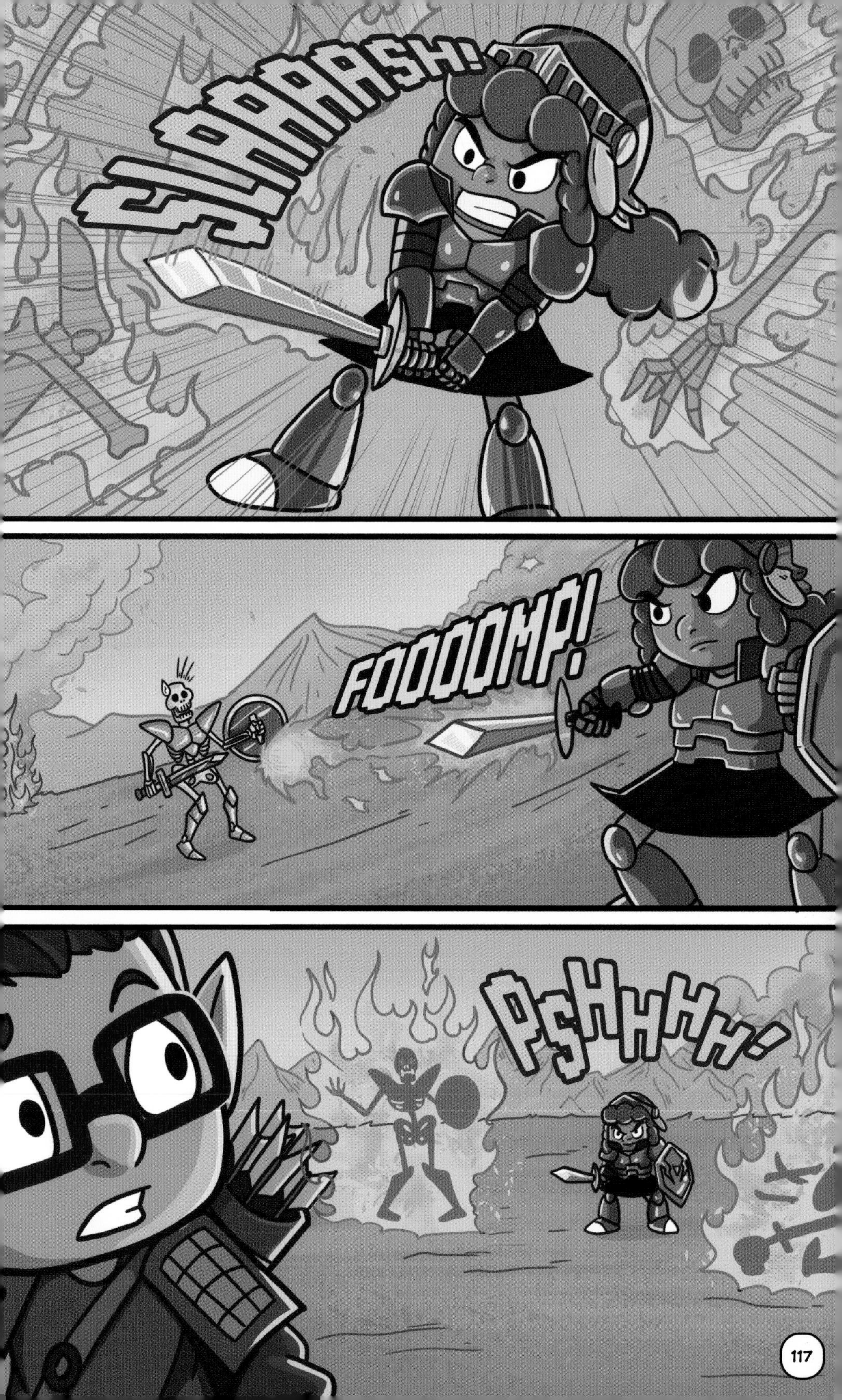
SLDAAASH!
FOOOOMP!
PSHHHHH!

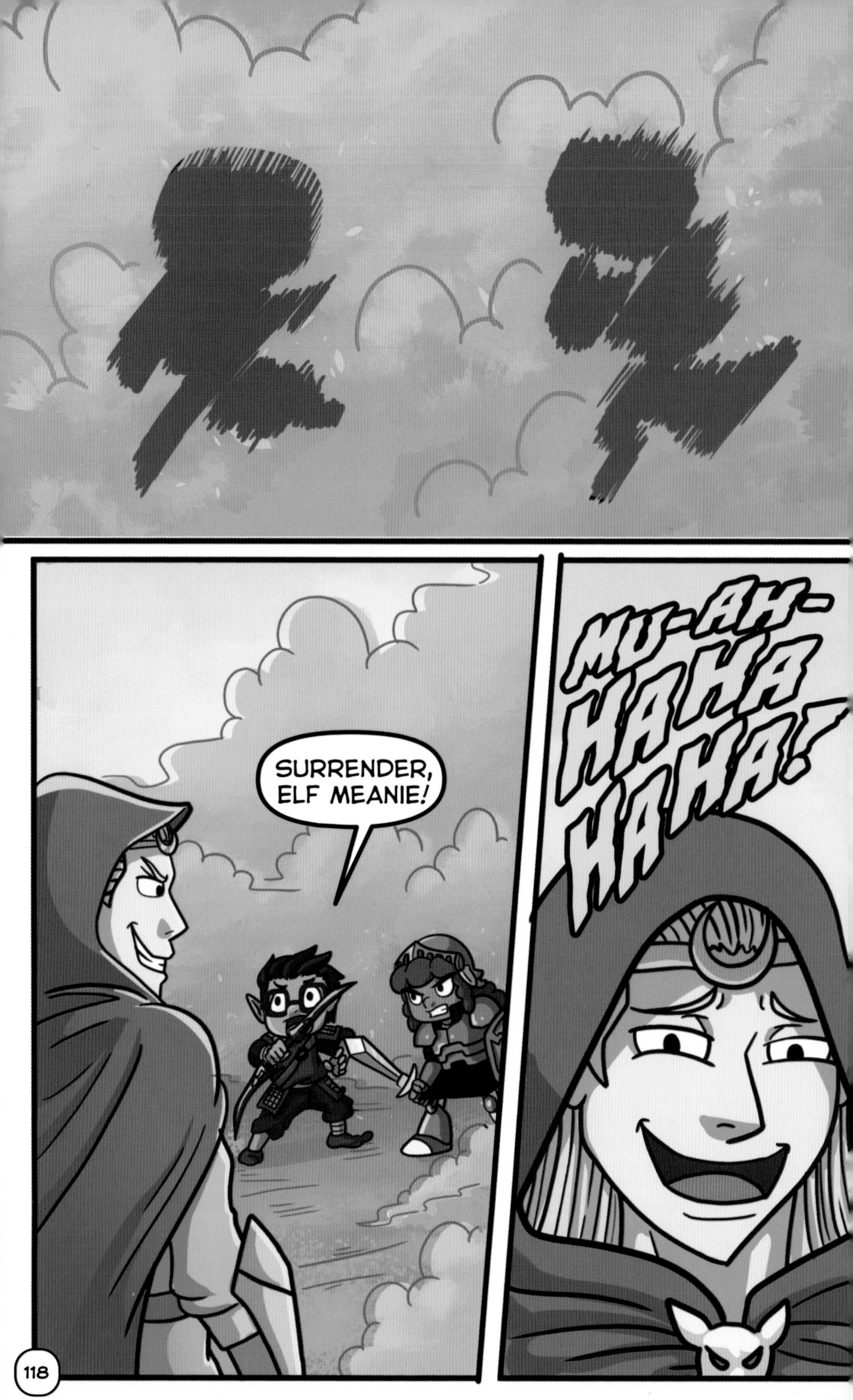
SURRENDER, ELF MEANIE!
MU-AH-HAHAHAHAHA!

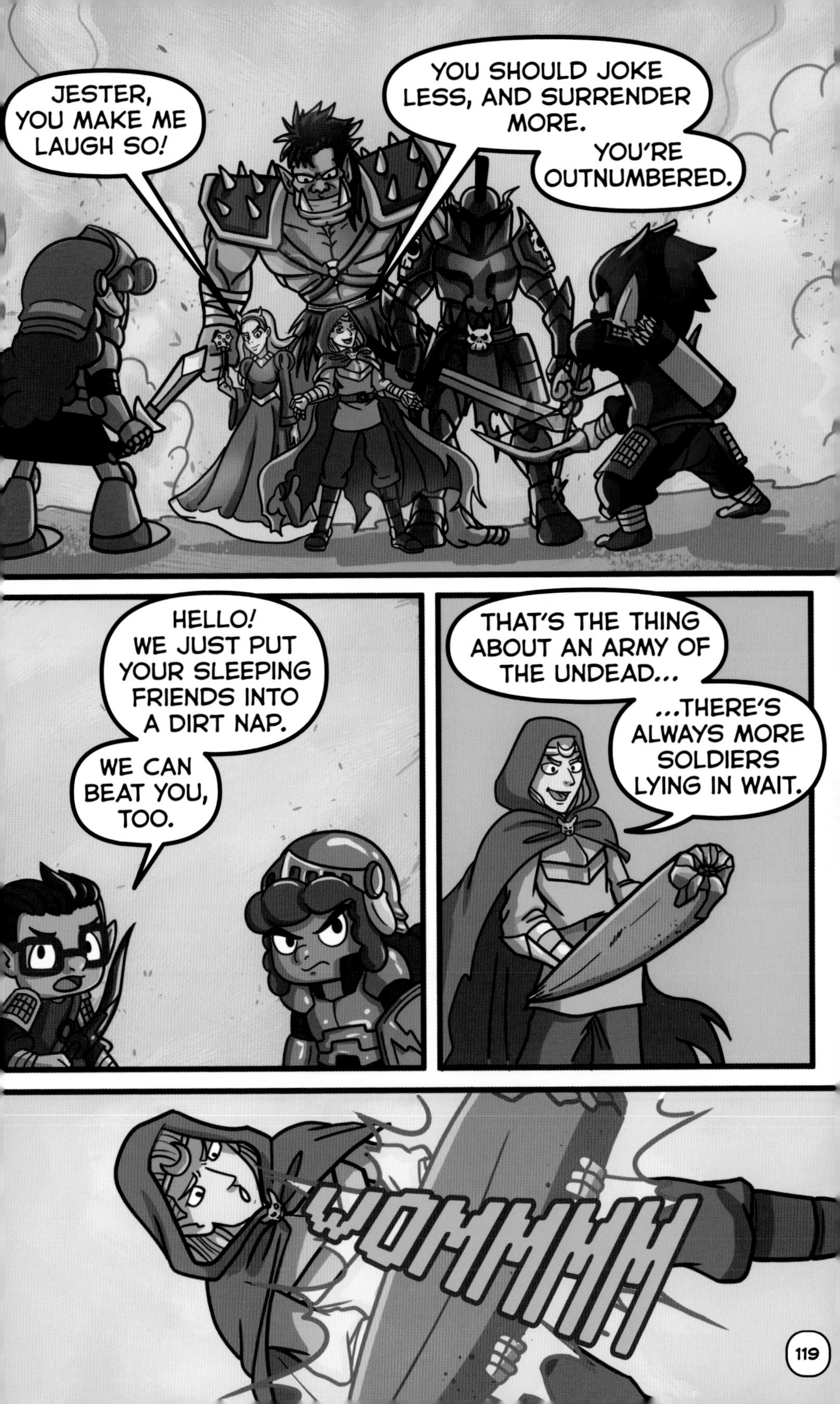
JESTER, YOU MAKE ME LAUGH SO!
YOU SHOULD JOKE LESS, AND SURRENDER MORE.
YOU'RE OUTNUMBERED.
HELLO! WE JUST PUT YOUR SLEEPING FRIENDS INTO A DIRT NAP.
WE CAN BEAT YOU, TOO.
THAT'S THE THING ABOUT AN ARMY OF THE UNDEAD...
...THERE'S ALWAYS MORE SOLDIERS LYING IN WAIT.
WOMMMM

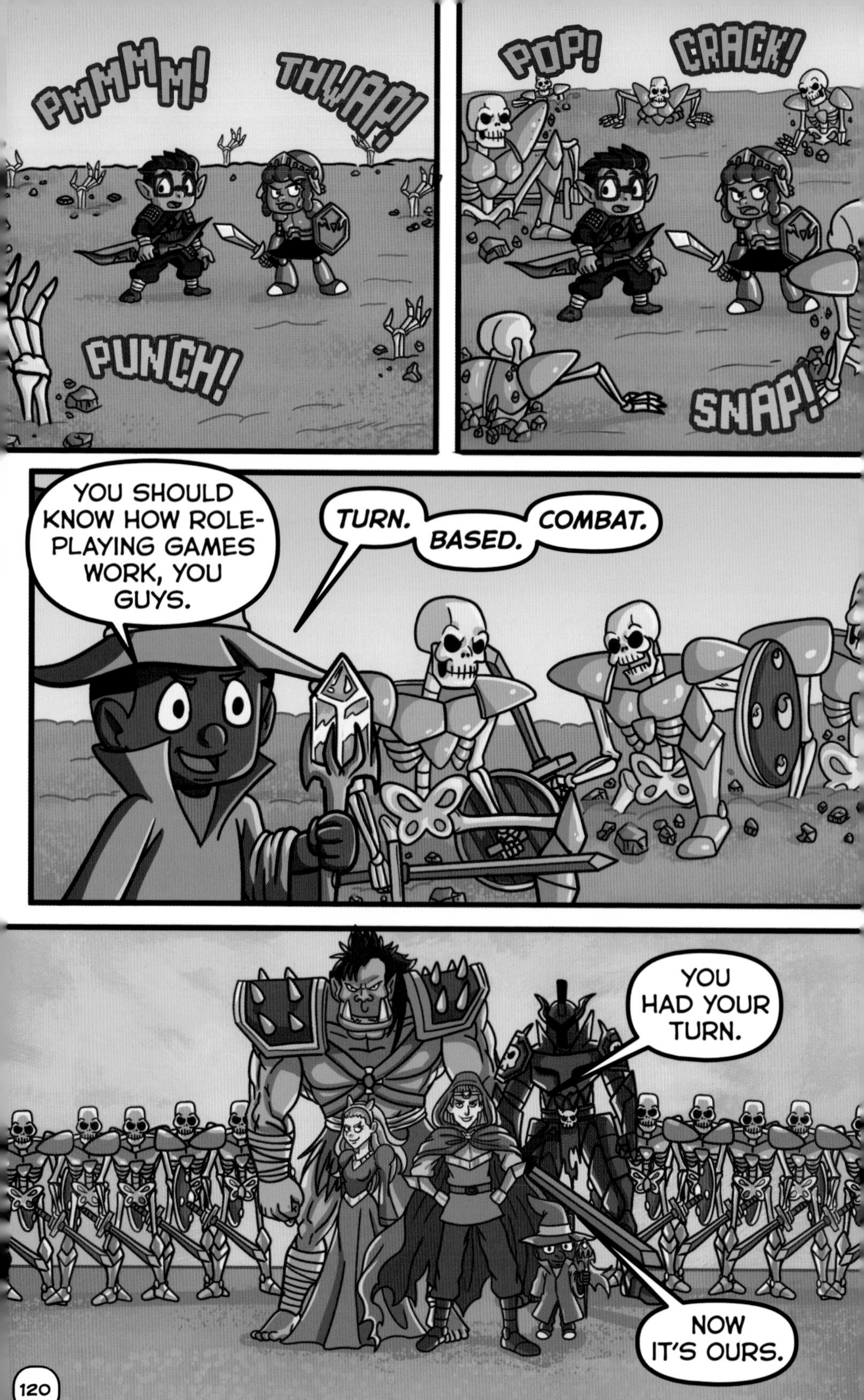
PMMMM!
THWAP!
PUNCH!
POP!
CRACK!
SNAP!
YOU SHOULD KNOW HOW ROLE-PLAYING GAMES WORK, YOU GUYS.
TURN.
BASED.
COMBAT.
YOU HAD YOUR TURN.
NOW IT'S OURS.

CHAPTER 9

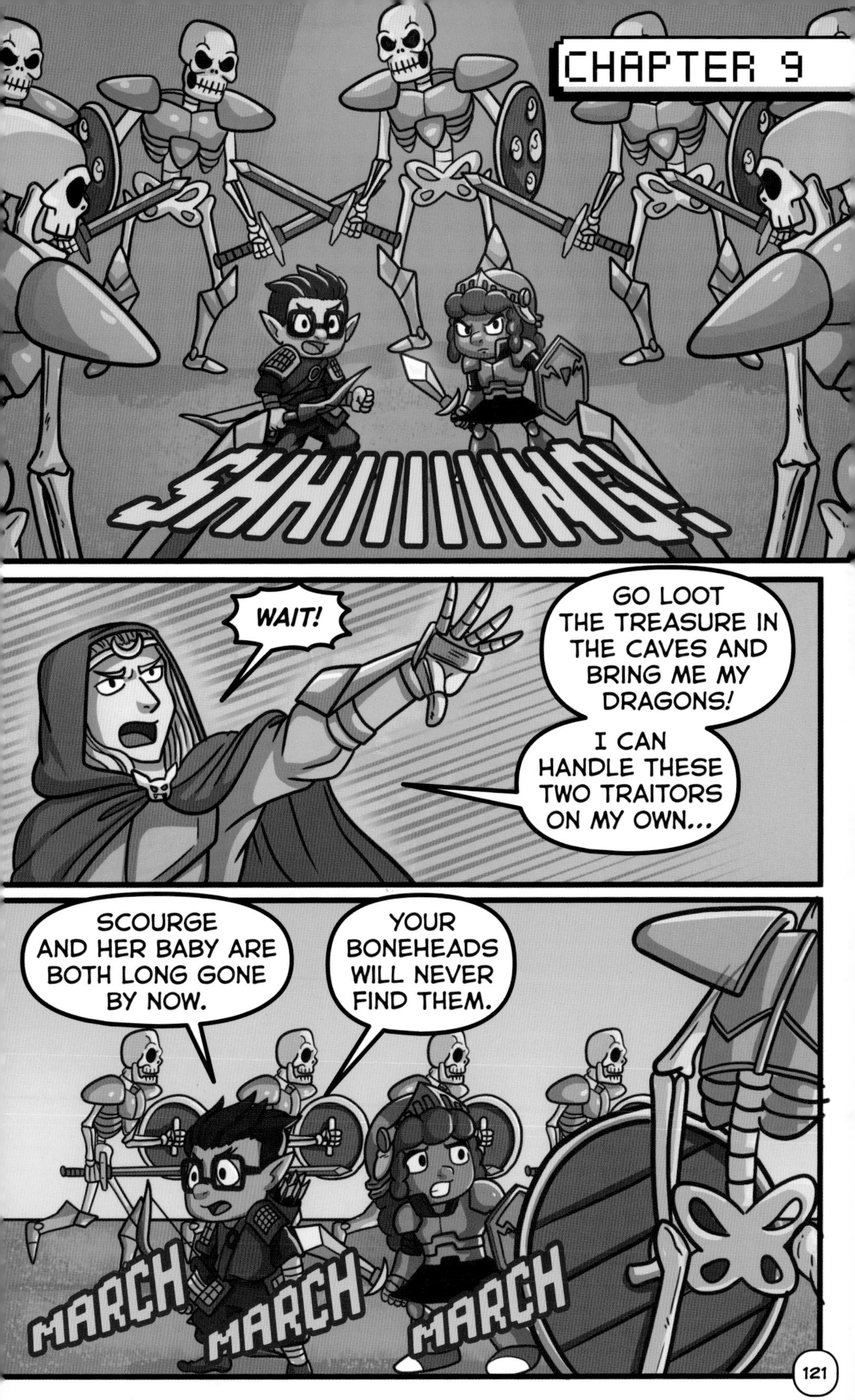
SHIIIIING!
WAIT!
GO LOOT THE TREASURE IN THE CAVES AND BRING ME MY DRAGONS!
I CAN HANDLE THESE TWO TRAITORS ON MY OWN...
SCOURGE AND HER BABY ARE BOTH LONG GONE BY NOW.
YOUR BONEHEADS WILL NEVER FIND THEM.
MARCH
MARCH
MARCH

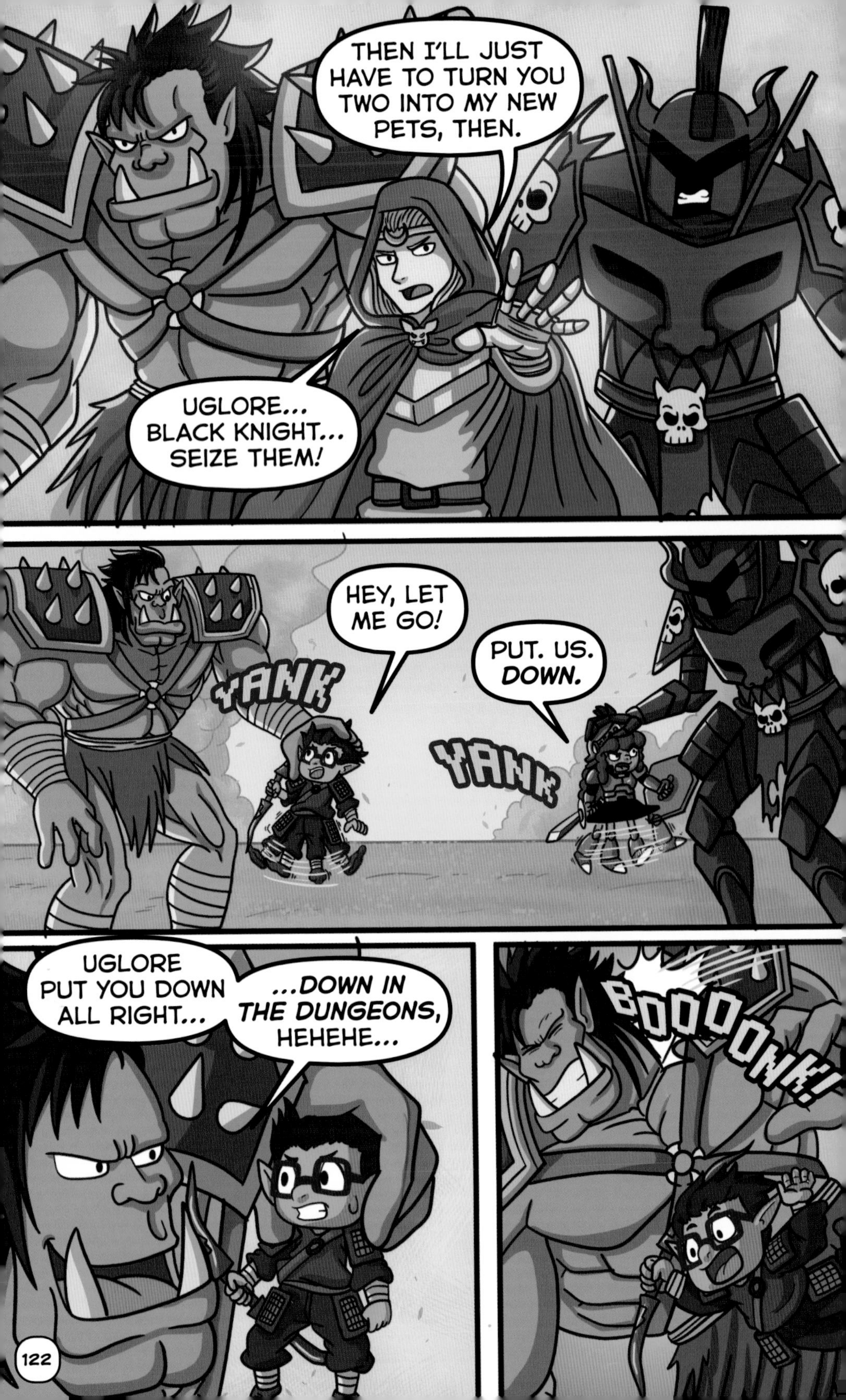
THEN I'LL JUST HAVE TO TURN YOU TWO INTO MY NEW PETS, THEN.
UGLORE... BLACK KNIGHT... SEIZE THEM!
YANK
HEY, LET ME GO!
PUT. US. DOWN.
YANK
UGLORE PUT YOU DOWN ALL RIGHT...
...DOWN IN THE DUNGEONS, HEHEHE...
BOOOONK!

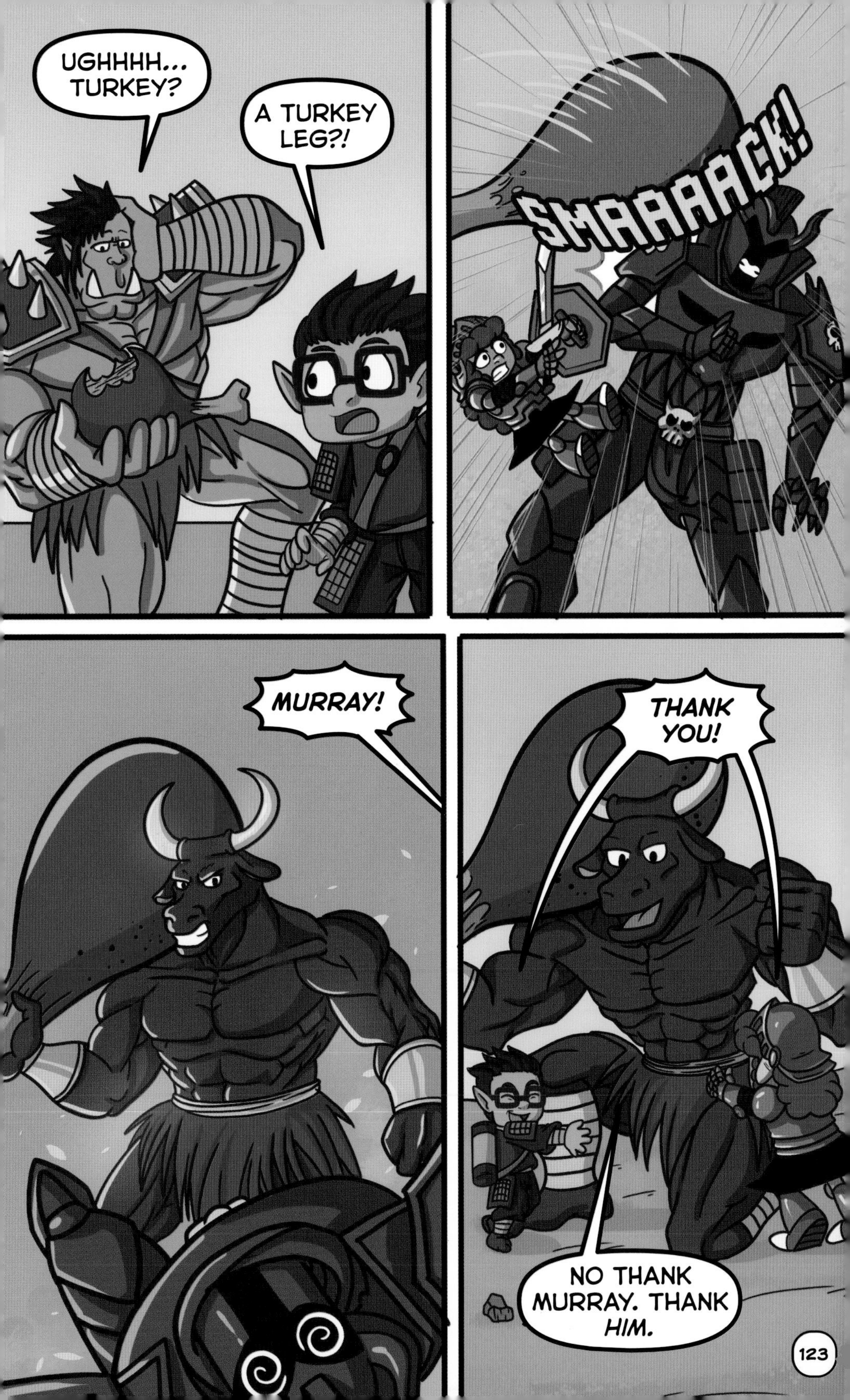
UGHHHH... TURKEY?
A TURKEY LEG?!
SMAAAACK!
MURRAY!
THANK YOU!
NO THANK MURRAY. THANK *HIM*.

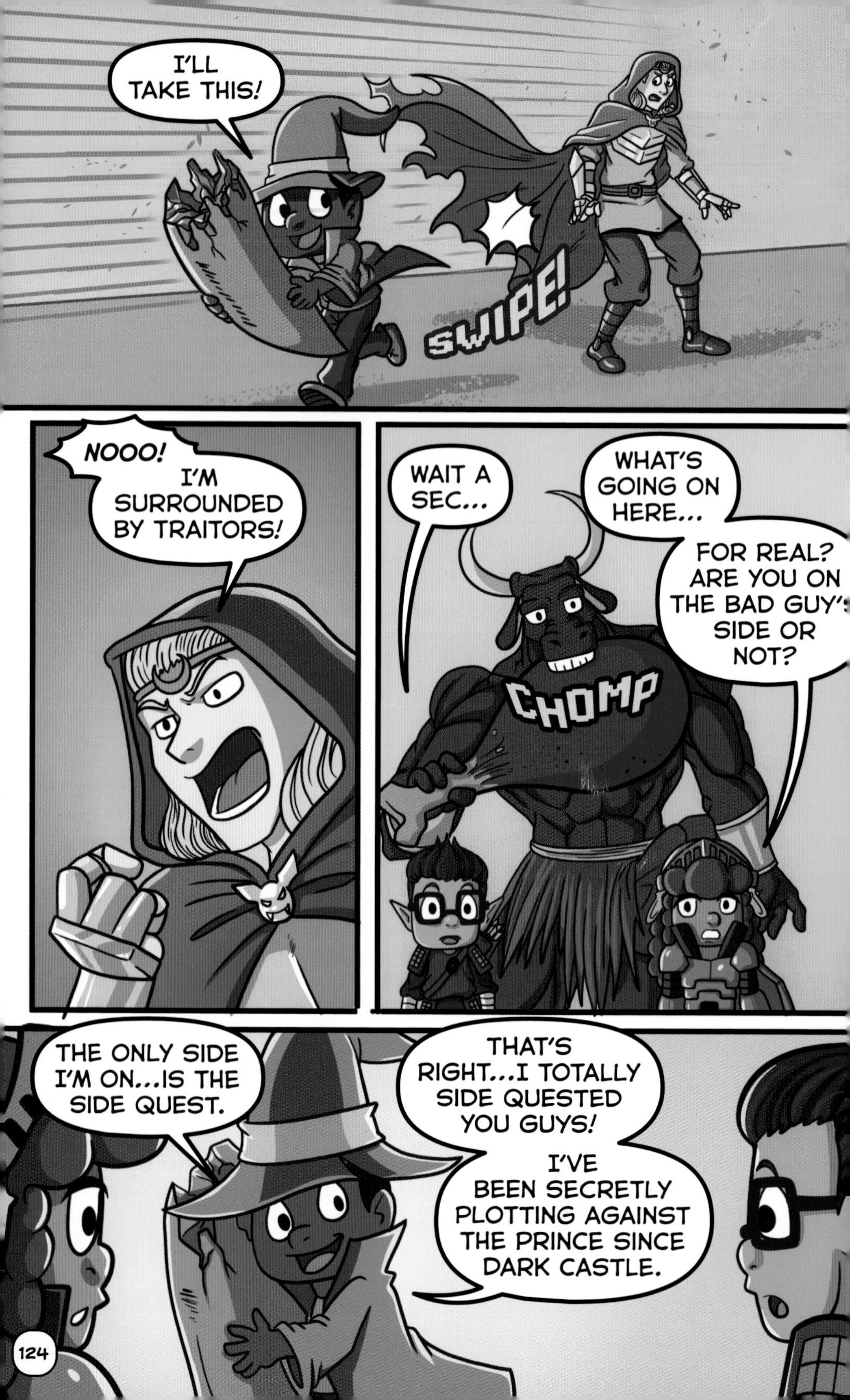
I'LL TAKE THIS!
SWIPE!
NOOO! I'M SURROUNDED BY TRAITORS!
WAIT A SEC...
WHAT'S GOING ON HERE...
FOR REAL? ARE YOU ON THE BAD GUY'S SIDE OR NOT?
CHOMP
THE ONLY SIDE I'M ON...IS THE SIDE QUEST.
THAT'S RIGHT...I TOTALLY SIDE QUESTED YOU GUYS!
I'VE BEEN SECRETLY PLOTTING AGAINST THE PRINCE SINCE DARK CASTLE.

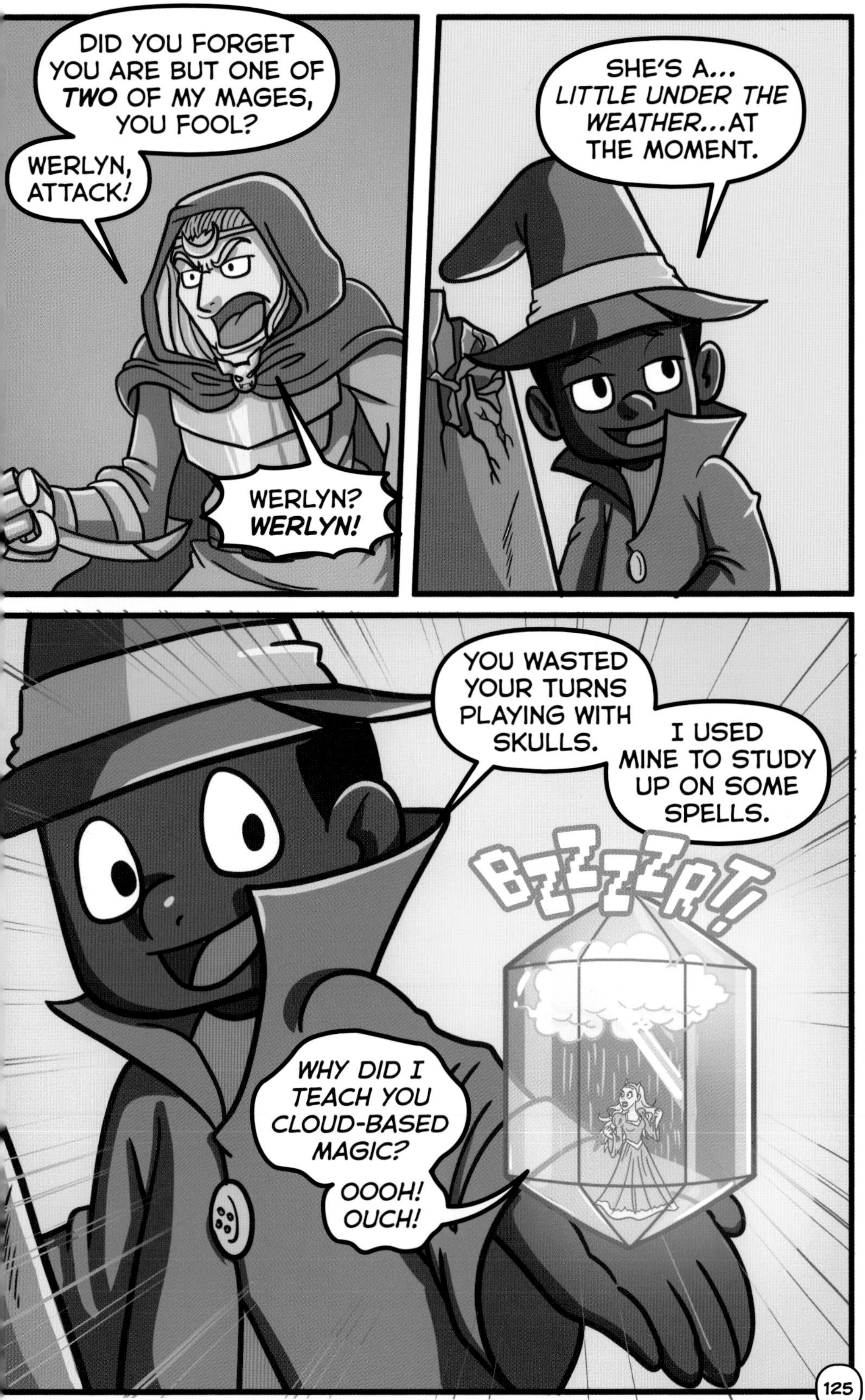
DID YOU FORGET YOU ARE BUT ONE OF *TWO* OF MY MAGES, YOU FOOL?
WERLYN, ATTACK!
WERLYN? *WERLYN!*
SHE'S A... *LITTLE UNDER THE WEATHER*...AT THE MOMENT.
YOU WASTED YOUR TURNS PLAYING WITH SKULLS.
I USED MINE TO STUDY UP ON SOME SPELLS.
BZZZZRT!
WHY DID I TEACH YOU CLOUD-BASED MAGIC?
OOOH! OUCH!

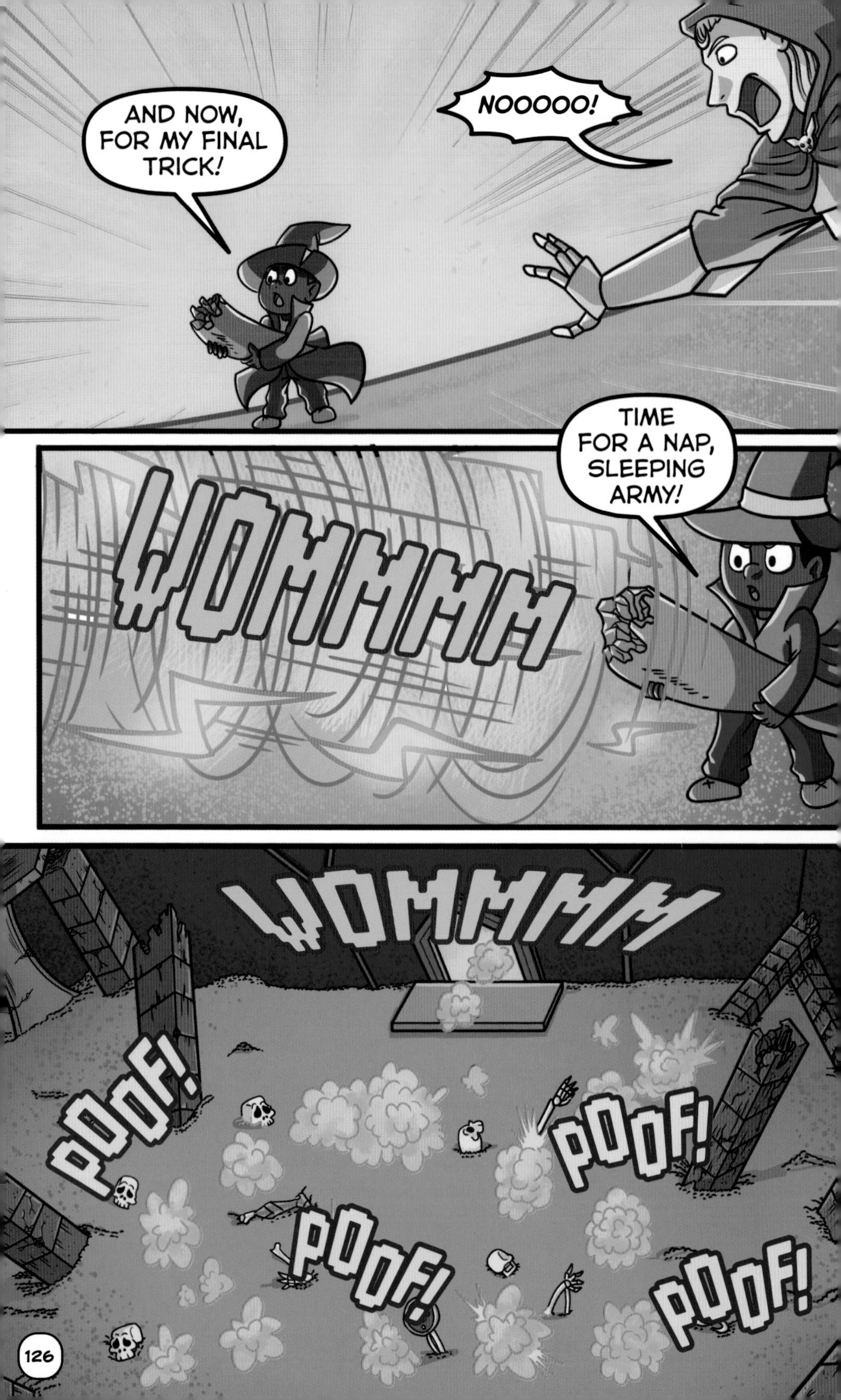
AND NOW, FOR MY FINAL TRICK!
NOOOOO!
TIME FOR A NAP, SLEEPING ARMY!
WOMMMM
WOMMMM
POOF!
POOF!
POOF!
POOF!

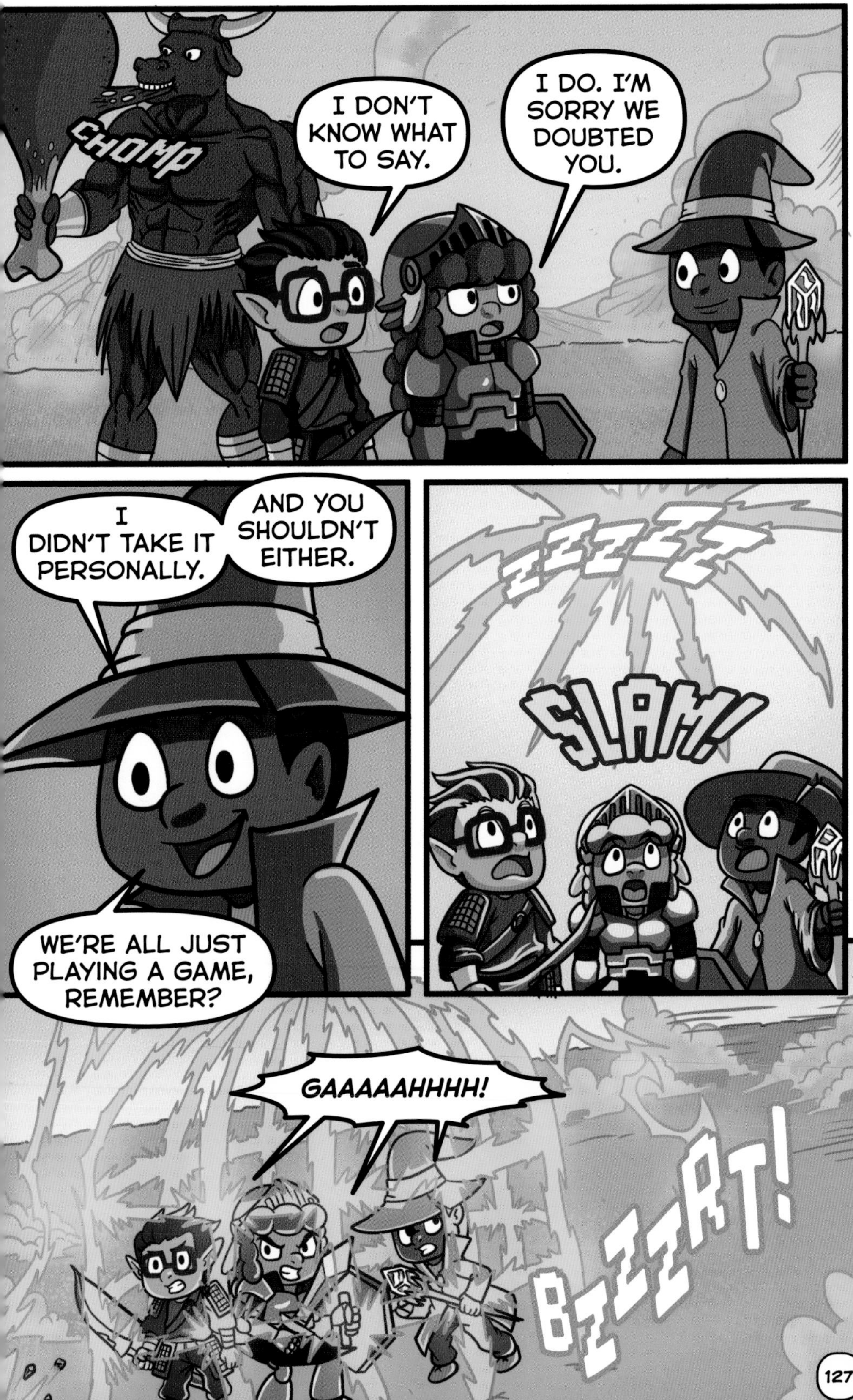
CHOMP
I DON'T KNOW WHAT TO SAY.
I DO. I'M SORRY WE DOUBTED YOU.
I DIDN'T TAKE IT PERSONALLY.
AND YOU SHOULDN'T EITHER.
WE'RE ALL JUST PLAYING A GAME, REMEMBER?
ZZZZZZ
SLAM!
GAAAAAHHHH!
BZZZRT!

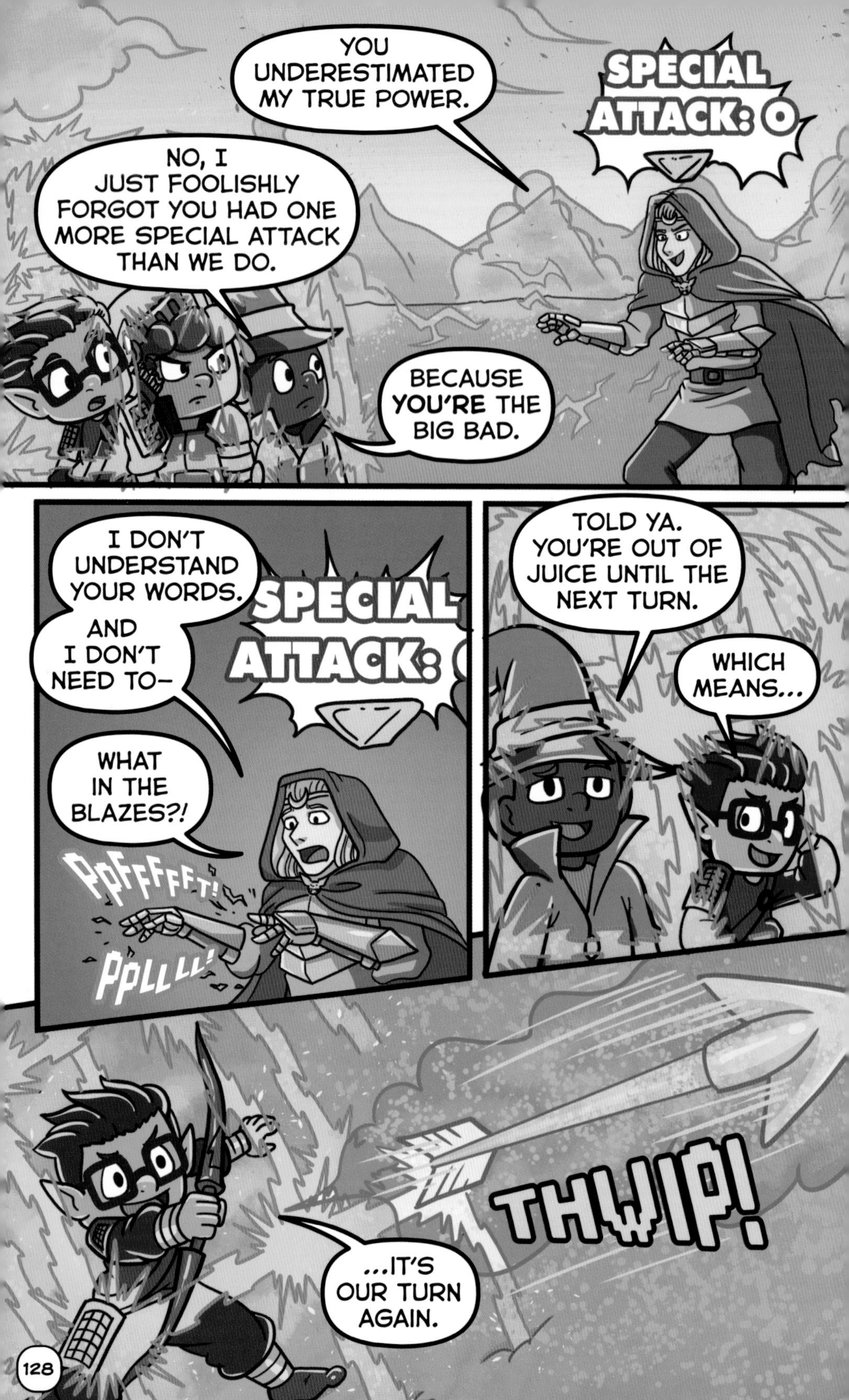
YOU UNDERESTIMATED MY TRUE POWER.
SPECIAL ATTACK: 0
NO, I JUST FOOLISHLY FORGOT YOU HAD ONE MORE SPECIAL ATTACK THAN WE DO.
BECAUSE YOU'RE THE BIG BAD.
I DON'T UNDERSTAND YOUR WORDS.
AND I DON'T NEED TO–
SPECIAL ATTACK:
WHAT IN THE BLAZES?!
PFFFFFFT!
PPLLLL!
TOLD YA. YOU'RE OUT OF JUICE UNTIL THE NEXT TURN.
WHICH MEANS...
THWIP!
...IT'S OUR TURN AGAIN.

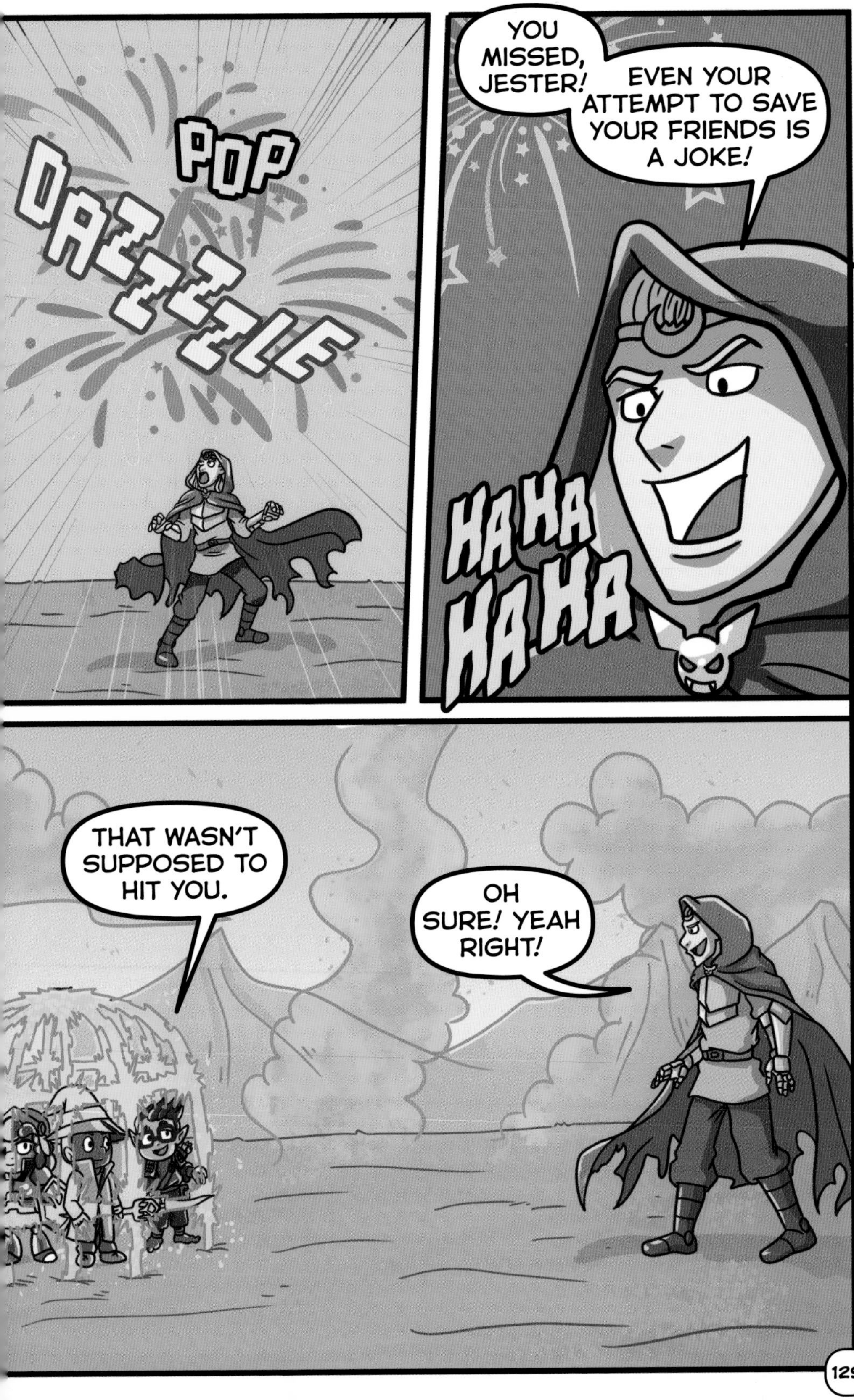
POP
DAZZZZLE
YOU MISSED, JESTER!
EVEN YOUR ATTEMPT TO SAVE YOUR FRIENDS IS A JOKE!
HA HA HA HA
THAT WASN'T SUPPOSED TO HIT YOU.
OH SURE! YEAH RIGHT!

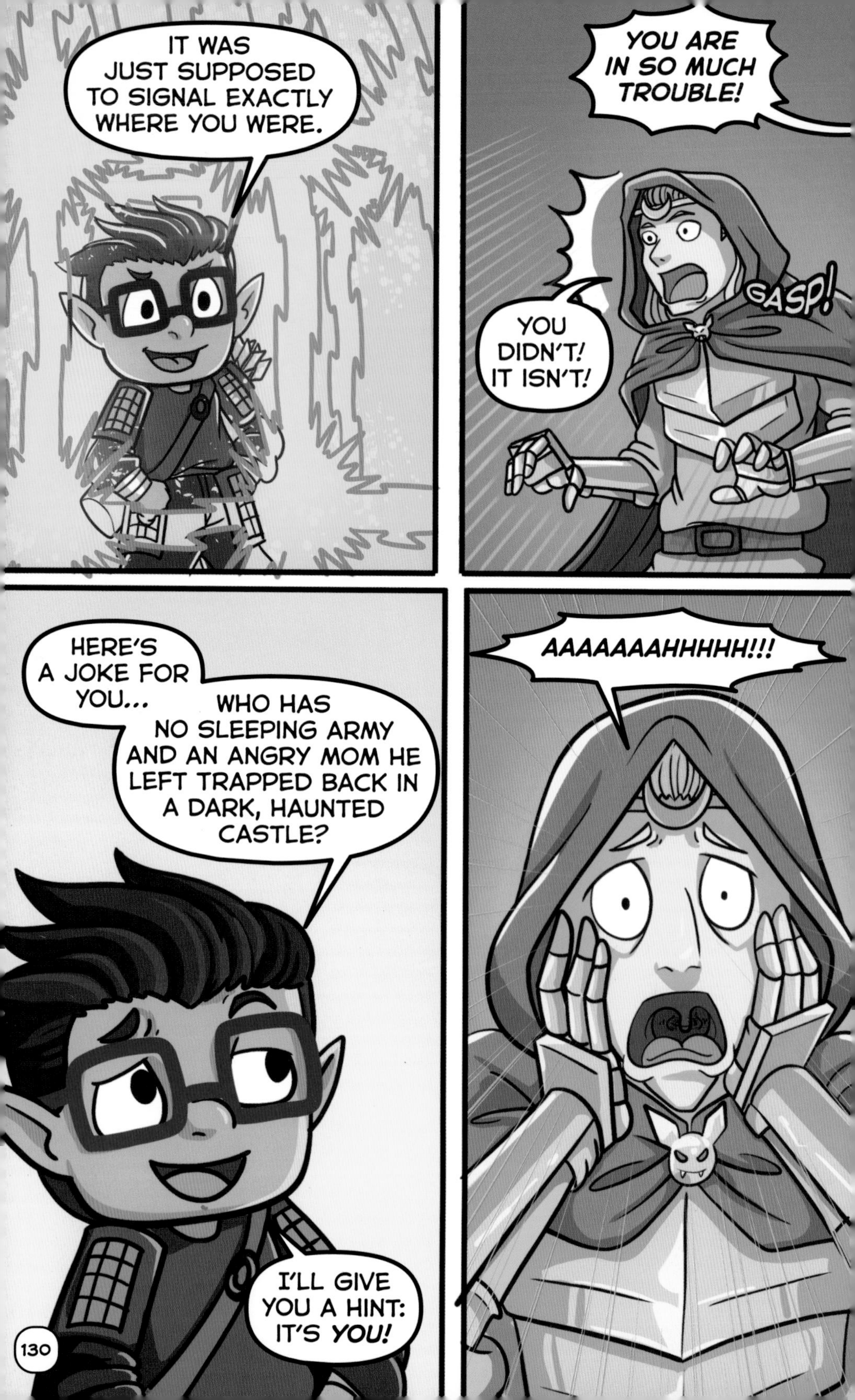
IT WAS JUST SUPPOSED TO SIGNAL EXACTLY WHERE YOU WERE.
YOU ARE IN SO MUCH TROUBLE!
GASP!
YOU DIDN'T! IT ISN'T!
HERE'S A JOKE FOR YOU...
WHO HAS NO SLEEPING ARMY AND AN ANGRY MOM HE LEFT TRAPPED BACK IN A DARK, HAUNTED CASTLE?
I'LL GIVE YOU A HINT: IT'S YOU!
AAAAAAAHHHHH!!!

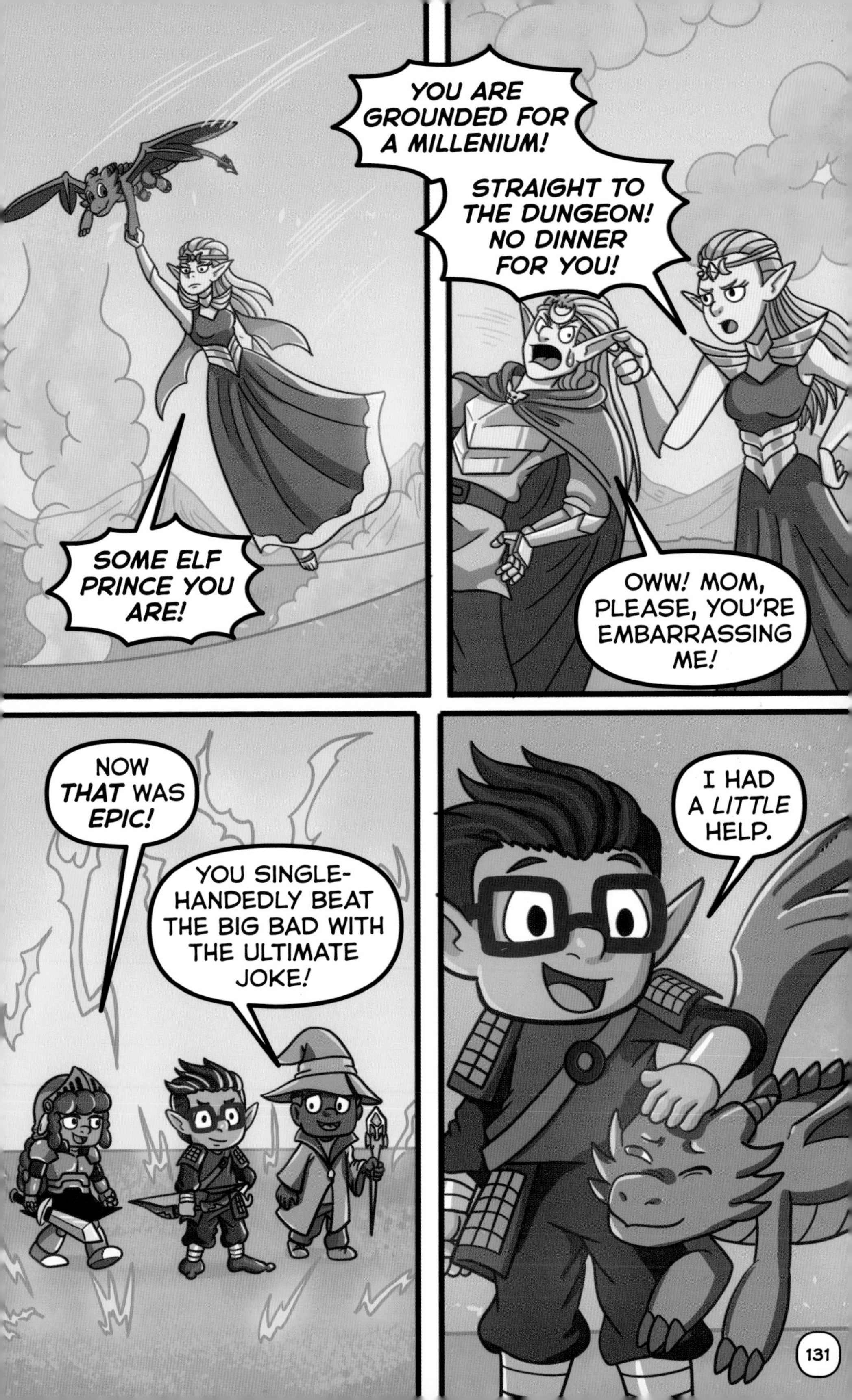
SOME ELF PRINCE YOU ARE!
YOU ARE GROUNDED FOR A MILLENIUM!
STRAIGHT TO THE DUNGEON! NO DINNER FOR YOU!
OWW! MOM, PLEASE, YOU'RE EMBARRASSING ME!
NOW THAT WAS EPIC!
YOU SINGLE-HANDEDLY BEAT THE BIG BAD WITH THE ULTIMATE JOKE!
I HAD A LITTLE HELP.

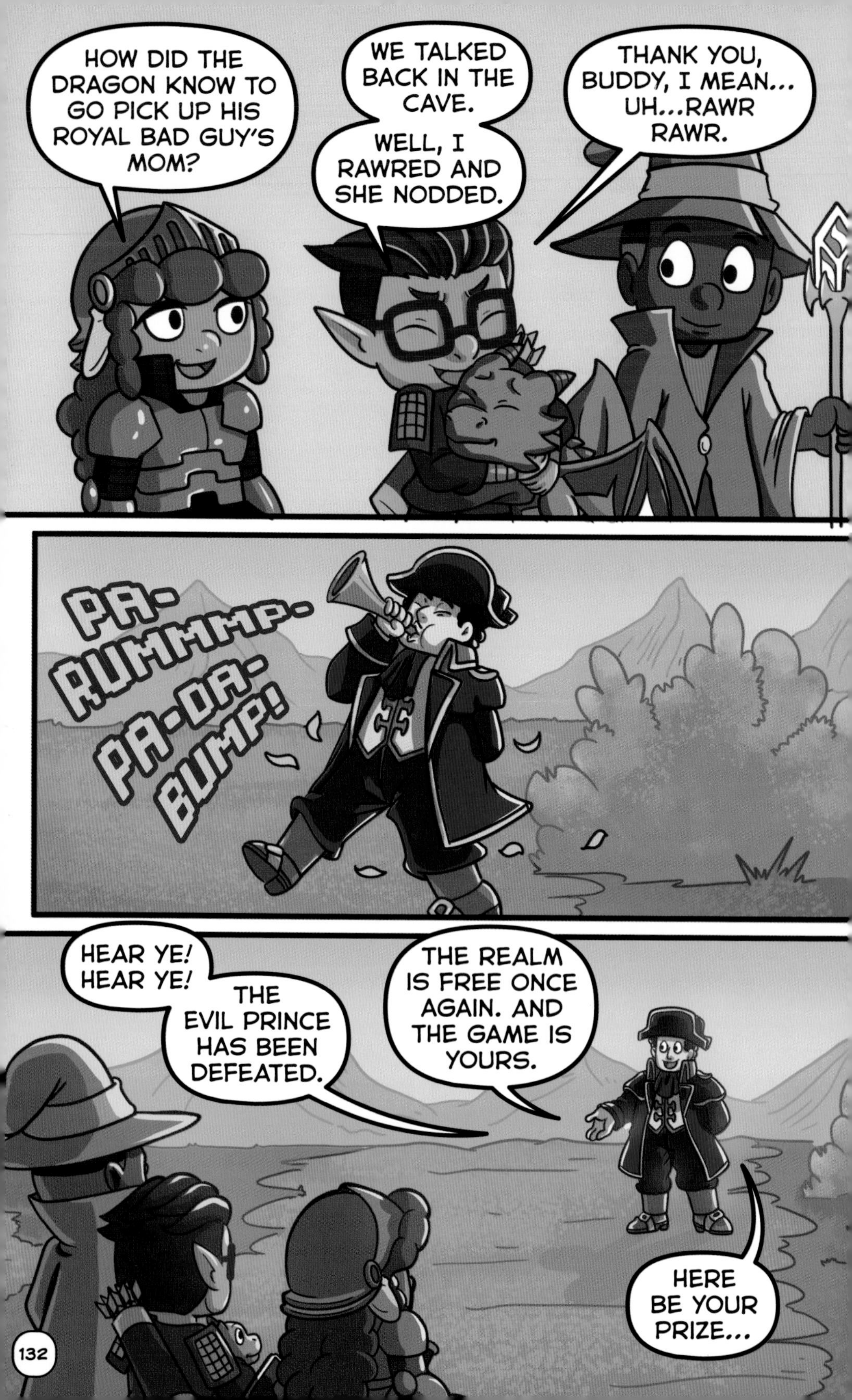
HOW DID THE DRAGON KNOW TO GO PICK UP HIS ROYAL BAD GUY'S MOM?
WE TALKED BACK IN THE CAVE.
WELL, I RAWRED AND SHE NODDED.
THANK YOU, BUDDY, I MEAN... UH...RAWR RAWR.
PA-RUMMMP-PA-DA-PA-DA-BUMP!
HEAR YE! HEAR YE!
THE EVIL PRINCE HAS BEEN DEFEATED.
THE REALM IS FREE ONCE AGAIN. AND THE GAME IS YOURS.
HERE BE YOUR PRIZE...

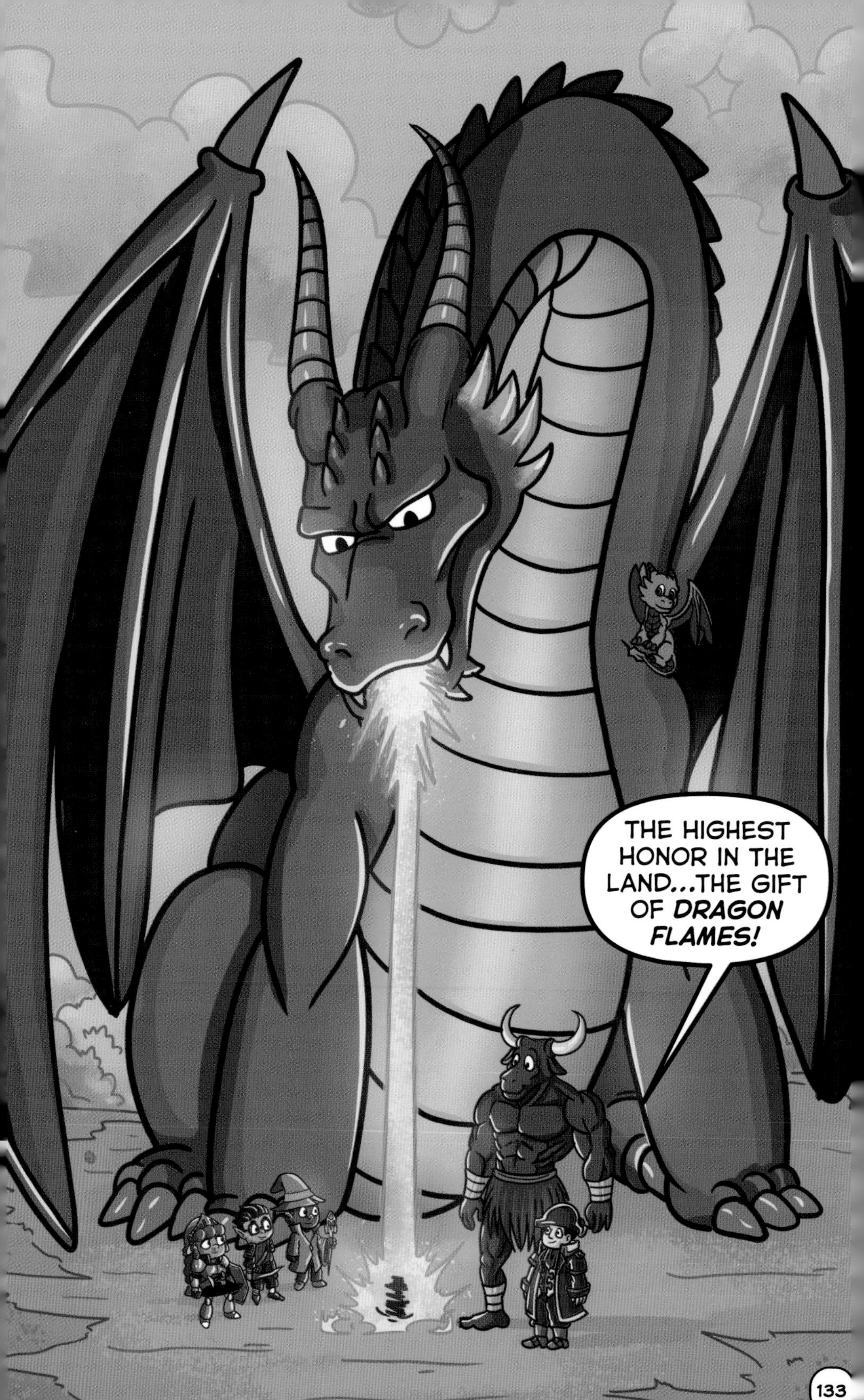
THE HIGHEST HONOR IN THE LAND...THE GIFT OF ***DRAGON FLAMES!***

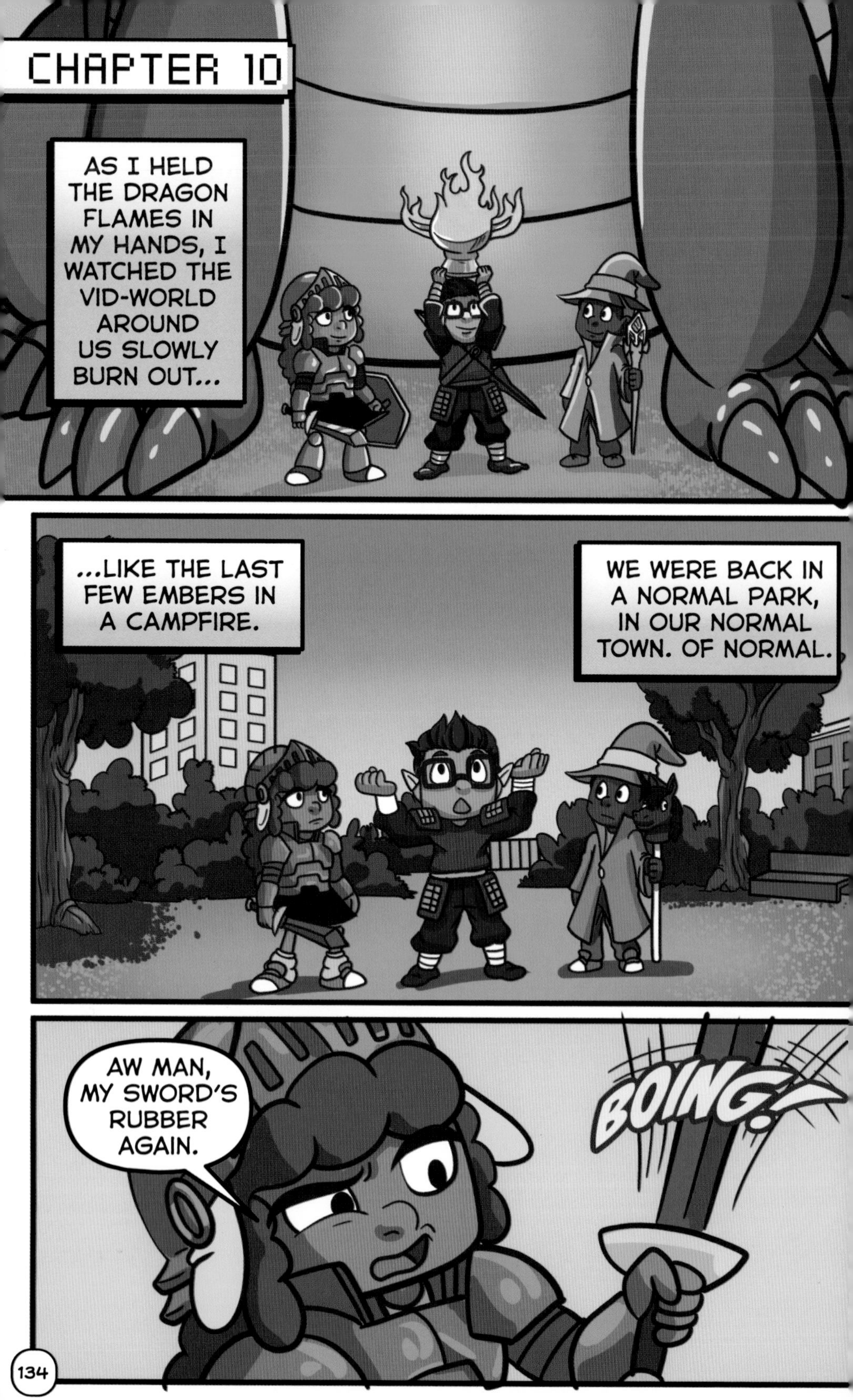
CHAPTER 10
AS I HELD THE DRAGON FLAMES IN MY HANDS, I WATCHED THE VID-WORLD AROUND US SLOWLY BURN OUT...
...LIKE THE LAST FEW EMBERS IN A CAMPFIRE.
WE WERE BACK IN A NORMAL PARK, IN OUR NORMAL TOWN. OF NORMAL.
AW MAN, MY SWORD'S RUBBER AGAIN.
BOING!

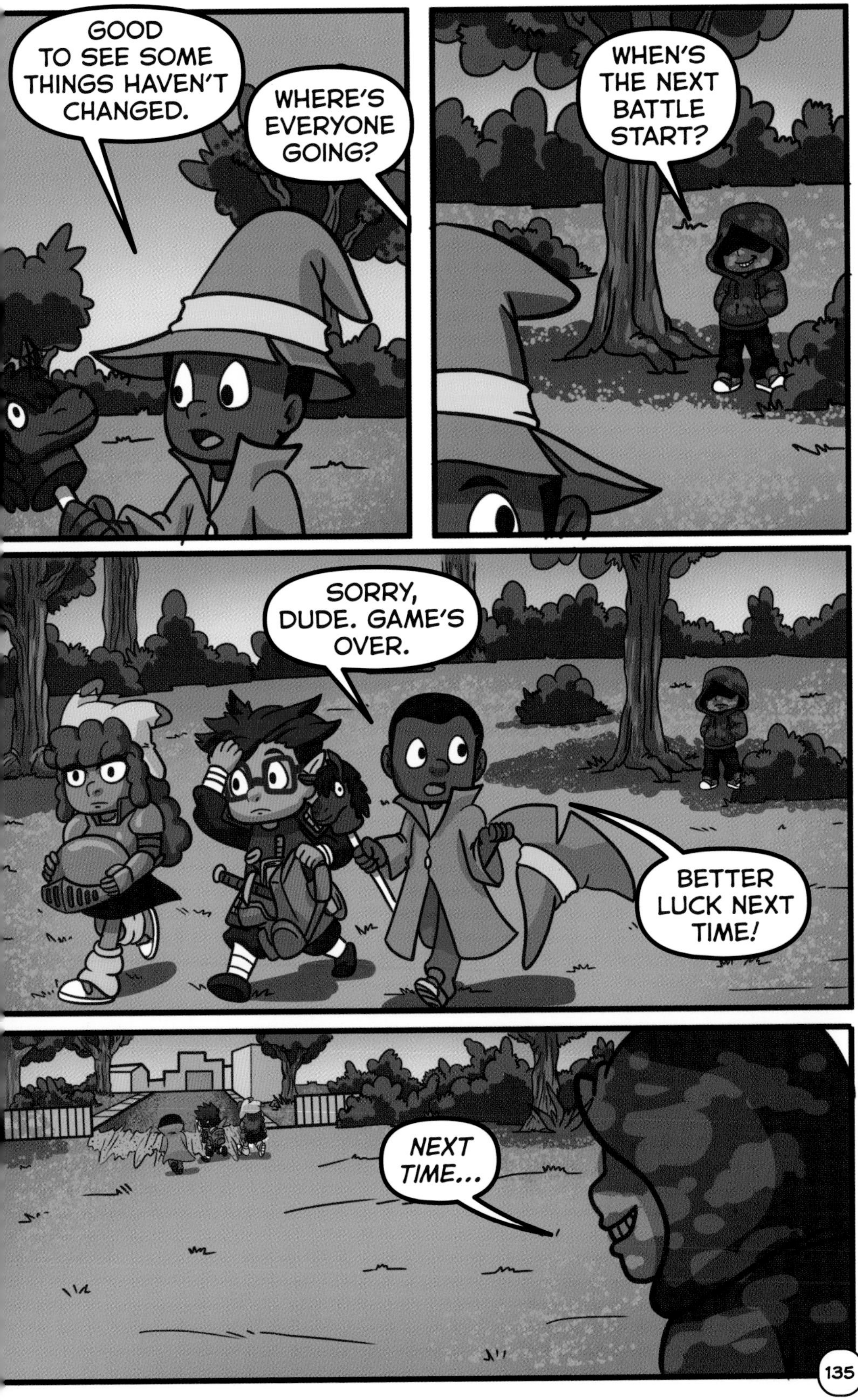
GOOD TO SEE SOME THINGS HAVEN'T CHANGED.
WHERE'S EVERYONE GOING?
WHEN'S THE NEXT BATTLE START?
SORRY, DUDE. GAME'S OVER.
BETTER LUCK NEXT TIME!
NEXT TIME...

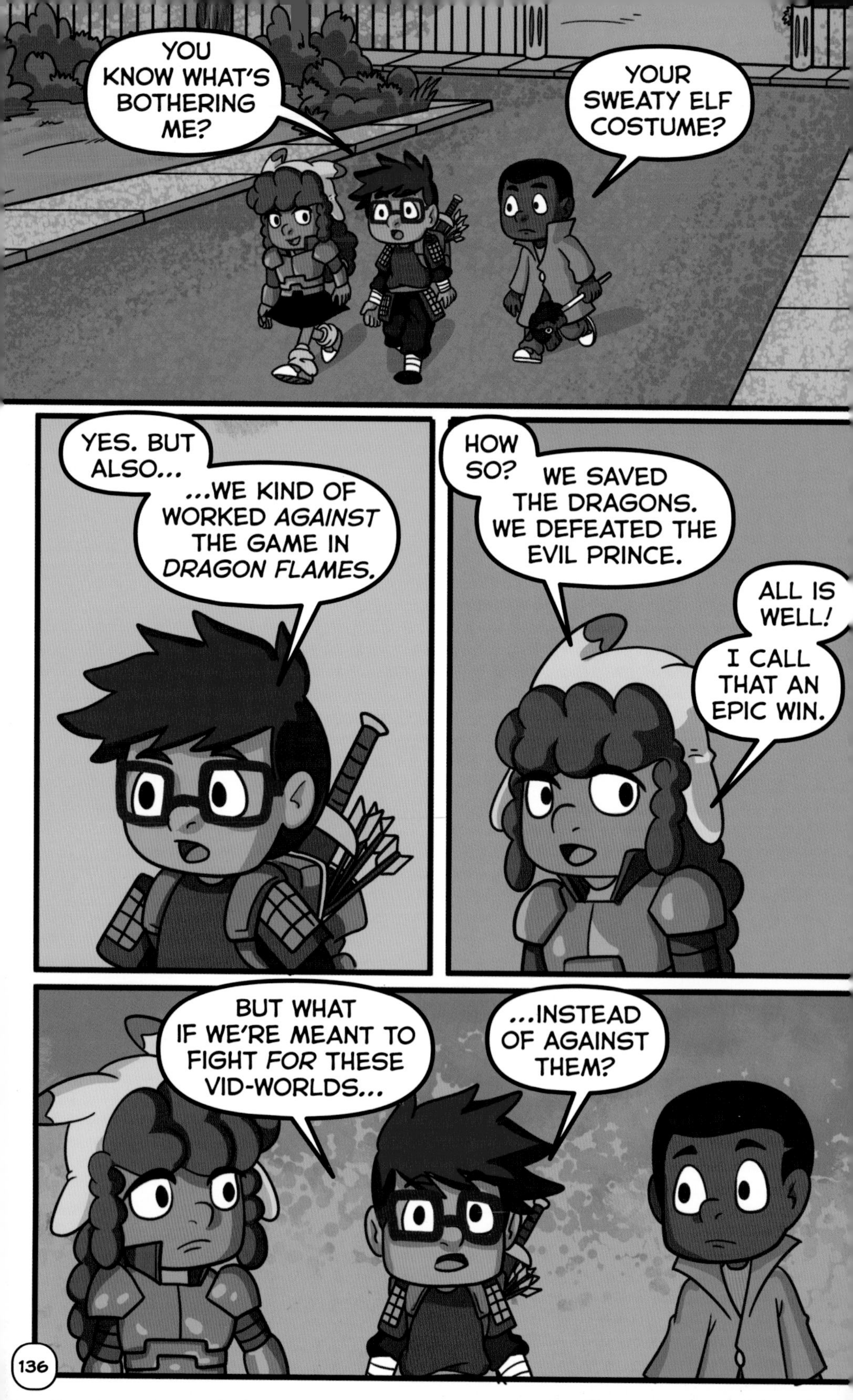
YOU KNOW WHAT'S BOTHERING ME?
YOUR SWEATY ELF COSTUME?
YES. BUT ALSO...
...WE KIND OF WORKED *AGAINST* THE GAME IN *DRAGON FLAMES.*
HOW SO?
WE SAVED THE DRAGONS. WE DEFEATED THE EVIL PRINCE.
ALL IS WELL!
I CALL THAT AN EPIC WIN.
BUT WHAT IF WE'RE MEANT TO FIGHT *FOR* THESE VID-WORLDS...
...INSTEAD OF AGAINST THEM?

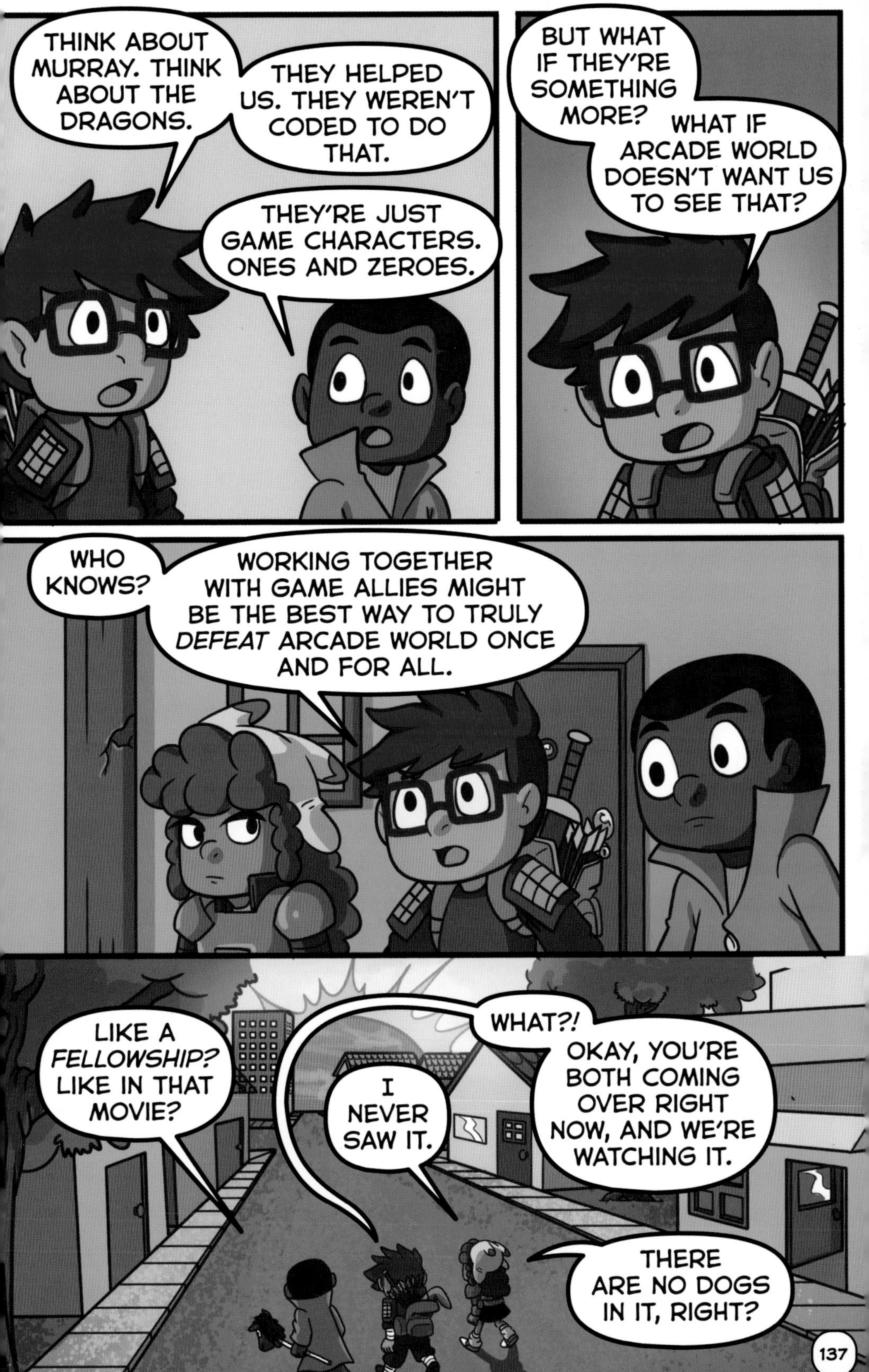
THINK ABOUT MURRAY. THINK ABOUT THE DRAGONS.
THEY HELPED US. THEY WEREN'T CODED TO DO THAT.
THEY'RE JUST GAME CHARACTERS. ONES AND ZEROES.
BUT WHAT IF THEY'RE SOMETHING MORE?
WHAT IF ARCADE WORLD DOESN'T WANT US TO SEE THAT?
WHO KNOWS?
WORKING TOGETHER WITH GAME ALLIES MIGHT BE THE BEST WAY TO TRULY *DEFEAT* ARCADE WORLD ONCE AND FOR ALL.
LIKE A *FELLOWSHIP?* LIKE IN THAT MOVIE?
I NEVER SAW IT.
WHAT?!
OKAY, YOU'RE BOTH COMING OVER RIGHT NOW, AND WE'RE WATCHING IT.
THERE ARE NO DOGS IN IT, RIGHT?

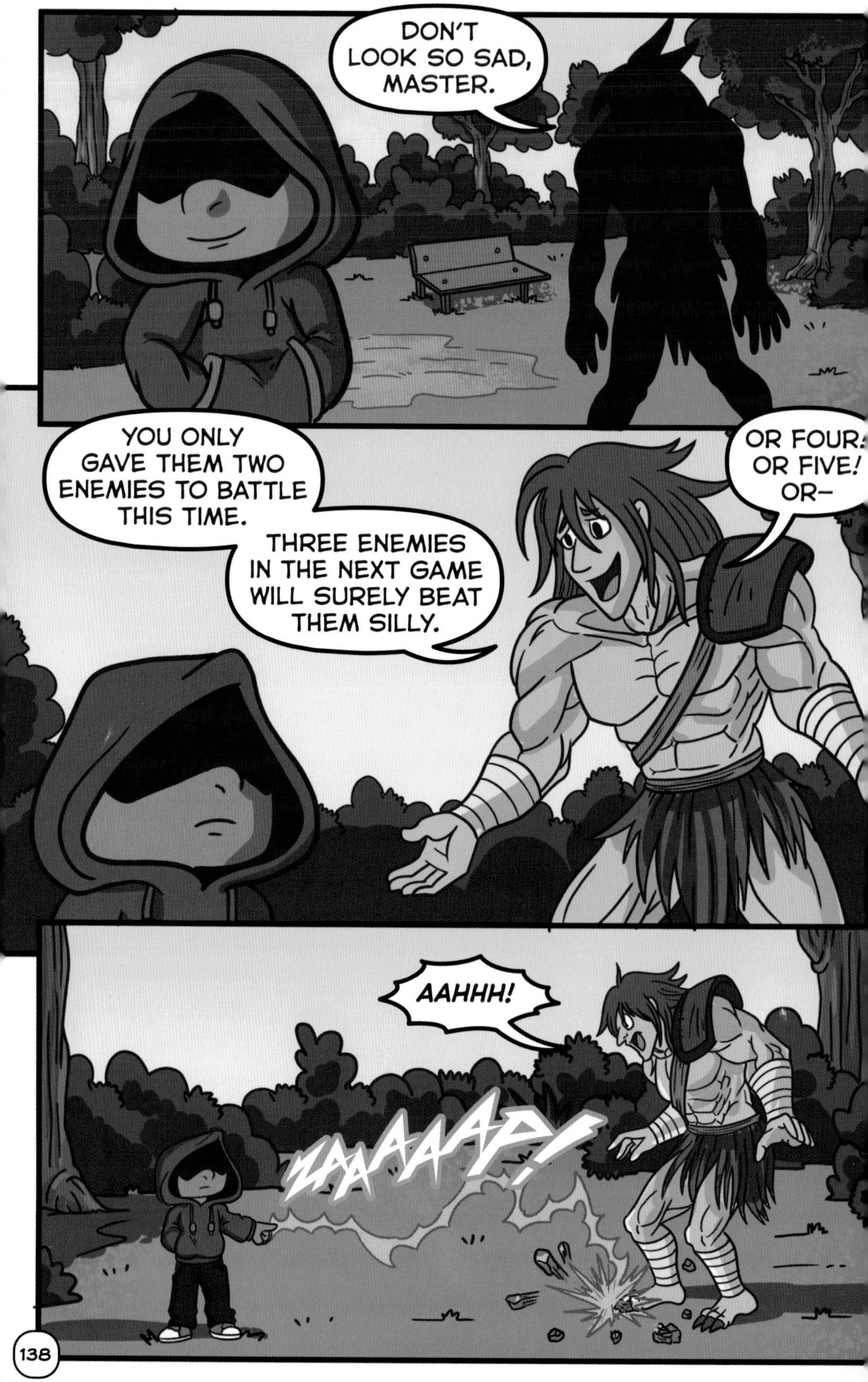
DON'T LOOK SO SAD, MASTER.
YOU ONLY GAVE THEM TWO ENEMIES TO BATTLE THIS TIME.
THREE ENEMIES IN THE NEXT GAME WILL SURELY BEAT THEM SILLY.
OR FOUR
OR FIVE! OR–
AAHHH!
ZAAAAAP!

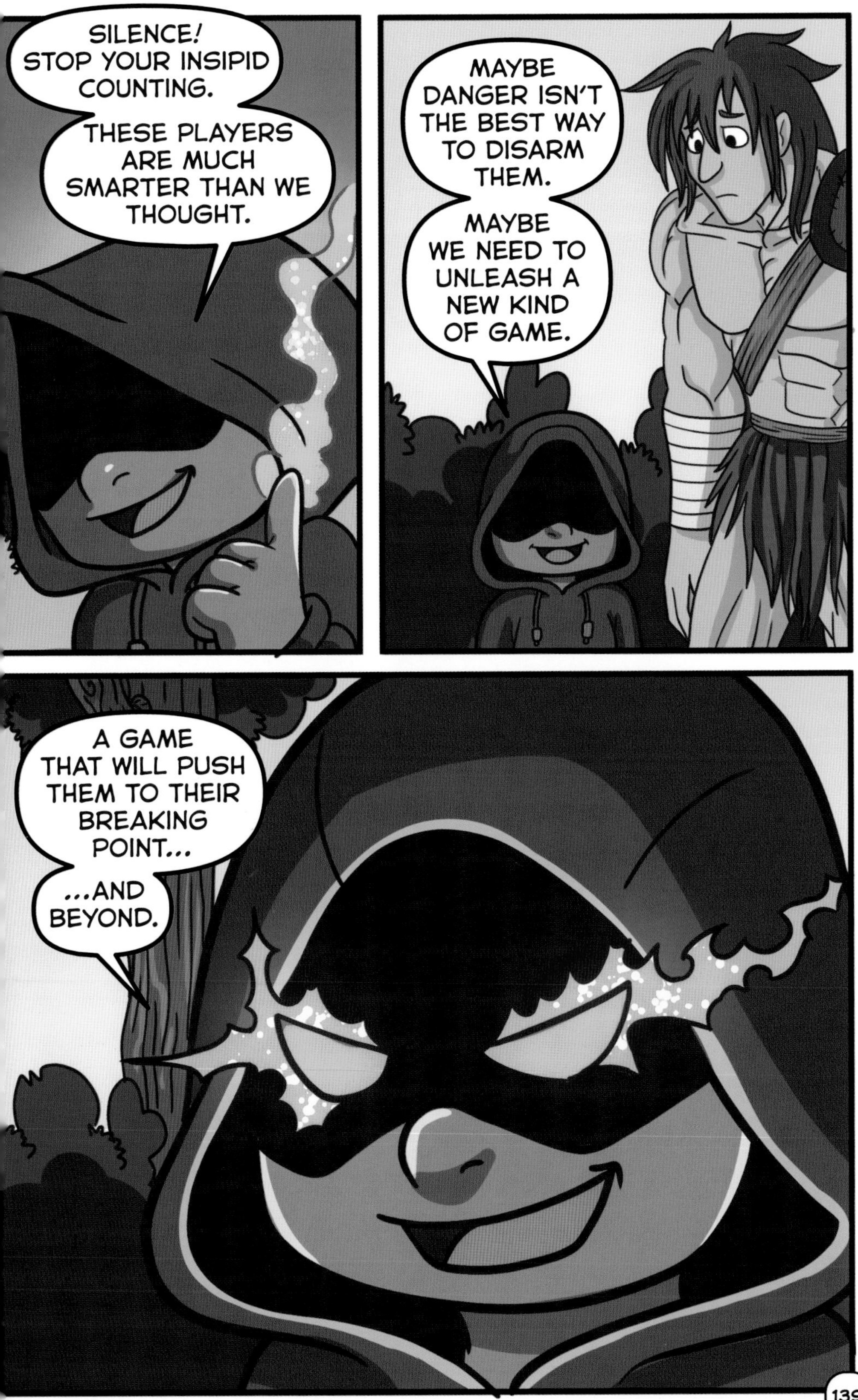
SILENCE! STOP YOUR INSIPID COUNTING.
THESE PLAYERS ARE MUCH SMARTER THAN WE THOUGHT.
MAYBE DANGER ISN'T THE BEST WAY TO DISARM THEM.
MAYBE WE NEED TO UNLEASH A NEW KIND OF GAME.
A GAME THAT WILL PUSH THEM TO THEIR BREAKING POINT...
...AND BEYOND.

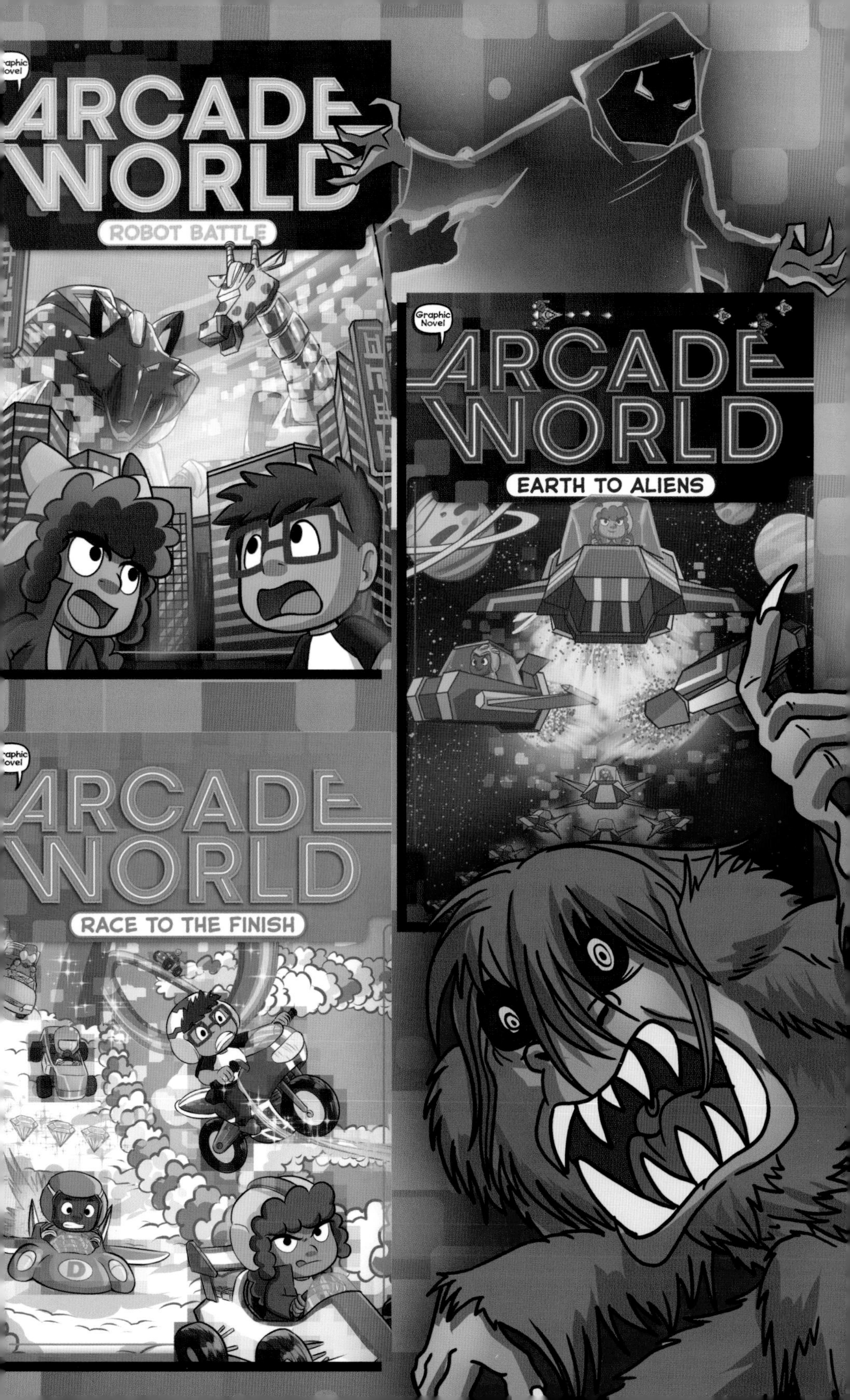
Graphic Novel
ARCADE WORLD
ROBOT BATTLE
Graphic Novel
ARCADE WORLD
EARTH TO ALIENS
Graphic Novel
ARCADE WORLD
RACE TO THE FINISH
D